Repetition, Regularity, Redundancy

Hituzi Linguistics in English

No.5	Communicating Skills of Intention	Tsutomu Sakamoto
No.6	A Pragmatic Approach to the Generation and Gender Gap in Japanese Politeness Strategies	Toshihiko Suzuki
No.7	Japanese Women's Listening Behavior in Face-to-face Conversation	Sachie Miyazaki
No.8	An Enterprise in the Cognitive Science of Language	Tetsuya Sano et al.
No.9	Syntactic Structure and Silence	Hisao Tokizaki
No.10	The Development of the Nominal Plural Forms in Early Middle English	Ryuichi Hotta
No.11	Chunking and Instruction	Takayuki Nakamori
No.12	Detecting and Sharing Perspectives Using Causals in Japanese	Ryoko Uno
No.13	Discourse Representation of Temporal Relations in the So-Called Head-Internal Relatives	Kuniyoshi Ishikawa
No.14	Features and Roles of Filled Pauses in Speech Communication	Michiko Watanabe
No.15	Japanese Loanword Phonology	Masahiko Mutsukawa
No.16	Derivational Linearization at the Syntax-Prosody Interface	Kayono Shiobara
No.17	Polysemy and Compositionality	Tatsuya Isono
No.18	fMRI Study of Japanese Phrasal Segmentation	Hideki Oshima
No.19	Typological Studies on Languages in Thailand and Japan	Tadao Miyamoto et al.
No.20	Repetition, Regularity, Redundancy	Yasuyo Moriya
No.21	A Cognitive Pragmatic Analysis of Nominal Tautologies	Naoko Yamamoto
No.22	A Contrastive Study of Responsibility for Understanding Utterances between Japanese and Korean	Sumi Yoon

Hituzi Linguistics in English No. 20

Repetition, Regularity, Redundancy

Norms and Deviations of Middle English Alliterative Meter

Yasuyo Moriya

Hituzi Syobo Publishing

First published 2014

Author: Yasuyo Moriya

Hituzi Syobo Publishing
Yamato bldg. 2F, 2-1-2 Sengoku Bunkyo-ku Tokyo, Japan
112-0011

phone +81-3-5319-4916 fax +81-3-5319-4917
e-mail: toiawase@hituzi.co.jp
http://www.hituzi.co.jp/
postal transfer 00120-8-142852

ISBN978-4-89476-683-9
Printed in Japan

Contents

Now schal we semlych se slehtez of þewez
And þe teccheles termes of talkyng noble.
Wich spede is in speche vnspurd may we lerne,
Syn we haf fonged þat fyne fader of nurture.

Now we'll certainly see both the seemliest manners
And the phrases and figures of faultless discourse.
We will hear one handy in the high art of speech,
Since the paragon of politeness has paid us a visit.
(*Sir Gawain and the Green Knight* ll. 916-19)

Preface

Essays in this volume represent my commitment to the study of Middle English (ME) alliterative meter in the past twenty years. The goal of these researches is to define the norm that governs ME alliterative verse and propose the limit of deviation based on metrical-syntactic analyses of corpora of approximately 23,000 lines of major and minor fourteenth-century alliterative poems. In order to highlight the "sensibility, artistic insight, and control of alliterative meter" (Kane, "Music" 89), the chapters examine various metrical phenomena. Each chapter is an independent argument focusing on particular poems or on particular metrical phenomena; thus, certain redundancy is inevitable though I tried to limit such overlap as minimum as possible. For the same reason, no concluding chapter is provided since each chapter contains concluding remarks. The size of corpora used for an analysis may slightly differ in certain chapters if the large number of lines of certain poems may affect the analysis result too adversely. The courier font is used when the positions of beats and offbeats must be marked in a precise manner. Readers' patience should be appreciated on this point.

Chapter One introduces current approaches to English meter, starting with a review of the development of metrical studies and then developing a discussion into the area of metrical phonology and English prosody. Especially illuminated are metrical features that are incorporated into the formal metrical structure by means of complex syllable structures and mobile stress. A method of scansion that reflects these phenomena and adapts various approaches to ME alliterative meter is proposed. These basics are essential in understanding arguments in the remaining chapters. I hope readers will peruse Chapter One before reading any particular chapter. Chapters Two and Three are a first attempt to apply the analysis method explained in Chapter One to the so-called Gawain Poems or Pearl Poems: *Pearl*, *Cleanness*, *Patience*, and *Sir Gawain and the Green Knight*. The base meters are postulated for these poems while possible deviations in various degrees are noted. Finally, the list of metrical complexity for each of the four poems is presented.

Chapters Four and Five concentrate on *Pearl* whose meter significantly differs from those of the other ME alliterative poems. In addition to the repetition of the same sound in alliteration, another metrical constraint of end rhyme and the recurring same word within the stanza and within the cluster of five or six stanzas are employed. This complex and intricate meter demands not only sound repetition but also lexical reiteration.

Chapters from Six to Ten examine alliteration techniques in various ME alliterative poems. The repetitious mode is often intense and overwhelming in certain ME alliterative poems. Overt and covert realization of alliteration sound may be extended beyond the verse line and continue over a group of lines. In contrast to *primary alliteration* that explicitly repeats the same sound in the word-initial syllable of metrical beats, *secondary alliteration*, subtly reflected in other than word-initiating consonants, is taken into consideration. Acknowledging secondary alliteration increases the number of *alliterating* syllables, which contributes toward aural homogeneity among the members of the metrical unit. Another distinctive metrical phenomenon in ME alliterative verse is that the vertical sound repetition, in addition to alliteration within a single verse line, unites consecutive lines.

Chapters Eleven and Twelve focus on *The Alliterative Morte Arthure* (*MA*), a voluminous piece consisting of more than four thousand lines. The repetition of the identical alliteration sound prevailing over from two to maximum eleven consecutive lines is classified into five types. Lines that contain one or more occasions of these types reinforce the repetitive mode. Identical alliteration of *MA*, thus, generates coherent rhythm among consecutive lines, which suggests that deliberate sound repetition, particularly the recurrence of *r*, plays a distinctive role in creating unity among successive lines.

Chapter Thirteen investigates the relationship between alliteration and natural speech rhythm. Alliteration may not always be the primary determiner in placing metrical beats in ME alliterative verse. Two different rules, the metrical subordination rule and the compound stress rule, operate, which will justify two or three different readings of a line. ME alliterative poets utilize the flexibility in stress placement by outweighing either alliteration or natural speech rhythm in different metrical environments. Chapter Fifteen extends the analysis into *MA* in order to examine its flexible lines between four-beat reading and five-beat reading.

Chapters Fourteen and Sixteen analyze the line end of ME alliterative verse, which has more restrictions on the number of syllables and stress quality than other part of the line. The implied offbeat, or no unstressed syllable between metrical beats, tends to appear toward the line end while a row of unstressed syllables exhibits the opposite tendency. Three variations to conclude the line prove that the line-final metrical beat is always under special prosodic constraints. Finally, Chapter Seventeen reexamines /r/ in alliteration of *MA*, and focuses on lines that contain the phrase, *the round table*. Through an observation of the fixed location of *the round table* in the second half-line and the overwhelming alliteration of the /r/ sound with it, it is evident that the *MA* poet is inflexible regarding the alliteration of a line that contains *the round table* and uses the phrase like a fixed formula.

The coherent assumption behind these seventeen chapters is that fourteenth-century alliterative verse is based on a metrical framework that could structurally link the verse line within the prescribed metrical unit and add extra aural effect by various devices in sound repetition. As Attridge asserts, "repetition is . . . a crucial feature of all poetry; . . . poetic form depends upon equivalences-that is, implied repetitions-along the axis of succession" ("Movement" 69). Redundancy in repetition bears a decisive role because it is "a necessary element in most systems of communication" (Burrow 119). The chapters illuminate what ME alliterative poets intend to communicate by means of their word play, repetitious mode, and artistic innovation within and beyond the alliterative tradition.

Since most of the poems analyzed here survive in a unique manuscript and there is no standard spelling in ME, a reliable observation in detecting meter would be by means of reading as many as lines from major and minor works and compiling statistical data. I utilized any time slot, long or short, for this task. Be it in a small flat airport in Kalamazoo, Michigan, on a breezy front porch of the Bodington Hall in Leeds, or on a crowded train to a conference site in Tokyo or Kyoto, I kept glossing, scanning, and marking ME lines. The pursuit was challenging while the progress was sometimes felt not very promising. But, it was those difficult lines to interpret that helped the research move forward. *Þat fyne fader of nurture* certainly visited me in such occasions and helped me hear beats and offbeats as if I had observed over their shoulders the poets composing their work.

It is a pleasant honor to acknowledge various scholars whom I met at conferences or had a personal contact with, including Professors Derek Attridge, Thomas Cable, Ralph Hanna III, Mitsunori Imai, Yoko Iyeiri, Ad Putter, Edgar Slotkin, Jeremy Smith, A. C. Spearing, E. G. Stanley, Matsuji Tajima, Akinobu Tani, and Thorlac Turville-Petre. Their insightful suggestions, critical responses, and encouraging comments have been invaluable assets in pursuing my quest. Research leaves from my university in three separate academic years enabled me to stay and conduct research at the University of Nottingham, the University of Oxford, and the University of London. In Oxford, I had a flat on Walton Street across from Professor Stanley's home. He kindly invited me to his home, claiming that we were the two medievalists who lived in the closest vicinity. Discussing OE and ME verse with Professor Stanley over a glass of wine is a precious memory.

Two research grants, Grants-in-Aid for Scientific Research by the Ministry of Education, Science, Sports and Culture (no. 15520317 and no. 19520433), provided the fundamental research environment. The grants enabled me to have assistants in sorting data and confirming analysis results. The publication itself was made possible by the Grant-in-Aid for Publication of Scientific Research Results (no. 255060), which significantly eased the financial difficulty for a volume that would not be a good seller. Special acknowledgements are also due to the editors of the following journals for their kind permissions to revise my articles that had once appeared in their volumes: *English Language Notes*, *English Studies* (Routledge), *Neuphilologische Mitteilungen, NOWELE*, *Poetica, Publications of the Medieval Association of the Midwest*, and *Studies in Medieval English Language and Literature*. Two editing agents proofread the entire manuscript while three individual proofreaders, a specialist in linguistics and two professionals in English composition, have also checked the manuscript thoroughly. A spell-check system for ME is not available; careful checks were made on quoted ME lines over several times. For errors, if still remaining, I am solely responsible. Last but not least, I am grateful to Ms. Eri Ebisawa of Hituzi Syobo Publishing for her editorial support.

London, July 2013
YM

Tables and Diagrams

Abbreviations

A	*The Wars of Alexander*
AG	*The Parlement of the Thre Ages*
B	*Beowulf*
C	*Cleanness*
CR	*Dispute Between Mary and the Cross*
CSR	Compound Stress Rule
E	*St. Erkenwald*
G	*Sir Gawain and the Green Knight*
J	*The Siege of Jerusalem*
K	*The Three Dead Kings*
L	*The Quatrefoil of Love*
M	*The Battle of Maldon*
MA	*The Alliterative Morte Arthure*
ME	Middle English
OE	Old English
OF	Old French
ON	Old Norse
PE	*Pearl*
PP	*Piers Plowman*
PPA	*Piers Plowman*, A-Text
PPB	*Piers Plowman*, B-Text
PPC	*Piers Plowman*, C-Text
PS	*A Pistel of Susan*
PT	*Patience*
R	*The Dream of the Rood*
S	*The Seafarer*
SMA	*The Stanzaic Morte Arthur*
SS	*Somer Soneday*
T	*The Destruction of Troy*
W	*Wynnere and Wastoure*
WA	*The Wanderer*
WL	*The Wife's Lament*

Scansion Symbols and Typographical Conventions

+s	stressed syllable
-s	unstressed syllable including the final *-e* in a monosyllabic word
s	indefinite stress; may replace either +s or -s
/s/	emphatic stress; may replace +s
[s]	metrically subordinated stress; may replace -s
s	syncope; the syllable is omitted
^+s, ^-s	elided syllables; may replace +s or -s
○	final *-e* in a word that consists of more than two syllables; may be pronounced and realized as an offbeat
○	final *-e* that may not form a syllable
B	beat
o	single offbeat
o2	double offbeat
o3	triple offbeat
o:	demotion
<B>	promotion
B̲	implied beat
ø	implied offbeat
○̲	final *-e* pronounced between beats
○	final *-e* in the line-final position
a, b, c, etc.	same alliterating or rhyming sound
x	metrical beat that does not alliterate

Chapter 1

Middle English Alliterative Verse and Its Meter

This chapter offers a brief introduction to the study of alliterative meter and presents current approaches to it. In order to illuminate the special characteristics of English alliterative verse, the chapter explains the development of metrical studies, explores constituents of English speech rhythm, and uncovers what phonological and metrical features are incorporated into the formal metrical structure. The chapter also verifies that English speech rhythm is determined not only by the system of fixed stress positions but also by the complex syllable structure and the mobility of stress. A method of scansion reflecting these phenomena and adapting various approaches to Middle English (ME) alliterative meter will be proposed. The following key concepts will be introduced in four sections:

1. Studies on Old English (OE) and ME Versification
2. Development of Metrical Studies in Literary and Linguistic Fields
3. English Speech Rhythm
4. Approaches to ME Versification

1.1 Studies on OE and ME Versification

The idea of analyzing the meter of early English grew out of my study on *Beowulf* and other OE verse, as well as on current linguistic research on English prosody and versification. In the initial research, however, I realized that the research on OE meter has seen significant diversity and achievement with relatively coherent terminology and methods of analysis. The study of OE meter has its foundation in the works of Baum, Kaluza, and Sievers; more recently these studies have been reinforced by the contributions of Cable, Creed, Duncan, Fulk, Hutcheson, Kendall, Lass, Lucas, and Russom. In contrast, not so much has been agreed upon and much more learning is needed concerning the ME versification (Barney; van Gelderen), presumably due to its complicated social, historical, and, most importantly, linguistic diversity that the period saw during the time of transition. The study of ME metrics has started to appear quite recently after the works by Borroff, Oakden, and Schipper, as seen in the research by Hanna, Hieatt, Lawton, McColly, Macrae-Gibson, Minkova, Pearsall, Salter, Schreiber, and T. Turville-Petre. Hanna explains the significance of alliterative meter as follows:

> . . . the mode in which such literary communication proceeds is not simply marked, but overmarked, as vernacular. Alliteration and alliterative diction, "'rum, ram, ruf", by lettre' (as Chaucer's Parson puts it), self-consciously mark the poetry off as English-against either the Latinity of its sources or the developing Francophilia of the circumambient literary tradition. . . . Moreover, alliterative poets over-emphasize their vernacularity through flaunting their own (thoroughly fictive) orality-and its social implications.
> ("Alliterative" 501–02)

A body of verse and prose distinguished for their variety and literary excellence is extant from the ME period. It was a time when an ancient Germanic culture, which flourished with a wealth of traditional verse, had gone through change and growth under the influence of surrounding cultures (J. Frankis; Lester). While OE verse used to be characterized by alliteration, unequal length of line, and four stressed syllables per line, English poetry by the late ME period had acquired a contrasting shape; namely end rhyme rather than alliteration, rising rhythm rather than falling, and a structure more strophic than stichic. These features are the cumulative results of what English poets would have expected and enjoyed in their vernacular, and could not have emerged suddenly. Blake claims that ME alliterative verse has "rhythmical alliteration: longer lines, less regular stress, and ultimately a freer alliteration" ("Rhythmical" 121). Because of the dynamism that the English language saw from late OE to Chaucer's time, the fourteenth century seems to be a crucial period (Sisam xvi-xxi). Yet as the great figure Chaucer enjoys such fame, the works of his contemporaries have not been examined very thoroughly with regard to versification. Knott and Fowler comment (53–54):

> The universal admiration of Chaucer, justified as it is, has had one unfortunate effect in connection with the study of Middle English literature. It has meant that other works, composed during the same period, have often been neglected. Yet without this other literature our knowledge of English life and manners in the fourteenth century would of necessity be somewhat limited, since Chaucer's outlook, in spite of his broad human sympathies, is fundamentally aristocratic.

Putter makes a similar argument (24–25):

> As the 'father of English poetry', Chaucer stands at the beginning of a literary tradition which has profoundly affected our view of what kind of verse or metre is natural and mainstream. . . . Chaucer's innovative choice of metre today seems self-explanatory because the rhymed iambic pentameter established itself as the standard medium of English poetry. While this development retroactively turned Chaucer into our 'father', it has also had the unfortunate consequence of making alliterative metre, which is a very different metrical system, seem strange.

The remarkable movement of alliterative poetry, proven by over 40,000 lines extant, arose in the same fourteenth century. It is still a matter of controversy whether this movement was a *revival* of the verse form that had once been popular in either the Anglo-Saxon period or a period when alliterative verse called special attention to the continuous tradition inherited from nearly a thousand years before (Duggan, "Patterning," "Shape"; Russom, "Evolution"; T. Turville-Petre, *Revival*). This alliterative, unrhymed form quickly gained considerable popularity, though it ceased rather abruptly in the fifteenth century.

Among the extant body of ME alliterative lines, the Gawain poet, often called the Pearl poet because his *Pearl* is the first poem in the manuscript among those ascribed to him, has left four poems in a single manuscript. The poems, *Pearl*, *Cleanness*, *Patience*, and *Sir Gawain and the Green Knight*, are all written in the West Midland dialect and are assumed to have been composed between 1360 and 1400. From around the same time, major and minor poems composed in alliterative verse are extant. A few examples include *The Alliterative Morte*

Arthure, *The Destruction of Troy*, *Piers Plowman*, *The Siege of Jerusalem*, and *The Wars of Alexander*. Analyses of these major works and others will illuminate not only the basic principle alliterative meter but also the points unique to each poem.

The alliterative meter has a long and complex history (Cable; Putter; Russom; T. Turville-Petre). It has been persistent in English verse from the Anglo-Saxon period through modern times due to its echoic beats and mnemonic effects of alliteration. Among contemporary forms, the native English rhythm frequently appears in nursery rhymes, children's songs, ballads, folk-songs, commercial jingles, and hymns. The alliterative form is considered being the oldest traditions of European poetry (Shepherd). "The concept of equivalence for alliteration derives from native-speaker intuitions about syllable structure, and corresponds to the concept of equivalence for early Germanic reduplication" (Russom, *Beowulf* 64). In spite of the archaic vocabulary and differences in grammar, the rhythm of early English is fairly perceivable to modern ears. Thus, for instance, *Beowulf* composed in OE does not look very familiar on the printed page, but many phrases appeal naturally to the ears of English speakers. The more OE and ME verse lines we recite or listen to, the more similarities we will experience between the rhythms of earlier English and contemporary English.

ME alliterative verse proposes another point of interest; that is, similar collocations are observed in stressed syllables as common phrases. The alliterative form allows rhythmic variety suitable for the English language in the ME period because it is capable of representing its speech rhythm. Shepherd claims that alliteration has been an aid to memorization throughout the history of English (143):

> Alliteration as a formal device superimposed upon the verbalizations of a culture is itself a mnemotechnique. From the beginnings of the settlement of England by the Anglo-Saxons, alliterative composition had been a preservative of power, patrimony, and communal wisdom.

Bliss proposes three rationales for studying meter: It helps readers appreciate a poem as art; it gives aesthetic and intellectual pleasure; and it is useful for textual criticism (1). Examining why a certain structure overwhelmingly appears and revealing several different variations will lead to aesthetic satisfaction. Russom remarks on the purpose of metrical studies as follows:

> What seems clear is that good poets and appreciative audiences have a remarkable ability to identify complex verses as variants of regular patterns. It is this ability that interests linguists most, since it represents a kind of intuitive linguistic work. Both linguists and poets begin with a set of internalized grammatical concepts that apply in normal language use.
>
> (*Old English Meter* 149)

Progress in modern phonology certainly has brought insightful ideas and methods into the study of versification, but a unified theory on English meter has not been agreed upon yet. The metrists may be divided, according to their methods, into groups of classical metrists, scanners through musical notation, equal-timers, stress-pattern analyzers, generative linguists, and post-generative grammar metrists. Whereas the traditional philologists base their argument on classical schemes of Latin and Greek verse, others use bars and measures of musical notation, stress markings, or tree diagrams. Furthermore, modern linguistics with its descriptive methods and scientific measurements in phonological investigations has contributed in revealing what had been overlooked in previous studies. The second section of this chapter will offer a brief explanation of these approaches and argue that the theory of beat rhythm is the most useful among them for the present study. Though this theory has been developed for the study of verse of the later period, it is applicable to medieval English with appropriate adjustments in scansion and notation. Though Sievers's types based on OE alliterative meter may be useful for ME alliterative meter as well, the taxonomic types pose various problems (Duggan, "Notes"; Leonard; Russom, *Beowulf*), and their application to ME alliterative verse would not necessarily yield convincing results as in OE verse. With respect to the reconstruction of the actual pronunciation and phonological particulars, the methodology developed in the fields of modern phonology and historical and comparative linguistics is useful. The forms of Modern English are another useful aid, especially in deciding on syncopation, elision of two syllables, and the syllable quality of the word-final -*e* and that of other unstressed inflectional endings.

In analyzing medieval verse, scholars must face various difficulties and uncertain feelings. The sounds, intonation, and stylistic features may not be fully recovered since precise reconstructions seem impossible for a language that is no longer in use. This is true of all languages reconstructed from written pages, but metrists have to settle and convert the signs and cues provided in extant manuscripts in order to hear the rhythmic flow in their mind's ear. The task is challenging but not unattainable. Alliterating syllables in a line will provide clues to the task of soliciting beats and offbeats repeated in its redundant meter (Burrow). The stylistic measures such as alliteration, syntax, word frequency, and word collocation will be of meaningful help. If recitation from the written page is expected for alliterative verse (R. Allen; Shepherd), the repeated letters significant at sight will help reconstruct acoustic effects. As Shepherd notes, "it is the sound that distinguished alliterative verse from other verse of the late ME period" (61). "The messages . . . which are so hard to interpret and yet in which there still vibrates, for the attentive reader, the intensity of what was a desire, an emotion no doubt, and the perception of a form of beauty" will be heard (Zumthor 4). Because of its repetitive mode, alliterative verse may be a proper source to attest sound symbolism, phonaesthesia (Smith, "Semantics"), and linguistic iconicity (Sadowski).

The study of meter has often fallen into a dilemma because the two disciplines concerned, linguistics and literary studies, "tend too often to treat each other as adversaries rather than allies" (Kiparsky and Youmans xi; Youmans, "Introduction" 1). Linguists demand empirical and scientific foundations while literary critics are apt to believe that their problems will not be solved by such an approach (Duggan, "Role"; Hagen; Hayes, "Review"). As Creed contends, the study of English meter of earlier days can only propose an acceptable approximation from written pages. Yet the approximation, with the aid of modern knowledge, can reach a compromising point between two fields. Revealing the metrical assumptions that the fourteenth-century alliterative poets had in mind will contribute to the study of ME speech rhythm and special characteristics of its prosody.

1.2 Development of Metrical Studies in Literary and Linguistic Fields

A concise overview of various approaches to meter, traditional and recent, is available in Holder's book *Rethinking Meter: A New Approach to the Verse Line*, especially in the first three chapters, and in Wesling's book *The Scissors of Meter: Grammetrics and Reading*, especially in the first four chapters. Attridge divides the function of poetic rhythm into two kinds:

> The poem in general: heightened language; consistency and unity; forward movement and final closure; memorability; mimetic suggestiveness; emotional suggestiveness; literary associations.
> Within the poem: emphasis; articulation; mimetic effects; emotional effects; meaning in process; connection and contrast. (*Poetic Rhythm* 12–19)

The interactions of the above functions create a specific flow of rhythm. This section focuses on approaches to the study of English versification that are helpful in understanding meter and analyzing materials used for the present research: the classical method, musical notation, approaches in modern linguistics, the statistical method, the theory of beat rhythm, and the current situation of metrical studies. It is noteworthy that those epoch-making arguments made a long time ago are still valuable and useful. Despite the advances in the study of meter, "no theory of meter can be definitive at present" (Russom, *Old English Meter* 149). The section will first present advantages and limitations of each approach, and then offer a definition of meter–what it is and how the definition should contribute to the study of versification.

1.2.1 The Classical Method

Traditionally, English meter has been discussed by means of the classical terms derived from the study of Greek and Latin prosody. A graphic method of scansion is commonly employed by marking stressed syllables and unstressed syllables and dividing them into feet and a pause called a caesura. The use of bars to indicate feet is also common in order to clarify the unit that contains a strong stress called an ictus. According to Fussell, a foot is "a measurable, patterned, conventional unit of poetic rhythm, and consists of one stressed syllable and one or two unstressed syllables" (*Poetic Meter* 19). The notion derives from the analogy of alternating actions such as walking, foot-tapping, and head-nodding (Cureton, "Rhythm" 108). The following line is an example of the classical scansion:

> The bóy | stood ón | the búrn | ing déck. (Chatman, *Introduction* 89)

This method is still dominant, appearing not only in the works of literary critics such as Fussell (*Poetic Meter*), Kaluza, Schipper, Sievers, Snell, and Wimsatt, but also in modern linguistics such as in the studies by Abercrombie, Bolinger, Chatman, and Guéron. Yet, there are some limitations in applying the quantitative meter of Latin or Greek to English (Attridge, *Rhythms*; Cureton, "Rhythm"; Fussell, *Poetic Meter*, "Historical"; Holder; Kuryłowicz; Wesling; Wimsatt and Beardsley). The measurement by means of long versus short syllables causes an artificial forcing of the metrical frame upon the natural flow of poetic rhythm; the division of the foot, whether a group of a stressed syllable and one or more unstressed syllables forms either rising or falling rhythm, is often unclear (Hascall, "Trochaic"; Townsend). The traditional method based on classical concepts does not necessarily present a coherent system of scansion because the reader's interpretation is inevitable and may result in a prescriptive reading. Metrical rules should account for the various possibilities that a line holds under a particular rhythmic organization, and should also be able to predict the distribution of different kinds of syllables within the line.

1.2.2 Musical Notation

Another common way of scanning poetry is by means of musical notation based on the notion that "meter is the measurement of the number of pulses between more or less regularly recurring accents" (Cooper and Meyer 4). The measurement of the duration of a syllable and a foot, which is often substituted with the word *measure* from the analogy of music, has been commonly practiced for various materials. Asserting the value of the musical notation, Lanier states, "since rhythm always depends necessarily upon quantity, those who deny the existence of quantity in English sounds must deny the possibility of rhythm in English verse" (97). Yet analyzing verse in syllable duration is not simple (Jassem, Hill, and Witten). Human senses are sometimes inaccurate in judging orderly movement, and the estimate of time, duration, and stress quality may not be as reliable as that made by machines. Rhythmic regularity, however, could be shared with others without mechanical justification, which suggests that rhythmic regularity reflecting psychological time but not precisely measurable time seems to play a vital role for ears in perceiving continual rhythm.

Visual transcription in the analogy of meter to musical notes is useful to a certain extent, but temporal measurement is not the sole element in determining total poetic meaning. The relationship between a stressed syllable and an unstressed one is often approximate and relative to, but not as exact as, that expected in a music score. Thus, Richards's criticism against the temporal approach is valid for a precise and practical study of meter (46):

> We shall never understand metre so long as we ask, "Why does temporal pattern so excite us?" and fail to realise that the pattern itself is a vast cyclic agitation spreading all over the body, a tide of excitement pouring through the channels of the mind.

The application of musical notation to earlier English poetry has not been very successful. For instance, Pope's study on the meter of *Beowulf* and other OE poetry does not suggest the mechanism of the meter used in OE verse, nor does it propose any significant metrical rules. Pope's scansion looks like one of the performance models of the poem, reflecting one possible way of recitation. Though Pope's work is acknowledged by many, it is a controversial issue whether or not Pope's method is the best model for the study of OE meter. Kiparsky's criticism against musical notation suggests an alternative as to what meter is and how it should be described:

> Nobody could possibly learn the distinction between metrical and unmetrical lines by memorizing the actual patterns; rather, one acquires a 'feel' for the verse in terms of some general principles. The initial task of metrical theory is just to discover these principles in particular metrical systems; at a deeper level, we can then proceed to try to explain them, and ultimately to develop a general theory of meter. ("Stress" 577)

1.2.3 Approaches in Modern Linguistics

Halle and Keyser's article entitled "Chaucer and the Study of Prosody" has triggered a subsequent flourishing of metrical studies in modern linguistics, particularly from the viewpoint of generative grammar (Bradford; Fabb; McKay). Halle and Keyser ("Iambic") introduce two fundamental concepts for metrical studies. First, one of the aims of prosodic studies is to distinguish between metrical and unmetrical lines. Abandoning the foot, which has been the core concept of traditional studies, they propose a new way of describing the line as having a certain number of positions; for example, five odd and five even slots in iambic pentameter. A meter has "two essential components: metrical positions (the smallest metrical constituent) and the metrical template (the largest metrical constituent)" (Fabb, *Linguistics* 88). Thus, a series of rules generates lines, simultaneously determining their well-formedness (Hayes, "Metrics"), or more specifically, their metricality (Brogan, "Generative"; Fabb, *Language* 4–5) and well-formedness (Hayes, *Metrical Stress Theory* 400–03). A meter consists of an abstract metrical pattern and realization rules, thus encoding the abstract pattern into a sequence of syllables. The scansion, therefore, proceeds position to position by numbering syllables from left to right, locating stressed and unstressed syllables and underlining all violated positions. The meter should be capable of producing all the metrical lines and predicting metrical lines only.

The linguistic approach has some serious contradictions; for example, many metrical lines have been found to have stress maxima in odd positions, the postulated stress rules are sometimes problematic for the lines analyzed, and the dichotomy between stressed and unstressed slots is so strict that the rules are not capable of covering all the possibilities found in verse. These problems originate from the assumption that verse lines can be clearly divided into two groups, metrical and unmetrical. The issue of metricality is not simple just as the judgment of grammaticality is vague in the study of language. Despite these problems, modern linguistics has made at least a contribution to the study of meter in determining two issues: the abandonment of the foot and the assignment of metrical slots with a focus on the relationship among the adjacent syllables for a weak or strong quality in a line. Thus, "there must be an objective opposition between metrically weak (W) and strong (S) syllabic positions: the former must at least TEND to be unstressed; the latter must at least TEND to be stressed (Tarlinskaja, "General" 123). Metrical phonology, the phonological study that uses binary branching in describing stress hierarchy, has also contributed to a better understanding of meter. McCarthy, Kiparsky ("Rhythmic"), and Liberman and Prince started such branching in clarifying the relationship between the adjacent syllables. Giegerich (*Metrical Phonology*) expanded it in the study of English phonology, providing useful tips for the study of English meter. Metrical subordination within the phrase is also a useful term in considering the hierarchy of stress quality (Russom, *Beowulf* 87–96).

1.2.4 The Statistical Method

The monumental works on English meter based on statistics have often been elaborated by prosodists who are neither British nor American. For example, German prosodists such as Kaluza, Schipper, and Sievers established the philological tradition in the study of English meter. Other European scholars introduced the inductive method characterized by the inclusion of statistical tables. Tarlinskaja's work, *English Verse: Theory and History*, which is full of tables and figures, is one of the most extensive studies of English verse that examines over 100,000 lines from the thirteenth to the nineteenth centuries. Using statistics about metrical ictus and non-ictus and referring to a Russian verse form, Tarlinskaja employs two terms that are important to her theory: *thresholds* and *dol'nic*. The first denotes the metrical border while the second denotes the four-stress verse in which stressed and unstressed syllables alternate regularly.

Bailey utilizes the inductive method in his study of ten English poets who wrote in the so-called iambic pentameter including Milton, Pope, Blake, and Wordsworth. He also provides statistical tables about stress placement and variation, syllabic variation, enjambment and rhyme, lexical selection, and stanza form. Gasparov claims that the mathematical method by means of language probability models is useful for the study of various European poetries such as English, Latin, French, Italian, Spanish, and Portuguese because such a method helps "differentiate language-caused phenomena from verse-specific, the involuntary from the creative, and helps to concentrate the scholars' attention on the latter" (337). The twenty-two tables at the end of Gasparov's study support this argument. Recently an analysis utilizing a large database called *corpus* has proven its potential in providing evidence and examples in a prodigious quantity (Cooper and Pearsall; Facchinetti and Rissanen; Markus). The high frequency in statistics, however, does not necessarily explain why certain phenomena are favored over others. The point of argument about the statistical approach is that the actual method of scansion in accumulating statistics is often left unexplained. Perhaps this is because the scansion reflects only one way of reading when there are several possibilities. Though statistics certainly provide a practical aid in surveying general points, allowing variations in interpretation and recitation may blur the argument.

1.2.5 The Theory of Beat Rhythm

Through a careful examination of these approaches explained above, Attridge proposes a metrical theory that uses beats and offbeats instead of feet or ictuses. He places above each syllable *+s* for a stressed syllable and *-s* for an unstressed syllable while he places beneath each syllable *B* for a metrical beat and *o* a metrical offbeat. Stewart (*Technique*) was the first to apply symbols for beats and offbeats to scansion. He uses *S* for a stressed syllable, *o* an unstressed syllable, *l* a lightly stressed syllable, *O* a heavy unstressed syllable, *p* a pause in the place of an unstressed syllable, *P* a pause in the place of a stressed syllable, and ||

a caesural pause. Stewart's scansion and Attridge's scansion look similar in spite of the different symbols used:

```
o   S o   l   o  S   o   S      O  S
If music be the food of love, play on.
```

(Stewart, *Technique* 224)

```
-s  +s    -s  +s-s      +s -s  +s    -s  +s
By chance, or nature's changing course untrimmed
 o   B     o   B o       B  o   B     o   B
```

(Attridge, *Rhythms* 205)

The distinction between the symbols for the stress pattern and for the metrical pattern is one of the Attridge's contributions. Another contribution of Attridge is to separate the underlying rhythm and the final product. He sets up basic rules for duple and triple meter by means of the base rules (the beat rule and the offbeat rule) and the deviation rules (the promotion rule, the demotion rule, and the implied offbeat rule). The underlying rhythm generates the abstract metrical pattern assigned to the row of syllables, and alters the quality of stress of each syllable according to realization rules so that the line maintains metrical expectations inherent throughout the whole poem. Thus, four-beat verse with an offbeat at the line-initial position and another at the end can be schematized as follows:

Verse → o B o B o B o B o

An optional offbeat is placed between parentheses:

Verse → o B o B o B o B (o)

The advantage of this method is that the stress distribution among syllables is visualized in a fairly simple and coherent way compared to other methods of scansion. Furthermore, it is superior to any other method in presenting the metrical complexity of the line using symbols for deviation. This method of scansion is capable of reflecting how norms are set in the metrical scheme, and how much deviation the line holds.

1.2.6 Current Status of Metrical Studies

Ten years after the publication of *The Rhythms of English Poetry* by Attridge, Cureton has completed a book entitled *Rhythmic Phrasing in English Verse* in which he tries to move beyond the traditional view of meter and focus on rhythmic responses that are metrical, as well as those that are not metrical. He claims that meters are "regular, low-level configurations of largely physically controlled pulsations" while phrasal structures are "more irregular, global organizations of rhythmic constituents" than meters (x). Cureton's method of scansion is much more complex than Attridge's two levels. The first tree formalization in Cureton's scansion starts with a grouping of syllables that are printed vertically, proceeds to a dot matrix of meter, and up to branches that group the syllables in their nodes. Thus, twenty-one lines of Williams Carlos Williams's free verse occupy three pages for the first analysis, a little more than a page for the analysis of bracketing formalization, five for the analysis of grouping reduction, another five for the analysis of prolongational reduction, and more than twenty-two pages for the analysis of high levels of phrasing (277–422). Though Cureton considers his method as "easy to use" (*Rhythmic Phrasing* 423), the analysis that can accommodate only four or five verse lines per page[1] may be too complicated and space-consuming to reflect the natural flow of language in a coherent manner.

Various reviews of *The Rhythms of English Poetry* by Attridge, both from a linguistic and literary viewpoint (Bjorklund; Cureton, "Review"; Easthope; Hayes, "Review," *Metrical Theory*; Holder), note several problems in Attridge's method and argument but have not been able to offer an alternative way that overcomes those. As Attridge counter-argues, "reviewers usually read something else: a work woven partly out of their fantasies and fears, perhaps extrapolated from the title or the picture on the cover; the work they would like to have written; the work they hoped (or dreaded) someone would write" ("Linguistic Theory" 183). Though this article of Attridge's appeared much earlier than the publication of Cureton's book, Cureton's method threatens the explicitness and economy of formalization that Attridge lists among the firm foundations of modern linguistics ("Linguistic Theory" 198). More recently the works by Cureton, Giegerich, and Hayes have achieved progress in studying meter, but Attridge's method still appears to be the most concise and useful one for analyzing English meter. This method is capable of postulating metrical norms and the limits of metrical deviation, and yet at the same time it does not force unnatural stress quality upon syllables.

1.2.7 The Definition of Meter

A glance at various definitions of meter may be useful in deciding what the term *meter* signifies:

> . . . meter is the principle of the organization of the accentual and syllabic material of all the lines, or a considerable part of them, if such a principle may be revealed by means of a comparison of these lines.
>
> (Tarlinskaja, *English Verse* 67)
>
> Meter turns out to be in many ways an historical, cultural concept.
>
> (Tarlinskaja, "General" 123)
>
> *Meter* is an organizing principle which turns the general tendency toward regularity in rhythm into a strict regularity that can be counted and named. It involves an intensification and regularization of the normal rhythm of the language. Metrical language is language written in such a way as to make possible the experiencing of *beats*, bursts of energy that produce repeated and structured patterns. (Attridge, *Poetic Rhythm* 19, italics original)
>
> When I say Meter I mean an abstract pattern of measurement to which the poet compares his lines. (Conner 23)
>
> Meter is an isolable phenomenon whose study will be less than, but may well enhance, a total reading of a poem and, ultimately, a study of the whole domain of poetics, the language of poetry. (Wilson, "Reading" 146)
>
> . . . meter is an abstraction that the poet uses to organize differences in syllable stress. Lines of poetry rarely realize the meter in its "ideal" form; indeed, poets vary the make-up of lines both as concessions to the nature of language and as attempts at aesthetic effects. Thus, it is useful to think of meter as a compositional device: something that the poet uses to control the pattern of stresses in his verse. (Glowka 79)
>
> Meter is a prime physical and emotional constituent of poetic meaning.
>
> (Fussell, *Poetic Meter* 3)
>
> Meter is what results when the natural rhythmical movements of colloquial speech are heightened, organized, and regulated. . . and (it) is the most fundamental technique of order available to the poet.
>
> (Fussell, *Poetic Meter* 4–5)
>
> METRE: The arrangement of language in lines of verse based on fixed rhythmical patterns regularly repeated. (Pearsall, *Poetry* 284)
>
> Meter, then, is an instance of complex secondary rhythm, since it contains

> not only grouped events, but also groups of grouped events (lines) and even groups of groups of grouped events (stanzas). (Chatman, *Theory* 113)

> Metre: In specific terms metre refers to the measurement of a poetic line by the number and the stress, pitch and accentual value of its syllables. In a more general sense the term refers to the practice and study of poetic form, a sphere also referred to as prosody, metrics and versification. (Bradford 210)

> . . . meter projects formal frames within which grouping and prolongation move to culmination and arrival. Normatively, meter is phasally afterbeating. Canonically, it marks the beginnings of phrases with strong beats that, in their hierarchical ordering, project measures composed of two subordinate levels of articulation. . . . meter is a rhythmic, not a linguistic, form, a rhythmic form with its own constraints on well-formedness, its own preferred relations to rhythmic stimuli, and its own particular function within rhythmic cognition as a whole. (Cureton, *Rhythmic Phrasing* 428)

> Verse has been called a heightened form of ordinary language, in the sense that it does nothing that is not done in ordinary speech, but what it does is foregrounded and focused on for its own sake. So natural rhythms are made more regular, and 'sound effects' like alliteration, assonance and rhyme, which occur in ordinary language but usually in a random way, are made a deliberate part of the sound patterns. (Freeborn 152)

From these definitions, it may be deduced that the meter is poetic discourse occurring for literary purpose and involving multiple linguistic features such as stress, tone, quantity, juncture, and rhythm. Meter is an abstract phenomenon that underlies each line of verse. The primary purpose of metrical studies is to define this phenomenon objectively and to formulate the rules that generate actual lines.

Here, I would like to propose three goals that metrical studies must achieve. First, since the meter is perceived from the recurring flow of speech rhythm, it should reflect the underlying abstract pattern in verse, as well as realization rules that define the substance of the abstract meter (Chatman, "Comparing"; Guéron; Halle and Keyser, "Chaucer"; Hayes, "Metrics"). Since the reader often perceives the principle underlying the verse without formal instruction or conscious effort, meter is what fulfills the reader's expectations for the aesthetic organization of sounds. As Fabb notes, "since most literary form is implied form, . . . most literary form takes on the complexities, indeterminacies, ambiguities and contradictions which are characteristic of inferential processes" (*Language* 215). This knowledge in appreciating meter is an intuitive set of rules, though scansion, quite contrarily, must be learned through a high command of and aesthetic sensitivity to the language. The task of metrists, therefore, resembles the task of grammarians who try to describe tacit knowledge of language with explicit accounts. The abstract character of meter is also proven by the fact that metrists do not learn how to scan the poem by memorizing patterns just like children do not learn the grammar of language by memorizing all the sentences they hear. As Cooper and Meyer affirm, it requires "experience, understanding, and sensitivity" for its interpretation (9).

The second purpose of studying meter is to provide a reasonable system of analysis and a method of scansion that is as simple and coherent as possible. The shorter and simpler the rules are, the more likely they represent the reality of poetic language (Hayes, "Hierarchy"). However, it is not a simple task because the peculiarities are not always obvious, and the sense of metricality, which often derives from a personal interpretation, is the main source of information to determine the meter. Also, the postulated meter should present the degree of metrical complexity, variously described as *degree of complexity* by Halle and Keyser ("Iambic"), a *principle of complexity* by Sapora, a *degree of tolerance in the underlying imperative* by Fussell ("Historical"), *tension and mismatch* by Furniss and Bath, *tension or internal complexity* by Wimsatt, and *interplay* by Wimsatt and Beardsley. The traditional scansion method that places slashes over stressed syllables has not been successful in representing this metrical complexity of the line (Attridge; Bernhart).

Meter is a recurring system. The expectancy of regularity in the reader decides whether the line is metrical or not, and a deviation occurs when this expectation is not met; it reinforces expressive, emotional effects. It is hard to find a perfectly regular line, or else the line is not perceived as poetic if it is totally obedient to the meter. Usually one or more deviations, such as initial inversion in the traditional terminology, add tension between the abstract meter and the actual line. Verse is perceived as most enjoyable when it has both a fixed regular basic rhythm and a potential for expressive variations (Fabb, *Language* 34–87). Andrew and Waldron use the terms *ground-pattern* and *variation* in order to describe the relationship between the base and its deviation (47). It is indeed variation that is important to the meter, but too many deviations may blur it and disturb the reader's expectation. As Andrew and Waldron contend, "a great deal of the variety of English verse is achieved through deliberate flexibility in approximation to and deviation from the conceptual 'norm'" (47). The poets themselves are sometimes blamed for producing unmetrical lines. Such lines should be carefully examined because it is important to find out about the possible ranges of variations and metrical limits. Determining the degree of complexity against the norm and marking metrically ambiguous lines are crucial for the study of meter. Metrically complex lines and metrically ambiguous lines cause great differences in scansion among readers. Again, Russom comments:

> Good poets often deviate from standard verse patterns, in part because what they wish to say makes it necessary to do so and in part to avoid metrical banality. In a poetic form intended for recitation, however, deviance must not create verses too complex for intuitive scansion. The complexity of an individual verse must be kept within tolerable limits, and a poem must not contain an intolerably high frequency of the most deviant verses.
>
> (*Beowulf* 5)

Thus, a reliable method for analyzing meter should account for the entire range of deviations, as well as their limitations.

Third, the study of meter is to prove that it is an abstract form of speech rhythm; Chatman (*Theory* 29) describes the meter as "basically linguistically determined secondary rhythm." It is essential to distinguish between the metrical framework and speech sounds because the meter is the product of negotiation between linguistic freedom and metrical regularity. The poet maintains the relationship between the metrical pattern and the actual product, sometimes consistently and sometimes with less consistency. Thus, efficient studies of meter should reflect the basic phonological rules, as well as the prosodic rules that involve factors other than simple phonetic and phonological elements.

1.3 English Speech Rhythm

A brief explanation on the elements involved in the speech rhythm of the English language will be useful. This section introduces three aspects of English speech rhythm that play a decisive role in determining poetic meter: stress hierarchy and mobile stress, isochrony and stress-timing, and full versus reduced vowels.

1.3.1 Stress Hierarchy and Mobile Stress

In addition to the simple stressed versus unstressed difference, phonologists have acknowledged another intermediate level for English, thus proposing three levels of stress: primary, secondary, and tertiary stresses, or fully stressed, lower stressed, and unstressed (Giegerich, *English Phonology* 67; Roach, *Phonetics* 85–87; Russom, *Beowulf* 216–19). The difference between primary and secondary stresses becomes important especially when stress placement in a compound word is considered (McCully, *Structure* 69–72). A widely-known example to explain this is the difference between a *lighthouse keeper* (someone whose job is to keep a light in a tower to warn ships of hazardous waters) and a *light housekeeper* (a maid who either does not do heavy work or may not weigh very much). Freeborn, supporting Attridge, proposes the use of beats and offbeats for analyses of meter:

> In order to distinguish between the stress-timed rhythm of ordinary speech and the more regular metre of verse, it is helpful to call stressed syllables in verse beats (B) and unstressed syllables off-beats (o). . . . because the beats are isochronous, we can then say that all English metrical verse is written on a pattern of alternating beats and off-beats. (150)

These rhythmic beats establish English rhythm. The basic principle of English speech rhythm is that stressed and unstressed syllables alternate with a fair degree of regularity (Couper-Kuhlen, *Introduction*, *Rhythm*; Cureton, *Rhythmic Phrasing*, "Rhythm"; Freeborn; Furniss and Bath; Jespersen; Stewart, *Technique*; Tarlinskaja, *English Verse*). In other words, English rhythm alternates between syllables with stronger stress and those with weaker stress. Certain syllables that carry lexical stress may be reduced because of the strong tendency to maintain the regular alternation of stressed and unstressed syllables. Bolinger explains that the rule to attach suffixes to an adjective is determined by stress alternation rather than by a rigid principle in stress placement (30–31):

> the óldest mán vs. *the móst óld mán
> the táller búilding vs. *the móst táll búilding
> the déepest ríver vs. *the móst déep ríver

The successive stress in the unacceptable or nonstandard forms, marked with an asterisk, violates the alternation rule of English rhythm; by way of contrast, the stressed syllables are separated by an unstressed syllable in the standard expressions. This metrical adjustment or compensation occurs when several stressed syllables appear without intervening unstressed syllables, and yet none of their stress qualities is reduced. Duncan ("Weak") and Hutcheson ("Realizations") recognize several different levels of weak stress and acknowledge their special role in OE meter. Otherwise, the successive stress will add a special effect to the rhythm. The sequence of stressed syllables may be possible if emphatic and dramatic effect is intended as seen in the following copy for an advertisement:

> "The most happy, funny, sunny show in London"
> (An add for the musical show, *Hairspray*, observed in London, 2009)

Except for such an emphatic case, the succession of stressed syllables usually triggers the weakening of one of the stressed syllables. This de-stressing of syllables is a piece of evidence that English stress entails certain degrees of stress or hierarchy (Cosmos; Hanna, "Alliterative"). Syllables do not bear an absolute value of stress that maintains their quality in every occurrence, but rather the overall pattern of an entire phrase determines the relative weight or prominence of a syllable in contrast to its adjacent neighbors (Roach, *Phonetics* 100). In other words, the absolute phonetic value of a syllable may be altered in actual speech depending upon the phonetic value of the surrounding syllables.

Stress is determined within the metrical structure, namely the hierarchical unit under the phonological structure. In order to reveal the relative contrast in stress, binary or dual grouping and tree-based or grid-based branching have been introduced (Dogil; Giegerich; Hayes; Jespersen; Wimsatt). The following examples are the hierarchical branching of phrase-stress assignment by Lieberman and Prince and the one by Hayes:

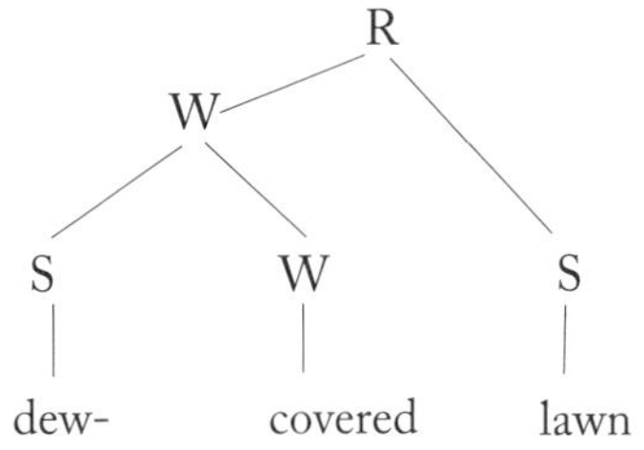

(Liberman and Prince 256)

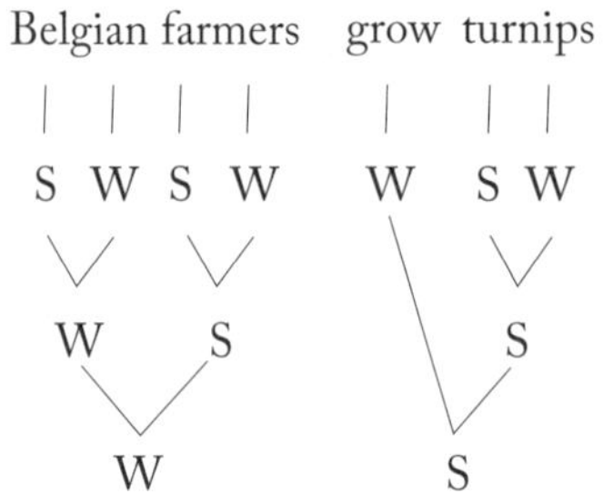

(Hayes, "Phonology" 35)

Treating hierarchical constituents in a binary branching system, Liberman and Prince assign each syllable to a strong or weak position and introduce the concept of a metrical grid that governs rhythmic hierarchies. Relative prominence is applied to each branch in this system to produce the hierarchical structure. Fabb explains this relative nature as follows:

> In English, the rhythmic pattern is realized as relative stress on syllables. . . . In thinking about English stress, it is necessary to distinguish between stress within a lexical word and stress within the utterance as a whole. The latter is constrained primarily by performance considerations, and can be very variable: the same sequence of words can be given very different patterns of stress within the utterance as a whole. This is called the postlexical stress pattern of the utterance. (Fabb, *Linguistics* 35–36)

Similarly, when monosyllables that have a similar quality of stress appear in a row, for example, in phrases such as "ma-ma-ma" (Faure, Hirst, and Chafcouloff 71) "Óh, Óh, Óh, Óh, Óh, Óh, Óh, Óh, Óh" (Cureton, "Rhythm" 107) "tick tack, tick tack" (Couper-Kuhlen, *Introduction* 51–52), or "Róck's vást Wéight" (Furniss and Bath 80), one cannot help but to utter one syllable with more prominence and others with less. Here, strong tension is created between natural rhythm and the meter. Certain principles are operating for addition, deletion, and movement of prominence, as it becomes necessary for the maintenance of the fairly regular alternation either between stressed and unstressed syllables or between beats and offbeats. Both lexical stress and stress hierarchy must be taken into account.

The mobility of stress, or stress shift, plays a vital role in maintaining rhythm.

The following phrases exemplify instances where such shifts take place so that the syllables may contribute toward more regular alternation between beats and offbeats:

Írene Dúnn *vs.* Iréne McDérmott
úpstairs bédroom *vs.* wént upstáirs (G. Allen, "Rhythm" 80)
He plays the clarinét. *vs.* He played a clárinet solo.
fiftéen *vs.* fífteen mén (Beaver, "Problem" 10–11)
thírteen mén
(Couper-Kuhlen, *Introduction* 37; Giegerich, *Metrical phonology* 206–07)
thírteen mén vs. thirtéen Américans (Bolinger 22)
The history was very detáiled. *vs.* a détailed history
I did it alréady. *vs.* I álready did it.
órnate *vs.* the ornáte figures (Chatman, *Theory* 153)
a qúite unknówn efféct *vs.* a lárgely únknown lánd
(Couper-Kuhlen, *Introduction* 33)
bíg black búgs
théy will have béen there befóre (Couper-Kuhlen, *Introduction* 37)
I counted fourtéen. *vs.* I've fóurteen books.
the comment was mispláced. *vs.* a mísplaced comment (Cutler 183–84)
fóurteen shíllings
ínlaid wood *vs.* áll inláid
únknown land *vs.* qúite unknówn (D. Jones 233)
bad-témpered *but* a bád-tempered teacher
half-tímbered *but* a hálf-timbered hóuse
heavy-hánded *but* a héavy-handed sentence (Roach, *Phonetics* 100)

As the above examples demonstrate, a word uttered in isolation has stress on a fixed syllable as defined in the lexicon, but the stress prominence may be altered in order to accomplish a regular alternation of stressed and unstressed syllables within the phrase in which the word occurs.

Two factors determine stress hierarchy in verse: the framework that has already been set up by the meter and the actual environment in which the syllable is placed. The meter, or the verse design in Jakobson's terminology ("Closing" 364), conditions prominence of stress according to its surrounding syllables. Couper-Kuhlen comments:

> If we view stresses as rhythmic beats, then we can account for this shift by appealing to a basic rhythmic principle of English, i.e. that stressed and unstressed syllables alternate regularly in speech. (*Introduction* 33)

When two consecutive syllables have a similar value of stress at the lexical level, the hierarchy intervenes in order to avoid a consecutive row of syllables of similar quality. On the other hand, when syllables with weak lexical stress appear in a row, one or two of them will gain additional prominence. It is noteworthy that, despite the frequent occurrences of stress shift, speakers are not always aware of this phenomenon. Stress shift, therefore, is systematic and presumably intuitive knowledge.

Grouping the words that may undergo stress shift according to grammatical functions is a common practice. For example, Couper-Kuhlen classifies word categories into two types (*Introduction* 35–36):

Word Categories Typically Stressed:
    nouns, pronouns, adjectives, main verbs, auxiliaries, adverbs, interjections.

Word Categories Typically Unstressed:
    pronouns, determiners, auxiliaries, adverbs (degree, relative), prepositions, conjunctions.

Dividing words into two categories, Duggan assumes that words from open classes occupy metrically prominent positions more frequently than words from closed classes ("Patterning" 77–78):

Open Classes:
    nouns, adjectives, most verb forms, adverbs ending in *-ly* or of two syllables, pronouns ending in *-self*.

Closed Classes:
    prepositions, some verbs, auxiliaries, pronouns, monosyllabic adverbs

Though these classifications reflect a certain relationship between stress hierarchy and syntactic categories, classifying words according to grammatical categories does not necessarily reflect the nature of stress shift. Conjunctions that introduce dependent clauses may be stressed, even though conjunctions in general are unstressed, for instance:

> Whén he comes, I'll . . .
> Ás I was saying . . .
> Áfter he had left . . . (D. Jones 252)

D. Jones also argues that the copulative conjunctions *and* and *but* may be stressed when immediately followed by two or three consecutive unstressed syllables:

> ánd at the same time . . .
> bút it's of the greatest importance . . . (D. Jones 253)

Adverbs are the most subtle category in determining their stress quality. D. Jones (253) assumes that adverbs such as *now* and *then* are not stressed in continuous speech. Matonis claims in her study of ME verse that words such as *what*, *which*, *this*, *all*, *many*, *now*, *soon*, and *then* may "arguably bear stress" ("Reexamination" 357).

It is known that adjustment can occur in the relative stress levels between the verb and the direct object, between verbs and particles, or between complements and objects. While Cosmos suggests in his study of *Beowulf* that certain verbs are unstressed, Schmerling (81) observes that verbs receive less stress than the subject and the direct object. This implies that predicates receive less stress than their arguments. Stress assignment in compound words (Kiparsky, "Stress" 578) and words borrowed from a foreign language, especially from French (Tarlinskaja, *English Verse* 40), is unstable and troublesome for an adequate description in terms of categories. Tarlinskaja, in agreement with Halle and Keyser, suggests the existence of accentual doublets for loan words: one in a native system and another in a Romance accent. Tarlinskaja further claims that the stress distribution of dissyllabic and trisyllabic native English words, as well as hybrid words such as *goddesse* and *pleasing*, is most complex in stress placement. Attridge tries to solve this problem of defining the mobility of stress by means of the concepts of indefinite stress and metrically subordinate stress (*Rhythms*), both of which will be used hereafter to designate a syllable that is flexible enough to make itself metrically useful for the maintenance of the regular alternation of stress.

1.3.2 Isochrony and Stress-Timing

Isochrony and *stress-timing* have been common terms for explaining English speech rhythm. English is said to be a stress-timed language (Freeborn; Giegerich, *English Phonology*; Hogg and McCully; McCully and Hogg); that is, stressed syllables recur in isochrony, equal intervals of time. A typical definition of isochrony is that "stressed syllables occur at approximately equal intervals of time, and the quantities of unstressed syllables vary to fit the time available between stresses" (Knowles 116). Other definitions of isochrony include that stresses occur "as nearly as possible at equal distances" (D. Jones 237), "in a fairly regular pace" (W. Allen 3), "at fairly equal intervals of time" (Gimson 238), or "at (roughly) equal timing intervals" (Giegerich, *English Phonology* 181). Common examples to explain the isochronous character of English rhythm are as follows. Different stress marks employed by each scholar are unified as ´ :

	Énglish	is	éasy.	
	Énglish	is very	éasy.	
The	Énglish lesson	is very	éasy.	
The	téacher		cáme.	
The	téacher is the one who		cáme.	(Shen and Peterson 7)

bréad'n bútter
drínka pínta mílka dáy. (Giegerich, *Metrical Phonology* 12)
Géts óut pláin sóap cán't réach. *vs.*
Tákes awáy the dírt that cómmon sóaps can néver réach.
(Bolinger 18)

the mán's hére
the mánor's hére
the mánager's hére (Hogg and McCully 225)
Thís is the hóuse that Jáck búilt (Giegerich, *English Phonology* 181)

The isochronous character of the English language causes certain rhythmic effects. Monobeat syllables in succession may have a special effect:

You háve nó búsiness asking me to do something like that.
It's júst nó úse trying to force him. (Bolinger 33)

The term *stress-timed* is used in contrast to the syllable-timed rhythm, a term first proposed by Pike in 1945. Roach uses the word *rhythmicality* inclusively for the two kinds of rhythms. While stressed syllables recur at isochronous intervals in stress-timed rhythm, syllables recur at equal intervals of time in syllable-timed rhythm. The contrast is found, for example, in the following sentences:

(English) Thís is the hóuse that Jáck búilt.
(French) C'est absolument ridicule. (Roach, "Distinction" 73)

Freeborn, in consideration of the stress-timing nature that favors the isochronous stressed syllables, asserts that isochrony, stress-timing, and alliteration all set the foregrounds for the "music" of the verse (146). Isochrony does not exist such that it can be objectively measured by mechanical devices. The actual time intervals may not be exactly equal but is close enough to be perceived as equal. There is an apparent gap between perceptual and physical senses concerning isochrony and stress-timing. The actual durational differences that have been proven by mechanical measurements are above the perceptual threshold for both speakers and listeners so that a strong rhythmic beat, not the exact amount of duration, is established in the flow of sounds, imposed by a perceptual tendency toward recurring phenomena. English rhythm is perceived as different from other languages such as French or Spanish, due to this flow of syllables.

Isochrony has not been proven in a pure linguistic sense. That is why a metronome, which has been suggested to be a suitable measuring scale to prove the stress-timing character of the English language, does not fit into English rhythm but rather reveals the inconsistent length between interstress intervals. It is human nature to impose a rhythmical pattern onto a flow of inorganic speech sounds such as "ma, ma, ma." When the listener hears three or four syllables that have a similar quality of stress, one syllable may be heard as if it had more prominence and thus be perceived as a more highly stressed syllable among the group. Even though there are differences among the interstress intervals, the listener imposes specific rhythmic pulses on the flow of speech sounds. Human senses are not very accurate in objectively measuring natural phenomena; psychological regularity, instead, is perceived according to expectancy. Human ears, therefore, seem to perceive rhythm according to psychological time through the salient and subordinate categories in rhythm. Though stressed syllables do not recur in exactly equal duration, the intervals are close enough to be perceived as rigid.

Cutler's study on syllable omission in spontaneous speech indicates that a closer approximation to rhythmic regularity is observed in errors, as well. Some of the errors she found in actual speech are as follows:

(1) E: /Next we /have this bi/cential/ rug
T: /Next we /have this bicen/tennial/ rug
(2) E: what the /speaker thinks his /interlocker/ knows
T: what the /speaker thinks his inter/locutor/ knows
(3) E: /in his /life there /seems to /be am/biguty
T: /in his /life there /seems to /be ambiguity (Cutler 186)

These errors can be explained by the speakers' intent to maintain the rhythmic regularity; namely these errors have resulted because the speakers tried to keep the length of each *foot* (Cutler's term) similar. Not all errors, of course, are made because of rhythmic regularity, but the tendency to establish psychological isochrony may be a cause of a twist of the tongue.

English speech rhythm, thus, consists of an expectancy system for isochronous alternation. How is this rhythm, then, incorporated into a more restricted scheme of verse? The answer may lie in unled choral reading. In choral reading, readers must use the rhythmic pattern that they expect everyone to use. Thus, obedience to the basic framework is indispensable for successful unison. Boomsliter, Creel, and Hastings have tried to bring to light this expectancy system by conducting an experiment in which readers were asked to read a passage in chorus. Readers had to utilize the prevailing pattern in order to read in an identical rhythm a nursery rhyme, "Pease Porridge Hot" and poems by Dickinson and by Tennyson. It turned out that stress tends to be imposed in a certain place in the choral reading.

The discussions of isochrony suggest that English rhythm entails a special rhythmicality in fairly regular time-intervals based on the recognition of a succession of two sorts of syllables: those perceived more stressed than the adjacent syllables and those perceived less stressed than their neighbors.

1.3.3 Full versus Reduced Vowels

Another characteristic of English speech rhythm is vowel reduction in unstressed syllables (Cosmos; Dauer; McCully; Roach). Stressed syllables contain full vowels whereas unstressed syllables are reduced. English rhythm may be redefined as the alternation of syllables with full vowels and those of reduced vowels in perceptual isochrony. The existence of two different kinds of unstressed vowels makes English speech rhythm flexible, but at the same time, quite complex. The first group consists of unstressed syllables that are genuinely unstressed, and the other one consists of syllables whose stress has been reduced within the phonological context. To complicate the situation, the reduction rule is not necessarily obligatory, but the phonological context of the syllable, regional and dialectal tendencies, and even personal habits determine whether the vowel may lose its full quality. The following minimal sets may sound identical:

Minnie	Willie	hairy	lassie	tory	hippie	
Minna	Willa	Harrah	Lhasa	tora	hippa	
minnow	willow	harrow	lasso	toro	hippo	(Bolinger 7)

Reduced vowels may not usually inform about which phoneme has been intended before the reduction; for example, unknown proper names are difficult to dictate because it is not always possible to speculate on the original quality before the syllable has been reduced. Though actual pronunciation may vary, the schwa sound [ə] plays a crucial role in representing the reduced vowel (McCully, *Structure* 120–24). Brinton and Arnovick consider vowel reduction to be one of the most significant sound change in the ME period (266–68). The centralization of vowels and laxing of a vowel in an unstressed syllable to schwa and later its complete loss caused various types of apocope and syncope, affecting the rhythmic structure.

The reduction rule goes even further and may entirely delete the vowel, which is again peculiar to English rhythm. This is typically observed when a vowel is followed by certain consonants like /l/, /n/, /m/, and /r/ that may form a syllable peak. For instance, *written*, *seven*, *eaten*, *bread and* (butter) can be pronounced as monosyllabic words whereas *common*, *canon*, *London*, and *iron* are usually disyllabic. Vowel reduction and deletion were already taking place in the time of early Middle English (C. Brown; Jordan; Starr; Wells). Jordan summarizes the chief characteristics of ME as follows (1):

1. Reduction of most post-tonic vowels to schwa *e*: OE *mona* (month), *sunu* (son), *stanas* (stones) became *mone*, *sune*, *stones* in ME.
2. Penetration of the French element into the vocabulary as a result of the Norman Conquest.

Certain unstressed syllables have been silent from the twelfth century; for example, OE *hlaefdiȝe* and *ælmesse* were already in the time of Orm *laffdiȝ* and *alms*, respectively. Stress on suffixes, which used to possess the quality of full vowels in Germanic counterparts, gradually became weak in contrast to other stressed syllables. Vowel reduction and deletion are unique in that their operation is optional; namely the vowels may undergo changes if the meter requires metrical adjustment. For the study of meter, including that of ME verse, it is necessary to reflect these reduced and deleted vowels in scansion because they may affect the metrical structure of the line.

In sum, the following six factors contribute to the formation of English rhythm:

1. English meter can be characterized by the integration of stress and the syllable. Syllable counting in English may vary according to the structure of syllables and the possible application of vowel reduction or deletion rules. Importantly, these variations are not necessarily obligatory; the same syllables may be realized differently under different metrical frameworks.
2. Stress plays the most vital role in English rhythm. However, not only stressed syllables but also unstressed ones contribute to the establishment of a peculiar rhythm. Lexical stress itself does not include information as to how it will be realized in the actual utterance. Hierarchy of stress among neighboring syllables, the tendency toward perceptual isochrony, and the preference of regular alternation between stressed and unstressed syllables determine what quality of stress a syllable should hold within a phonological context or metrical framework.
3. Rhythm is a recurring system. The movement of the sounds, not the sounds themselves, establishes rhythm. Meter reflecting a certain rhythm is an arithmetic norm that may include a controlled departure from the norm. Meter is linguistically determined secondary rhythm.
4. Some of the features that constitute English rhythm are language universals, but others may not be so. The notion of stress-timed and syllable-timed languages, though not proven to be satisfying, reveals certain differences in rhythmic make-up of different languages. It is clear at least that rhythmic force created by stressed syllables, as well as by unstressed ones, plays a vital role in English rhythm.
5. Speech rhythm is an expectancy system because it is perceived through

the imposition of an anticipated rhythmic structure on the flow of speech sounds. When this norm is deviated, the resulting speech rhythm is perceived as irregular, or emphasis is added. This predictable system is the target of metrical analysis.

6. Rhythm is not necessarily regular all the time. Deviations from the norm within a certain limit offer variations and rhetorical effects. The actual distribution of stress quality, therefore, does not always obey the stress patterns marked in the lexicon. Though the actual quality and quantity of stressed syllables are not exactly the same, the succession of rhythmic units is perceived as even. Metrical contexts, which are based on an expectancy system, decide the actual quality and quantity of the syllable. Therefore, it is crucial for the study of meter to determine how the compromise between linguistic freedom and metrical constraints, called "metrical convenience" by Duggan ("Final -*e*" 191), takes place in the actual metrical context.

1.4 Approaches to ME Versification

This section reviews the unique points of poetic forms and verse production in medieval times. This is important not only because of the changes that the language underwent but also because of the series of changes that the composition and publishing process underwent. Four points of interest about ME verse will be introduced: its unique metrical phenomena; the role of the word-final –*e*; the relationship among the poet, the scribe, and the audience; and the relationship among meter, scansion, and performance.

1.4.1 Metrical Phenomena Unique to ME Verse

Some of the special features and phenomena of ME verse already have formal terms. The following thirteen ideas, traditional and recent, denote specific poetic effects, and each will be explained briefly: elision, caesura and half-lines, line beginnings, line endings, alliteration and rhyme, foreign influence, strophes and stanzas, beats and offbeats, implied beats and implied offbeats, rising and falling rhythms, quality and quantity of stress, method of position occupancy, and four-beat meter and five-beat meter.

i. Elision

A blending of two or more syllables into a single one, commonly called elision or resolution (Carroll 171–76), has been recognized not only in OE but also from the time of Chaucer (Couper-Kuhlen, *Introduction* 58; Moore 62). Elision alliteration, which is two sounds across the word boundary providing the alliterating syllable, is known in ME alliterative verse (Duggan, "Final *–e*"; T. Turville-Petre, "Emendation"). The following lines exemplify the elision alliteration where it is underlined. Simple alliteration is italicized:

A 364 *N*owþire my*ne a*wen ne na *n*othire god lat þe *n*oȝt spare,
A 582 And *n*orisch him as *n*amely as he my*ne a*wyn warre,
A 1829 *T*akis þam with him to his *t*ent and þam a*t e*se makis.
PE 233 Ho watz me *n*erre þe*n a*unte or *n*ece:
G 356 Bot for as *m*uch as ȝe ar *m*yn em I a*m o*nly to prayse;
G 962 Þe twey*ne y*ȝen and þe *n*ase, þe *n*aked lyppez,
MA 130 It es *l*efull ti*ll* vs his *l*ikynge till wyrche;

Two types of elision are common in English verse: synaeresis (when two vowels are contracted to a single syllable) and syncope (when a consonant or an unstressed vowel is omitted). Fussell's examples of synaeresis and syncope are as follows (*Poetic Meter* 26):

Of man's first disobedience, and the fruit — Milton, "Paradise Lost"
Ill fares the land, to hastening ills a prey
Goldsmith, "The Deserted Village"

In Milton's line, the diphthong /ie/ becomes a so-called y-glide and is pronounced as a single vowel while *hastening* in Goldsmith's line is reduced to two syllables so that the line will fit into the metrical constraint of ten syllables per verse line. Contraction also occurs when /h/ is deleted between vowels, between a sonorant and a vowel, or between a vowel and a sonorant (Suzuki 102–03). Whether it is called syncope (within words) or apocope (between words) depends on the position of the syllable that undergoes elision. The possible extent of elision becomes crucial in reading ME poems, especially where syllable counting and the syllable value of the final *-e* are concerned.

ii. Caesura and Half-Lines

Caesura, a term commonly used for a pause in verse lines, may fall near the beginning of the line (initial caesura), in the middle (medial caesura), or near the line end (terminal caesura). A simple analogy to explain a caesura is that it signals a rest to the ear just as punctuation marks a rest to the eye. Phrase divisions, normally indicated between syntactic units by punctuation marks including semi-colons and commas, correspond to the position of a caesura. If a caesura falls in the middle, a verse line may be further divided into two half-lines or hemistiches. Half-lines of ME verse are sometimes not as predictable as those of OE verse; some metrists such as Saintsbury recognize distinct halves in a line of ME verse while others do not (Duggan, "Patterning" 77). The caesura, especially a medial one, is important for the line structure of ME alliterative verse because it designates the possible place for a pause between the two half-lines, called the *a*-verse and the *b*-verse. The terms *the first and the second half-lines* are also commonly used instead of the *a*-verse and the *b*-verse.

iii. Line Beginnings

The verse line may begin with one or more unstressed syllables. These line-initial unstressed syllables are traditionally called anacrusis. In a traditional sense, anacrusis signifies the extra unstressed syllables that are placed before the first measure (Carroll). The combination of unstressed and stressed syllables in that order establishes an upbeat, rising rhythm. Stewart points out that lines without anacrusis are perceived as more vigorous and forceful than those that begin with an unstressed syllable, which he calls direct attack (*Technique* 46).

iv. Line Endings

Unstressed syllables at the beginning of the line, as well as unstressed syllables at the end, can play a prominent role in ME verse since paroxytonic endings, traditionally called feminine endings, frequently appear in ME verse. Stewart explains paroxytonic endings as colloquial turns of speech (*Technique* 46) while Fabb pays attention to the "brevis in longo (short in long)" (*Language* 175–77). Along with line-initial unstressed syllables, the effect of the line-terminal unstressed syllable or syllables may often be significant enough to affect the metrical structure of the whole verse line.

v. Alliteration and Rhyme

Alliteration is the repetition of the same sound. Precisely, it is the repetition of the same consonants or consonant clusters generally in stressed root syllables. The general rules about alliteration can be summarized as follows:

1. The same initial consonant or consonant cluster usually appears twice in the first half-line and at least once in the second half.
2. Vocalic alliteration, in which any vowels and diphthongs are considered to alliterate, is possible because vowels and diphthongs are supposed to be preceded by a glottal stop.
3. The consonant /h/ may alliterate with other /h/ sounds, as well as with vowels.

The alliteration of ME verse is slightly different from that of OE verse. In OE verse, the first half-line contains at least one but no more than two alliterating syllables whereas the second half-line has one but no more than one alliterating syllable. In Germanic languages, which consider stress as the primary element of verse, alliteration is a predominant metrical principle (Creed 49). Though alliterative poetry became popular with possible end-rhyme in the ME period, its characteristics include certain differences from those of OE verse. For example, ME alliteration is less rigid than that of OE; the ME line became more end-stopped than in OE verse; the first half-line gained more flexibility in the number of stressed syllables and distribution of alliterating syllables; and finally, the division of the two half-lines became less abrupt than in OE.

vi. Exotic Influence

ME poets encountered foreign poetic devices quite different from what had been employed in OE verse. Because of the hybrid state consisting of various languages such as Celtic, Latin, and Scandinavian, there is even a claim that ME is a creole (Brinton and Arnovick 297–99; Görlach, *Linguistic* 140–54; van Gelderen 106–08). As a result of the Norman Conquest in 1066, many Romance words, as well as exotic meters, came into English. This multilingual situation encouraged polyglot literature (Stein 35–36) and enabled poets to use new verse forms other than the OE conventions. ME poets were eager to use a variety of Romance vocabulary for alliteration and rhyme and to place stress according to the Romance stress rule on the syllable that is originally unstressed. Not only verse writers but also prose writers willingly tried to use French rhythm and vocabulary in their writing (Blake, "Audience" 439; Lester 26–46). Thus, two sets of stress rules were known in the late ME period: the native Germanic system and the Romance system. For example, the word *coming* could be read as *cóming* according to the Germanic rule or as *comíng* according to the Romance rule. The Romance stress rule added doublets to stress placement of the language, which was one of the most significant changes that happened to the English language during the ME period (Duggan, "Stress" 325–27). Another difference between OE verse and ME verse resulting from foreign influences is the loss of inflectional endings that enforced the rigid grammatical order of words in a sentence. In OE verse, it was possible to move words around in order to fit them into the meter, but ME poets had less freedom than Anglo-Saxon poets concerning word order. Since both vocabulary and syntax contribute to different metrical make-up within alliterative meter, it is essential to indicate in scansion possible variants but not to impose a predetermined way of reading.

vii. Strophes and Stanzas

Sir Gawain and the Green Knight, one of the major ME alliterative poems, consists of 101 structural units in verse, which is traditionally called stanza. *Piers Plowman*, another major ME alliterative poem, does not suggest such a grouping of lines. The term *strophe* is also used to signify a division of verse lines. The strophic construction of a poem is recognized in certain ME poems such as *Sir Gawain and the Green Knight*, *The Wars of Alexander*, those recorded in the Lincoln Cathedral Manuscript, and in the margins of the *Morte Arthure* (Day; Duggan, "Strophic"; Vaughan). A strophe in *Sir Gawain* is followed by extra lines called a bob (a short line consisting of one stressed syllable with unstressed syllables on each side) and a wheel (a set of four lines longer than the bob but shorter than the typical line in the main strophe). The bob and the wheel not only separate strophes but also bring varied rhythm into the poem. According to Turco, the bob and the wheel are "an English accentual-syllabic quintet stanza sometimes found in association with accentual poems as a tail (*cauda*) on a stanza or as a strophe of Anglo-Saxon prosody" (102).

viii. Beats and Offbeats

In order to avoid the confusion of using stressed and unstressed syllables or strong and weak stress in the study of meter and reflect possible variations in quality and quantity of stress and syllable under metrical circumstances, the terms *beat* and *offbeat* will be used for the metrically stressed and unstressed syllables, respectively. The terms *stressed*, *unstressed*, *strong*, or *weak syllables* will be reserved for the examination of stress placement but not for the construction of meter. The two layers of symbols, the first one above the line indicating the stress pattern and the second one beneath the line marking the metrical pattern, are one of the advantages of Attridge's method of scansion that allows variations in stress quality and does not force stress over a syllable under a special circumstance (Glowka 79–91; Holder 64–102; Wesling 38). It also reflects, most efficiently among other methods, the linear order of syllables and their relationship with the adjacent partners without forcing the foot boundary or the prescribed metrical type. Though the actual presentation may differ, this way of understanding the rhythmic make-up of the verse line has been adopted by various scholars including Fabb, Freeborn, Furniss and Bath, Glowka, and Wesling.

ix. Implied Beats and Implied Offbeats

Occasionally, a syllable or two may be missing in the expected position within a verse line. If the missing syllable is an unstressed one, a succession of stressed syllables will result. If a stressed syllable is missing, the line lacks one of the metrical beats that the meter requires, and a sense of deviation is created. Pope proposes the idea of rest in his metrical study on *Beowulf*, marking a rest in the place of a missing stressed syllable. He assumes that, in the days when the poem was performed by singers, the harp[2] was struck in these places. The term *rest* will not be used for the present research because the analogy to music may be another cause of confusion. Instead, the terms *implied beat* and *implied offbeat* will be used, based on Attridge's idea. If the missing syllable is an unstressed one, the symbol for an implied offbeat ø will be placed in scansion. If the missing syllable is a stressed one, the symbol for an implied beat $\underline{B}$ will appear.

x. Rising and Falling Rhythms

The traditional terms *ascending rhythm* and *descending rhythm* have been used in describing differences, for example, differences between iambic rhythm and trochaic rhythm. The former is often considered suitable and natural, but the latter that divides syllables into groups of a stressed syllable and its following unstressed partner may be insistent and distinct. Bolinger presents an opposing opinion that the dactylic meter, a falling rhythm whose foot consists of a stressed syllable followed by two unstressed syllables, is ideal for English. Schane, on the other hand, asserts that English stress rhythm is trochaic. Recognizing a clear difference between iambic and trochaic rhythm, Hascall ("Trochaic") yet questions whether or not the use of different foot types is adequate. Demonstrating three types of line structure that may happen in iambic meter but never in trochaic meter, Hascall contends that iambic and trochaic rhythms are distinguishable. He is skeptical, however, about the distinction between triple meters such as dactylic and anapestic meters. The contradiction that the foot and its substitutions present is that it is not always consistent. The difference between iambic and trochaic meters is often ambiguous, as is the difference between dactylic and anapestic meters. Scholars have been suspicious about the significance of the foot for ME verse (Duggan, "Patterning"; Saintsbury). However, the distinction between rising and falling rhythms is useful because the link between a stressed syllable and an unstressed syllable may play a pivotal role in rhythmic effect. The following stanzas are both in four-beat meter, but their rhythmic effects are quite different from one another:

> Condemned to Hope's delusive mine,
> As on we toil from day to day,
> By sudden blasts or slow decline,
> Our social comforts drop away.
>
> When the bonny blade carouses,
> Pockets full, and spirits high,
> What are acres? What are Houses?
> Only dirt, or wet or dry. (Attridge, *Rhythms* 108)

If the link between an offbeat and its following beat is strong as seen in the first stanza, the line is in rising rhythm. If the link between an offbeat and its preceding beat is strong as seen in the second stanza, the line is in falling rhythm. Stewart reports that ordinary English speech is composed roughly of forty-five percent rising phrases, ten percent falling phrases, and forty-five percent neutral (*Technique* 38). The large percentage of rising phrases is, Stewart argues, due to the use of articles, prepositions, and conjunctions.

xi. Quality and Quantity of Stress

English stress changes its quality and quantity in relation to the syllables that surround a given syllable. English meter is not purely quantitative, but the varying quality and quantity of stress within a syllable play a significant role in establishing isochronic rhythm. Syllables with greater force of quality and quantity than the adjacent syllables are perceived as beats whereas those that do not outstand are perceived as offbeats. The terms *beats* and *offbeats* reflect changes of syllable quality and quantity due to the metrical adjustment.

xii. Method of Position Occupancy

Halle and Keyser ("Chaucer") first proposed syllable occupancy, abandoning the traditional foot as the base of meter. In *English Stress*, the two authors present a formal description of iambic pentameter according to the position occupancy system. The three types of abstract entities correspond to a single syllable: *S* for a strong syllable, *W* for a weak syllable, and *X* for an optional syllable. Stressed syllables occur in *S* positions only and in all *S* positions. The asterisk denotes a syllable that is preferable whereas parentheses indicate where another syllable is optional. Thus, their abstract metrical pattern for iambic pentameter is postulated as follows:

Verse → (*W*)**SWSWSWSWS*(*X*)(*X*) (*English Stress* 169)

Another contribution by Halle and Keyser is their recognition of optional and preferred elements in meter by means of parentheses and asterisks respectively.

Fabb, acknowledging the complexity of metricality, uses the position occupancy scheme in order to clarify explicit rhythm and the metrical template (*Language* 1–33). Attridge's method of separating the stress pattern from the metrical pattern better reflects the reality of stress distribution within a line because strict distinction between stress rules and metrical rules is crucial to the study of meter. Attridge explains his method as follows:

> The scansion of a line provides a graphic representation of the relationship between the metrical pattern and the stress pattern; that is, it shows which metrical rules are employed at particular points to realise beats and offbeats. It therefore directly reflects the way in which the line is perceived as rhythmically regular, indicating the degree and exact nature of metrical deviation

at every stage . . . Full scansion shows the stress pattern above the line, and the metrical pattern with deviation symbols beneath it:

```
      +s -s   [s]    +s    -s   +s  (s)-s +s  -s -s
  (1) Gilding pale streams with heavenly alchemy
        B     ŏ        B      o     B     o B    o [B]
```

However, the stress pattern can be fully specified without showing +s and -s, since the absence of a symbol will indicate the most straightforward realisation implied by the metrical pattern and deviation symbol:

```
              [s]                   (s)
  (1) Gilding pale streams with heavenly alchemy
         B    ŏ        B      o      B    o B   o [B]
```

(Attridge, *Rhythms* 361–62)

xiii. Four-Beat Meter and Five-Beat Meter

Creed, Halle and Keyser, and Pope initiated the study of OE meter. Recently, a considerable number of theories and arguments have been made by Cable ("Meter"), Creed, Fulk, Kendall, and Russom. Particularly insightful is the study of four-beat meter of OE verse and other Germanic meters in contrast to popular verbal art such as nursery rhymes and mnemonic verse. Distinctive similarities have been recognized between the meter of nursery rhymes and counting-out rhymes and that of OE (Freeborn; Guéron; Kelly and Rubin; Keyser; Lester). Burling compares various children's verses in his cross-linguistic study, and concludes that the four-by-four structure, which contains four major beats in a line and four lines in each stanza, is especially common. Nursery rhymes and popular songs preserve a natural rhythm for English verse and, thus, are pleasant to the ear and easy to remember. The four-by-four pattern has a "strongly insistent metrical pattern and coaxes into a chant-like rendition" (Furniss and Bath 31). The relationship between the native four-stress meter and the so-called iambic pentameter is more complicated than that between nursery rhymes and OE verse (Furniss and Bath 34–45). The fifth beat in iambic pentameter is sometimes realized where the medial pause falls (Malof 586–87) or when a weak syllable is promoted to a stressed one. Metrically ambiguous lines in pentameter may often be read in the native four-stressed rhythm; in other words, the old native meter is always ready to threaten iambic meter because:

> . . . in the iambic pentameter generally the formal pattern gives a continuous sense of order and reference while the four-stress tendency of the rhythm provides a continuous pull away from that pattern, creating the tension between meter and rhythm. (Malof 588)

Thus, when English poets attempt to write their verse in a five-stress meter, the old four-stress meter may still stand out in the reader's perception. As Malof observes, "in times of metrical uncertainty the English poets always return to the native English form and character, the four-stress pattern on an accentual basis" (583). Since ME alliterative verse lines can be four-beat and five-beat, it will be useful to keep in mind the possible tension between these two meters.

1.4.2 The Role of the Word-Final *-e*

The treatment of the word-final *-e* is one of the most unsettled, controversial issues in the study of ME versification because a reading can vary significantly according to the syllabic value of the final *-e*. Its disappearance from actual pronunciation took place gradually during the ME period. First, phonetic changes in the early stage of ME caused vowel reduction in unstressed syllables, especially those of inflectional endings; thus the final *-e* changed into a schwa (C. Brown 473). In addition to these inflectional and etymological final *-e*'s, other kinds of final *-e*'s appeared such as inorganic final *-e*'s that have no historical antecedent and scribal final *-e*'s that are used in the places where other vowels would have appeared had the scribe known the proper forms. Conner (35) asserts that scribes omitted or added final *-e*'s according to their own habits without paying attention to etymology and inflections. Thus, unstressed syllables were first centralized, and then became entirely lost. For example:

swete	[swe:te]	>	[swe:tə]	>	[swe:t]
ryde	[ri:de]	>	[ri:də]	>	[ri:d]
roote	[ro:te]	>	[ro:tə]	>	[ro:t]

Old English	>	Middle English	>	Modern English
hnappian [hnæpjan]	>	nape [napə]	>	nap
hlæne [hlæ:nɛ]	>	leane [lɛ:nə]	>	lean

drivan [drivan] > drive [dri:və] > drive

(Fennell 98)

C. Brown (473) believes that the final *-e* was syllabic in verse probably until the time of Chaucer, except when it was elided in front of a vowel or a combination of the weak /h/ and a vowel. The fusion of the final *–e*, when it is followed by a vowel or /h/, is also commonly agreed upon.

Among the dialects spoken during the ME period, the northern dialects are said to be the first to have dropped the syllabic *-e* by the end of the fourteenth century or even earlier (Duggan, " Final *-e*" 140) whereas the final *-e* maintained its syllabic value in the southern and Kentish dialects throughout the fourteenth century (Moore 119–25). However, even if it was pronounced, its grammatical function had been lost long before. Various arguments have been made on this issue concerning the vocalization of a word-final *-e* (Cable, *Tradition* 66–84; Duggan, "Final *–e*" 140–45; P. Frankis 11–12). The idea that the metrical environment in the line determines the vocalization of the final *-e* and unstressed inflectional suffixes seems a reasonable way to decide their metrical value (Attridge, *Rhythms* 71–72; Tarlinskaja, *English Verse* 71).

It appears, nonetheless, difficult to reach an absolute conclusion about whether or not unstressed syllables such as the final *-e* and other inflectional endings retained their syllabic value in reading medieval English (Barney; Cable, "Standards"; Donaldson, "Final *–e*"; Duggan, "Final *–e*"; P. Frankis; Minkova, *History*). In Chaucer's time, as many argue, it used to be pronounced on certain occasions but not all the time. In other words, the final *-e* was in a transitional stage; it might form a syllable in certain places, but might not retain its syllabic value in others. Chaucer's verse sounds awkward if the reader tries not to pronounce any final *-e*'s or unstressed inflectional endings. On the other hand, it would also sound unnatural if all of these unstressed syllables are pronounced as separate syllables. As to ME alliterative verse, Putter and Stokes assume that the final *–e* is used for metrical purposes, metrical demands, and metrical flexibility.

Attridge treats the final *-e* as an optional syllable filler "to prevent successive stresses" (*Rhythms* 71–72). He assumes that the optional pronunciation of the final *-e* had survived in verse reading long after its obsolescence from actual speech. Tarlinskaja presents two different types of reading of the final *–e* in pre-Chaucerian romances of the fourteenth century: one in which the final *-e*'s are syllabic, and the other in which the final *-e*'s are considered optional.

She chooses the latter method in her analysis because it allows certain flexibility. Trying to reconstruct the actual speech of ME, Conner suggests that not only the *e* feminine but also the *e* mute, which comes in the middle of words such as *judgement* or *trewely*, are likely to have been pronounced.

The orthography of the final *-e*'s may not reflect how it was pronounced in actual speech. Despite unsettled arguments, marking the final *-e* and other unstressed inflectional endings as optional elements will illuminate certain tendencies as to where these weak syllables appear; namely when the meter demands a certain number of syllables for each line and there are not enough unstressed syllables except for the final *-e* and inflectional endings, they may retain their syllabic value. When there are enough unstressed syllables between beats, they may not be realized as syllables. Lester asserts (114):

> The situation was changing throughout the period, with final *–e* ceasing to be pronounced earlier in northern districts than in the South. It remained a feature in written English long after it had died out in the spoken language, but as time went by final *–e* in verse came to be used as a separate syllable only where metrical conditions required it.

1.4.3 The Poet, the Scribe, and the Audience

Medieval verse is created in a different literacy context from that of modern times. During the ME period, the literary product was created by the poet, copied and presumably altered several times by scribes, and, for the most part, enjoyed aurally by the audience (R. Allen; Bradbury; Chapman; Coleman, *Public*; Creed; Koff; Lawton, "Diversity"; Leonard; Pearsall, *Poetry*; Salter, "Revival"; Sisam). This relationship among the poet, the scribe, and the audience is quite different from that of the later period. The scribe's intervention often affected the structure and rhythm of the verse (Blake, *Introduction* 77–79; Duggan, "Scribal" 215; Fulk 30; Kane, "Text" 187; Matonis, "Poetry" 345; Russom, *Old English Meter* 133); alliteration was quite frequently altered by the scribe (Duggan, "Patterning" 82–83). This process may be described as follows: The poet first tried to compose his work in the form of a draft or loose rhythmical prose that may not have always been written down. He then revised it so that the alliteration would not deviate from regular patterns (Lawton, "Introduction" 7). Duggan believes that irregular alliteration is scribal "corruption" rather than the poet's original work ("Patterning" 102).

There is no evidence that the poet always used regular prototype and base meter; neither is there indisputable evidence that all the irregular lines are scribal. The extant texts contain what was acceptable to the scribes, but do not necessarily reflect the original in the identical manner. In the process of copying, the scribes might have rearranged the verse according to their own dialect and style, which might have affected the whole structure of the verse line, thus creating something different from the original intention of the poet. These alterations by scribes are usually discussed in a negative sense as can be seen in expressions such as "mistakes" (Bolton 4), "corruptions" (Duggan, "Patterning" 102), "carelessness" (Vaughan 8–9), "abuse" (Duggan, "Stress" 309), and "misreading" and "error" (Jefferson and Putter 425). As Duggan concedes, "a highly competent scribe demonstrably worked with a concept of metricality that is substantially different from that of the poet whose work he copies" ("Patterning" 74). Thus, the study of ME verse confronts complicated problems such as scribal alterations, dialectal variables, and other idiosyncratic habits and preferences, all of which are so crucial to the study of meter that they may overthrow any postulated metrical assumptions. Furthermore, editorial conjectures and interpretations of modern times often contradict with each other.

The notion of the text during the ME period was different from that of modern times (R. Allen: Bolton; Coleman, *Public*; Finke and Shichtman; Furniss and Bath), and reading would have connoted the hearing of recitation. In other words, the poem was composed on the assumption that it was subject to change after the initial completion. Zumthor suggests that medieval poetry is closer to modern mass media than to literature for the individual reading, and calls medieval poetry a poetry-in-context:

> The context is so deeply inscribed in the code that the text seems to be very scantly marked by indicators referring explicitly to it. The relationship of the text to the listener implies direct confrontation, a real dialogue between characters in immediate contact with each other. Medieval poetics is thus a poetics of effects, tending in performance to fulfill an expectation that contains known constants and is part of the poetic enterprise. (22)

The oral character of verse was still dominant as in the OE period, and had the potential to affect the structure of the poem. Even if the poem did not originate in oral performances, the verse form itself could have maintained traces of oral composition (R. Allen; Pearsall, "Social Backgrounds"). Pearsall explains this as follows:

> . . . while modern critical works distort the realities of medieval poems in one way, by imposing on them categories of form derived from post-Renaissance theory, the nature of modern critical editions distorts them in another. The very concept of the critical edition is alien to the nature of much Middle English poetry, since the scribe as much as the poet is the 'author' of what we have in extant copies. (*Poetry* 120)

Thus, as Saintsbury points out, the medieval poet was not only "a reformer and innovator of what had already been accumulated by his predecessors" but also a "performer or improver" (199). The poet had self-esteem as a maker of creative work. Schmidt provides an interesting observation about the difference among poet, maker, translator, and versifier in Chaucer's and Langland's days; that is, "'poet' and 'maker' are honorific, 'translator' and 'versifier' at best descriptive terms" (*Clerkly* 144).

Scribal alteration does not necessarily mean that it is totally impossible for modern readers to know what the original intention of the poet was, nor does it mean that the analysis is not very valid because the texts that possibly underwent such alteration are the only source. Particularly in a poem that has survived in a unique manuscript, which is the case for most ME alliterative verse except for *Piers Plowman* and *The Siege of Jerusalem*, only a modified product by the scribe is available, and scrutiny of the poet's norm in composition is not very simple (Ebbs; Lawton, "Idea"). However, what scribes did to the original work provides information on how people at the time approached literary products (Blake, *Introduction* 78). At least, metrical assumptions that are inherent throughout the poem can be extracted by marking possible, optional, and preferred elements, as well as by checking the postulated meter against a sufficient number of lines. For shorter poems consisting a few hundred lines, a definite conclusion may not be reached. Detailed scansion over many lines in a corpus and internal evidence it offers should overcome these difficulties and suggest the metrical frameworks despite the elements that have possibly been added or altered.

Another significant contributor to the formation of verse since the days of the Anglo-Saxons is the audience. Wrenn defines the immediate object of poetry as "pleasure, not truth" (43). Renoir contends:

> . . . the art of writing and its literary byproducts did not replace oral traditions overnight whenever medieval monks inaugurated a new scriptorium in a district. Quite on the contrary, it seems that oral and written traditions found means of cohabiting for a period of time, and there is evidence that this was the case within the very walls of the monastery. This assumption necessarily leads one to suppose that poets could have been composing oral-formulaic poetry in writing for the benefit of an audience familiar enough with the relevant tradition of oral-formulaic rhetoric to interpret the resultant texts accordingly, and there is convincing circumstantial evidence to bolster the supposition. (237)

If the poet had failed in providing sufficient pleasure to his audience, his work would not have been considered very genuine (Wrenn 44). During the transmission of verse to other regions or to later times by means of written manuscripts, thus, various alterations could have occurred. Pearsall discusses possible changes that could have happened to the manuscript of the alliterative revival: "The audience implied may not be the audience addressed; the circumstances of manuscript survival may be no guide at all to the circumstances of production; and sophistication is a difficult thing to quantify" ("Social Backgrounds" 49). Blake also suggests that the different interest of the audience in the late ME period enforced more rigid regularity in alliterative poetry:

> . . . the later poetry developed from the earlier poetry as a result of a different audience and of the poets' growing professionalism and ability to handle the alliterative meter, just as in OE poetry a poem like *Beowulf* was the result of a development in style and meter from cruder beginnings.
>
> (Blake, "Rhythmical" 121)

Fussell quotes Hollander's definition of meter as "the metrical contract" between the poet and the audience (*Poetic Meter* 15). The audience would experience pleasure in the metrical formality, as well as in the poetic arrangements and deviations that the poet offers, based on this contract. In this way, the repetition of the same poem is not a mere repetition but "re-creation, and it is this mode of signification its audience is asked to share" (Foley, "Implications" 46).

A wide variety of audiences has been recognized for ME alliterative poetry. Different social classes were able to enjoy the alliterative poems (Richardson;

Salter, "Revival" 236–37; T. Turville-Petre, *Revival* 46). Pearsall assumes that the mobility of the nobles and the educated had become more common and frequent by the time alliterative poetry gained favor once again in the fourteenth century ("Origins"; "Social Backgrounds"). Not only the nobles and their retinues but also clerics and government officials would move to regions that had eager audiences with different tastes. Salter supports the idea of frequent movement of patrons and audiences ("Revival" 236–37). Lords and officials constantly moved to the west and north where their estates were. Even though the alliterative verse did not originate in the region that was the center for literary production, it was spread as people moved around. As Putter summarizes (29):

> Two facts emerge clearly from an investigation into the audience of other alliterative poetry: one is that alliterative poetry often reached audiences outside its dialect area, another that the movements of alliterative poets were not limited to this area either. Manuscript evidence clearly shows that alliterative poetry was a national rather than a local phenomenon in the fourteenth and early fifteenth centuries, and actually enjoyed some popularity in London.

Thus, the relationship among the author, the audience, and the actual product, as well as the oral presentation proven in the frequent references to audience (Duggan, "Final *-e*" 141), can be attested in the marked pause, the promise to continue, and the request for attention in the alliterative poems (Pearsall, "Social Backgrounds" 50). Poems should delight readers, and it is important for the study of meter to consider the economy and coherence of verse. "Density of texture is attained by an interweaving of poetic elements–predications, metaphors, rhythm–so firmly and tightly that, once interwoven, the separate strands resist unraveling, and, as it were, transform themselves into each other" (Fussell, *Poetic Meter* 90).

1.4.4 Meter, Scansion, and Performance

Another controversial issue in the study of meter is the difference between the meter and the actual performance of a poem. Jakobson proposed a set of useful terms to distinguish the four different levels that the meter and the performance represent: *verse design* (the abstract metrical pattern), *verse instance* (how the verse design is actually realized), *delivery design* (abstract performance pattern), and *delivery instance* (how the performance design is actually performed) ("Closing" 364–67). These levels suggest that individual readers have idiosyncratic differences while the meter does not strictly and formally control the actual performance (Fabb, *Linguistics* 94). Considering verse instance and delivery instance will trigger discussions on ambiguous cases and defensible reading. The ultimate goal of scansion is to visualize the abstract recurring structure that underlies verse lines. The study of meter is not instruction in how to recite the verse, but rather to reveal the abstract principles that govern the whole verse (verse design) from its realization in each line (verse instance). If the investigation of meter clings to a particular preference in recitation, it may not be able to postulate the abstract principles of meter. The study of meter should not become a set of detailed guidelines for a particular recitation, but should include all the possible variations in recitation. As Fabb concedes, "texts do not determine their interpretation, but only provide evidence for them" (*Linguistics* 259).

Certain prosodic features may be added or reduced according to the performer's linguistic customs. For instance, the syllabicity of unstressed syllables, elision, and the placement of stress and pause may differ from performer to performer. Emphasizing the strict distinction between the metrical organization of a poem and the way it is recited, Kiparsky warns readers not to confuse meter and performance because "stress-based verse can . . . be recited in many ways" ("Stress" 585). One may read verse in a dramatic manner or in a strict way as a schoolboy would have done a century ago (Attridge, *Well-Weighed*). Though a search for meter cannot but start from the actual reading of the lines, the critical description of meter should reflect all the possibilities in performance in order to reveal the common construction that each line intends in its rhythmic organization. Fabb claims:

> Literary form is complex because it is a matter of how the text is thought, and because it is not a fact about any instance of the text. This complexity is further complicated by the fact that form is developed from performances which by their 'absolute contingency' are in themselves formless. And the formal complexity is complicated by its coexistence with a collection of 'external' meanings (the content of the text) with which it has no general relation. Verbal art is experienced as aesthetic because it exploits to the full every option for making verbal behaviour difficult. (*Langauge* 217)

The chapters that follow the present introduction use examples and data from the corpus consisting of the major and minor ME alliterative poems. Their titles alphabetically ordered according to their abbreviations and the number of lines analyzed are as follows. Hyper-metrical lines and corrupt or missing lines are excluded:

Excerpts from *The Wars of Alexander* (*A*)	2,005 lines
The Parlement of the Thre Ages (*AG*)	661 lines
Cleanness (*C*)	1,812 lines
Dispute Between Mary and the Cross (*CR*)	900 lines
Saint Erkenwald (*E*)	352 lines
Sir Gawain and the Green Knight (*G*)	2,530 lines
The Siege of Jerusalem (*J*)	1,334 lines
The Three Dead Kings (*K*)	143 lines
The Quatrefoil of Love (*L*)	520 lines
The Alliterative Morte Arthure (*MA*)	4,345 lines
Pearl (*PE*)	1,211 lines
Excerpts from *Piers Plowman*, A-Text (*PPA*)	1,180 lines
Excerpts from *Piers Plowman*, B-Text (*PPB*)	1,030 lines
A Pistel of Susan (*PS*)	364 lines
Patience (*PT*)	531 lines
Somer Soneday (*SS*)	133 lines
Excerpts from *The Destruction of Troy* (*T*)	3,531 lines
Wynnere and Wastoure (*W*)	503 lines
Total	23,085 lines

In the remaining chapters, the above abbreviations in parentheses will be used for the name of the text. The full title may be used if helpful for the readers, especially when the title appears for the first time in the chapter.

Finally, the following points should be noted regarding typological adjustments. Punctuation marks, including periods, commas, quotation marks, colons, and semi-colons, remain as they are in the text used so that the syntactic boundary can be indicated within a line. If a single line ends with a quotation mark and the other quotation mark that initiates the quote is not found in the same line, it implies that the quote continues from the previous line or lines. Since each chapter is an independent research, there may be repeated explanations, though cross-referential information will be given where necessary.

Notes

1 Cureton implies that four or five lines can be scanned into tree diagrams according to his method (*Rhythmic Phrasing*). However, if the analysis part is included, twenty-one lines of free verse by Williams occupy forty-five pages, fourteen lines of sprung rhythm by Hopkins occupy fifty-four pages, and twelve lines of pentameter by Yeats occupy forty-four pages. On average, one page is assigned to each .33 line; namely, three pages are used for a single line.

2 As to the use of the harp and harpers at the courts of the Anglo-Saxon kings, as well as the decline of harping by the fifteenth century, see Southworth 20–28 and 87–100. Despite the evidence that the harp was used in the Anglo-Saxon period, Pope's conjecture has been criticized. See, for instance, Creed 202–03.

Chapter 2

Metrical Norms and Deviations of *Pearl, Cleanness, Patience,* and *Sir Gawain and the Green Knight*

This chapter is the first attempt in applying the ideas and methods of analysis explained in Chapter One. The analysis method using metrical beats and offbeats and their positions in the verse line, especially the one proposed by Attridge, will be adopted and adapted here in order to clarify the metrical structures, their peculiarities, and the limit of deviation of ME alliterative verse. The basic assumptions may be summarized as follows:

1. The study of meter should be able to distinguish between metrical lines and deviated lines.
2. English meter is comprised of a regular alternation between beats (metrically stressed syllables) and offbeats (metrically unstressed syllables), which is perceived occurring in isochronous intervals.
3. The verse line consists not of feet but of certain positions of metrical beats and offbeats, and meter should represent how these slots are distributed in the line.
4. One of the important goals for studying meter is to determine degrees of the metrical complexity among verse lines.

The poems analyzed in this chapter are the four alliterative poems in the Cotton MS. Nero A. x. Art. 3 of the British Library. These poems, *Pearl* (*PE*), *Cleanness* (*C*), *Patience* (*PT*), and *Sir Gawain and the Green Knight* (*G*), are extant in this unique manuscript. They are composed in the dialect of the Northwest Midlands and date from the late fourteenth century.[1] The goal of this chapter is to determine the rhythmic principles permeating the four poems and suggest the extent of the deviation that they allow within their metrical constraints. It will become clear that the verse line consists of four *or* five beats. This meter operates in a similar manner among *C*, *PT*, and *G* whereas the meter of *PE* markedly differs from those of the other three. The meter common to *C*, *PT*, and the long alliterative lines of *G* is flexible enough to produce a line with four or five beats, allowing the reader's freedom in actual recitation. On the contrary, the meter of *PE* is in a rigid duple rhythm with a complex network of end rhyme.

The first section explains the scansion method and presents how to mark special characteristics of ME and particular metrical phenomena in the notation. The second section postulates the base meter of ME alliterative verse. The third section discusses the implications of the postulated meter while the fourth section offers the list of metrical complexity among the verse lines of *PT*. In conclusion, the four-beat alliterative meter of these four poems is an intricate device that could structurally link the constituents within the prescribed metrical unit and add extra prominence and aural effects in verbal play.

Let us review several controversial issues in analyzing ME alliterative meter discussed in Chapter One. The word final *-e* is considered to have already lost its phonetic value to form a syllable (Duggan, "Final *–e*" 120; Tolkien and Gordon 133). However, some critics, including Donaldson ("Final *-e*"), argue that the final *-e* was always sounded at the end of Chaucer's lines. Other critics, such as Cable and Conner, assert that the word-final consonant used to be released with a puff of air in order to provide more syllables than the actual spelling.

The meter of ME alliterative verse is epitomized in the following remark by T. Turville-Petre (*Poetry* 5):

> The line is divided into half-lines, which may be referred to as the *a*-verse and the *b*-verse. Each half-line has two stresses, and is bound to its partner by alliteration of both stresses of the *a*-verse and the first stress (or rarely both stresses) of the *b*-verse. . . . This pattern is represented as aa/ax. Consonants alliterate with identical consonants or with consonant groups such as /sk/ or /sp/; any vowel can alliterate with any other or with /h/, though some poets tend to alliterate identical vowels.

Each of the products in the ME alliterative movement, however, reveals its own peculiarities. Some are comparatively obedient to the assumed norms whereas others often allow deviations. The present chapter examines the four poems in the so-called *Pearl* manuscript, asserting that English meter is comprised of a regular alternation between beats (metrically stressed syllables) and offbeats (metrically unstressed syllables).

The traditional method of scansion of simply marking stressed and unstressed syllables does not always prove sufficient for a coherent treatment of meter; a predetermined stress quality is sometimes imposed on a syllable that is not qualified for it.[2] There is thus a marked tendency in modern studies of metrics to concentrate on whether the proposed scansion is adequate with respect to stress placement (Cable, "Timers"). Despite opposing views on English versification among modern researchers, the following notions seem to have become unquestionable. First, the English metrical system consists not of absolute stressed syllables and absolute unstressed syllables but of a regular alternation between metrically stressed syllables and metrically unstressed syllables. Second, each line is characterized by varying degrees of metricality.

2.1 Scansion

Scansion is the primary step in the analysis of meter. Since the justification in using Attridge's method has been given in Chapter One, a brief summary of the actual scansion method is given below using examples from *PT*.

Symbols used in stating the stress pattern:[3]

+s	stressed syllable
-s	unstressed syllable including the final -*e* in a monosyllabic word
s	indefinite stress; may replace either +s or -s
/s/	emphatic stress; may replace +s
[s]	metrically subordinated stress; may replace -s
(s)	syncope; the syllable is omitted
^+s, ^-s	elided syllables; may replace +s or -s
ₒ	final -*e* in a word that consists of more than two syllables; may be pronounced and realized as an offbeat*
(ₒ)	final -*e* that may not form a syllable*

Symbols used to note the metrical pattern:

B	beat
o	single offbeat
o2	double offbeat

o3 triple offbeat
o: demotion
<B> promotion
B (underlined) implied beat
ø implied offbeat
o (with mark below) final -*e* pronounced between beats*
° final -*e* in the line-final position*

Scansion proceeds in two steps–first, by putting stress marks above syllables; and second, by putting metrical symbols below the line. Stress symbols, such as *+s*, *-s*, etc., are meant to appear immediately above the concerned syllables. Symbols for beats should appear directly beneath the stressed syllables while symbols for offbeats come in between the two beats. The following explains how line 378 of *PT* is scanned in this first process:[4]

```
      -s   -s +s -s-s +s -s   +s   -s -s   +s-s
PT 378 And he radly vpros and ran fro his chayer,
```

The metrical structure is described beneath the line accompanied by the alliteration pattern in square brackets:

```
      -s   -s +s -s-s +s -s   +s   -s -s   +s-s
PT 378 And he radly vpros and ran fro his chayer,       [aaax][5]
           o2  B    o2  B  o    B      o2    B o
```

This line consists of four beats that are separated by a single offbeat and two double offbeats. There is a double offbeat at the beginning whereas the line concludes with a single offbeat. Many lines in *PT* are scanned in this way for instance, line 274:

```
      -s    +s -s -s  -s   +s-s  -s   +s  -s  -s +s-s
PT 274 And stod vp in his stomak þat stank as þe deuel. [aaax]
       o     B         o3   B     o2    B      o2  B o
```

These examples present the alternation of beats and either single or double offbeats in the line. The primary task is to determine the number of beats per line and seek any regularity in offbeats.

Four peculiar points need special attention: the phonetic value of the word final *-e* and other inflectional suffixes, elision of two syllables, metrically subordinated stress, and indefinite stress. First, as discussed in Chapter One, the metrical environment determines whether or not a word-final *-e* or an inflectional suffix is vocalized to form a weak syllable. These unstressed syllables may supply an optional syllable if the meter demands one. For instance, the final *-e* in *Lede called* of *PT* 281 below is likely to form a syllable because there is no other candidate to be realized as an offbeat. This makes a contrast with *PT* 280 which has no such a candidate in the same position. An implied offbeat is assumed in this case:[6]

```
                                                         +s ₒ +s
PT 281 And þer he lenged at þe last, and to þe Lede called:
                                                          B o  B
```

```
                                                          +s   +s
PT 280 In wych gut so euer he gotz, bot euer is God swete;
                                                           B   ø B
```

The final *-e* at the end of the line by itself is treated as a syllable since an unstressed syllable tends to appear at the line closure in ME alliterative verse. When there already are unstressed syllables between beats, the final *-e* or an inflectional suffix may be silent:

```
                        +s(°)-s   -s +s
PT 68 Þat in þat place, at þe poynt, I put in þi hert.
                         B        o2  B
```

```
             -s   -s -s (°)+s
PT 242 Þaȝ he nolde suffer no sore, his seele is on anter;
                  O3       B
```

The final-*e* of *sore* and *seele* in *PT* 242 may behave in the same way since the offbeat position has other legitimate candidate or candidates for an offbeat.

Second, two adjacent syllables may elide and yield one single syllable. *PT* 7 exemplifies such a case:

```
                 +s  -s    ^-s+s
PT 7 Þen is better to abyde þe bur vmbestoundes
                 B      o2    B
```

A rather complex combination of unstressed syllables may be a double offbeat by elision as seen in the line below:

```
                     +s   (s)  -s   ^-s+s
PT 143 And efte busched to þe abyme, þat breed fysches
                       B          o2      B
```

Third, stress quality may vary in the syllable that is syntactically subordinated to what follows it, which is called metrically subordinated stress (Attridge, *Rhythms* 230–39). This type of words may or may not receive stress and they are realized as either a beat or an offbeat, depending upon the metrical environment:

```
                   +s-s   [s] +s
PT 142 Þat þe wawes ful wode waltered so hiȝe
                     B    o2     B
```

```
                   +s -s   [s]   +s
PT 236 Tyl a swetter ful swyþe hem sweȝed to bonk.
                     B     o2      B
```

```
                                     +s(°)[s]-s [s](°)+s
PT 20 For þay schal frely be refete ful of alle gode;
                                       B       o3       B
```

Metrically subordinated stress typically falls on a monosyllabic adjective or adverb that has a strong syntactic relationship with the subsequent word. Example words that hold metrically subordinated stress in *PT* include:

Adjectives:

all(e), blo, byg(g)(e), co(o)lde, dyngne, est, fayn, ful, gret(e), holy, hyȝ(e), long(e), lyt(t)el (lyttle), nobel(e), north(e), pure, rych(e), schyr(e)(e), trwe,

Determiners:

aȝt(e), fyrst(e), Goddes (Goddez), much(e), more, such(e), sum(me), thre, two

Adverbs:

ay, now(e), tyd

Titles:

lord(e), dame

Finally, a stressed syllable of certain words may not be realized as a beat, even though these words have stress contrast when pronounced as a separate word. This flexible stress is called indefinite stress (Attridge, *Rhythms* 215–22), and the following are some of the words that have it in *PT*:

Prepositions:

ab(o)ut(t)e, abof, after, aloft(e), among, betwene (bitwene), bout(e), byfore (bifore), into, ouer, toward(e), vnder, vnte, vpon, withinne, wythoute(n) (withouten),

Determiners:

another, any, ayther, both(e), ilk(e), mony(e), other, quoso, this(e) (this(e)), thos(e), vch(e), vch(e)on(e), whatso, whoso, ȝonder

Adverbs:

adoun, also, away(e), eft(e), euer, her(e), her(e)inne, ilych(e), neuer, oft(e), then(ne), ther(e), ther(e)as, therabof, therafter, therfor(e), therin(ne), theroute, thervnder, therwith, thider,

Conjunctions:

forthy, sythen, whyle

For example, *boþe* and *vpon* in *PT* 138 and *also* in *PT* 291 are not likely to form a beat, though they have stress contrast when separately pronounced.

```
        -s   s(°) +s         +s(°)-s s    [s]
PT 138 When boþe breþes con blowe  vpon blo watteres.
             o2    B          B       o2  B
```

```
              +s(°) s -s +s
PT 291 Þer he sete also sounde, saf for merk one,
               B    o2   B
```

A word with indefinite stress may fill in a beat position within the line; for instance, *neuer* in *PT* 226 forms a beat due to its appearance in the line-final beat position:

```
                                  +s-s   -s  s-s
PT 226 Þat He gef hem þe grace to greuen Hym neuer,     [aaax]
                                    B    o2   B o
```

But, the same word may not form a beat in the following line:

```
                                   +s (°) s-s  -s +s
PT 420 And ay Þy mercy is mete, be mysse neuer so huge.
                                    B      o3     B
```

A word with indefinite stress is generally realized as a beat in the line-terminal position. Indefinite stress reflects in the scansion the varying stress placement in certain words. Again the metrical environment determines whether or not the syllable should receive stress to form a metrical beat.

The first six lines of *PT*, thus, are scanned as follows. The lines show an alternation of beats and several different types of offbeats:

```
     +s-s  (°)-s-s +s     -s  -s  -s  +s ° s °
PT 1 Pacience is a poynt, þaȝ hit displese ofte.        [aaax]
      B    o3       B         o3      B º B °
```

```
      -s  [s]-s +s  -s  -s +s   -s   +s-s   s(s)+s -s
PT 2 When heuy herttes ben hurt wyth heþyng oþer elles, [aaaaa]
        o  B o  B        o2  B   o    B      o2  B  o
```

```
     +s  -s  (°) -s -s +s(s) -s -s  -s  +s  ° +s °
PT 3 Suffraunce may aswagen hem and þe swelme leþe,     [aaax]
      B         o3     B        o3       B  º B °
```

```
     -s  -s  +s (s) s (°)-s  +s -s   +s  -s  -s +s °
PT 4 For ho quelles vche  a qued and quenches malyce;   [aaax]
         o2   B       o2      B  o     B  o2     B °
```

-s s-s +s -s -s(°) +s +s ° -s(°) +s °
PT 5 For quoso suffer cowþe syt, sele wolde folȝe, [aaax]
o3 B o2 B ø B o2 B °

-s -s -s +s -s -s +s(°) -s +s -s -s +s -s(s)
PT 6 And quo for þro may noȝt þole, þe þikker he sufferes.
o3 B o2 B o B o2 B o
[aaax]

PT 2 may be read in four-beat meter if the metrical subordinated stress in *heuy* is not considered to receive metrical stress. The opposite case is *PT* 5, which may be read in five-beat meter if the word *quoso* is considered to form a beat. The next section will consider lines that have two or more alternative readings.

2.2 The Structure of the Verse Line

Some lines in *PT* contain four beats whereas others contain five. Traditionally, the four-beat meter has been considered to be the base of ME alliterative verse as seen in T. Turville-Petre's explanation quoted earlier, but different scansions that acknowledge different numbers of beats per line are known. Some examples include the following:

Andrew and Waldron (47–48):

x x / x x /(x) | x / x x /(x)
C 236 Þurȝ þe **f**aut of a **f**reke þat **f**ayled in trawþe

x x / x x / || x / x x / (x)
PT 125 Bot he **d**redes no **d**ynt þat **d**otes for elde

x x /(x) x x / || x / x x / (x)
PT 195 Þenne a**sc**ryed þay hym s**ck**ete and a**sk**ed ful loude

x x / x x / x || x / x /
C 101 Be þay **f**ers, be þay **f**eble, **f**orlotez none

Gardner (87–90):[7]

G 4 Watz tríed for his tríchèrie, þe tréwest on érthe

G 1631 For súche a bráwne of a bést, þe bolde burne sáyde

G 1272 For þe cóstes þat Í haf knówen vpon þe, knyȝt, here

G 2352 For boþe two here I þe bede bot two bare myntes

Tolkien and Gordon (148):

G 11*a* Tírius to Túsckan

G 858*b* of túly and társ

G 51*a* Þe most kýd knýȝtez

G 40*b* and réchles mérþes.

Keyser (354):

```
G 241 Þerfore to ánsware watȝ árȝe mony áþel fréke
       X          S1           S2        S3     S4

G 263 And here is kýdde córtaysye, as Í haf herd cárp
       X          S1    S2            S3         S4

G 988 Þus wyth láȝande lóteȝ þe lórde hit tayt máke[sic]
       X        S1     S2       S3             S4
```

Hieatt (124):

G 842 |Gáwayn glỳȝt on þe | góme þat | gódly hym | grét,

G 843 And | þùȝt hit a | bólde bùrne | | þat þe | búrȝ àȝte,

G 844 A | hóge hàþel for þe | nónez, | | and of | hýghe èldee; |

G 845 | Bróde, | | brýȝt, watz his bèrde, | | and al | béuer-hwèd, |

McIntosh (33):

```
G 155a With  |  blýþe  |  bláunner ful  |  brýȝt

G 2a   Þe  |  bórȝ  |  bríttened and  |  brént

G 44b  ful  |  fíften  |  dáyes

G 144b were  |  wórthily  |  smále
```

Sapora (73):[8]

```
G 1188 Þat droȝ þe dor after hir ful dernly and stylle, [SSSW]

G 1189 And boȝed towarde þe bed; and þe burne schamed,  [SSSW]

G 1190 And layde hym doun lystyly, and let as he slepte; [SSSW]

G 1191 And ho stepped stilly and stel to his bedde,     [SSSW]

G 1192 Kest vp þe cortyn and creped withinne,           [SSSW]
```

Silverstein (18–19):

```
G 4   Watz tríed for his trícherie, þe tréwest on érthe

G 27  Forþi an áunter in érde I áttle to schâwe

G 417 The gréne knýȝt vpon gróunde gráyþely hym drésses

G 905 Þat is þe rýche rýal kýng of þe Róunde Táble
```

Borroff ("Reading" 196):[9]

```
                C          C        C        C
G 203 Wheþer hade he no helme ne hawbergh nauþer,
                a   (a)    a    /   a        x
```

```
                C                 C           C           C
G 204 Ne no pysan ne no plate þat pented to armes,
                a                 a    /      a           x
```

```
                   C                  C               C             C
G 205 Ne no schafte ne no schelde to schwue ne to smyte,
                   a                  a               a             x
```

```
                           C           C         C       C
G 206 Bot in his on honde he hade a holyn bobbe,
                           a           a    /    a       x
```

Schiller (277): *G* 60–63

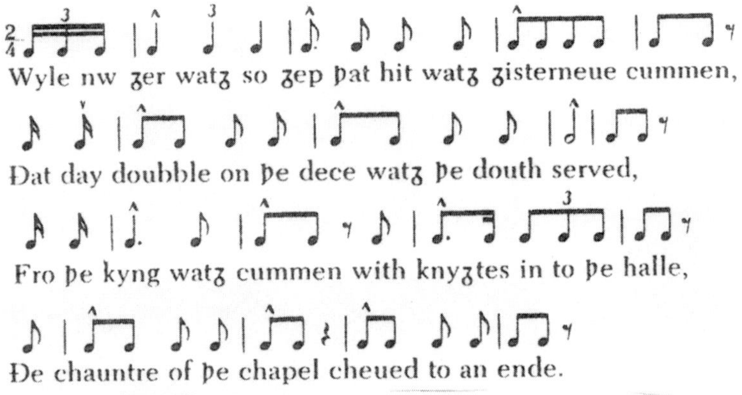

Wyle nw ȝer watȝ so ȝep þat hit watȝ ȝisterneue cummen,
Þat day doubble on þe dece watȝ þe douth served,
Fro þe kyng watȝ cummen with knyȝtes in to þe halle,
Þe chauntre of þe chapel cheued to an ende.

Osberg (*Gawain* xiv, xx):

```
       ^    ^  ^  ^     / ^     / ^   ^   ^     /    ^  ^    ^ /
G 6 That sithen depreced provinces and patrounes bicome
```

```
       ^  /        /  ^     ^     /      ^   /  ^  ^    /  ^
G 2 the borgh brittened and brent to brondes and askes
```

Vantuono (*Gawain* 258–59):

```
         /            /                     /          /
G 42  Justed ful jolilé,  /  þise gentyle kniȝtes.
         a            a                     a          x
```

```
                /               /           /            /
G 43   Syþen kayred to þe court   /  caroles to make.
                a               a           a            x


       /        /      \              /          /              /
G 67   ȝeȝed 'ȝeres-ȝiftes' on hiȝ,  /  ȝelde hem bi hond.
       a        a      a              b          a     (b)      b


       /         /           \            /           /
G 112 Bischop Bawdewyn abof   /  bigineȝ the table.
       a         a           a        (a)x            x
```

Cable (*Tradition* 158):

```
       x     x    /      x    x   /        x    / x x    x    / x
C 213 With þis worde þat he warp    þe wrake on hym lyȝt;


          /  x    x     x    / x  /        x    /    x   x x / x
C 214 Dryȝtyn with his dere dom    hym drof to þe abyme.


      x    x   / x x x    x    /         x    /    x x   x  /  x
C 215 In þe mesure of his mode    his merȝ neuer þe lasse;


       x    xx   x   /     x   /  x   /       x    x    /     /  x
C 216 Bot þer he tynt þe tythe dool    of his tour ryche.
```

In order to compromise these differences in scansion and avoid confusion regarding the stress quality and metrical quality of syllables, I should like to propose that both four-beat lines and five-beat lines can be generated from one single metrical base. Keyser proposes the following abstract metrical pattern for ME alliterative verse (353):

$$\text{Verse} \rightarrow X\ (S_0)\ S_1\ S_2\ S_3\ S_4$$

Sapora alters this pattern into the following (18):

$$\text{Verse} \rightarrow X_1\ X_2\ R\ V$$

Keyser's symbol *X* at the beginning is simply an initial double offbeat, but approximately one-third (31.8%) of the lines of *PT* start with a beat. Though Sapora does not give any explanation for deleting the symbol *X* from Keyser's scheme, his meter without unstressed syllables at the line beginning better reflects the metrical reality than does Keyser's. Sapora's meter, however, is not very adequate because the symbols *R* and *V* are not very helpful in clarifying the metrical structure.[10] Keyser's scheme without the initial *X* seems to reflect the metrical reality most adequately. Thus, replacing the symbols *S* with *B* for a beat, I should like to postulate the distribution of beats in an ME alliterative line as follows:

Postulated Beat Structure for the ME Alliterative Line:

Verse $\rightarrow$ (B_0) B_1 B_2 B_3 B_4

This template allows a line to have four or five beats without any extra rules to increase or reduce a beat. The common alliteration patterns easily fit this base, [aaa/ax] being full realization and [aa/ax] appearing in a line in which B_0 is not filled in. For example, the following lines may be read in both four-beat meter (reading *a*) and five-beat meter (reading *b*). The syllable with indefinite stress of the words *amonge*, *whyder*, *forþy*, and *þenne* does not form a beat in reading *a*, but does so in reading *b*:

```
          -s s (°)-s +s    -s   s-s-s    +s -s   +s -s
PT 82-a   Amonge   enmyes so mony and mansed fendes,        [aaax]
               o3     B      o  B    o2    B  o    B  o

          -s s (°)-s +s    -s   s-s-s    +s -s   +s -s
PT 82-b   Amonge   enmyes so mony and mansed fendes,        [aaaax]
          o B       o  B      o  B    o2    B  o    B  o

             s-s -s   +s  (°) -s   -s  +s    -s       s -s   -s +s   °
PT 202-a Whyder in worlde  þat þou wylt, and what is þyn arnde?
                   O3   B         o2       B     o     B   o2    B    °
                                                                  [aaax]
```

```
                s-s -s  +s  (°)-s  -s  +s   -s     s -s  -s +s   °
PT 202-b Whyder in worlde þat þou wylt, and what is þyn arnde?
                B  O2    B      o2      B      o  B   o2  B   °
                                                          [aaaax]
```

```
               s -s +s(s) -s -s -s +s(°)-s   +s(s) -s -s s   °
PT 211-a Forþy berez me to þe borde and baþes me þeroute,
                 O2  B      o3      B    o    B    o2    B   °
                                                           [aaax]
```

```
               s -s +s(s) -s -s -s +s  (°)-s   +s(s) -s -s s   °
PT 211-b Forþy berez me to þe borde  and baþes me þeroute,
               B  o  B      o3      B     o    B    o2    B   °
                                                          [xaaax]
```

```
             -s     s (°)   -s   +s-s    -s +s(s)-s    -s  s    +s  °
PT 360-a And þenne schal Niniue be nomen and to noȝt worþe;
                     o3         B    o2   B     o2      B  ø B  °
                                                            [aaax]
```

```
             -s     s (°)   -s   +s-s    -s +s(s) -s    -s  s    +s  °
PT 360-b And þenne schal Niniue be nomen and to noȝt worþe;
             o    B        o   B   o2    B      o2      B  ø B  °
                                                           [xaaax]
```

Especially when the additional beat reinforces alliteration as in *PT* 82 and *PT* 202, the five-beat reading seems more reasonable. *PT* 46 and *PT* 63 are additional examples:

```
             s(s)   ^-s   +s  (°)-s    -s   +s-s    +s (s) -s  -s+s-s
PT 46-a Syþen I  am sette with hem samen, suffer me byhoues;
                 o2      B              o2  B o     B        o2  B o
                                                              [aaax]
```

```
           s-s    ^-s  +s (°)-s    -s  +s-s   +s (s) -s -s+s-s
PT 46-b Syþen I   am sette with hem samen, suffer me byhoues;
           B        o2  B           o2   B   o  B     o2   B o
                                                          [aaaax]

          [s]-s    +s  -s -s   +s  -s  -s -s  +s  +s °
PT 63-a Goddes glam to hym glod þat hym vnglad made,       [aaax]
           o2       B    o2    B        o3      B ø B °

          [s]-s    +s  -s -s   +s  -s  -s -s  +s  +s °
PT 63-b Goddes glam to hym glod þat hym vnglad made,      [aaaax]
           B  o     B    o2    B        o3      B ø B °
```

The first hundred lines of *PT* show the following percentages concerning flexibility in the number of beats:

Table 2.1. Four-Beat Reading *vs.* Five-Beat Reading (*PT*)

I. Definite 4B	36%
II. 4B or 5B; 5B reading adds another alliterating beat	14%
III. 4B or 5B; 5B reading adds an unalliterating beat	42%
IV. 4B or 5B; 5B reading produces two set of alliteration	2%
V. Definite 5B	6%
Total	100%

If the four-beat reading is strictly applied, the number of lines that are in four-beat will be the sum of the first four categories, I-IV. In contrast, the sum of the lines excluding the first category, II-V, will be the number of five-beat lines if the five-beat reading is favored. The flexible lines between four-beat and five-beat, namely lines belonging to the II, III, and IV categories, appear in fifty-eight percent of the whole lines, which plays a distinctive role in the meter. Allowing two alternatives from one base solves the problem caused by such flexible lines.

Not much discussion has been made regarding the structure and function of the offbeat. The metrical make-up of the offbeat observed in *PT* reveals that the majority of unstressed syllables between beats can be scanned as a single, double, or triple offbeat, even though the number of syllables at the stress level varies considerably from one to six. The following lines exhibit the simplest structure and the most complicated structure of the offbeat in *PT*. Structures (i), (iii), and

(vii) are the simplest ones for the single, double, and triple offbeat, respectively. Structures (ii), (vi), and (x) are the most complicated ones for the single, double, and triple offbeat, respectively. Only the scansion of the concerned part is shown:

(i) A single offbeat that consists of an unstressed syllable:

```
                +s -s   +s
PT 283 Þaȝ I be fol and fykel and falce of my hert,
                 B  o    B
```

```
                    +s-s +s
PT 328 Þat into His holy hous myn orisoun moȝt entre.
                     B o  B
```

```
                           +s    -s +s
PT 437 Þer he busked hym a bour, þe best þat he myȝt,
                            B     o  B
```

(ii) A single offbeat that consists of two unstressed syllables:

```
                         +s(°)-s   +s
PT 75  'If I bowe to His bode and bryng hem þis tale,
                          B    o    B
```

```
               +s (s) -s +s
PT 301 Ande as sayled þe segge, ay sykerly he herde
                B      o  B
```

(iii) A double offbeat that consists of two unstressed syllables:

```
       -s  -s +s-s  -s  +s     +s -s  -s  s
PT 348 For to go at Þi gre: me gaynez non oþer.'
          o2   B    o2   B      B     o2  B
```

```
                 +s -s-s  +s
PT 420 And ay Þy mercy is mete, be mysse neuer so huge.
                  B   o2   B
```

(iv) A double offbeat that consists of three unstressed syllables:

```
                +s(s)  -s  -s  s(°)-s -s   s
PT 263 And also dryuen þurȝ þe depe and in derk walterez.
                 B      o2      B    o2     B
```

```
                 +s(°)-ss  +s
PT 194 And ay þe lote vpon laste lymped on Jonas.
                  B    o2    B
```

(v) A double offbeat that consists of four unstressed syllables:

```
              +s (s) -s  -s(°)+s   [s](°)-s(°)-s +s
PT 34 He were happen þat hade  one; alle were þe better.
               B     o2        B    B     o2      B
```

```
              +s(°)s(s) -s +s
PT 52 Oþer to ryde oþer to renne to Rome in his ernde,
               B     o2     B
```

(vi) A double offbeat that consists of five unstressed syllables:

```
                +s (°)-s(°) s(°)  +s
PT 37 For in þe tyxte þere þyse two arn in teme layde,
                 B        o2      B
```

(vii) A triple offbeat that consists of three unstressed syllables:

```
       -s  -s -s   +s
PT 126 For he watz fer in þe flod foundande to Tarce,
           o3       B
```

```
                                +s  -s -s  -s  +s
PT 422 To manace alle þise mody men þat in þis mote dowellez,
                                 B       o3     B
```

(viii) A triple offbeat that consists of four unstressed syllables:

```
       -s    s(s) -s +s
PT 109 Watz neuer so joyful a Jue as Jonas watz þenne,
              o3      B
```

```
         -s  s (°)-s +s
PT 387 Þat alle þe bodyes þat ben withinne þis borȝ quyk,
             o3       B
```

(ix) A triple offbeat that consists of five unstressed syllables:

```
         +s (s)-s  -s  s (°)+s
PT 178 Herȝed out of vche hyrne to hent þat falles.
         B        o3       B
```

(x) A triple offbeat that consists of six unstressed syllables:

```
                                +s (s)  -s  [s](°)-s (°) [s]
PT 395 Al schal crye, forclemmed, with alle  oure clere strenþe;
                                 B           o3          B
```

The metrical structure cannot be clarified by simply counting the number of unstressed syllables, but the lines demonstrate certain regularity in terms of offbeats. The meter is identified as consisting of four or five beat positions that are separated by either a single or double offbeat with a high potential for a triple offbeat, and the initial combination of an offbeat and a beat is optional. By a convention in linguistics of using a subscript for the minimum number and a superscript for the maximum,[11] the meter may be defined as follows:

Meter of *C*, *PT*, and the long alliterative lines of *G*:

Verse → $(o_1^2\ B_0)\ o_1^2\ B_1\ o_1^2\ B_2\ o_1^2\ B_3\ o_1^2\ B_4$ <o>

(With possibility of triple offbeat for an offbeat position and with alliteration pattern [(a)aaax] or [(x)aaax]. Parentheses indicate optional constituents in the line whereas <o> indicates an optional offbeat which shows preference for inclusion.)

PE uses an alliterative meter that is quite different from any of the meters used in the other three, which will be examined in detail in Chapters Four and Five. Finch, who translated the text edited by Andrew, Waldron, and Peterson, assumes anapestic tetrameter for *C*, *PT*, and *G* but iambic tetrameter for *PE*. However, Finch does not explain the metrical differences among these four. Without the use of such classical terms, the meter of *PE* may be postulated as follows:

Meter of *PE*:

$$\text{Verse} \rightarrow o\ B_1\ o\ B_2\ o\ B_3\ o\ B_4\ (o)$$

(With less regular alliteration but always with rhyme in B_4. The final parentheses indicate an optional offbeat which shows neutral preference.)

The offbeat of *PE* tends to be single while the triple offbeat is rare. The double offbeat presents a significant metrical deviation in *PE*, though it is quite common in the other three poems. The rhymed lines of *G* are somewhat similar to *PE* because they are composed in duple rhythm with end rhyme. The meter may be represented as posed below:

Meter of the rhymed lines of *G* (the wheel):

$$\text{Verse} \rightarrow o\ B_1\ o\ B_2\ o\ B_3\ <o>\ \underline{B_4}$$

Lines of the so-called wheel have been scanned in trimeter traditionally. However, according to Attridge (*Rhythms* 84–96), there are no three-beat verses in English because there is always an implied beat lurking at the end of a three-beat line. This idea of four-beat meter with an implied beat needs further consideration. Particularly useful will be the examination of the wheel of other ME poetry such as *Harley Lyrics*, *The Quatrefoil of Love*, *The Pistill of Susan*, and *Summer Sunday*.[12] If the wheel line is composed in four-beat meter, it implies that the stanza with the wheel consists of two completely different four-beat meters.

2.3 Implications of the Postulated Meters

The postulated meter is the template lurking behind lines that show different realizations of it. Thus, not only metrical similarities but also differences will illuminate what standard and limit of deviation the ME alliterative poets had in a particular work. This section compares the metrical similarities and differences among the four poems. The postulated meters suggest several points unique to the four poems. First, alliteration may have several alternative forms; it may be found in offbeats in addition to beats:

```
       -s  s-s   s -s  +s(s) -s  +s °
PE 485 Ne neuer nawþer Pater ne Crede-              [aaxx]
        o  B  o  B  o   B     o   B °
```

```
       +s (s)  -s -s +s -s-s  +s -s  [s]  +s °
C 221  Fellen fro þe fyrmament fendez ful blake,    [aaax]
        B     o2       B  o2     B   o2       B °
```

```
      -s   s     +s -s -s  +s (°)-s  +s(°)-s +s  °
PT 192 In such slaȝtes of sorȝe to slepe so faste.  [aaax]
          o2     B     o2  B     o    B    o  B  °
```

Particularly in *G*, the alliteration can be overwhelming. The following line of *G* appears with excessive alliteration on /b/:

```
        +s-s  +s-s -s    +s(°)-s +s   -s -s s   °
G 2082 Brokez byled and breke bi bonkkez aboute,   [aaaaa]
         B o   B    o2    B    o  B    o2  B    °
```

G differs from the other three poems in the number of lines with duple alliteration; that is, the alliteration patterns such as [abab], [abba], and [aabab] are frequent. The lines with duple alliteration (two sets of alliteration in a line), however, are very few in the other three poems–about five percent in *PE*, about one percent in *C*, and less than one percent in *PT*. In other words, *C* does not present many variations in alliteration, maintaining the [aaax] pattern throughout. This basic alliteration pattern is consistently maintained in *PT* as well. *G* is distinctive because it shows several types of alliteration: alliteration in offbeats, duple alliteration in a single line, and alliteration in the identical sound over several consecutive lines. A typical explanation about alliteration of ME alliterative verse, a four-stress line with the first three alliterating (Osberg, *Gawain* xiii), is adequate in the case of *C* and *PT*. However, alliteration may appear in an extreme manner in *G* while it is relatively less rigid in *PE*. The number of lines with two alliterating beats exceeds that of lines with three alliterating beats in *PE*. Other peculiar points concerning the alliteration of *PE* are that the final beats often alliterate, and that lines without alliteration often appear, which is not observed in the other three poems.[13]

Table 2.2. Occurrences of the Implied Offbeat (*PE*, *C*, *PT*, *G*)[14]

	Between B_0 and B_1	Between B_1 and B_2	Between B_2 and B_3	Between B_3 and B_4
PE (1,211 lines)[15]	/	17	11	29
C (1,000 lines)[16]	34	45	61	117
PT (531 lines)	15	9	24	65
G (900 lines)[17]	34	26	58	102

Secondly, implied offbeats and triple offbeats, both of which are deviated forms of the normal offbeat, are distributed in a distinctive manner. Table 2.2 presents how the implied offbeat occurs in the four poems whereas Table 2.3 demonstrates the occurrences of the triple offbeat in the first hundred lines of each poem:[18]

Table 2.3. Occurrences of the Triple Offbeat (*PE*, *C*, *PT*, *G*)

	Before B_0	Between B_0 and B_1	Between B_1 and B_2	Between B_2 and B_3	Between B_3 and B_4
PE	0	0	0	0	0
C	1	21	13	10	1
PT	2	22	15	10	4
G	1	21	4	10	4

Tables 2.2 and 2.3 reveal that in *C*, *PT*, and *G* the implied offbeat occurs more frequently toward the end of the line whereas the triple offbeat tends to appear at the beginning of the line, marking a clear contrast against the line end. The successive stressed syllables without any unstressed syllables in between have the function of slowing the tempo of the line whereas a succession of unstressed syllables has the effect of quickening the tempo (Fussell, *Poetic Meter* 35). The slow tempo toward the end of the line, in addition to the unalliterating beat in the line-final position, thus, signals the line boundary. This phenomenon is observed in *C*, *PT*, and *G*, but not in *PE*. Perhaps this is because *PE* does not need another metrical device to mark the line end, in addition to its rigid duple rhythm and end rhyme.

Thirdly, the line conclusion plays an important role in the meter. Table 2.4 shows the line endings of the four poems:

Table 2.4. Line End Patterns According to the Line-Final Element (*PE*, *C*, *PT*, *G*)

	Lines that end with a single offbeat	Lines that end with a final-*e*	Lines that end with a beat	Total
PE	7.4%	61.0%	31.6%	100.0%
C	44.2%	46.4%	9.4%	100.0%
PT	39.0%	52.7%	8.3%	100.0%
G	42.0%	47.4%	10.6%	100.0%

One obvious difference between *PE* and the other three poems is that *PE* has more lines that end with an -*e* and more lines that end with a beat. Whether or not the line-terminal -*e* forms a syllable has been a matter of controversy, as discussed in Chapter One. If the line-final -*e* is considered to form a syllable, the number of lines that have an unstressed syllable at the end is close to ninety percent in *C*, *PT*, and *G*. This number is close to Cable's observation that "the end of the second half-line had an unstressed syllable 98 percent of the time" (*Tradition* 74). Since "the rhythm of the *b*-verse is quite tightly controlled" (T. Turville-Petre, *Poetry* 5) and "the line tends to a right-edge metrical strictness" (Osberg, "Prosody" 160), the final unstressed syllable may be considered a metrical requirement in these three poems. On the contrary, the line in *PE* is more likely to end with a beat. This is reflected in the postulated meter; namely, the line-terminal offbeat of *PE* is placed in parentheses. This makes a clear contrast against the other three because the postulated meter for *C*, *PT*, and *G* shows the stronger expectation for a line-terminal offbeat, which is indicated between angled brackets.

The fourth point that the postulated meters reveal is flexibility in reading. Certain lines may be read in both four-beat and five-beat if one of the syllables of a triple offbeat is considered stressed to form another beat. The following lines exemplify the two alternative readings in the three poems:

```
          s -s [s] -s  -s +s-s -s  +s-s-s  +s-s (°)
C 33-a   Forþy hyȝ not to heuen in haterez totorne,      [aaax]
          O2   B       o2  B   o2   B   o2  B o

          s -s [s]  -s  -s +s-s -s  +s-s-s  +s-s (°)
C 33-b   Forþy hyȝ not to heuen in haterez totorne,     [xaaax]
          B  o  B     o2   B   o2   B   o2  B o
```

-s [s](°)-s +s -s s +s -s +s -s -s +s °
C 1752-a And alle þe folk þerof fayn þat folȝed hym tylle.
o3 B o2 B o B o2 B °
[aaax]

-s [s](°)-s +s -s s +s -s +s -s -s +s °
C 1752-b And alle þe folk þerof fayn þat folȝed hym tylle.
o B o B o2 B o B o2 B °
[xaaax]

-s +s(°)-s -s [s](°)+s(s) -s s (°)-s +s +s-s
PT 152-a Þe coge of þe colde water, and þenne þe cry ryses.
o B o2 B o4 B ø B o
[aaax][19]

-s +s(°)-s -s [s] ° +s(s) -s s (°)-s +s +s-s
PT 152-b Þe coge of þe colde water, and þenne þe cry ryses.
o B o2 B o B o3 B ø B o
[aaxax]

s s ^-s +s-s [s] +s(°) s +s -s -s +s °
PT 298-a Þurȝ mony a regioun ful roȝe, þurȝ ronk of his wylle;
o3 B o2 B o B o2 B °
[aaax]

s s-s-s +s-s [s] +s(°) s +s -s -s +s °
PT 298-b Þurȝ mony a regioun ful roȝe, þurȝ ronk of his wylle;
o B o2 B o2 B o B o2 B °
[xaaax]

-s -s -s s -s [s]+s -s +s-s -s +s °
G 404-a 'Þat is innogh in Nwe ȝer-hit nedes no more,' [axax]
O3 B o2 B o B o2 B °

```
              -s -s -s  s  -s   [s]+s  -s  +s-s  -s +s °
G 404-b 'Þat is innogh in Nwe ȝer-hit nedes no more,'   [aaxax]
                  O3     B   o    BøB   o   B    o2  B °
```

```
              -s  s (°)-s +s -s +s -s(s) -s  -s [s] ° +s  °
G 1732-a Withinne þe comly cortynes, on þe colde morne. [aaax]
                    o3     B  o  B         o3     B  °  B  °
```

```
              -s  s (°)-s +s -s +s -s(s) -s  -s [s] ° +s  °
G 1732-b Withinne þe comly cortynes, on þe colde morne. [xaaax]
               o  B     o  B  o  B         o3     B  °  B  °
```

C 33, *PT* 298, and *G* 1732 contain a syllable with indefinite stress while *C* 1752, *PT* 152, and *G* 404 exemplify cases with metrically subordinated stress.

The five-beat reading is acceptable in *C*, *PT*, and *G*, if there are three alliterating beats as found in the following lines:

```
            -s +s  -s  +s (°)-s  -s  +s -s +s (°)-s -s+s-s
C 68    To see hem pulle in þe plow aproche me byhouez.' [xaaax]
          o  B   o  B      o2      B  o  B     o2    B o
```

```
             -s     -s  +s -s +s-s  +s -s +s(°)-s-s +s   °
PT 359 'ȝet schal forty dayez fully fare to an ende,      [axaax]
               o2        B  o  B o   B  o  B     o2  B   °
```

```
            -s +s   -s +s(°)-s  -s  +s(°) -s  +s  -s  -s +s  °
G 549   To Sech þe gome of þe grene,  as God wyl me wysse.'
          o  B    °  B       o2   B     o   B        o2 B  °
                                                          [xaaax]
```

When the alliterating sound appears in the potential syllable for another beat, it may be natural to read the line in five beats because this five-beat reading will reinforce alliteration. The following are examples from *C*, *PT*, and *G* in which alliteration is reinforced in the five-beat reading:

```
           s(s) -s +s(s)-s  -s  +s(°)-s +s(°)-s +s
C 557-a    Syþen þe Souerayn in sete so sore forþoȝt        [aaax]
             o2      B    o2      B    o  B    o  B

           s-s  -s +s(s)-s  -s  +s(°)-s +s(°)-s +s
C 557-b    Syþen þe Souerayn in sete so sore forþoȝt       [aaaax]
           B     o2 B    o2      B    o  B    o  B

           s(°)+s  -s -s   +s -s    +s -s -s    +s -s
PT 388-a   Boþe burnes and bestes, burdez and childer,      [aaax]
           o    B     o2   B  o     B     o2    B  o

           s  ° +s -s -s   +s -s    +s -s -s    +s -s
PT 388-b   Boþe burnes and bestes, burdez and childer,     [aaaax]
           B °  B     o2   B  o     B     o2    B  o

           s -s -s  +s -s  -s   +s -s(°)-s +s     s(°)-s  +s-s
G 240-a    Forþi for fantoum and fayryȝe þe folk þere hit demed.
             o3    B      o2  B    o2   B    o2        B o
                                                        [aaax]

           s -s -s  +s -s  -s   +s -s(°)-s +s     s(°)-s  +s-s
G 240-b    Forþi for fantoum and fayryȝe þe folk þere hit demed.
           B    o2  B      o2  B    o2   B    o2        B o
                                                       [aaaax]
```

Many lines in *C*, *PT*, and *G* have this flexibility between four- and five-beats, but the likely place for the fifth beat is fairly limited to the first part of the line so that the latter part will not be affected. If this happens to the second half-line, it disturbs the metrical expectation and thus threatens the meter. This phenomenon, however, is not observed in *PE*. The four-beat rhythm of *PE* is not as flexible as those of the other three, allowing only one way of reading. Conflicts among various scansions can be avoided accordingly by discriminating the optional from the obligatory and the variable from the invariable.

2.4 List of Metrical Complexity of *Patience*

One of the advantages of the present method is that it is capable of suggesting degrees of metrical complexity. I have made the lists of metrical complexity of the four poems, and these lists present an increasing order of metrical complexity of the lines, progressively showing more metrical tension towards the end. The greater the variation of stress marks and symbols that the scansion uses, the more complex is the structure of the line. The list of metrical complexity of *PT* is given below in order to show how the lists look like:

1. Base rules only

```
           -s  -s  +s  -s -s  +s -s   +s -s -s +s  °
PT 272 Til he blunt in a blok as brod as a halle;
              o2     B  o2      B  o    B     o2  B  °
```

2. Double offbeat that consists of more than two syllables

```
          -s +s (°)-s  -s +s  -s -s +s  (°) -s -s  +s -s
PT 58 To sette hym to sewrté, vnsounde he hym feches.
           o  B     o2     B     o2  B       o2     B  o
```

3. Elision

```
           -s +s   ^-s  -s+s-s  ^-s   -s +s  °  +s  °
PT 418 Þy bounté of debonerté and Þy bene grace,
            o  B     o2     B      o3      B o̲   B  °
```

4. Indefinite stress

4–1. One occasion of indefinite stress in a line

```
           -s  -s  +s-s -s  +s   s-s  -s +s °+s-s
PT 147 For hit reled on roun vpon þe roȝe yþes.
             o2      B   o2  B     o3      B ° B o
```

4–2. Two occasions of indefinite stress in a line

```
          -s  s(s) -s +s  (s) s-s +s (°)-s +s(°)-s  -s +s   °
PT 356 Er euer he warpped any worde to wyȝe þat he mette,
                 o3     B      o2   B     o  B    o2     B   °
```

5. Metrically subordinated stress

```
       [s] +s  -s -s    +s  -s  (°)+s  -s   -s -s+s-s
PT 529 Ful softly with suffraunce saȝttel me bihouez;
        o   B      o2   B        o  B       o3   B o
```

6. Triple offbeat

6–1. Complicated triple offbeat

```
      [s]   -s   +s(°)-s  +s (s)  -s  [s](°)-s(°) +s °   +s  °
PT 395 Al schal crye, forclemmed, with alle oure clere strenþe;
             o2   B    o   B           o3          B °     B  °
```

6–2. Two triple offbeats in a line

```
      -s   +s-s (s)^-s -s +s (°)-s +s (s)-s -s  -s +s  °
PT 435 And farandely on a felde he fettelez hym to bide,
       o    B         o3   B      o  B       o3       B °
```

6–3. Three triple offbeats in a line

```
       -s   -s -s +s  s -s -s  +s(s) -s   -s  -s +s   +s   -s
PT 266 How fro þe bot into þe blober watz with a best lachched,
           o3      B       o3    B         o3     B  ø  B    o
```

7. Implied offbeats

7–1. Line-final implied offbeat

```
       -s  -s  -s   +s-s -s   +s(°) -s  -s   +s   +s -s
PT 200 Þat þou þus slydes on slepe when þou slayn worþes?
            o3       B   o2     B      o2      B  ø B  o
```

7–2. Line-medial implied offbeat

```
       -s -s  +s  -s  [s] +s     +s-s -s   +s °
PT 355 Þat on journay ful joynt Jonas hym ȝede,
         o2    B       o2  B   ø  B    o2   B °
```

7–3. Line-initial implied offbeat

```
       -s +s  +s  -s -s  +s    -s   +s (°)[s](°) -s  +s °
PT 148 Þe bur ber to hit baft, þat braste alle her gere,
        o  B ø B       o2  B     o    B      o2       B °
```

8. Two implied offbeats in a line

-s +s (s)-s -s +s +s +s -s -s +s-s
PT 221 In bluber of þe blo flod bursten her ores.
o B o2 B ø B ø B o2 B o

9. A triple offbeat at the beginning and an implied offbeat at the end

-s s -s +s(s)-s -s +s -s -s +s +s °
PT 377 And ay he cryes in þat kyth tyl þe kyng herde,
o3 B o2 B o2 B ø B °

10. Two triple offbeats and an implied offbeat

s[°]-s -s +s -s [s](°)+s -s -s -s+s +s-s
PT 29 These arn þe happes alle aȝt þat vus bihyȝt weren,
o3 B o2 B o3 B ø B o

11. Promotion due to alliteration

[s](°)-s +s -s -s -s-s +s(°)-s -s +s °
PT 209 Alle þis meschef for me is made at þys tyme,
o2 B o2 <B> o B o2 B °

12. One word containing two beats

s (°)+s-s(s) -s +s s -s +s +s °
PT 446 Þenne wakened þe wyȝ vnder wodbynde,
o B o2 B o2 B ø B °

13. Quadruple offbeat

-s +s -s -s -s -s +s -s -s s +s ° +s °
PT 190 And broȝt hym vp by þe brest and vpon borde sette,
o B o4 B o3 B ° B °

14. Crowded unstressed syllables in the middle

-s +s (s)-s -s +s -s-s(s) -s -s -s +s +s -s
PT 366 To borges and to bacheleres þat in þat burȝ lenged;
o B o2 B o5 B ø B o

15. Deviated alliteration

```
        -s   [s](°)-s  +s -s   -s  s  ° +s(°)-s   +s °
PT 364 And alle þat lyuyes hereinne lose þe swete.'     [axax]
           o3          B     o2  B º  B    o   B °
```

16. Four alliterating beats in a line

```
        -s   +s -s(s) -s    -s +s -s (°)-s -s   -s +s ° +s -s
PT 468 And wyddered watz þe wodbynde bi þat þe wyȝe wakned;
        o    B          o3       B             o4     B º  B  o
                                                            [aaaa]
```

17. Excessive alliteration

```
        -s+s -s   +s-s   ^-s +s (°)-s   +s -s   -s +s    °
PT 381 He askez heterly a hayre and hasped hym vmbe,    [aaaaa]
        o B  o    B      o2  B      o   B       o2  B    °
```

18. Two sets of alliteration

```
        +s-s -s    -s   +s-s   +s-s  -s   [s]   +s(°) +s  °
PT 155 Scopen out þe scaþel water þat fayn scape wolde- [aabab]
        B      o3         B  o  B        o3       B º   B   °
```

19. Stress shift due to alliteration

```
        s  (°)-s -s+s   -s    -s +s   -s   -s [s]   +s    °
PT 326 Þenne  I remembred me ryȝt of my rych Lorde,      [aaax]
           o2   <B>      o3:     B     o2     B ø  B     °
```

In terms of metrical complexity, twenty-two degrees are suggested for *PE* (See Chapter Four), twenty-one for *C* (See Chapter Three), nineteen for *PT* (as shown above), twenty-three for the long alliterative lines of *G* (See Chapter Three). Each list differs in its ordering of metrical features, and some lists contain distinctive features that others do not have. By comparing these lists, the unique features of each poem, as well as the common ground, are clarified. Five points can be summarized from the lists of metrical complexity.

First, the verse line is governed by the alternation between beats and offbeats in all four poems. The end of the line is more restricted as to metrical variations, and the medial caesura is rather obscure. Second, alliteration is one of the fundamental elements, but is not the most crucial determiner of the meter. Particularly in *PE*, the poet chose such a complex metrical framework of alliteration and rhyme at the same time that he had to ignore one or two of the metrical requirements in certain lines. Third, various rules about stress, such as metrically subordinated stress and indefinite stress, are essential in maintaining the fairly regular offbeat and in allowing variations in reading. The vocalization of the word final *-e* and unstressed inflectional suffixes also plays a flexible role in supplying an optional syllable or making a syllable silent. The fourth point that the present analysis has revealed is that the common offbeat between beats is either single or double in *C*, *PT*, and the long alliterative lines of *G*. Other types of offbeats, such as implied offbeats and triple offbeats, may introduce metrical tension to the line. *PE* and the rhymed lines of *G* differ from the other three poems in their strong tendency to have single offbeats between beats, which often promotes an unstressed syllable to a beat. Finally, the metricality of the line does not depend on a fixed number of syllables per line. Some five-beat lines may have fewer syllables than other four-beat lines. These observations confirm two peculiarities of ME alliterative verse. First, beats and offbeats, but not stressed and unstressed syllables, consist of meter, and second, the relativity of stress is utilized in an intricate manner.

Notes

1 A single author is assumed for these four poems, though evidence to support or deny it has not been available. See Andrew and Waldron 15–16 and Hamilton 339–40.

2 I do not imply that the method based on beats and offbeats should be employed in every occasion in which meter is argued. The traditional method may suffice for explaining meter to those who do not need to study it in detail. A coherent method of scansion, however, is indispensable for a systematic treatment of meter.

3 Some symbols used here are different from Attridge's for typing ease. Symbols irrelevant to the present analysis are omitted while those with asterisks are added to accommodate peculiarities of the ME language.

4 Because of technical difficulties, I have not been able to place these symbols in the exact places. However, if readers are aware of the general rules about the placement of symbols, the task of identifying the right places for the symbols that appear misplaced will not be very difficult. I appreciate the readers' patience concerning this factor. The punctuation marks remain as they are in the text. This is because syntactic boundaries provide information for phrasing and linking.

5 The symbol *a* indicates alliterating beats while the symbol *x* indicates non-alliterating

beats. Symbols *a* and *b* used for a single line indicate two sets of alliteration in different consonants. Even if *x* appears more than twice in the alliteration pattern, it does not mean that these two alliterate with each other. The alliteration pattern may not be shown with every example if alliteration is not controversial for the argument.

6 In order to highlight the part concerned, partial scansion, usually from one beat to the following beat, will be shown instead of the full scansion.

7 Gardner's phrase symbol and the number 2 are meant to suggest the presence of two stresses impossible to establish as hovering either in the pattern ^ ´ or in the pattern ´ ^ . He asserts that the use of conventional spondees in place of hovering stresses clarifies the problem by evading it: ´ ´ ´ . See Gardner 90.

8 According to Sapora, the symbol *S* indicates a metrical syllable which alliterates and is considered to represent strong emphasis while the symbol *W* indicates a metrical syllable which does not alliterate and presents a weak emphasis (31).

9 Borroff uses the symbol *C* for a chief syllable–a syllable that "clearly predominates in stress over adjacent syllables" ("Reading" 194). The symbols *a* and *x* indicate alliteration.

10 Sapora defines symbols that he uses in his analysis as follows:

> *R* and *V* indicate abstract metrical positions which are characteristically realized in the metrical surface of verses as *S* and *W* respectively (i.e., *R*→*S*, *V*→*W*), and which are reversed in their characteristic tendency (i.e., *R*→*W*, *V*→*S*) only by correspondence rules which occur relatively late in the ordering of such rules and which aim to specify relatively complex metrical types (21).

11 *PT* does have examples that suggest that reading the initial or medial three unstressed syllables as a double offbeat is plausible:

```
             -s   -s   +s
PT 325 For when þ'acces of anguych watz hid in my sawle,
                 o2   B
```

The poet or the scribe did not separate the two words *the* and *acces*, probably wishing to maintain a double offbeat.

12 See Chapter Eight as to some of the ME alliterative poems with the wheel.

13 See Chapter Four as to the meter of *PE*.

14 The number that follows the *B* symbols represents the position of that beat among the four within the line. Before B_1, thus, means between the line beginning and the first beat.

15 The position between B_0 and B_1 is not possible in *PE* because it is in rigid four-beat meter.

16 Lines from *C* are randomly chosen from its 1,812 lines.

17 These are the long alliterative lines that appear in the first two fits of *G*.

18 Since the triple offbeat occasionally appears in the other three poems, the first hundred lines reflect the general tendency.

19 The phrase, *colde water*, may receive metrical stress on *colde* but not on *water* due to the alliteration sound /k/. A detailed analysis on this phenomenon will be given in Chapters Thirteen and Fifteen. The reading to realize metrical stress in *water* but not in *colde* will result in the alliteration pattern, [axax].

Chapter 3

A Comparative Analysis of *Cleanness* and *Sir Gawain and the Green Knight*: Metrical Standard and Idiosyncrasies

This chapter specifically compares the meters of *Cleanness* (*C*) and *Sir Gawain and the Green Knight* (*G*). Chapter Two has proposed the same metrical structure for both of the poems; however, the actual realizations of the meter are not identical, and there are some differences between them that cannot be represented through formal notations. This chapter first reviews common points that are observed in both of the poems while quoting typical examples. Common features to the two poems include the conditions of vocalizing the word final *-e*, elision of two syllables, metrically subordinated stress, indefinite stress, structures of the offbeat, and the structure of the entire line that consists of four or five beats separated by single or double offbeats. The chapter will then reveal features that are different between *C* and *G*: Alliteration is rather regular in *C* whereas *G* is abundant in variations. The number of lines that can be read in both four- and five-beat meters is larger in *G*, but *C* maintains the regular pattern of [aaax] in its rather rigid four-beat meter. The third section will present the lists of metrical complexity of *C* and *G*. These lists, both of which start with a basic line and end with a line that contains six beats, will illuminate peculiar points to each poem in its own hierarchy.

3.1 The Basics and the Metrical Template

ME alliterative meter is typically explained as having the following features:

1. Underlying regularity of pace, marked by four chief stresses to the line.
2. A central caesura—i.e. a greater syntactical break between second and

third stresses than between first and second or third and fourth.
3. Repetition of the initial sounds (alliteration) of some of the stressed syllables (in principle the first three), which gives extra prominence to these syllables and bridges the caesura.
4. Variation in the number of unstressed syllables between the stresses.

(Andrew and Waldron 47)

A comparison of the meter of *C* and that of the alliterative long lines of *G* further reinforces what has been observed in Chapter Two, revealing the metrical template common to ME alliterative verse and observing various metrical phenomena within the limit of metrical deviation. The meter of *G* has been a well-known research topic, but the meter of *C* has not been examined thoroughly except in McColly's statistical analysis.

The postulated meter for *C* and *G* is as follows:

Meter of *C* and the long alliterative lines of *G*:

Verse → $(o_1^2\ \ B_0)\ \ o_1^2\ \ B_1\ \ o_1^2\ \ B_2\ \ o_1^2\ \ B_3\ \ o_1^2\ \ B_4\ \ \langle o\rangle$

(With possibility of triple offbeat for an offbeat position and with alliteration pattern [(a)aaax] or [(x)aaax]. Parentheses indicate optional constituents in the line whereas <o> indicates an optional offbeat which shows preference for inclusion.)

The above meter indicates that the verse line consists of either four or five beats (metrically stressed syllables), and that a single offbeat (metrically unstressed syllable) or a double offbeat separates these beats. The meter tends to have an unstressed syllable at the beginning of the line and is likely to place another at the end. Alliteration usually falls on the three or four beats in the five-beat line and on the first three beats in the four-beat line.

3.2 Special Metrical Phenomena Observed in *Cleanness* and *Sir Gawain and the Green Knight*

The phenomena that are observed in both *C* and *G* are as follows: the vocalization of the word final *-e* and other inflectional suffixes according to metrical circumstances, elision of two syllables, metrically subordinated stress, indefinite stress, and structures of the offbeat. A quick observation on these phenomena will be useful before the presentation of the metrical complexity.

First, the word final *-e* and other unstressed suffixes may be silent if there are already a sufficient number of unstressed syllables between beats to form an offbeat. However, they may form a syllable in a metrical circumstance where there is no other constituent of an offbeat. Minkova's article on schwa deletion ("Prosodic Character"), particularly her idea that schwa loss dramatically changed rhythmic principles of the language, is helpful in deciding the metrical role of the final *-e*. Hutcheson provides useful information about OE unstressed syllable that may be skipped in the actual reading. The following lines of *C* and *G* indicate how a word final *–e* or inflectional suffix is realized in the meter:

```
      -s   +s-s  -s +s(°)-s  -s   +s (s)-s  -s +s-s-s  +s °
C 110  And diden þe dede þat watz demed, as he deuised hade,
       o    B     o2 B      o2     B       o2   B   o2  B °

      -s   -s -s  +s(s) -s  -s +s(s) -s   -s +s ° +s -s
C 1243 And þo þat byden wer so biten with þe bale hunger
           o3      B       o2   B       o2    B º   B  o

        -s -s  +s(°)-s -s  +s (°)-s  +s(°)-s  -s +s
G 138  Fro þe swyre to þe swange so sware  and so þik,
         o2    B     o2     B     o   B      o2    B

       -s  [s]°  +s-s (°)-s s  +s   °  +s(°)-s  -s  s  °
G 1070 Þe Grene Chapayle  vpon grounde greue yow no more
        o   B °   B      o3      B  º    B   o2      B °
```

In *C* 110, the unstressed syllable *-en* in *diden* forms a syllable whereas the final *-e* in *dede* and the unstressed syllable *-ed* in *demed* can be silent. These syllables may not be vocalized because there are already two syllables that are definitely vocalized between the two beats. In *C* 1243, the unstressed syllables in *byden* and *biten* are not likely to form a syllable, but the final *-e* in *bale* is vocalized in order to avoid a clash of beats. In *G* 138 as well, the final *-e*'s in *swyre*, *swange*, and *sware* are not likely to form a syllable. On the contrary, the final *-e* is vocalized twice in *G* 1070 in order to avoid a clash of beats.

The second metrical phenomenon observed in both *C* and *G* is that the two elided syllables are realized as a single offbeat or a constituent of a double offbeat with another unstressed syllable:

-s   +s-s ^-s   +s-s-s   -s   +s(°) -s   -s+s-s
C 238 Þer pryuély in paradys his place watz devised,
o   B   o2   B   o3   B   o2   B o

-s   +s   ^-s   -s   +s-s   +s-s   ^-s +s °
G 63   Þe chauntré of þe chapel cheued to an ende,
o   B   o2   B o   B   o2 B   °

By means of elision marked with the symbol ^, the above lines maintain a double offbeat, though there are three unstressed syllables between the beats.

Another phenomenon common to both *C* and *G* is metrically subordinated stress. Certain monosyllabic and dissyllabic adjectives and adverbs behave as unstressed syllables, depending upon the metrical environment. Metrically subordinated stress is marked by square brackets. The following are the lines with metrically subordinated stress in the word *all* in the beat position (*C* 1211 and *G* 567) and in the offbeat position (*C* 280 and *G* 483):

-s -s   -s   [s](°)-s -s +s ° +s -s (°) +s-s
C 1211 By þat watz alle on a hepe hurlande swyþee,   [aaax]
o3   B   o2   B °   B   o   B o

+s -s +s -s -s +s -s -s   [s](°)-s(°)-s   +s
G 567   Askez erly hys armez and alle were þay broȝt.   [aaaax]
B   o   B   o2   B   o2   B   o2   B

-s   -s +s(°)-s [s]   +s   [s]   +s -s -s+s -s
C 280   Þat þe Wyȝe þat al wroȝt ful wroþly bygynnez.   [aaax]
o2   B   o2   B   o   B   o2   B   o

-s [s](°)+s   -s   +s   (°)-s   +s -s   -s   +s   °
G 483   Of alle dayntyez double, as derrest myȝt falle,   [aaax]
O2   B   o   B   o   B   o2   B   °

Metrically subordinated stress reflects the flexibility of stress found in certain word categories. As seen in these examples, alliteration may be an influential determiner as to whether or not the syllable is realized as a beat or offbbeat.

Words with indefinite stress are also flexible about their metrical function. The same word can be both stressed and unstressed, again depending on the metrical circumstance in which it falls. *C* 578 and *G* 218 below demonstrate occasions of indefinite stress as a beat in *bot*, *neuer*, and *after* whereas *C* 88 and *G* 746 show those as an offbeat in *also* and *mony*, respectively:

```
           s   -s   +s(s) -s -s   +s    -s   s(s)-s s   +s-s
C 578 Bot non nuyez Hym on naʒt ne neuer vpon dayez       [aaax]
           o2      B      o2      B     o  B     o2     B o

        -s    -s s -s   -s +s   ° +s   -s   [s]+s   °
G 218 And so after þe halme halched ful ofte,             [aaaa]
            o2  B     o2    B  o̲  B      o2    B   °

        -s    s -s +s(°)-s s   +s(°) -s   +s-s   -s   +s   °
C 88  And also fele  vpon fote, of fre and of bonde.      [aaax]
             o3     B       o2  B     o     B    o2    B   °

         -s     s-s   +s  -s -s   +s(°)-s s   +s °   +s-s
G 746 With mony bryddez vnblyþe  vpon bare twyges,        [aaax]
                o3    B     o2    B      o2   B o̲    B  o
```

The word with indefinite stress presents stress contrast if it is pronounced individually. Yet it may behave as a word without a stressed syllable if the meter demands an offbeat but not a beat in that slot of the line. Typical examples of words with indefinite stress include prepositions such as *withoute*, *amonge*, *vpon*, *into*, *ouer*, and *byfore*, determiners such as *other*, *mony(e)*, and *any*, and adverbs such as *neuer*, *also*, *therafter*, and *therto*.

Finally, the structure of the offbeat exhibits special characteristics. The offbeat, which can be single or double, may be simply one or two unstressed syllables, respectively, or it may consist of several unstressed syllables. The following lines illuminate the simplest construction of a single and double offbeat while the latter lines indicate more complicated structures of an offbeat:

(i) A single offbeat that consists of an unstressed syllable:[1]

```
                      +s  -s +s
C 1   Clannesse whoso kyndly cowþe comende,
                       B   o  B
```

```
                             +s   -s  +s
G 2   Þe borʒ brittened and brent to brondez and askez,
                              B    o   B
```

(ii) A single offbeat that consists of two unstressed syllables:

```
                          +s (°)-s  +s
C 430 Vche hille watz þer hidde with yþez ful graye.
                           B     o   B
```

```
                +s (°)-s  +s
G 410 And if I spende no speche þenne spedez þou þe better,
                 B     o   B
```

(iii) A double offbeat that consists of two unstressed syllables:

```
     [s]-s  +s                 +s  -s -s +s
C 59  Al is roþeled and rosted ryʒt to þe sete;
        o2   B                  B    o2    B
```

```
                          +s-s-s  +s
C 780 Whyl þe Souerayn to Sodamas sende to spye.
                           B   o2  B
```

```
           +s -s -s   +s-s   -s  +s-s   -s +s
G 49  With lordez and ladies, as leuest him þoʒt.
            B     o2   B      o2  B      o2  B
```

(iv) A double offbeat that consists of three unstressed syllables:

```
                                     +s   s(s) -s +s
C 215 In þe mesure of His mode, His metz neuer þe lasse.
                                     B         o2  B
```

```
        +s (s) -s -s +s
C 44    Hurled to þe halle dore and harde þeroute schowued,
         B      o2    B
```

```
                          +s-s(s) [s]+s
G 65    Nowel nayted onewe, neuened ful ofte.
                                B     o2   B
```

(v) A double offbeat that consists of four unstressed syllables:

```
           +s(s) s(s) -s  +s
C 1776 Asscaped ouer þe skyre watteres and scayled þe walles,
           B      o2       B
```

```
                    +s(°)-s -s (°)+s
C 28    For he schal loke  on oure Lorde with a leue chere';
                     B      o2     B
```

```
                             +s(s)  -s -s (°) s
G 91    Þat he þurȝ nobelay had nomen: he wolde neuer ete
                              B       o2      B
```

(vi) A double offbeat that consists of five unstressed syllables:

```
            +s(s)[s](°) ^-s +s
C 1270 And pyled alle þe apparement þat pented to þe kyrke-
            B      o2       B
```

```
                          +s(s)[s](°) s(°)[s]
C 1281 Now hatz Nabuzardan nomen alle þyse noble þynges,
                           B      o2      B
```

```
          +s(s) s (s)  ^-s+s
G 790   Enbaned vnder þe abataylment, in þe best lawe;
           B      o2      B
```

(vii) A triple offbeat that consists of three unstressed syllables:

```
                             +s   -s  -s -s +s
C 143 How watz þou hardy þis hous for þyn vnhap to neʒe
                              B      o3      B
```

```
     -s   -s  -s +s-s   -s  -s  +s -s  -s  -s   +s
G 142 And þat þe myriest in his muckel þat myʒt ride;
          03      B     o3       B    o3         B
```

(viii) A triple offbeat that consists of four unstressed syllables:

```
                        +s(°)-s   -s  -s  +s
C 16   Boþe God and His gere, and Hym to greme cachen.
                         B         o3      B
```

```
          +s-s  -s(°)-s +s
G 1170 Þe ledez were so lerned at þe loʒe trysteres;
           B     03      B
```

(ix) A triple offbeat that consists of five unstressed syllables:

```
       +s -s  (°)-s  s(s) +s
C 1212 Folʒande þat oþer flote, and fonde hem bilyue,
        B         o3       B
```

```
                      +s-s   s(s) -s -s+s
G 608  Wyth a lyʒtly vrysoun ouer þe  auentayle,
                       B     o3          B
```

(x) A triple offbeat that consists of six unstressed syllables:

```
           +s(s)  s(s)-s s(s)  +s
C 1755 For daʒed neuer anoþer day, þat ilk derk after,
            B       o3          B
```

```
       +s [s](°)-s(°)[s](°)+s
G 656  Now alle þese fyue syþez forsoþe were fetled on þis knyʒt
        B         o3       B
```

In terms of stressed and unstressed syllables, the above lines under (ii), (iv), (v), (vi), (viii), (ix), and (x) may be overtly chaotic to fit the meter, but in terms of beats and offbeats they present a regular distribution of beats and single or double offbeats.

As seen in Tables 2.2 and 2.3, the frequent appearance of the implied offbeat (a null offbeat that creates a metrical pause between beats) in the line-terminal position and the general tendency of the triple offbeat (a group of three metrically unstressed syllables) to appear in the line-initial position suggest that the line tends to slow the tempo toward the end. The implied offbeat most frequently appears between the third and fourth beats whereas the most common place of the triple offbeat is before the first beat. This is observed in both *C* and *G* and can be seen in the following lines:

```
                                             +s   +s
C 960  And ferly flayed þat folk þat in þose fees lenged.
                                              B  ø B
```

```
                                   +s   +s
G 869  Þat a comloker knyȝt neuer Kryst made,
                                    B  ø  B
```

```
        s -s   -s  +s
C 865  Bot I schal kenne yow by kynde a crafte þat is better:
             o3      B
```

```
        s  -s   -s +s
G 2368 Bot for ȝe lufed your lyf-þe lasse I yow blame.'
            o3      B
```

The following observation can be made about the conclusion of the line. The table extracts the percentages of *C* and *G* from Table 2.4 given in Chapter Two:

Table 3.1. Distribution of Metrical Elements at the Line End (*C*, *G*)

	With a single offbeat	With a final *-e*	With a beat
C	44.2%	46.4%	9.4%
G	42.0%	47.4%	10.6%

Table 3.1 indicates a similar distribution in *C* and *G* regarding three possible ways to conclude the line. If the final *-e* is assumed to form a syllable at the end of the line because a puff of air can easily accompany the final consonant before the line boundary (Conner), the total percentage of lines that end with an unstressed syllable is close to ninety percent in both *C* and *G*.

Another similarity between *C* and *G* is that the meter is flexible in producing a line that can be read in two ways. The following scansion shows how a line can be read in both four-beat meter (reading *a*) and five-beat meter (reading *b*):

```
          s-s  +s-s(°)-s   +s -s  -s   +s-s  +s-s
C 638-a Syþen potage  and polment in plater honest.      [aaax]
           o2   B       o2   B    o2     B o   B o

          s-s  +s-s(°)-s   +s -s  -s   +s-s  +s-s
C 638-b Syþen potage  and polment in plater honest.     [xaaax]
          B o   B       o2   B      o2   B o   B o
```

```
        -s     s(s) +s(s) -s -s   +s    -s  +s-s  -s +s   -s
G 434-a And syþen boȝez to his blonk, þe brydel he cachchez,
             o2      B       o2    B     o   B    o2  B    o
                                                          [aaax]

        -s     s-s  +s(s) -s -s   +s    -s  +s-s  -s +s   -s
G 434-b And syþen boȝez to his blonk, þe brydel he cachchez,
          o    B o   B     o2      B     o   B    o2  B    o
                                                         [xaaax]
```

When a syllable that has potential to form the fifth beat alliterates, the five-beat reading reinforces the alliteration and may be felt more natural than the four-beat reading:

```
          -s s  -s +s-s(s)-s+s-s   -s   +s -s  -s   s-s
C 1479-a Vpon þe pyleres apyked, þat praysed hit mony,   [aaax]
            o3     B   o2   B    o2     B    o2    B o
```

```
        -s s   -s +s-s(s)-s+s-s   -s    +s -s  -s   s-s
C 1479-b Vpon þe pyleres apyked, þat praysed hit mony, [aaaax]
         o B   o  B   o2   B    o2     B    o2    B o

        -s s (°)+s-s  -s  +s  -s  -s  +s -s  +s-s
G 2028-a Aboute beten and bounden, enbrauded semez,     [aaax]
           o2    B     o2  B        o2    B   o B o

        -s s  °  +s-s -s   +s  -s  -s  +s -s  +s-s
G 2028-b Aboute beten and bounden, enbrauded semez,    [aaaax]
         o B  °   B   o2    B     o2     B  o   B o
```

From the various metrical phenomena observed above, the meters of *C* and *G* closely resemble with each other. Nevertheless, there are certain differences between them. First, the flexible lines to be read in both four- and five-meters differ with regard to changes in the alliteration patterns. The following table compares the flexible lines in the two poems:

Table 3.2. Percentages of Four-Beat and Five-Beat Lines (*C*, *G*)

	C	*G*
Definite 4B	43%	10%
4B or 5B; 5B reading adds another alliterating beat	11%	20%
4B or 5B; 5B reading adds another unalliterating beat	30%	49%
4B or 5B; 5B reading produces two sets of alliteration	3%	6%
Definite 5B	13%	15%
Total	100%	100%

Table 3.2 reveals that *C* has more lines that are in definite four-beats. It is also evident that the five-beat reading in *G* is likely to bring in another alliterating beat. If the strict five-beat reading is applied, the total percentage of the lines that are in five-beat is only fifty-seven percent in *C* in contrast to ninety percent in *G*. In other words, lines in *G* are relatively more natural even in a strict five-beat reading.

The second difference between *C* and *G* is that alliteration, which is considered to be the one of the most crucial determiners of alliterative meter, is more rigid in *C* while alliteration in *G* demonstrates notable diversity. In particular, the five-beat reading presents more variations in *G* than in *C*. It is one of the peculiarities of *C* that the final beat rarely alliterates whereas the final beat frequently alliterates in *G*. The excessive alliteration found in *G*, such as alliteration in all beats, additional alliteration in offbeats, two sets of alliteration within a line, and the same alliteration repeated in several consecutive lines, is not common in *C*.[2] Lines in *C* obey the basic [aaax] pattern throughout. The following lines from *G* exemplify its heavy alliteration:

```
          +s-s  +s-s -s    +s(°)-s +s   -s -s s   °
G 2082   Brokez byled and breke bi bonkkez aboute,        [aaaaa]
          B  o  B   o2      B    o  B    o2  B   °
```

```
         -s   +s(°) -s -s  +s   -s    -s -s  -s  +s   +s  -s
G 2432[3] For wele  ne for worchyp, ne for þe wlonk werkkez;
          o  B         o2  B           o4         B  ø  B   o
                                                             [aaaa]
```

```
        -s   -s  -s +s  -s-s  (°) +s(°)-s  +s  -s   -s  +s °
G 335    And wyth a countenaunce dryȝe he droȝ doun his cote,
            o3       B      o2       B    o  B     o2     B °
                                                             [abba]
```

```
          s   °  s -s  -s -s  +s -s -s  s   °
G 952[4] Riche red on þat on rayled ayquere,                 [aaax]
          B  o̲  B      o3     B    o2  B   °
```

```
         +s   +s  -s   +s-s  -s  s-s -s  +s -s
G 953    Rugh ronkled chekez þat oþer on rolled;            [aaxxa]
          B ø  B   o    B     o2  B    o2  B  o
```

3.3 Lists of Metrical Complexity of *Cleanness* and *Sir Gawain and the Green Knight*

A list of metrical complexity for each of the poems is presented below. The list presents an increasing order of metrical complexity of the lines in *C* first, showing progressively stronger metrical tension. In other words, the greater the variation of symbols the scansion uses, the more complex is the structure of the line.

1. Base rules only

```
       -s    -s +s   -s   -s   +s -s   -s   +s     -s  -s +s °
C 1202 Wyth þe best of his burnes, a blench for to make;
          o2    B       o2   B      o2   B      o2     B °
```

2. Double offbeat that consists of more than two syllables

```
      -s -s +s -s(s)[s](°)+s -s   -s  +s -s    -s -s   s °
C 242 Þat enpoysened alle peplez þat parted fro hem boþe,
         o2    B    o2          B      o2  B        o3     B °
```

3. Elision

```
      -s  +s  -s  +s -s  +s -s ^-s   +s-s [s](°)+s-s
C 400 To dryȝ her delful destyné and dyȝen alle samen;
       o   B   o   B  o   B     o2    B   o2     B o
```

4. Indefinite stress

4–1. One occasion of indefinite stress in a line

```
     -s s  +s-s -s  +s(°) -s   +s  -s  +s -s
C 38 Abof dukez on dece, with dayntys serued?
      o2   B    o2  B     o    B   o   B  o
```

4–2. Two occasions of indefinite stress in a line

```
      -s  s (s) +s  (°)s-s  +s(°)-s +s -s -s +s  °
C 556 Withouten maskle oþer mote, as margerye-perle.
         o2     B    o2     B    o  B   o2  B  °
```

4–3. Three occasions of indefinite stress in a line

```
      -s  s(s) +s(°) s-s   +s  s(s)-s  +s ° +s °
C 432 Þat euer flote, oþer flwe, oþer on fote ȝede,
        o2      B    o2    B      o2   B º B °
```

5. Metrically subordinated stress

```
      -s +s -s  [s] +s -s-s   +s  -s  -s +s °
C 797 He ros vp ful radly and ran hem to mete,
       o  B   o2    B   o2   B     o2   B °
```

6. Triple offbeat

6–1. Complicated triple offbeat

```
               +s  -s  (°) -s   s(s)  +s(°) -s   +s  (°)-s   -s+s  °
C 1212 Folȝande þat oþer flote, and fonde hem bilyue,
                B          o3          B    o    B      o2     B  °
```

6–2. Two triple offbeats in a line

```
         -s  -s  (°)+s  (°)-s(°)-s   -s  +s(s)-s   -s  -s   +s  -s  +s   °
C 424 Nyf oure Lorde hade ben her lodezmon hem had lumpen harde.
          o2     B      o3          B        o3       B  o   B   °
```

6–3. Three triple offbeats in a line

```
        -s   +s  -s   -s   -s    +s-s  -s  (°)-s    +s-s  -s  -s  +s   °
C 724 And reȝtful wern and resounable  and redy Þe to serue,
         o    B        o3       B        o3        B   o3      B    °
```

7. Implied offbeat

7–1. Line-final implied offbeat

```
           -s   -s  +s(°)-s    -s+s   -s    -s  -s  +s      +s-s
C 646 When þe mete watz remued and Þay of mensk speken,
          o2     B    o2     B      o3      B   ø   B  o
```

7–2. Line-medial implied offbeat

```
        +s-s   +s  -s  -s   +s    +s-s   -s     +s   °
C 375 Water wylger ay wax, wonez þat stryede,
         B  o  B      o2  B  ø B    o2      B   °
```

7–3. Line-initial implied offbeat

```
           -s    +s   +s    -s   -s +s(°)-s     +s    -s   -s   +s  -s
C 1541 His cnes cachches toclose, and cluchches his hommes,
           o     B ø B      o2    B    o     B    o2       B   o
```

8. Two implied offbeats in a line

```
        -s   -s   +s(s)  s -s -s    +s    -s    +s    +s    +s-s
C 787 As he stared into þe strete þer stout men played,
          o2    B      o3        B    o    B ø  B ø  B o
```

9. A triple offbeat at the beginning and an implied offbeat at the end

```
          s -s  -s   +s (s)-s -s +s  [s](°)-s  +s   +s -s
C 1008 Nov is hit plunged in a pit like  of pich fylled.
          o3        B     o2    B        o2   B ø  B  o
```

10. Two triple offbeats and an implied offbeat

```
         -s  +s  -s s -s +s  -s  +s  -s   -s -s  +s   +s-s
C 1025 For lay þeron a lump of led, and hit on loft fletez,
          o  B     o3    B   o   B        o3     B  ø B o
```

11. Three triple offbeats and an implied offbeat

```
         s   ^-s(°)-s+s -s  -s   -s +s  -s   -s -s  +s   +s -s
C 749 Bot I haue bygonnen wyth my God, and He hit gayn þynkez;
          o3         B     o3      B   o3           B  ø B  o
```

12. Promotion due to alliteration

```
       -s   -s +s  -s  -s  -s   -s  -s -s +s  +s -s
C 974 And þe wenches hym wyth þat by þe way folʒed;
          o2   B    o2   <B>      o3     B ø B  o
```

13. One word containing two beats

```
         -s +s  (°)-s -s+s -s  -s  -s  +s -s +s-s
C 1358 To vouche  on avayment of his vayneglorie;
          o  B    o2   B    o3       B  o  B o
```

14. Quadruple offbeat

```
        -s   -s  -s   -s +s  +s   -s   +s -s  +s -s
C 1215 And þer watz þe kyng kaʒt wyth Caldé prynces,
             o4          B  ø  B   o   B  o   B  o
```

15. Crowded unstressed syllables in the middle

```
        +s -s  +s  -s(s) -s  -s   -s  -s  -s +s -s  +s -s
C 86 Broʒten bachlerez hem wyth þat þay by bonkez metten,
        B  o  B         o3       <B>    o2   B  o   B  o
```

16. Deviated alliteration

```
       -s   -s   +s    -s   s -s   -s    +s(°)-s    +s-s
C 770 ȝet he cryed Hym after with careful steuen:          [axax]
        o2      B     o B      o2     B    o     B o
```

17. Four alliterating beats in a line

```
         s-s   +s -s-s    +s   °   +s [s](°)-s    +s -s
C 367 Mony clustered clowde clef alle  in clowtez;         [aaaa]
        o2    B     o2    B  º    B        o2       B  o
```

18. Excessive alliteration

```
       -s    -s   -s +s(s)-s   -s +s  (°)-s -s -s   +s    ° +s   °
C 1597 And hatz a haþel in þy holde, as I haf herde  ofte,
              o3      B        o2    B         o3       B  º  B   °
                                                                [aaaa]
```

19. Two sets of alliteration

```
         +s(°)-s    +s -s -s     +s(s) -s    s(s)  +s-s +s
C 1720 Made  of stokkes and stonez þat neuer styry moȝt. [abbba]
         B     o    B     o2     B    o2           B o  B
```

20. Stress shift due to alliteration

```
        -s   +s-s -s   -s+s-s-s   -s  +s -s(°)+s  °
C 1432 In Judé, in Jerusalem, in gentyle wyse:             [aaax]
         o   B    o2  B          o4    B    o  B °
```

21. Six beats

```
         s  (°)+s  (°)-s  (°)+s(°)  s   -s +s  °    +s   -s +s-s +s-s
C 661 Þenne sayde  oure Syre þer He sete: ‘Se! so Saré laȝes,
         o     B     o     B       o2   B  °    B    o  B o  B o
```

The metrical complexity of the lines in the alliterative long lines of *G* is as follows:

1. Base rules only

```
      -s -s  +s  -s-s  +s (°)-s  -s +s  ° +s °
G 1431 In a knot bi a clyffe  at þe kerre syde,
         o2   B   o2     B   o2       B  o̲  B °
```

2. Base rules with a varied alliteration pattern

```
       -s -s +s  -s-s  +s  -s +s  -s  -s+s  °
G 2522 Þus in Arthurus day þis aunter bitidde-          [axax]
          o2  B     o2   B   o  B    o2   B  °
```

3. Double offbeat that consists of more than two syllables

```
    -s  +s -s(°) -s (°)+s (s) -s   -s +s -s  -s +s  °
G 99 As fortune  wolde fulsun hom, þe fayrer to haue.
     o   B     o2       B      o2      B   o2    B °
```

4. Elision

```
     -s  +s     ^s  -s  +s-s   +s-s   ^-s +s   °
G 63 Þe chauntré of þe chapel cheued to an ende,
      o   B     o2       B  o   B      o2  B  °
```

5. Indefinite stress

```
        s-s   +s (s) -s  -s  +s  -s    +s (s) -s -s   +s   °
G 1339 Siþen britned þay þe brest and brayden hit in twynne.
          o2   B      o2      B   o     B        o2    B   °
```

6. Stress shift

```
     -s  -s  -s +s   -s  -s+s (°)[s]+s -s  +s-s
G 44 For þer þe fest watz ilyche ful fiften dayes,
        o3       B     o2   B     o   B o   B o
```

7. Triple offbeat

7–1. Line-initial triple offbeat

```
       -s -s -s  +s (°)-s  -s  +s   -s +s  -s   -s +s -s
G 1800 Þat I may mynne  on þe, mon, my mournyng to lassen.’
           o3     B      o2     B    o  B      o2   B  o
```

7–2. Line-medial triple offbeat

```
        s -s +s(°)-s -s  -s +s (°)-s  -s +s ° +s -s
G 2193 Now I fele hit is þe Fende, in my fyue wyttez,
          o2  B       o3     B     o2     B  º B  o
```

7–3. Complicated triple offbeat

```
       +s(°) -s  s   +s   ^-s  -s   -s  +s   +s-s
G 1794 Kysse me now, comly, and I schal cach heþen;
        B      o2     B         o3       B ø  B o
```

7–4. Two triple offbeats in a line

```
      -s s   -s +s -s  -s  -s +s(°)-s  +s -s  -s +s °
G 445 Toward þe derrest on þe dece he dressez þe face
        o3       B     o3      B    o   B     o2  B °
```

7–5. Three triple offbeats in a line

```
       -s  -s  -s  s   -s -s  -s +s (s) -s   -s -s  +s ° +s  °
G 1393 Hit may be such hit is þe better, and ʒe me breue wolde
            o3     B     o3        B        o3       B º  B  °
```

8. Implied offbeats

8–1. Line-final implied offbeat

```
       +s -s +s (°)-s   -s +s (°) -s  -s +s     +s -s
G 1694 Ferly fayre watz þe folde, for þe forst clenged;
        B  o B     o2       B      o2      B  ø   B  o
```

8–2. Line-medial implied offbeat

```
      -s  +s   +s-s   +s(°)-s   +s  -s -s s-s
G 287 Þat dar stifly strike  a strok for anoþer,
       o   B ø  B  o   B    o    B   o2   B o
```

8–3. Line-initial implied offbeat

```
      +s   +s  ^-s  -s  +s(°)-s  -s -s  +s ° +s -s
G 983 Hent heʒly of his hode  and on a spere henged
       B ø  B     o2     B       o3      B °  B  o
```

9. Two implied offbeats in a line

```
       +s   +s(s)-s  -s +s   +s  -s  -s +s  -s
G 2080 Mist muged on þe mor, malt on þe mountez;
        B ø  B    o2     B   ø B   o2     B   o
```

10. A triple offbeat at the beginning and an implied offbeat at the end

```
       -s  s  -s +s  (°)-s -s    +s  -s  -s +s   +s  °
G 1430 Bitwene a flosche in þat fryth and a foo cragge.
           o3      B    o2        B    o2    B ø  B  °
```

11. Two triple offbeats and an implied offbeat

```
        +s-s (°) -s -s  +s(s)-s -s  -s  +s    +s  °
G 1706 Wreȝande hym ful weterly with a wroth noyse,
         B      o3       B     o3         B  ø B  °
```

12. Three triple offbeats and an implied offbeat

```
      -s   s  -s    +s   -s -s s  +s    -s   -s -s   +s    s  °
G 2019 And al watz fresch as vpon fyrst, and he watz fayn þenne
            o3       B      o3     B       o3          B ø B  °
```

13. Two sets of alliteration, one of which is on vowels

```
      -s   +s-s  -s +s   -s  -s  +s  -s -s  +s +s  -s
G 1565 And madee hym mawgref his hed for to mwe  vtter,  [aabab]
       o    B    o2   B     o2    B      o2   BøB   o
```

14. Two sets of alliteration on two different consonants

```
       -s  -s +s  -s  +s  +s    -s   s +s  +s-s
G 1682 For þe lur may mon lach whenso mon lykez.'      [ababa]
         o2    B    o   B ø B     o2    B ø B o
```

15. Two sets of alliteration with its echo in the offbeats

```
     -s   -s -s  +s  -s  +s-s  -s  +s -s  +s  -s  s-s
G 939 And he hym þonkked þroly; and ayþer halched oþer  [aabbb]
      o3           B   o    B   o2   B  o   B   o  B o
```

16. A particular consonant, which is not the alliterating sound, is repeated in the offbeats

```
       -s   -s (s) +s -s(s) -s +s  -s  +s(°) s(s) -s +s -s
G 430 And nawþer faltered ne fel þe freke neuer þe helder
          o2        B    o2     B   o   B       o2     B  o
```

17. Excessive alliterating syllables in a line

```
          +s-s  +s-s -s    +s(°)-s +s  -s -s s   °
G 2082 Brokez byled and breke bi bonkkez aboute,
          B  o  B    o2    B  o    B   o2   B   °
```

18. Varied alliteration and its echo in offbeats

```
      -s  -s  -s +s   -s  -s+s (°)[s]+s -s  +s-s
G 44 For þer þe fest watz ilyche ful fiften dayes,        [axax]
         o3     B    o2    B      o  B  o   B o
```

19. Two sets of alliteration with a triple offbeat and an implied offbeat

```
          +s-s     s    -s  s-s  +s    +s -s  -s s   °
G 1942 'Mary,' quoþ þat oþer mon, 'myn is bihynde,      [abaab]
          B       o3       B o   B  ø  B    o2  B   °
```

20. Demotion between beats[5]

```
         s(°)s(s) +s-s-s   +s(°)  [s] +s(°)-s   +s    +s     +s
G 1445 Þise oþer halowed 'Hyghe!' ful hyȝe, and 'Hay! Hay!' cryed,
          o2      B    o2 B       o    B    o     B    o:     B
```

21. Varied alliteration and caesura

```
        +s   +s-s  -s s  -s   +s (°)-s -s  +s °
G 254 Liȝt luflych adoun and lenge, I þe praye,          [aaxa/x]
        B  ø B   o2  B   o     B    o2     B °
```

22. Alliteration in words of Romance origin

```
          s(°)-s   s  -s   -s    +s    ^-s    -s   -s  +s -s
G 311 Where  is now your sourquydrye and your conquestes, [axaa]
         B   o  B     o2       B            o3         B  o
```

23. Six beats

```
      +s(°)-s +s  +s -s-s    s  -s -s(°)+s  ° +s  °
G 1135 Ete  a sop hastyly, when he hade herde masse,
       B   o   B ø B     o2  B      o2   B  º  B  °
```

The list consists of twenty-one degrees of metrical complexity for *C* and twenty-three for the long alliterative lines of *G*. The differences concerning the hierarchy of the complexity are as follows. First, the list of metrical complexity of *G* places the line with two sets of alliteration, in the thirteenth (alliteration on one consonant and vowels), fourteenth (alliteration on two different consonants), and fifteenth degree (alliteration on two different consonants plus the echo of one alliterating sound in offbeats). On the contrary, the list of metrical complexity of *C* does not include variants of two sets of alliteration. Since alliteration of *C* is rigid and variations are few, the deviated alliteration patterns are listed from the sixteenth to nineteenth degrees. The sixteenth degree is the line with a deviated alliteration pattern [axax]; the seventeenth degree is the line in which all beats alliterate; the eighteenth degree is the line with excessive alliteration, which is rather rare in *C* but quite common in *G*.[6] The nineteenth degree of *C* is a line with duple alliteration, which is again less frequent than in *G*. The line on the edge of metricality in *C*, the most metrically complicated line at the end of the list, is the line with six beats. The most complicated line in *G* is also a six-beat line. The lists both start with a base line and end with a line with six beats, but differ in between.

In sum, the meter of *C* and that of the long alliterative lines of *G* are governed by similar principles. There are certain differences between them that are not major ones like the differences between *Pearl* and the other poems in the same manuscript. Because the differences are concerned with the details of the metrical structure, the formal notations of the two meters look exactly the same. The two poems are composed in a similar meter, yet the meter of *C* is obedient to the base in contrast to that of *G*, which is filled with various metrical innovations.

Notes

1 In order to highlight the particular metrical point, a partial scansion is shown rather than the scansion of the entire line.

2 These alliteration techniques will be explained in detail in Chapter Six.

3 The sound /f/ is repeated in offbeats three times in this line. The quadruple offbeat is another variation of the offbeat, but a five-beat reading can be applied in order to avoid it.

4 *G* 952 and *G* 953 have the identical alliteration on /r/.

5 This type of demotion, which occurs between beats or between a beat and the line boundary, is common in the rhyming part but rare in the alliterative part.

6 *C* 1597 is comprised solely of words that start with vowels, which is highly reminiscent of *G* lines.

```
          -s   -s   -s +s (s)-s  -s +s (°)-s -s -s   +s  ° +s  °
C 1597 And hatz a haþel in þy holde, as I haf herde ofte,   [aaaa]
              o3       B        o2   B         o3      B  o̲  B  °
```

Chapter 4

The Meter of *Pearl*: Its Unique Features against Other ME Alliterative Poems

Based on the idea that differences in metricality create a certain flow of rhythm for each poem, this chapter analyzes the meter of *Pearl* (*PE*). The aim of this chapter is to describe the rhythmic principle permeating the prosodic system of *PE*. Various metrical phenomena will be marked by the symbols for the stress pattern and the metrical pattern. Metrical complexity will also be proposed from the simplest to the most complicated. Finally, the chapter will point out peculiar points of *PE* compared to the other three alliterative poems that appear in the same manuscript.

4.1 The Basics for *Pearl*

Since scansion requires knowledge about how to interpret symbols for the stress pattern and those for the metrical pattern, this section first introduces several lines that present the basic template. Explanation follows about four peculiar points that need to be taken into account in analyzing ME meter: namely the vocalization of the word final *-e* and other inflectional suffixes, elision of two syllables, metrically subordinated stress, and indefinite stress. Because of the variability of stress, ME verse acknowledges several different ways of reading. The scansion reflects the variable nature of English stress. In other words, the symbol that appears above a particular syllable explains why it is considered stressed or unstressed in that metrical position of the line. As Attridge contends, "reading a line of metrical verse aloud, therefore, is not simply a matter of choosing one interpretation and rejecting others: the fact of optionality itself is a characteristic of the rhythm, and remains effective whatever shades of stressing the line receives" (*Rhythms* 313).

In the first step of scansion, the stress symbols are placed above the line. For example, *PE* 409 is scanned as follows:

```
       -s  +s -s  +s  -s  +s  -s +s °
PE 409 'A blysful lyf þou says I lede;
```

Then metrical symbols are placed beneath the line, followed by the alliteration pattern in square brackets:

```
       -s  +s -s  +s  -s  +s  -s +s °
PE 409 'A blysful lyf þou says I lede;                  [xaxa]
        o   B  o   B   o   B   o  B °
```

The above structure indicates that the line contains four beats that are separated by three single offbeats. The line starts with a single offbeat while there is a word-final *-e* at its end. Many lines of *PE* are comprised of this so-called duple rhythm and can be scanned in the same manner; for instance, *PE* 622 and *PE* 796:

```
       -s  +s -s  +s  -s    +s -s  +s  °
PE 622 Þay laften ryȝt and wroȝten woghe.               [xxaa]
        o   B  o   B   o     B  o    B  °

       -s +s   -s  +s   -s +s -s   +s
PE 796 My Joy, my Blys, my Lemman fre-                  [xxxx]
        o  B    o   B    o  B  o    B
```

The traditional terms, such as *trochaic* or *iambic*, may not suffice for this meter due to the frequent appearance of unstressed syllables both at the beginning and at the end. Furthermore, a double offbeat can appear between beats as seen in *PE* 61:

```
       -s  +s  -s  +s-s  -s    +s  -s   +s °
PE 61 Fro spot my spyryt þer sprang in space;
        o   B   o   B    o2     B   o    B °
```

The meter is thus tentatively defined as a four-beat line with both single and double offbeats.

The four metrical features peculiar to ME verse, explained in the previous chapters, are also observed in *PE*. The vocalization of a word-final –*e* and certain unstressed inflectional suffixes depends on the metrical environment. For instance, consider the metrical role of the word final -*e* in the phrase *faste faȝt* in *PE* 54 in contrast to *hert denned* in *PE* 51:

```
                               +s   °  +s
PE 54 Wyth fyrce skyllez þat faste faȝt.
                                B   º  B
```

```
                            +s   +s
PE 51 A deuely dele in my hert denned,
                             B  ø B
```

The final two beats clash in *PE* 51 whereas the word final -*e* in *PE* 54 is likely to act as an unstressed syllable and form a single offbeat. The final -*e* and inflectional suffixes may supply an optional syllable in this manner in order to avoid the clash of two consecutive beats whereas the clash as seen in *PE* 51 causes strong metrical tension and emphasizes the two words concerned.

When a final -*e* or inflectional suffix appears with one and only one unstressed syllable between two beats, this unstressed syllable is not likely to be realized as a syllable. This is different from the other three poems because the offbeat in *PE* has a strong tendency of being single. The following line exhibits the basic alternation between beats and single offbeats if the final -*e* and the inflectional suffix are not realized as a syllable:

```
       -s   +s(s)  -s  +s  (°)-s   +s(°)-s    +s  °
PE 156 Þat meued my mynde  ay more  and more.
        o    B      o  B     o    B     o    B  °
```

The final -*e* at the end of the line, as seen in *PE* 156, is tentatively treated in scansion as an unstressed syllable, though conclusive evidence is not available about whether the line final -*e* is always expected to form a syllable.

The second feature to note is the elision of two adjacent syllables; for example, the syllable *-dy* in *PE* 62 may be elided to the subsequent syllable *on*, supplying a single offbeat:

```
          +s ^-s  +s
PE 62 My body on balke þer bod. In sweuen
           B   o   B
```

The following line demonstrates another occasion of elision:

```
            +s     ^-s +s
PE 1053 As John þe appostel in termez tyȝte.
             B     o     B
```

The third metrical phenomenon is that a syllable with metrically subordinated stress may be realized as an unstressed syllable, though the word receives stress when pronounced as a separate word:

```
            +s(°)[s]    +s
PE 28 Þer schyne ful schyr agayn þe sunne.
              B     o      B
```

The word *ful* in *PE* 28 is not stressed due to its syntactic relationship with its follower *schyr*. In *PE*, the words *ful* and *al(le)* most frequently appear among those that have metrically subordinated stress. Other words with metrically subordinated stress in *PE* include:

Adjectives:

god, gold(e), gret(e), hyȝ(e), ilk(e), lyk(e), olde, riȝt(e), rych(e), ydel,

Adverb:

wel

Determiners:

aȝt(e), both(e), lest, more, much(e), no(n)(e), such(e), sum(me), thre, twelue, two, vch(e),

Such words are found in the following examples:

```
        [s]+s
PE 291 Þre wordez hatz þou spoken at ene:
         o  B
```

```
                             +s  [s](°) +s
PE 292[1] Vnavysed, forsoþe, wern alle þre.
                              B   o      B
```

The fourth feature to consider is indefinite stress; certain word categories are flexible in stress quality. The syllable that receives stress in the following words may be realized as either a beat or an offbeat depending on the metrical environment:

Prepositions:

abof, after, among(e), anende, byfore, byȝonde, bytwene, inn(e), into, inwyth, ouer, toward(e), þurȝ(e), vnder, vnto, vpon, wiþinne, wiþoute(n)

Determiners:

anoþer, any, ayþer, fele, felle, mony(e), on(e), only, oþer, quat(so), þes(e), þos(e), vch(e)

Adverbs:

adoun, also, away(e), euen, euer, euermore, here, her(e)inne, hider, hyder, neuer, togeder(e), þen(e), þenn(e), þer(e), þer(e)as, þerat(t)e, þerfor(e), þerin(ne), þerof, þeron, þeroute, þerto, þydervtwyþ

Conjunctions:

alþaȝ, bot, forþi, nauþer, nawþer, quen, syþen, þaȝ, w(h)eþer, when, wher(e)

The following lines serve as examples of indefinite stress:

```
         s(s) +s-s(°)-s +s (°)s(s)+s -s  +s  °
PE 130 Wheþer solace ho sende oþer ellez sore,
           o   B    o2   B      o  B  o   B °
```

```
      -s  +s (s) -s s(°)-s  s -s   +s  °
PE 172 As lyttel byfore þerto watz wonte.
       o   B    o   B    o  B  o    B  °
```

The words *wheþer* and *oþer* in *PE* 130 do not form a beat while the words *byfore* and *þerto* in *PE* 172 do so. It is the metrical position that decides whether or not the syllable with indefinite stress may form a beat. In *PE* 513 below, *aboute* forms a beat whereas *under* is not likely to form one due to its position in the line. In *PE* 608, *other* does not form a beat while *neuer* does:

```
       -s s (°)s (s) -s +s (°)-s +s -s  +s
PE 513 Aboute vnder þe lorde to marked totz,
        o B         o2     B     o B  o   B

        s(s) +s-s -s   +s   -s   s-s   +s  °
PE 608 Oþer gotez of golf þat neuer charde.
         o   B    o2  B     o    B o    B  °
```

Thus, the scansion of the first stanza of *PE* appears as follows:

```
        +s   °  +s-s   (°)  -s  +s -s  +s °
PE 1    Perle plesaunte, to prynces paye            [aaaa]
         B   °   B        o2     B  o   B °

        -s   +s -s   +s -s  +s (°)-s  +s °
PE 2    To clanly clos in golde so clere:           [aaxa]
         o   B  o    B   o B   o      B °

        s (°)-s +s^-s   -s +s -s-s +s  °
PE 3    Oute  of oryent, I hardyly saye,            [aaax]
        B     o B      o2   B    o2 B  °

        -s   +s(s)-s  s(s) -s    +s-s   +s °
PE 4    Ne proued I neuer her precios pere.         [axaa]
         o   B    o B      o     B  o   B °

        -s +s   (°)  -s +s(s)-s [s](°)-s+s °
PE 5    So rounde, so reken in vche  araye,         [aaxa]
         o B      o    B    o B   o   B °
```

```
        -s  +s   -s  +s(°)-s  +s-s  -s °
PE 6    So smal, so smoþe her sydez were;          [aaax]
         o   B    o   B    o   B o  <B>°

         -s (s)^+s-s -s +s -s  +s -s  +s °
PE 7    Queresoeuer I jugged gemmez gaye           [xaaa]
          o     B    o2 B  o   B  o   B °

        -s +s (°)-s  +s (s) ^-s  +s  -s °
PE 8    I sette hyr sengeley in synglure.          [aaax]
        o  B     o   B        o   B ø <B>°

        -s +s  -s +s (°)-s -s -s -s +s °
PE 9    Allas! I leste hyr in on erbere;           [aaxx]
        o  B   o  B     o <B>   o2  B °

         s    +s (°)-s  +s  (°)-s   -s -s +s
PE 10   Þurȝ gresse to grounde hit fro me yot.     [aaxx]
         o     B    o   B      o   <B> o  B

        -s +s-s(°) -s +s (s)-s  +s  +s  -s °
PE 11[2] I dewyne, fordolked of luf-daungere       [aaxx]
        o  B    o2    B     o   B   o: <B>°

        -s  -s    +s-s +s (°)-s  s -s   +s
PE 12   Of þat pryuy perle withouten spot.         [aaxx]
         o2        B o B     o  B  o    B
```

The metrical structure presents certain regularity in the four-beat rhythm. The next section observes the alliteration and end rhyme.

4.2 Alliteration and Rhyme in *Pearl*

Alliteration in *PE* is not as regular as it is commonly defined. Sometimes the alliteration of *PE* is much deviated from that of the other three poems that appear in the same manuscript, namely *Cleanness* (C), *Patience* (*PT*), and *Sir*

Gawain and the Green Knight (*G*). In these three poems, the basic [aaax] pattern and its variations linger throughout the entire lines. In *PE*, on the contrary, lines with two alliterating beats are as common as lines with three alliterating beats. Moreover, lines without alliteration appear quite frequently. For example, the following lines reflect no alliteration in beats:

```
      -s   +s (°)-s   +s (°)-s    +s (s)-s   s
PE 41 On huyle þer perle hit trendeled doun                [xxxx]
       o   B      o   B     o     B     o    B

      -s   +s   -s (°) +s    [s](°) +s(°)-s    +s °
PE 90 Of flaumbande hwez, boþe smale  and grete;           [xxxx]
         o B       o   B            B     o    B °
```

On the other hand, alliteration may be excessive; all four beats may alliterate as seen in *PE* 1, and the offbeat may echo alliteration as in *PE* 6. Lines that have two different sets of alliteration (duple alliteration) are also observed:

```
       -s   +s -s   +s   -s  +s -s    +s
PE 106 As fyldor fyn her bonkes brent.                     [aabb]
        o    B  o    B   o    B  o    B

       -s +s    ^-s +s(s) -s    +s(°) -s    +s-s
PE 107 I wan to a water by schore þat scherez;             [aabb]
        o  B     o  B      o    B      o     B o
```

The medial caesura is generally assumed between the second and the third beat in alliterative verse. However, the short line structure of *PE* does not present a noticeable pause in the middle, and the caesura indicated by a syntactic boundary such as a comma may fall in other places than the middle. These phenomena imply that the metrical unit of *PE* is a single line and that the two half-lines are tightly linked. In other words, the link between two half-lines in *PE* is rather smooth.

The following alliteration patterns, classified by the number of alliterating beats, appear in *PE*. The number in parentheses is the percentage of that pattern:

Table 4.1. Alliteration Patterns in *PE*

Four beats alliterating	9.2%	
aaaa		(9.2%)
Three beats alliterating	28.2%	
aaxa		(11.6%)
xaaa		(6.6%)
axaa		(6.0%)
aaax		(4.0%)
Two beats alliterating	36.2%	
aaxx		(9.6%)
xxaa		(8.4%)
xaxa		(5.2%)
axax		(5.0%)
xaax		(4.4%)
axxa		(3.6%)
Duple alliteration	7.4%	
aabb		(3.6%)
abba		(2.0%)
abab		(1.8%)
No alliteration	19.0%	
xxxx		(19.0%)
Total	100.0%	

Alliteration of *PE* exhibits the following three distinctive points. First, unlike the other ME alliterative poems, the number of the lines that have three alliterating beats is not the largest. Lines with two alliterating beats are most frequent. Second, among lines with three alliterating beats, which nevertheless are not very numerous, the most usual pattern is the one whose first, second, and fourth beats alliterate but not the first, second, and third.[3] *PE* does not conform to the basic rule of alliterative verse, namely the general rule to alliterate in the first three stressed syllables. Third, a significant number of lines carry no alliteration, which is a striking feature of *PE* in contrast to other alliterative poems.

Another peculiar point that distinguishes *PE* from other alliterative poems is that end-rhyme is rigidly maintained throughout the 101 twelve-line stanzas. The base pattern is *ababababbcbc*, with the identical *c* rhyme being repeated in five or six consecutive stanzas that form a cluster. Furthermore, the refrain word that forms the *c* rhyme in the twelfth line of all the five or six stanzas of a cluster also appears in the initial lines of the second through the last stanzas within the same cluster. This refrain word comes up once again in the first line of the subsequent cluster. The rhyme structure is of such metrical interest that it will be the topic of Chapter Five. Here, one metrical feature is associated with rhyme; namely the final beat often alliterates in *PE* (58.0% as calculated from Table 4.1) unlike the line-final beat of the other poems. Adding the rhyme constraint on the fourth beat and fulfilling the alliteration requirement at the same time make the metrical framework quite inflexible not only within the line but also within a larger unit of the stanza and the cluster. As a result, the poet can be less strict about the alliteration in other places. Instead, he focuses on alliteration and rhyme on the final beat, freeing one or two of the first three beats from the alliteration constraint.

4.3 The Offbeat Structure of *Pearl*

The duple rhythm is outstandingly dominant in *PE* while the other three poems in the same manuscript contain the mixture of duple and triple rhythms. In *PE*, a single offbeat may consist of one to three unstressed syllables and a double offbeat of two to three syllables.[4] The following lines represent the structure of a single and double offbeat:

(i) A single offbeat that consists of an unstressed syllable:

```
           +s -s  +s -s  +s
PE 2   To clanly clos in golde so clere:
            B  o   B  o   B
```

(ii) A single offbeat that consists of two unstressed syllables:

```
           +s(s)-s  s(s) -s   +s
PE 4   Ne proued I neuer her precios pere.
            B    o  B     o    B
```

```
                   +s  ^-s   +s ^-s   +s
PE 383 Bot Crystes mersy and Mary and Jon,
                    B    o    B     o  B
```

(iii) A single offbeat that consists of three unstressed syllables:

```
                  +s (s)  s(°)+s
PE 127 Þe fyrre I folȝed þose floty valez,
                   B     o     B
```

```
            +s(s)^-s +s
PE 363 If rapely I raue, spornande in spelle:
             B     o  B
```

(iv) A double offbeat that consists of two unstressed syllables:

```
                                  +s -s-s +s
PE 3    Oute of oryent, I hardyly saye,
                                   B    o2 B
```

```
                              +s -s  [s]   +s
PE 42   Schadowed þis wortez ful schyre and schene:
                               B       o2    B
```

(v) A double offbeat that consists of three unstressed syllables:

```
                     +s-s  (°) -s  +s
PE 1    Perle plesaunte, to prynces paye
                      B       o2     B
```

```
                              +s -s  ^-s +s
PE 47   Þer wonys þat worþyly, I wot and wene,
                               B      o2   B
```

4.4 The Beat Structure of *Pearl*

In *C*, *PT*, and *G*, both four-beat and five-beat lines are observed. For this phenomenon, Sapora presents a seriatim list of the metrical forms of the seven ME alliterative poems. In order to explain the variation in the number of beats per line, I have proposed in Chapters Two and Three a metrical structure that is flexible enough to generate both four-beat lines and five-beat lines. As for *PE*, however, the number of beats per line has little variation, and the four-beat line dominates throughout the poem.

Another difference between *PE* and the other three is in variations of the offbeat. The offbeat may be either single or double in the other three poems; the triple offbeat is a legitimate option. In *PE*, however, the single offbeat is dominant, with the double offbeat occupying less than ten percent of all of the offbeat positions. The triple offbeat is rare because it is found in only two lines.[5]

Table 4.2 demonstrates how the double offbeat appears in the 4,844 offbeat slots in *PE*:[6]

Table 4.2. Occurrences of Double Offbeats in *PE*

Before B_1	Between B_1 and B_2	Between B_2 and B_3	Between B_3 and B_4
107	153	139	76

Since the number of double offbeats is limited and there is little difference among the first three positions (i.e., before B_1, between B_1 and B_2, and between B_2 and B_3), it is hard to make a definite generalization about the double offbeat. Yet one factor that immediately becomes evident from Table 4.2 is that the line end tends to keep a single offbeat before the final beat. In the other three poems, the combination of the final beat and an implied offbeat that precedes it often suggests the line end (Tables 2.2 and 2.3 of Chapter Two). In *PE*, however, the link between the line-final beat and a single offbeat prior to it is strong. This leads to the idea that the final beat in ME alliterative verse in general is not likely to be preceded by multiple unstressed syllables.

Another variant of the offbeat, the implied offbeat, is a frequent constituent in the other three poems. In *PE*, however, its appearance is rare, only 57 times in 1,211 lines as shown in Table 2.2. The triple offbeat is rather infrequent in *PE*. The line in *PE* does not mark a significant contrast between the initial part and the concluding part by means of variations in offbeats. The implied offbeat before the line-final beat, which slows the tempo toward the line end, is not so utilized as in the other three. Instead of the slower tempo by means of the implied offbeat, the end rhyme signals the line boundary in *PE*. The end rhyme is so rigid and conspicuous in indicating the line closure that other additional metrical devices may be redundant.

As to how the line ends, I have observed in Chapters Two and Three that the other three poems exhibit a strong tendency to include an unstressed syllable in the line-final position. As shown in Table 2.4 of Chapter Two, more than sixty percent of the lines of *PE* end with a final *-e* whereas about one-third of them end with a beat. In more detail, 143 lines of *PE* start with a beat, which is about 11.8% of the entire lines. One may argue that these prove that the final *-e* is never vocalized in *PE* at least at the line closure.[7] Lines of the other alliterative poems, however, place an unstressed syllable at the end, which suggests that a final unstressed syllable may be a metrical requirement of ME alliterative verse. Another peculiar point to *PE* is the frequency of line closures with a beat; among the four poems, the number of lines that end with a beat is largest in *PE*. The meter of *PE* may be tentatively defined as follows:

> **Postulated Beat Structure for the *PE* line:**
>
> Verse → B_1 B_2 B_3 B_4

The meter alternates between a single offbeat and a beat. It contains four beat positions and four offbeat positions, possibly with another offbeat at the end. This meter is rigid, allowing a limited number of variations. The implied offbeat and double offbeat are possible but present a significant sense of metrical deviation.

Because of its rigid meter, there are several points about *PE* that are not observed in the other three poems. First, promotion is occasionally found. In a metrical circumstance where a beat is expected, an unstressed syllable is promoted to a stressed one to form a beat. The following lines exemplify how promotion occurs in *PE*:

```
        -s  -s   -s    +s -s -s  -s +s °
PE 45   ȝif hit watz semly on to sene,
         o  <B>   o     B  o <B>  o   B  °

        -s    +s    -s +s(°)-s -s   [s] +s
PE 748  Þat wroȝt þy wede he watz ful wys;
         o    B     o  B    o <B>   o   B
```

In addition, demotion, which is rarely found in the other three poems, occurs in order to avoid the irregular distribution of beats and offbeats. *PE* 530 provides such an example:

```
       -s +s  (°)-s s(°)-s +s  (°)+s +s
PE 530 On oure byfore þe sonne go doun,
       o  B      o B    o  B     o: B
```

Demotion is a metrical phenomenon in which a stressed syllable is demoted to an unstressed one because it falls in the position where an unstressed syllable is strongly expected. It is comparatively easy in the other three poems to locate stressed syllables; alliteration is of significant help in this task. In *PE*, however, the rigid duple rhythm is so dominant that promotion and demotion intervene in order to amend the array of syllables with a similar stress quality. This means that stress subordinates to meter, and this tendency is quite strong in *PE*.

The rigid duple meter results in another metrical adjustment; namely, stress shifts to an unstressed syllable in the circumstance where a beat is desired. The same word *thowsande* is realized differently in *PE* 869 and *PE* 870:[8]

```
          -s    -s    -s   +s  (s)(s)-s   +s   -s(°)+s -s   °
PE 869 And wyth Hym maydennez an hundreþe þowsande,
          o   <B>    o    B          o    B       o2:  <B>  °
```

```
          -s    +s  (°)-s    +s  -s +s  -s  (°)+s
PE 870 And fowre  and forty þowsande mo.
          o     B       o    B  o  B    o    B
```

Another significant point about *PE* is that a single word can contain two beats:

```
          -s +s  (s)  -s   +s  -s   [s]  +s  -s  -s
PE 307 ȝe setten Hys wordez ful westernays
          o  B        o    B      o2   B  o <B>
```

```
          -s   +s  (°)-s +s  (°) -s     -s+s-s-s
PE 840 In helle, in erþe, and Jerusalem.
          o    B      o  B      o2       B o <B>
```

The final syllable of the above lines must form a beat for the sake of the end rhyme. The word *westernays* in *PE* 307 rhymes with the following three words: *prayse* in *PE* 301, *vncortoyse* in *PE* 303, and *rayse* in *PE* 305. The word *Jerusalem* in *PE* 840 rhymes with the word *seme* in *PE* 838.[9]

Finally, metricality is determined neither by the number of syllables per line nor by the length of the line. The following lines are all metrical despite the different number of syllables and the different length of the line:

```
         +s -s  +s   -s +s    +s  °
PE 999   Jasper hyȝt þe fyrst gemme                 [axxa]
          B  o   B    o  B  ø  B  °
```

```
        -s   -s   -s+s -s-s-s+s
PE 1184  In þys veray avysyoun!                     [xxxx]
         o   <B>   o B  o<B>o B
```

```
         -s +s(s) -s +s (s) -s  +s  s(s)  +s
PE 380   We meten so selden by stok oþer ston.      [xaaa]
          o  B      o  B       o   B    o    B
```

```
        -s    +s  (s)-s  -s +s  (°)-s -s +s     +s-s
PE 980   And blusched on þe burghe, as I forth dreued,   [aaxx]
          o    B        o2    B      o2     B   ø  B o
```

4.5 List of Metrical Complexity of *Pearl*

The metrical complexity among the lines of *PE* is exemplified below in twenty-two degrees. The list begins with the metrically simplest line, and presents increased metrical tension toward the end. The list of complexity is critical because it is one of the crucial tasks of metrical studies "to determine the limits of variability fixed by the line's metrical structure, and to indicate the part played by that strictness, and the freedom within it, in the working of the poem" (Attridge, *Rhythms* 314). The list not only reveals the peculiar points of *PE* but also suggests similarities and differences if the list is compared to the metrical complexity lists of the other alliterative poems already presented in Chapters Two and Three.

1. Base rules only

```
         -s  +s   -s +s   -s +s   -s +s °
PE 1151  Þat syȝt me gart to þenk to wade
          o   B    o  B    o  B    o  B °
```

2. Base rules plus silent final *-e*'s

```
      -s   +s(°)-s  +s(°)-s +s (°) -s    +s
PE 503 Of tyme  of ʒere þe terme watz tyʒt,
       o   B      o B   o  B     o    B
```

3. Base rules plus silent unstressed syllables

```
      -s   +s -s  +s (s) -s   +s(s) -s  +s  °
PE 856 Of spotlez perlez þat beren þe creste.
       o    B  o   B      o   B     o   B  °
```

4. Promotion

```
      -s  -s  -s   +s -s-s  -s +s °
PE 45 ʒif hit watz semly on to sene,
       o  <B>  o    B o<B>  o  B °
```

5. Elision

```
       -s  +s     ^-s +s (s)-s  +s -s  +s  °
PE 1053 As John þe appostel in termez tyʒte.
        o   B    o    B     o   B  o   B  °
```

6. Metrically subordinated stress realized as an offbeat

```
       -s   +s (°)-s  +s    [s]   +s -s +s
PE 179 Þat stonge myn hert ful stray astount,
        o    B     o   B    o     B  o  B
```

7. Indefinite stress realized as an offbeat

```
       -s  +s  -s    +s(°)-s  +s  s(s)+s  °
PE 211 Her semblaunt sade for doc oþer erle,
        o   B   o     B    o   B    o  B  °
```

8. Indefinite stress realized as a beat

```
       -s   +s-s   +s  -s  s -s  +s   °
PE 189 Þat gracios gay withouten galle,
        o    B   o  B   o  B  o   B   °
```

9. A double offbeat

```
       -s  +s  -s  +s-s  -s    +s  -s   +s °
PE 61 Fro spot my spyryt þer sprang in space;
        o   B   o   B     o2    B   o    B °
```

10. Metrically subordinated stress

10–1. Metrically subordinated stress realized as a beat

```
        -s [s](°)-s +s  ° +s(s)-s  +s
PE 119 Þat alle þe loȝe lemed of lyȝt,
        o  B     o  B °  B    o   B
```

10–2. Metrically subordinated stress realized as a beat and as an offbeat within the same line

```
       [s]-s (°)+s(s) -s +s(°)[s] +s
PE 807 Al oure balez to bere ful bayn
       B     o  B     o  B    o   B
```

11. Indefinite stress

11–1. Indefinite stress realized as a beat and as an offbeat within the same line

```
       s(s) +s-s -s  +s   -s   s-s   +s  °
PE 608 Oþer gotez of golf þat neuer charde.
         o   B   o2  B    o    B o    B  °
```

11–2. Indefinite stress realized as one beat and two offbeats within the same line

```
         -s  s -s  +s (°)s(s) +s (°)s(s)  +s
PE 1060 Withouten fylþe oþer galle oþer glet.
          o   B  o B      o   B     o     B
```

12. Non-medial caesura

```
      -s +s ^-s  +s (°)-s  +s  -s   +s-s
PE 62 My body on balke þer bod. In sweuen
       o  B  o  B     o   B     o  B o
```

13. Deviated alliteration

13–1. Alliteration not quite achieved

```
             +s(°)   s(s) +s-s ^-s   -s -s +s   °
PE 565 '"'More, weþer louyly is me my gyfte-                [axax]
              B        o    B      o2 <B> o   B   °
```

13–2. Duple alliteration

```
         -s   +s(s)^-s +s  °    +s -s(°)-s    +s   °
PE 363 If raþely I raue, spornande in spelle:               [aabb]
         o    B      o   B º     B        o2    B   °
```

14. Excessive alliteration

```
          -s   +s(°) -s   +s    -s +s  °   +s
PE 190 So smoþe, so smal, so seme slyȝt,                    [aaaa]
          o    B      o    B     o   B °    B
```

15. More than one double offbeat

15–1. Two double offbeats

```
          +s (°)-s   -s    +s   -s+s-s  -s +s-s
PE 123 Bylde  in me blys, abated my balez,
          B         o2     B    o B    o2  B o
```

15–2. Three double offbeats

```
        -s -s +s  (°)-s   -s   +s    °    s(°)-s   -s   +s °
PE 65 I ne wyste  in þis worlde quere þat hit wace,
           o2   B            o2   B   º    B       o2     B  °
```

16. Indefinite stress realized as a beat twice in a line

```
          -s +s(s)-s s    -s    s -s    +s  °
PE 1145 I loked among His meyny schene
           o   B    o B    o    B  o     B  °
```

17. Shift of stress due to rhyme

```
          +s(°)-s   -s   +s-s   -s    +s(°)  +s-s  °
PE 237 Caȝte of her coroun of grete tresore
           B       o2       B       o2    B      o:<B>°
```

18. Implied offbeat

```
         -s   -s +s   +s (°)[s] +s  -s +s
PE 1076 And þe self sunne ful fer to dym.
           o2    B ø B     o   B   o  B
```

19. Demotion

19–1. Demotion

```
        -s  +s -s  +s -s   s  +s(s) +s   +s °
PE 331 What seruez tresor bot garez men grete,
         o   B  o    B     o2  B      o:   B °
```

19–2. Demotion and promotion

```
       -s -s -s +s-s -s   +s   +s  +s °
PE 614 Þat I my peny haf wrang tan here;
        o <B> o  B   o2    B    o:  B °
```

20. Not enough candidates for beats

```
       +s  -s   -s -s  s(s)-s -s  +s °
PE 239 Wel watz me þat euer I watz bore
        B   o  <B> o  B     o2     B °
```

21. Few offbeats

```
       +s -s  +s   -s +s    +s  °
PE 999 Jasper hyȝt þe fyrst gemme
        B  o   B    o  B  ø  B  °
```

22. Lines on the edge of metricality[10]

```
        s   s   +s (°) -s  -s +s (°) -s  -s  -s    +s °
PE 271 Now þurȝ kynde  of þe kyste þat hyt con close      [aaxa]
           o2    B     o2     B     o   <B>  o    B °


       -s -s   -s +s  °  +s-s-s
PE 276 Þou art no kynde jueler.'                          [xxxx]
        o <B>   o  B  º  Bo<B>
```

```
          -s +s  ^-s -s  -s  +s-s(s)-s   °
PE 366 I do me ay in Hys myserecorde.                [xxxx]
          o  B    o <B>  o   B o   <B> °

             s(s) +s (s) s(s) +s   -s -s  -s+s   °
PE 604 Wheþer lyttel oþer much be hys rewarde.        [xxxx]
             o     B     o     B    o <B>  o B   °

          -s   -s   -s  +s (s)(s)-s  +s  -s(°)+s -s   °
PE 869 And wyth Hym maydennez an hundreþe þowsande,   [xxxx]
          o   <B>  o    B      o      B       o2:<B>  °
```

4.6 The Meter of *Pearl*

The following meter is postulated for *PE*, which significantly differs from that of the other three poems. Angled brackets are used for the line-final offbeat of the other three poems, indicating preferred inclusion of an offbeat. However, since *PE* shows neutral preference (Attridge, *Rhythms* 357) for inclusion of such an offbeat, parentheses are used for the line-final unstressed syllable:

> **Meter of *PE*:**
>
> $\text{Verse} \rightarrow \text{o}\ \ B_1\ \ \text{o}\ \ B_2\ \ \text{o}\ \ B_3\ \ \text{o}\ \ B_4\ \ (\text{o})$
>
> (With less regular alliteration but always with rhyme in B_4. The final parentheses indicate an optional offbeat which shows neutral preference.)

The postulated meter for *C* and *G* in Chapter Two is applicable to *PT* as well. The meter of these three poems can be defined as follows:

> **Meter of *C*, *PT*, and the long alliterative lines of *G*:**
>
> $\text{Verse} \rightarrow (\text{o}_1^2\ \ B_0\ )\ \ \text{o}_1^2\ \ B_1\ \ \text{o}_1^2\ \ B_2\ \ \text{o}_1^2\ \ B_3\ \ \text{o}_1^2\ \ B_4\ \ \langle \text{o} \rangle$
>
> (With possibility of triple offbeat for an offbeat position and with alliteration pattern [(a)aaax] or [(x)aaax]. Parentheses indicate optional constituents in the line whereas <o> indicates an optional offbeat which shows preference for inclusion.)

The meter of *C*, *PT*, and *G* defined above is capable of generating either four-beat or five-beat lines in which beats are separated by either single or double offbeats. Conflict among various arguments about scanning ME alliterative meter can be avoided accordingly by discriminating the optional from the obligatory and the variable from the invariable. The postulated meter for *PE* reveals the following points in contrast to the other three poems:

1. The single line that consists of four beats is the metrical unit, and the medial caesura is obscure.
2. Rigid alternation between beats and single offbeats is dominant throughout the poem, which frequently results in promotion and demotion.
3. The double offbeat is a possible but not a common deviation of the offbeat. The triple offbeat is rare, though it is commonly observed in the other three poems.
4. Regular alliteration is not the most crucial determiner of the meter.
5. Rhyme, in addition to alliteration, plays a vital role in determining beats and offbeats and in signaling the line end.
6. Indefinite stress, metrically subordinated stress, and stress shift function as metrical aids to maintain the regular alternation of rhythm.
7. The metricality depends on neither the number of syllables per line nor the length of the line.
8. The end of the line has different metrical restrictions from the other three: rhyme, the refrain word within the stanza and the cluster, and strong preference of the combination of a single offbeat and a beat before the line closure.

This chapter has confirmed as to *PE* that it is not only beats but also offbeats that characterize the meter of ME alliterative verse. It has also observed that the relativity of English stress is most significantly utilized in *PE* among the four poems that appear in the same manuscript. These variants in stress placement, which do not seem to operate by rules except for the metrical necessity in that particular position of the line, suggest that stress is subordinate to meter. The meter of fourteenth-century alliterative verse can be more demanding than the stress rules so that stress quality may be altered according to the position within the verse line.

Notes

1 The word *þre* functions as a beat in this line because the word has no partner within the line to share a syntactic bond. The word *alle*, on the other hand, is syntactically subordinate to its subsequent word *þre*.

2 The word *daungere* in this line is meant to rhyme with *clere* in *PE* 2, *þere* in *PE* 4, *were* in *PE* 6, *synglure* in *PE* 8, and *erbere* in *PE* 9. Gollancz (12) emends *synglure* in *PE* 8 as *syng[u]l[e]-re* so that these six lines are in complete rhyme. Because of the rigid end rhyme of *PE*, stress is likely to shift to the second syllable of *daungere*. Thus, demotion and promotion take place in this word as the scansion indicates. If stress does not shift onto the second syllable of *daungere*, the alliteration will be achieved on three beats. This line can be an example to prove that alliteration is subordinate to rhyme in *PE*.

3 It is noteworthy that the [aaax] pattern is used in only four percent of the entire lines of *PE*.

4 Unstressed syllables here signify not those that are realized as unstressed syllables in the actual recitation but those that may theoretically form a syllable. It is possible, for instance, to realize in the reading two unstressed syllables between the words *mersy* and *Mary* in *PE* 383. These two unstressed syllables in the stress pattern are realized as a single offbeat in the actual reading because of the metrical structure that demands a single offbeat.

5 These lines are as follows:

```
           -s    -s -s +s -s  +s (°)-s -s  -s +s
PE 895 And to þe gentyl Lombe hit arn anjoynt,
               o3      B  o   B      o <B>  o  B

            ^-s+s (s)-s -s+s-s-s  (°)-s   +s(°)-s  +s °
PE 944 Þe apostel in Apocalyppce  in theme con take.
            o  B    o2    B           o3     B    o    B °
```

6 Since *PE* 472 is missing, the number of the lines that supply data is 1,211. Each line theoretically contains four offbeat positions. The line-final offbeat is not included since it is considered optional.

7 Lines end with a beat from *PE* 985 through *PE* 996, as well as from *PE* 1009 through *PE* 1020 (except for *PE* 1016), which contributes a special poetic effect.

8 The stress should fall on the second syllable of *þowsande* in *PE* 869 since the word is assumed to rhyme with *farande* in *PE* 865, *stande* in *PE* 867, and *fande* in *PE* 871. The shift of stress in this word occurs by a combination of demotion and promotion. The colon after a double offbeat in the scansion means that one of the constituents of the double offbeat has been demoted.

9 The word *Jerusalem* is repeated in the stanza-final lines of the entire fourteenth cluster. In *PE* 792, *PE* 804, *PE* 816, *PE* 828, and *PE* 840, the word contains two beats.

10 These five lines exhibit the most complicated metrical structure in *PE*. There are neither enough candidates for beats nor enough alliterating syllables in these lines, which creates metrical ambiguity. As seen in the scansion, promotion has to take place in order to realize the beats in these lines. This frequent operation of promotion proves how different *PE* is from the other three poems since promotion is the least likely metrical device in the others.

Chapter 5

Rhyme Constraints in *Pearl*: Reiteration within the Verse Line, the Stanza, the Cluster, and the Whole Poem

One of the metrical features that distinguish *Pearl* (*PE*) from the other alliterative poems in the Cotton Nero A. x. manuscript is end-rhyme, which is rigidly maintained throughout the 101 twelve-line stanzas in addition to alliteration. As observed in Chapter Four, the verse line in *PE* mainly consists of four stressed syllables with relatively weaker alliteration compared to the other alliterative poems. On the other hand, the end-rhyme with a pattern of *ababababbcbc* never fails to appear in every stanza. The identical *c* rhyme is repeated in five consecutive stanzas (six for the fifteenth group) called *cluster* (Hamilton 342) or *section* (Gardner 85). Furthermore, the *refrain word*[1] that forms the *c* rhyme in the twelfth line of the first stanza of a cluster reappears in the initial lines of the second through the last stanzas within the same cluster. This refrain word appears once again in the first line of the subsequent cluster. Rhyme governs the stanza (twelve lines) and the cluster (five or six stanzas), thus uniting the entire twenty clusters (101 stanzas or 1,212 lines[2]) into a whole. This complex rhyme structure not only inspired literary interest (Kean; McGalliard) but also drew mathematical attention (Grant, Peterson, and Cross). This chapter examines the rhyme of *PE* and considers various constraints it creates in relation to alliteration. Analyses of rhyme from stanza to cluster will prove that there are certain tendencies among rhyming words and that the refrain word establishes a unique enclosure over two consecutive clusters. It will also be suggested that the stanza-final lines often do not conform to ME alliterative meter due to the repetition of the same refrain word.

The following stanza illustrates the base pattern. Since the line numbers within the stanza are helpful in figuring out to which rhyme group a line belongs, the stanza number and the line number within the stanza are connected by a hyphen; the actual line number is indicated within parentheses. For instance, the first line of the second stanza (line 13 in the entire poem) will be identified as 2–1 (*PE* 13). Rhyming parts are in boldface:[3]

2–1	(*PE* 13)	Syþen in þat stote hit fro me spr**ange**,	*a*
2–2	(*PE* 14)	Ofte haf I wayted, wyschande þat **wele**	*b*
2–3	(*PE* 15)	Þat wont watz whyle deuoyde my wr**ange**	*a*
2–4	(*PE* 16)	And heuen my happe and al my h**ele**–	*b*
2–5	(*PE* 17)	Þat dotz bot þrych my hert þr**ange**,	*a*
2–6	(*PE* 18)	My breste in bale bot bolne and b**ele**.	*b*
2–7	(*PE* 19)	Ȝet þoȝt me neuer so swete a s**ange**	*a*
2–8	(*PE* 20)	As stylle stounde let to me st**ele**.	*b*
2–9	(*PE* 21)	Forsoþe þer fleten to me f**ele**.	*b*
2–10	(*PE* 22)	To þenke hir color so clad in cl**ot**!	*c*
2–11	(*PE* 23)	O moul, þou marrez a myry ju**ele**,	*b*
2–12	(*PE* 24)	My priuy perle withouten sp**otte**.	*c*

These lines can be rearranged according to rhyme as follows:

-ange	group *a*	lines 1, 3, 5, and 7 of the stanza
-ele	group *b*	lines 2, 4, 6, 8, 9, and 11 of the stanza
-ot(te)	group *c*	lines 10 and 12 of the stanza

In the first eight lines of the stanza, two rhyme sounds alternate. The repetition of the *b* rhyme in the ninth line of the stanza predicts a major change in the line that follows. The *b* rhyme reappears in the eleventh line of the stanza, and the new rhyme sound introduced in the tenth line appears again in the twelfth line to mark the end of the stanza with the refrain word. The refrain word that carries the *c* rhyme appears beyond the stanza. It is repeated in five or six stanzas within the cluster. Thus, the poem consists of 1,212 lines divided into 101 stanzas or twenty clusters. A refrain word, namely the rhyming word of the twelfth line of a stanza, is identical throughout all the stanzas within a cluster. Thus, the rhyme scheme of *PE* can be defined as *ababababbcbc*. Though alliteration is absent from a significant number of lines (Chapter Four), end rhyme never fails to appear. Another example to demonstrate this basic pattern is the eleventh stanza:

11–1	(*PE* 121)	Þe dubbement dere of doun and d**alez**,	*a*
11–2	(*PE* 122)	Of wod and water and wlonk pl**aynez**,	*b*
11–3	(*PE* 123)	Bylde in me blys, abated my b**alez**,	*a*
11–4	(*PE* 124)	Fordidden my stresse, dystryed my p**aynez**.	*b*
11–5	(*PE* 125)	Doun after a strem þat dryȝly h**alez**	*a*
11–6	(*PE* 126)	I bowed in blys, bredful my br**aynez**;	*b*
11–7	(*PE* 127)	Þe fyrre I folȝed þose floty v**alez**,	*a*
11–8	(*PE* 128)	Þe more strenghþe of joye myn herte str**aynez**.	*b*
11–9	(*PE* 129)	As Fortune fares þeras ho fr**aynez**,	*b*
11–10	(*PE* 130)	Wheþer solace ho sende oþer ellez s**ore**,	*c*
11–11	(*PE* 131)	Þe wyȝ to wham his wylle ho w**aynez**	*b*
11–12	(*PE* 132)	Hyttez to haue ay more and m**ore**.	*c*

-***alez***	group *a*	lines 1, 3, 5, and 7 of the stanza
-***aynez***	group *b*	lines 2, 4, 6, 8, 9, and 11 of the stanza
-***ore***	group *c*	lines 10 and 12 of the stanza

In Chapter Four, the metrical structure of the *PE* line has been defined by means of formal notations. The basic principle can be summarized as follows:

1. Each line of *PE* allots four beats (metrically stressed syllables) divided by a single offbeat (metrically unstressed syllable).
2. Two unstressed syllables may replace a single offbeat.
3. An unstressed syllable may start the line while a word final -*e* or an unstressed syllable tends to appear after the final rhyming beat.
4. A certain number of the beats in a line alliterate, but alliteration is not as rigid as that of the other alliterative poems.

Alliteration in the fourteenth-century alliterative verse is typically explained as occurring in three stressed syllables out of four, which can be described as [aaax] (Osberg, *Gawain* xiii). *PE*, however, does not always adhere to this general rule, and its peculiarities observed in Chapter Four may be summarized as follows. First, lines that have three alliterating beats do not form the majority. The number of the lines with two alliterating beats supersedes that of the lines with three alliterating beats.[4] Second, among the lines with three alliterating beats, which are not numerous in the first place, the most common pattern is the one whose first, second, and fourth beats alliterate ([aaxa]), but not the typical [aaax]. Finally, a significant number of lines lack alliteration. This is peculiar to *PE* because other alliterative poems in the same manuscript maintain alliteration in most of the lines or even distribute it more than expected, as seen in *Sir Gawain and the Green Knight* (*G*). The weaker alliteration of *PE* may have a correlation with its rigid rhyme. Examining end-rhyme will elucidate multiple constraints created in this *alliterative* poem. This chapter first examines the spelling variations in rhyme by listing all the word-endings of *a*, *b*, and *c* rhymes, and then summarizes deviations. It is evident through these observations that *PE* achieves rigid rhyme proper in which the combination of a vowel and a successive consonant or consonant cluster is identical. It is also worth noting that the poet is careful about not repeating the same rhyming word within a stanza.[5]

The end rhyme in *PE* provides useful information about how a group of spellings is perceived to hold the same or a similar sound quality by a late fourteenth-century poet. The *PE* poet utilizes a variety of ME vowels for the rhyming syllables but maintains the same word endings in this alliterative verse. This chapter summarizes how various spellings are incorporated within the same rhyme, first on vowels and second on consonant combinations, and considers various deviations. The chapter then examines the rhyme within the stanza and within the cluster in order to suggest what verbal art the poet intends to create with his reiteration technique.

5.1 Vowels in Rhyme

The following groups of vowels are intended to rhyme with one another:

(i) -*u* and -*o*

3–2 (*PE* 26), 3–4 (*PE* 28), 3–6 (*PE* 30), 3–8 (*PE* 32), 3–9 (*PE* 33), 3–11 (*PE* 35):

runne, sunne, dunne, wonne, bygonne, sponne

44–1 (*PE* 517), 44–3 (*PE* 519), 44–5 (*PE* 521), 44–7 (*PE* 523):

wonne, sunne, conne, runne

49–2 (*PE* 578), 49–4 (*PE* 580), 49–6 (*PE* 582), 49–8 (*PE* 584), 49–9 (*PE* 585), 49–11 (*PE* 587):

blom, dome, come, sum , tom, nom

(ii) -*o* and -*ou*

36–2 (*PE* 422), 36–4 (*PE* 424), 36–6 (*PE* 426), 36–8 (*PE* 428), 36–9 (*PE* 429),

36–11 (*PE* 431): *errour, honour, flour, fauour, dousour, Fasor*

81–2 (*PE* 962), 81–4 (*PE* 964), 81–6 (*PE* 966), 81–8 (*PE* 968), 81–9 (*PE* 969), 81–11 (*PE* 971): *flor, bor, tor, fauor, cloystor, vygour*

99–2 (*PE* 1178), 99–4 (*PE* 1180), 99–6 (*PE* 1182), 99–8 (*PE* 1184), 99–9 (*PE* 1185), 99–11 (*PE* 1187):

regioun, swone, renoun, avysyoun, sermoun, doungoun on and ohn[6]

82–10 (*PE* 982), 82–12 (*PE* 984): *schon, John*

83–10 (*PE* 994), 83–12 (*PE* 996): *ston, John*

84–10 (*PE* 1006), 84–12 (*PE* 1008): *ston, John*

85–10 (*PE* 1018), 85–12 (*PE* 1020): *schon, John*

86–10 (*PE* 1030), 86–12 (*PE* 1032): *fon, John*

(iii) *-o*, *-u*, and *-ou*

15–2 (*PE* 170), 15–4 (*PE* 172), 15–6 (*PE* 174), 15–8 (*PE* 176), 15–9 (*PE* 177), 15–11 (*PE* 179): *fonte, wonte, brunt, blunt, frount, astount*

(iv) *-aw* and *-ow*

46–1 (*PE* 541), 46–3 (*PE* 543), 46–5 (*PE* 545), 46–7 (*PE* 547):

knaw, owe, rawe, lowe

(v) the presence and absence of a final *-e*

5–2 (*PE* 50), 5–4 (*PE* 52), 5–6 (*PE* 54), 5–8 (*PE* 56), 5–9 (*PE* 57), 5–11 (*PE* 59):

caȝt(ø), saȝt(ø), faȝt(ø), wraȝte, flaȝt(ø), slaȝte

Words with *-e* and those without *-e* frequently rhyme with each other, for instance, in stanzas 2, 3, 7, 10, 16, 17, 21, 22, 25, and 26, to name a few from the initial part of the poem. Despite various arguments about the word final *-e*, the two types of spelling, one with an *-e* and the other without one, could have had the same phonological value to the poet.[7] This may provide evidence about the role of the final *-e* as a supplier of an extra syllable since verse reading may be more conservative than daily speech.

(vi) the word-medial unstressed *-e*[8]

5–1 (*PE* 49), 5–3 (*PE* 51), 5–5 (*PE* 53), 5–7 (*PE* 55):

spenn(ø)d, denned, penned, kenned

The word-medial *-e* does not necessarily form a syllable. This scribal error in *PE* 49 (Gollancz 12) suggests that the pronunciation of ***spennd*** could have been close to that of ***denned***, ***penned***, and ***kenned***. Another example is found in stanza 60 in which *ayed* and *ayde* rhyme.

60–2 (*PE* 710), 60–4 (*PE* 712), 60–6 (*PE* 714), 60–8 (*PE* 716), 60–9 (*PE* 717), 60–11 (*PE* 719): *aw**ayed***, *br**ayde***, *pr**ayed***, *rest**ayed***, *s**ayde***, *ar**ayed***

This is observed in stanzas 82 and 98 as well.

82–1 (*PE* 973), 82–3 (*PE* 975), 82–5 (*PE* 977), 82–7 (*PE* 979):
*vnh**yde***, *s**yde***, *b**yde***, *assp**yed***

98–2 (*PE* 1166), 98–4 (*PE* 1168), 98–6 (*PE* 1170), 98–8 (*PE* 1172), 98–9 (*PE* 1173), 98–11 (*PE* 1175):
*ar**ayd***, *rest**ayed***, *br**ayde***, *l**ayde***, *str**ayd***, *s**ayd***

(vii) -*e* and -*y*

18–1 (*PE* 205), 18–3 (*PE* 207), 18–5(*PE* 209), 18–7 (*PE* 211):
*g**y**rle*, *p**e**rle*, *w**e**rle*, ***e**rle*

20–1 (*PE* 229), 20–3 (*PE* 231), 20–5 (*PE* 233), 20–7 (*PE* 235):
*p**y**se*, *Gr**e**ce*, *n**e**ce*, *sp**y**ce*

34–10 (*PE* 406), 34–12 (*PE* 408):
*mekene**s**se*, *bl**y**sse*

49–1 (*PE* 577), 49–3 (*PE* 579), 49–5 (*PE* 581), 49–7 (*PE* 583):
*here**i**nne*, *w**y**nne*, *byb**y**nne*, *m**y**nne*

53–2 (*PE* 626), 53–4 (*PE* 628), 53–6 (*PE* 630), 53–8 (*PE* 632), 53–9 (*PE* 633), 53–11 (*PE* 635): *l**y**ne*, *v**y**ne*, *encl**y**ne*, *h**y**ne*, *þere**i**ne*, *f**y**ne*

92–1 (*PE* 1093), 92–3 (*PE* 1095), 92–5 (*PE* 1097), 92–7 (*PE* 1099):
*r**y**s*, *w**y**se*, *eupr**e**sse*, *g**y**se*

(viii) -*e* in a monosyllabic word and -*é*

25–2 (*PE* 290), 25–4 (*PE* 292), 25–6 (*PE* 294), 25–8 (*PE* 296), 25–9 (*PE* 297), 25–11 (*PE* 299): *b**e***, *þr**e***, *fl**e***, *s**e***, *countr**é***, *fr**e***

64–2 (*PE* 758), 64–4 (*PE* 760), 64–6 (*PE* 762), 64–8 (*PE* 764), 64–9 (*PE* 765), 64–11 (*PE* 767): *Destyn**é***, *assembl**é***, *bonert**é***, *þ**e***, *bewt**é***, *vergynt**é***

(ix) -*y* and -*i*

57–2 (*PE* 674), 57–4 (*PE* 676), 57–6 (*PE* 678), 57–8 (*PE* 680), 57–9 (*PE* 681), 57–11 (*PE* 683): *sk**y**lle*, *t**y**lle*, *h**y**lle*, *d**y**lle*, ***i**lle*, *st**y**lle*

61–2 (*PE* 722), 61–4 (*PE* 724), 61–6 (*PE* 726), 61–8 (*PE* 728), 61–9 (*PE* 729), 61–11 (*PE* 731): *w**y**nne*, *þer**i**nne*, *s**y**nne*, *vnp**y**nne*, *bl**y**nne*, *l**y**nne*

95–1 (*PE* 1129), 95–3 (*PE* 1131), 95–5 (*PE* 1133), 95–7 (*PE* 1135):

*deu**i**se, pr**y**se, H**y**s, w**y**se*

-*y*, -*e*, and no vowel

27–1 (*PE* 313), 27–3 (*PE* 315), 27–5 (*PE* 317), 27–7 (*PE* 319):

*dayl**y**, bayl**y**, fayl**e**, counsayl(ø)*

-*e*, -*y*, and -*i*

100–2 (*PE* 1190), 100–4 (*PE* 1192), 100–6 (*PE* 1194), 100–8 (*PE* 1196), 100–9 (*PE* 1197), 100–11 (*PE* 1199):

*g**e**uen, þr**y**uen, dr**y**uen, cl**y**uen, tor**i**uen, str**y**uen*

-*yye* and -*é*

40–10 (*PE* 478), 40–12 (*PE* 480):

*b**yye**, cortays**é***

-*ey* and -*e*

46–2 (*PE* 542), 46–4 (*PE* 544), 46–6 (*PE* 546), 46–8 (*PE* 548), 46–9 (*PE* 549), 46–11 (*PE* 551): *m**ey**ny, repren**é**, p**e**ny, att**e**ny, pl**e**ny, str**e**ny*

-*ay* and -*a*

91–1 (*PE* 1081), 91–3 (*PE* 1083), 91–5 (*PE* 1085), 91–7 (*PE* 1087):

*merw**ay**le, b**a**ly, qu**ay**le, trau**ay**le*

-*yi* and -*y*

101–2 (*PE* 1202), 101–4 (*PE* 1204), 101–6 (*PE* 1206), 101–8 (*PE* 1208), 101–9 (*PE* 1209), 101–11 (*PE* 1211):

*Kryst**yi**n, f**yi**n, encl**yi**n, m**y**n, w**y**n, h**y**ne*

-*e*, -*é*, -*ye*, and -*y*

67–2 (*PE* 794), 67–4 (*PE* 796), 67–6 (*PE* 798), 67–8 (*PE* 800), 67–9 (*PE* 801), 67–11 (*PE* 803): *b**e**, fr**e**, deboner**té**, felon**ye**, H**e**, quer**y***

-*ye* and -*yȝe*

69–1 (*PE* 817), 69–3 (*PE* 819), 69–5 (*PE* 821), 69–7 (*PE* 823):

*Galal**ye**, Ysa**ye**, profess**ye**, dr**yȝe***

87–1 (*PE* 1033), 87–3 (*PE* 1035), 87–5 (*PE* 1037), 87–7 (*PE* 1039):

*s**yȝe**, assp**ye**, margyr**ye**, pl**ye***

38–10 (*PE* 454), 38–12 (*PE* 456):

*h**yȝe**, cortays**ye***

(x) -*ay* and -*oy*

26–1 (*PE* 301), 26–3 (*PE* 303), 26–5 (*PE* 305), 26–7 (*PE* 307):

*pr**ay**se, vncort**oy**se, r**ay**se, western**ays***

(xi) diphthong and monophthong

66–1 (*PE* 781), 66–3 (*PE* 783), 66–5 (*PE* 785), 66–7 (*PE* 787):

quene, menteene, bene, sene

73–2 (*PE* 866), 73–4 (*PE* 868), 73–6 (*PE* 870), 73–8 (*PE* 872), 73–9 (*PE* 873), 73–11 (*PE* 875): *wro, þro, mo, also, þoo, blo*

79–10 (*PE* 946), 79–12 (*PE* 948):

flote, moote

(xii) *-ou*, *-au*, and *-aw*

39–1 (*PE* 457), 39–3 (*PE* 459), 39–5 (*PE* 461), 39–7 (*PE* 463):

Poule, naule, sawle, gawle

(xiii) *-ue* and *-we*

75–2 (*PE* 890), 75–4 (*PE* 892), 75–6 (*PE* 894), 75–8 (*PE* 896), 75–9 (*PE* 897), 75–11 (*PE* 899):

knewe, swe, due, hwe, vntrwe, remwe

Several points are revealed from the above groups as to the vowels in rhyme. First, *-u* and *-o* are interchangeable, and both of them are close to the diphthong *-ou*. As the examples in the fourth group demonstrate, the diphthongs *-aw* and *-ow* could hold the same phonological value. Several different spellings can be used for the rhyme with /i/. The high front vowel /i/ may be represented by several different spellings, and the etymological source may be a legitimate reason for that (Cable, *Tradition*; Grant, Peterson, and Cross). In the word-final position, which is in the line-final position at the same time, *-e*, *-é*, *-y*, and *-i* may rhyme with each other. Furthermore, *-e*, *-é*, and *-y* can rhyme with *-ye* and *-yȝe*. In the word-medial position, *-e*, *-i*, and *-y* can rhyme with each other while diphthongs, such as *ey* and *yi*, may appear in the same rhyme group.

The word-final *-e* may rhyme with the syllable that is not accompanied by a final *-e*, which suggests that a consonant could have been pronounced in the same manner whether the word-final *-e* is present or not. The absence or presence of the final *-e* does not seem to make much difference, as seen in the contrast of *ayed* and *ayde*, or *ayd*, *ayde*, and *ayed*. The groups from (x) to (xii) are related to double vowels and diphthongs. As C. Jones explains, "the spelling system represents abstract and not necessarily realized phonological features" (46). C. Jones claims that the following sounds are used in ME:

Consonantal:

hw, wh, ȝ, g, ssh, sc, ss, s, sch, ssch, þ, ð, f, v, u, y, w, gh, h, ch, b, d, l, m, n, p, t, z, c, k, cw, qu, kn, x, qh, quh, qw, th, gg, dg, j

Vowels and diphthongs:

a, aa, æ, e, ea, eo, ee, i, y, ii, ey, iy, o, oo, oa, u, ou, ow, v,
iu, ui, oe, ue, ai, æi, aȝ, æȝ, ay, ei, eu, ew, iw, eou, eow, ag, agh, oȝ, og, ogh, oy, oi

As C. Jones's list of graphs, digraphs, and trigraphs suggests, poets between the years 1100 and 1450 had a variety of vowels and diphthongs that they could utilize in verse making. The variants in vowels seem to have been an essential aid, especially in composing verse with rhyme.

5.2 Consonants in Rhyme

The following phenomena are observed concerning the consonant combination in rhyme.

(i) -*c* and -*s*

57–1 (*PE* 673), 57–3 (*PE* 675), 57–5 (*PE* 677), 57–7 (*PE* 679):
cas, face, pace, place

(ii) -*c* and -*tz*

37–2 (*PE* 434), 37–4 (*PE* 436), 37–6 (*PE* 438), 37–8 (*PE* 440), 37–9 (*PE* 441), 37–11 (*PE* 443): *face, grace, space, place, hat**z**, chace*

-*s* and -*tz*

43–2 (*PE* 506), 43–4 (*PE* 508), 43–6 (*PE* 510), 43–8 (*PE* 512), 43–9 (*PE* 513), 43–11 (*PE* 515): *ros, porpos, got**z**, clos, tot**z**, pos*

-*s* and -*z*

61–10 (*PE* 730), 61–12 (*PE* 732): *pres, mascelle**z***

64–10 (*PE* 766), 64–12 (*PE* 768): *dese, maskelle**z***

65–10 (*PE* 778), 65–12 (*PE* 780): *depres, maskelle**z***

(iii) -*y* and -*ȝ*

85–1 (*PE* 1009), 85–3 (*PE* 1011), 85–5 (*PE* 1013), 85–7 (*PE* 1015):
*crysol**y**t, qu**y**t, t**yȝ**t, pl**y**t*

-*gh* and -*ȝ*

52–10 (*PE* 622), 52–12 (*PE* 624): *wo**gh**e, inno**ȝ**e*

55–10 (*PE* 658), 55–12 (*PE* 660): *withdro**ȝ**, inno**gh***

w and *gh*

53–10 (*PE* 634), 53–12 (*PE* 636): *alo**w**, inno**gh**e*

(iv) a single consonant and a double consonant

-s and *-ss*

73–10 (*PE* 874), 73–12 (*PE* 876): *re**ss**e, le**s***

75–10 (*PE* 898), 75–12 (*PE* 900): *dysstre**ss**e, le**s***

76–10 (*PE* 910), 76–12 (*PE* 912): *expre**ss**e, neuerþele**s**e*

93–2 (*PE* 1106), 93–4 (*PE* 1108), 93–6 (*PE* 1110), 93–8 (*PE* 1112), 93–9 (*PE* 1113), 93–11 (*PE* 1115): *gla**ss**e, wa**ss**e, pa**ss**e, wa**ss**e, tra**s**, ma**s***

-k and *-kk*

79–2 (*PE* 938), 79–4 (*PE* 940), 79–6 (*PE* 942), 79–8 (*PE* 944), 79–9 (*PE* 945), 79–11 (*PE* 947): *spa**kk**, sa**k**e, sla**k**e, ta**k**e, bla**k**e, fla**k**e*

-ch and *-chch*

71–1 (*PE* 841), 71–3 (*PE* 843), 71–5 (*PE* 845), 71–7 (*PE* 847): *pe**chch**e, stre**ch**e, te**ch**e, fe**ch**e*

(v) *-c* and *-g*

76–1 (*PE* 901), 76–3 (*PE* 903), 76–5 (*PE* 905), 76–7 (*PE* 907): *þon**c**, wlon**c**, amon**g**, bon**c***

The following tendencies may be summarized from the above. The letters *-c* and *-s* are interchangeable while *tz* may correspond to *-c*, *-s*, and *-z* as seen in the second group. Also interchangeable are *-ȝ*, *-y*, *-gh*, and *-w* as exemplified in the third group. A single consonant may rhyme with a double counterpart as seen in the fourth group. The consonants in rhyme are less variable than the vowels, which means that the poet does not use *consonance* or *assonance* but maintains *rhyme proper* throughout the entire poem.[9]

5.3 Deviations in Rhyme

The following examples exhibit somewhat deviated features in rhyme.

(i) Rhyme may extend over more than one syllable:

6–2 (*PE* 62), 6–4 (*PE* 64), 6–6 (*PE* 66), 6–8 (*PE* 68), 6–9 (*PE* 69), 6–11 (*PE* 71): *sw**euen**, m**euen**, cl**euen**, dyscr**euen**, l**euen**, w**euen***

46–2 (*PE* 542), 46–4 (*PE* 544), 46–6 (*PE* 546), 46–8 (*PE* 548), 46–9 (*PE* 549), 46–11 (*PE* 551): ***meyny**, repr**ené**, **peny**, att**eny**, **pleny**, str**eny***

82–2 (*PE* 974), 82–4 (*PE* 976), 82–6 (*PE* 978), 82–8 (*PE* 980), 82–9 (*PE* 981), 82–11 (*PE* 983): ***heued**, **veued**, **leued**, dr**eued**, **keued**, pr**eued***

(ii) One word may have two beats, which results in rhyme on a syllable that is not originally stressed. The word *Jerusalem* from stanza 66 through stanza 70 is meant to bear stress on two syllables:

66–10 (*PE* 790), 66–12 (*PE* 792): *dr**em**, Jerusal**em***
67–10 (*PE* 802), 67–12 (*PE* 804): *n**em**, Jerusal**em***
68–10 (*PE* 814), 68–12 (*PE* 816): *b**em**, Jerusal**em***
69–10 (*PE* 826), 69–12 (*PE* 828): *cl**em**, Jerusal**em***
70–10 (*PE* 838), 70–12 (*PE* 840): *s**eme**, Jerusal**em***

(iii) Stanza 66 consists of the following rhyming words:

66–1 (*PE* 781), 66–3 (*PE* 783), 66–5 (*PE* 785), 66–7 (*PE* 787):
*qu**ene**, ment**eene**, b**ene**, s**ene***
66–2 (*PE* 782), 66–4 (*PE* 784), 66–6 (*PE* 786), 66–8 (*PE* 788), 66–9 (*PE* 789):
*bl**ot**, n**ot**, fl**ot**, kn**ot**, cl**ot***
66–11 (*PE* 791): *hyl-c**oppe***
66–10 (*PE* 790), 66–12 (*PE* 792): *dr**em**, Jerusal**em***

The word *hyl-coppe* in 66–11 is meant to rhyme with *blot*, *not*, *flot*, *knot*, and *clot*. The two consonants, /p/ and /t/, are similar in the sense that both of them are voiceless stops. Since this is one of the rare occasions of assonance in *PE*, it gives a sense of deviation. Another example of assonance is found in stanza 59 in which *it*, *yet*, and *yed* belong to the same rhyme group:

59–2 (*PE* 698), 59–4 (*PE* 700), 59–6 (*PE* 702), 59–8 (*PE* 704), 59–9 (*PE* 705),
59–11 (*PE* 707): *h**it**, justyf**yet**, cr**yed**, assp**yed**, d**yed**, tr**yed***

(iv) Stanza 63 shows another deviation:

63–1 (*PE* 745), 63–3 (*PE* 747), 63–5 (*PE* 749), 63–7 (*PE* 751):
*p**ure**, fyg**ure**, nat**ure**, lettr**ure***
63–2 (*PE* 746), 63–4 (*PE* 748), 63–6 (*PE* 750), 63–8 (*PE* 752), 63–9 (*PE* 753),
63–11 (*PE* 755): *pr**ys**, w**ys**, v**ys**, propert**éz**, l**ys**, off**ys***
63–10 (*PE* 754), 63–12 (*PE* 756):
*cort**ez**, maskell**ez***

The word *propertéz* in 63–8 is meant to rhyme with *prys*, *wys*, *vys*, *lys*, and *offys*, but it also rhymes with *cortez* and *maskellez*. As seen before, *-y* and *-é* may be interchangeable in certain cases. The poet presumably used *propertéz* to correspond with *-ys*, and came up with a word by chance that could rhyme with the tenth and twelfth lines of the stanza. As a result, eight out of twelve lines (*PE* 746, *PE* 748, *PE* 750, *PE* 752, *PE* 753, *PE* 754, *PE* 755, and *PE* 756) hold a similar rhyme in this particular stanza.

(v) The *b* and *c* rhymes are similar in stanzas 78 and 83:

78–2 (*PE* 926), 78–4 (*PE* 928), 78–6 (*PE* 930), 78–8 (*PE* 932), 78–9 (*PE* 933), 78–11 (*PE* 935): *r**oute**, d**oute**, þer**oute**, ab**oute**, l**oute**, st**oute***

78–10 (*PE* 934), 78–12 (*PE* 936): *g**ote**, m**ote***

83–2 (*PE* 986), 83–4 (*PE* 988), 83–6 (*PE* 990), 83–8 (*PE* 992), 83–9 (*PE* 993), 83–11 (*PE* 995): *ren**oun**, ad**oun**, br**oun**, b**oun**, ten**oun**, t**oun***

83–10 (*PE* 994), 83–12 (*PE* 996): *st**on**, J**ohn***

Furthermore, the *a* and *b* rhymes are quite similar in stanzas 60 and 89:

60–1 (*PE* 709), 60–3 (*PE* 711), 60–5 (*PE* 713), 60–7 (*PE* 715): *r**ede**, areþ**ede**, ȝ**ede**, b**ede***

60–2 (*PE* 710), 60–4 (*PE* 712), 60–6 (*PE* 714), 60–8 (*PE* 716), 60–9 (*PE* 717), 60–11 (*PE* 719): *aw**ayed**, br**ayde**, pr**ayed**, rest**ayed**, st**ayde**, ar**ayed***

89–1 (*PE* 1057), 89–3 (*PE* 1059), 89–5 (*PE* 1061), 89–7 (*PE* 1063):[10] *sw**ete**, str**ete**, ȝ**ete**, m**ete***

89–2 (*PE* 1058), 89–4 (*PE* 1060), 89–6 (*PE* 1062), 89–8 (*PE* 1064), 89–9 (*PE* 1065), 89–11 (*PE* 1067): *fl**et**, gl**et**, s**et**, ref**et**, ȝ**et**, res**et***

In stanzas 60 and 89, thus, ten out of twelve lines rhyme on a similar sound, which gives a special sense of unity.

(vi) The fifteenth cluster consists of six stanzas. Gardner (85) contends that this extra stanza should have been "revised out" by the poet whereas Gilligan (7) and Røstvig (330) assert that this must be deliberate. As far as the rhyme structure is concerned, the sixth stanza of the fifteenth cluster faithfully follows the rhyme rule with the refrain word in its tenth (*PE* 910) and twelfth (*PE* 912) lines.

5.4 Rhyme within the Stanza

The end rhyme is more demanding in *PE* than its alliteration is. By means of a classical term, this strict constraint of rhyme can be defined as solid rhyme proper in which both the vowel and the consonant or consonant cluster are repeated. The poet took advantage of ME vowel variations, but he does not seem to have been interested in consonantal variations. ME in general is not recorded according to the standard orthography. This makes it difficult to reconstruct the actual sounds that are represented by various spellings. However, rhyming words are often used in order to prove regional differences, phonological variability, and authorship. Both rhyme and alliteration represent the poets' language and their aesthetics in verbal echo. Alliteration links the line by means of the repetition of the same sound. Rhyme, on the other hand, provides a different device of cohesion because it is capable of vertically "binding the passage together in a net of sound" (Tamplin 45), and thus becomes "one of the strongest shape-giving devices due to its chiming recurrence" (Tamplin 13). Since end rhyme is one of the most peculiar phenomena in *PE*, the poet seems to have known that "the linkages possible through rhyme are of a much more various and interesting kind than the linkages possible through alliteration" (Fraser 60). He is quite successful in achieving this task within an alliterative framework. This section examines the rigid rhyme structure within the stanza while the next section will analyze the rhyme structure within the cluster. The final section postulates the overall structure of rhyme together with alliteration.

Clark and Whiteall classify rhyme into four categories (706)[11]: rhyme in whole words (**dawn**-**fawn**), rhyme in ends of words (appl**aud**-defr**aud**), rhyme in groups of whole words (st**ayed with us**-pl**ayed with us**), and rhyme in ends of words followed by one or more whole words (bes**eech him**-imp**each him**). The following six patterns are observed in *PE*:

(i) rhyme in whole words:

__paye__ (*PE* 1)-*__saye__* (*PE* 3)

(ii) rhyme in ends of words:

*err**our*** (*PE* 422)-*hon**our*** (*PE* 424)-***flour*** (*PE* 426)-*fau**our*** (*PE* 428)-*dous**our*** (*PE* 429)

(iii) rhyme in whole words with the same preceding consonant:

*s**weuen*** (*PE* 62)-***weuen*** (*PE* 71)

*c**leuen*** (*PE* 66)-***leuen*** (*PE* 69)

(iv) rhyme in identical words:

. . . *o **Jerusalem*** (*PE* 792)

. . . *in **Jerusalem*** (*PE* 804)

. . . *and **Jerusalem*** (*PE* 840)

(v) rhyme in groups of words:

Þat er watz ***grounde of alle my blysse.*** (*PE* 372)
Þise arn þe ***grounde of alle my blysse.*** (*PE* 384)
Hit is in ***grounde of alle my blysse.'*** (*PE* 396)
Þat is þe ***grounde of alle my blysse.*** (*PE* 408)
Is rote and ***grounde of alle my blysse.'*** (*PE* 420)

(vi) rhyme in full lines:[12]

For ***þe grace of God is gret inoghe.*** (*PE* 612)
For ***þe grace of God is gret innoȝe.*** (*PE* 624)
For ***þe grace of God is gret innoghe.*** (*PE* 636)
Þe grace of God *wex* ***gret innoghe.*** (*PE* 648)
And ***þe grace of God is gret innogh.*** (*PE* 660)

The patterns (i), (ii), and (iii) appear in *a* and *b* rhymes and in *c* rhymes of the tenth line of the stanza whereas the remaining three patterns, (iv), (v), and (vi), are limited to the twelfth or final line of the stanza. The recurrence of similar or identical lines five times (six for the fifteenth cluster) within a cluster like types (v) and (vi) has the effect of uniting the concerned stanzas into a coherent group.[13]

The following is the list of rhymes in the *a* and *b* positions (202 rhyme sounds in total) classified by frequency. The stanza number and the rhyme type (*a*, *b*, or *c*) in which that particular rhyme appears are placed in parentheses. Spelling variations other than the word-final *-e* are placed in square brackets:

Nine times:

-er(e)	(1b, 8a, 14b, 34b, 52b, 62a, 74b, 93a, 97a)

Eight times:

-et(e)	(8b, 28a, 47b, 54a, 64a, 70a, 89a, 89b)

Seven times:

-ent(e)	(22a, 33a, 53a, 56b, 85b, 95b, 100a)
-ys(e) [*-ece, -yce, -éz, -esse, -ise*]	(9a, 12a, 17a, 20a, 63b, 92a, 95a)

Six times:

-en(e)	(4b, 17b, 25a, 66a, 80a, 96a)
-yȝt(e)	(10b, 21a, 42b, 83a, 88b, 90a)
-yn(e) [*-inne, -ynne, -ine, -yin*]	(28b, 43a, 49a, 53b, 61b, 101b)

Five times:

-ede	(3a, 35a, 41a, 60a, 88a)

-oun [*-one*] (4a, 45b, 83b, 92b, 99b)

Four times:

-ace [*-atz*, *-as*]	(6a, 15a, 37b, 57a)
-ay(e) [*-ay*]	(1a, 22b, 37a, 41b)
-elle	(31a, 55a, 67a, 94b)
-onc [*-onk*, *-ong(e)*]	(40b, 45a, 76a, 98a)
-os(e) [*-otz*]	(16a, 23a, 43b, 76b)
-yt(e) [*-it*, *-yet*, *-yed*, *-yȝt*]	(30a, 54b, 59b, 85a)

Three times:

-are	(13a, 70b, 86a)	*-e* [-é, *-y(e)*]	(25b, 64b, 67b)
-o [*-oo*]	(29b, 47a, 73b)	*-on*	(18b, 32b, 69b)
-ure	(19b, 63a, 91b)	*-yȝe* [*-ye*]	(26b, 69a, 87a)

Twice:

-ade	(12b, 96b)	*-aȝt(e)*	(5b, 101a)
-alle	(16b, 77a)	*-ate*	(33b, 52a)
-ayed [*-ayd(e)*]	(60b, 98b)	*-ayl(e)* [*-ayly*, -aly]	(27a, 91a)
-ayn(e)	(58a, 68a)	*-ele*	(2b, 78a)
-emmen	(19a, 84a)	*-esse*	(29a, 42a)
-est(e)	(24a, 72b)	*-eue*	(27b, 40a)
-euen [*-yuen*, *-iuen*]	(6b, 100b)	*-om(e)* [*-um*]	(49b, 59a)
-onde	(13b, 79a)	*-onne* [*-unne*]	(3b, 44a)
-or [*-our*]	(36b, 81b)	*-we* [*-ue*]	(36a, 75b)
-yde [*-yed*]	(34a, 82a)	*-yf*	(65b, 71b)
-ylde	(61a, 81a)	*-ylle* [*-ille*, *-yle*]	(57b, 58b)
-yng(e)	(38b, 72a)		

Once:

-able	(50b)	*-age*	(35b)	*-ake* [*-akk*]	(79b)
-ale	(84b)	*-alez*	(11a)	*-alt(e)*	(97b)
-ambe	(65a)	*-ande*	(73a)	*-ange*	(2a)
-ard(e)	(51b)	*-arpe*	(74a)	*-asse [-as]*	(93b)
-atez	(87b)	-aue	(56a)	*-aule* [*-awle*, *-oule*]	(39a)
-aunt	(14a)	*-aw(e)* [*-owe*]	(46a)	*-awez*	(24b)
-ayned	(21b)	*-aynez*	(11b)	*-ayre*	(86b)
-ays(e) [*-oyse*]	(26a)	*-eche* [*-echche*]	(71a)	*-ef* (23b) *-eme*	(99a)
-enned [*-ennd*]	(5a)	*-eny* [*-ené*, *-eyny*]	(46b)	*-epe*	(10a)
-erez	(9b)	*-ert(e)*	(50a)	*-es(e)*	(80b)

-eued	(82b)	*-oched*	(94a)	*-od(e)*	(62b)
-oȝt(e)	(44b)	*-olde*	(68b)	*-on(e)*	(77b)
-onte [*-ount*, *-unt*]	(15b)	*-orde*	(31b)	*-ore*	(20b)
-ot [*-oppe*][14]	(66b)	*-oþe*	(32a)	*-ounde*	(55b)
-oute	(78b)	*-oynt(e)*	(75a)	*-yche*	(51a)
-ydez	(7a)	*-yft(e)*	(48a)	*-ykez*	(48b)
-ym	(90b)	*-ynde*	(7b)	*-yrle* [*-erle*]	(18a)
-yst(e)	(39b)	*-yþe*	(30b)	*-yue*	(38a)

The *c* rhyme is treated separately from the *a* and *b* rhymes below because it recurs within a cluster. Theoretically, there are twenty variations in the *c* rhyme, each of which governs five or six stanzas:

C rhyme appearing in two different clusters:

-em(e)	(26c, 27c, 28c, 29c, 30c; 66c, 67c, 68c, 69c, 70c)
-ore	(11c, 12c, 13c, 14c, 15c; 46c, 47c, 48c, 49c, 50c)
-yȝt(e)	(16c, 17c, 18c, 19c, 20c; 56c, 57c, 58c, 59c, 60c)

C rhyme appearing in one cluster:

-ate	(41c, 42c, 43c, 44c, 45c)
-ay(e)	(97c, 98c, 99c, 100c, 101c)
-ent(e)	(6c, 7c, 8c, 9c, 10c)
-er(e)	(21c, 22c, 23c, 24c, 25c)
-es(e) [*-ez*]	(61c, 62c, 63c, 64c, 65c)
-esse [*-es(e)*]	(71c, 72c, 73c, 74c, 75c, 76c)
-ogh(e) [-oȝ(e), *-ow*]	(51c, 52c, 53c, 54c, 55c)
-on [*-ohn*]	(82c, 83c, 84c, 85c, 86c)
-one	(87c, 88c, 89c, 90c, 91c)
-ot [*-otte*]	(1c, 2c, 3c, 4c, 5c)
-ote	(77c, 78c, 79c, 80c, 81c)
-y(e) [*-é*, *-yȝe*, *-yye*]	(36c, 37c, 38c, 39c, 40c)
-ysse [*-esse*]	(31c, 32c, 33c, 34c, 35c)
-yt(e)	(92c, 93c, 94c, 95c, 96c)

The rhyme sounds that are frequently used in *PE*, such as *-ere*, *-ete*, *-ente*, and *-yse*, are often Romance origin words, and these words have the special capability to place stress on rhyming syllables. Keyser assumes two stress systems in the

English language of this period: the native Germanic one and the newly adapted Romance one (354–55). If the Romance accent enabled the poet to shift stress toward the word end, he would have utilized it in order to meet with the rhyme requirement at the line closure. Table 5.1 compares etymological make-up of line-terminal words in *PE* (the entire 1,211 lines) and *G* (first 1,211 lines from the beginning to the fourth line of stanza 49). *G* provides useful information because it consists of unrhymed alliterative lines and the rhymed bob and wheel:

Table 5.1. Etymological Sources of Line-Terminal Words in *PE* and *G*[15]

	OE	OF	ON	Others	Total
PE	715	385	70	41	1,211
	(59.0%)	(31.8%)	(5.8%)	(3.4%)	(100.0%)
G	764	123	73	11	971
(Unrhymed lines)	(78.7%)	(12.7%)	(7.5%)	(1.1%)	(100.0%)
G	173	46	19	2	240
(Rhymed lines)	(72.1%)	(19.2%)	(7.9%)	(0.8%)	(100%)

Table 5.1 reveals that words from Old French are more frequently used in *PE* than in *G*. The rhymed lines of *G* contain more Romance origin words than the unrhymed lines, but *PE* shows a marked tendency to use words of Romance origin at the line conclusion. Romance disyllabic and polysyllabic words that may receive stress on their final or penultimate syllable expanded the poet's word choice. In other words, syllables whose stress quality may be altered according to the metrical environment are more frequently used in order to ensure rhyme at the line end. Words of Romance origin are a crucial aid in composition.

5.5 Rhyme within the Cluster

The refrain word usually appears as a single word in stanza-initial lines whereas it is accompanied by other words in phrasal repetition in stanza-terminal lines. The following two clusters illustrate the appearance of the refrain word in stanza-initial lines and the similarities among the stanza-final lines within the same cluster. Repeated words in some or all of the stanza-final lines of the same cluster are in boldface:

spot in Cluster 1 (Stanzas 1–5):
1–12 (*PE* 12) **Of þat pryuy perle withouten spot.**

2–1 (*PE* 13) Syþen in þat **spote** hit fro me sprange,
2–12 (*PE* 24) **My priuy perle withouten spotte.**
3–1 (*PE* 25) Þat **spot** of spysez mot nedez sprede,
3–12 (*PE* 36) **Of þat precios perle wythouten spotte.**
4–1 (*PE* 37) To þat **spot** þat I in speche expoun
4–12 (*PE* 48) **My precious perle wythouten spot.**
5–1 (*PE* 49) Bifore þat **spot** my honde I spennd
5–12 (*PE* 60) On **þat precios perle withouten spot.**
6–1 (*PE* 61) Fro **spot** my spyryt þer sprang in space;

pyȝt in Cluster 4 (Stanzas 16–20):

16–12 (*PE* 192) A **precios** pyece **in perlez pyȝt.**
17–1 (*PE* 193) Perlez **pyȝte** of ryal prys
17–12 (*PE* 204) With **precios perlez** al vmbe**pyȝte.**
18–1 (*PE* 205) A **pyȝt** coroune ȝet wer þat gyrle
18–12 (*PE* 216) Of **precios perle in** porfyl **pyȝte.**
19–1 (*PE* 217) **Pyȝt** watz poyned and vche a hemme—
19–12 (*PE* 228) Þat **precios perle** þer hit watz **pyȝt.**
20–1 (*PE* 229) **Pyȝt** in perle, þat precios pyse
20–12 (*PE* 240) To sware þat swete in **perlez pyȝte**!
21–1 (*PE* 241) 'O perle,' quoþ I, 'in perlez **pyȝt,**

Refrain words may appear in three forms in stanza-final lines: a single word, a phrase, and an entire line. Stanza-initial lines, on the contrary, do not show this overwhelming repetition around the refrain word. The tenth line, which rhymes with the refrain word in the twelfth line, usually ends with a different word in each stanza, but the twelfth line always ends with the identical word. This makes a clear contrast between non-stanza-final lines and stanza-final lines because the repetition of the same rhyming word is not common in the first eleven lines of the stanza.

The refrain word in stanza-initial lines does not necessarily initiate the stanza, but may appear after several syllables. The first lines of stanzas 21, 85, and 92, for instance, place the refrain word after a few words or even at the end:

21–1 (*PE* 241) 'O perle,' quoþ I, 'in perlez **pyȝt,**

85–1 (*PE* 1009) ȝet joyned **John** þe crysolyt,
92–1 (*PE* 1093) Ryȝt as þe maynful **mone** con rys

A derived form of the refrain word may be used as long as the stem remains the same, as seen in the first lines of stanzas 7, 9, 35, and 78. The refrain word is *adubbemente* for stanzas 7 and 9, *blysse* for stanza 35, and *mote* for stanza 78:

7–1 (*PE* 73) **Dubbed** wern alle þo downez sydez
9–1 (*PE* 97) So al watz **dubbet** on dere asyse
35–1 (*PE* 409) 'A **blysful** lyf þou says I lede;
78–1 (*PE* 925) 'Þys **motelez** meyny þou conez of mele,

The rule governing the refrain word is that it may change its form at the beginning of the stanza, but may not do so at the end, though a longer word that includes the refrain word is permissible, as seen in *vmbepyȝte* instead of *pyȝte* in the final line of stanza 17.

The stanzas may be classified according to the position of the refrain word in the first line, as shown in Table 5.2. Among the seventy-one stanzas in which the refrain word does not appear at the beginning, fifty-five stanzas contain the refrain word in the first beat position:

Table 5.2. Positions of the Refrain Word in Stanza-Initial Lines (*PE*)

Line-initial positions	28	(27.7%)
Line-medial positions	71	(70.3%)
Line-final positions	2	(2.0%)
Total	101	(100.0%)

Table 5.3 explains the distribution of stanzas according to which beat position the refrain word occupies:

Table 5.3. Beat Positions of the Refrain Word in Stanza-Initial Lines (*PE*)

In the first beat position of the line	83	(82.2%)
In other than the first beat position of the line	18	(17.8%)
Total	101	(100.0%)

Each stanza, thus, is enclosed by the identical refrain word at the beginning and at the end. A new refrain word is introduced in the final line of the cluster-initial stanza; the final lines of stanzas 6, 11, 16, 21, and so forth play a vital role in initiating another cycle with a new refrain word. The repetition of the identical word at the end of five or six stanzas produces prominent metrical homogeneity among the stanza-final lines within the cluster. The first eleven lines of the stanza are tied with one another by rhyme but not under such distinct homogeneity.

Stanza 101, which ends with the word *pay*, offers another example of carefully planned word repetition. This word *pay* that concludes the entire poem appears in the very first line:

101–12	(*PE* 1212)	Ande precious perlez vnto His **pay**.
1–1	(*PE* 1)	Perle plesaunte, to prynces **paye**

The first line of the poem theoretically does not have the refrain word from the previous cluster. But the refrain word of the final stanza appears in the beginning of the poem, and the final lines of the stanzas of cluster 20 repeat this word:

97–12	(*PE* 1164)	Hit watz not at my **Pryncez paye**.
98–12	(*PE* 1176)	Now al be to **þat Pryncez paye**.'
99–12	(*PE* 1188)	Þat þou art to **þat Prynsez paye**.'
100–12	(*PE* 1200)	Oþer proferen Þe oȝt agayn Þy **paye**.
101–12	(*PE* 1212)	Ande precious perlez vnto His **pay**.

The poet carefully uses this intricate repetition of words in his work. As Gilligan comments, "the poet may have had in mind his role as imitator of that divine architect who counsels us not to be surprised that he takes such pains with his carefully crafted 'hondewerk'" (10).

The portion that the refrain word governs is not the entire sixty lines of a single cluster (seventy-two lines in the case of the fifteenth cluster), but the fifty-nine lines of a cluster (seventy-one lines in the case of the fifteenth cluster) and the first line of the subsequent cluster. This is also applied to the final and last stanzas of the poem. Thus, the refrain word plays a role not only in completing each stanza and each cluster but also in initiating another stanza and another cluster, creating multiple types of metrical unity. Finally, the entire poem turns into a cyclic composition, suggesting a story that never ends.

In contrast to the frequent appearance of the refrain word governed by the end rhyme, alliteration, which is another crucial metrical requirement of the poem, is sometimes missing. Table 5.4 compares the alliteration patterns in stanza final-lines and those in other lines:

Table 5.4. Alliteration in Stanza-Final Lines and in Other Lines (*PE*)

Number of alliterating beats per line	Stanza-final lines	Other lines
Four alliterating beats	3.0%	9.2%
Three alliterating beats	15.8%	29.2%
Two alliterating beats	56.4%	34.9%
Two sets of alliteration	3.0%	7.5%
No alliteration	21.8%	19.2%
Total	100.0%	100.0%

Table 5.4 indicates that alliteration is less frequent in stanza-final lines than in other lines that are already less alliterative compared to those of other alliterative poems. Out of fifty-seven stanzas of *PE* that contain two alliterating beats in their final line, twenty-four alliterate on a sound other than the initial sound of the refrain word. The twelfth line of stanza 88 is an example in which alliteration and rhyme are not achieved in the line-final word:

88–12 (*PE* 1056) Watz *br*yȝter þen *b*oþe þe sunne and mone. [aaxx]

On the contrary, alliteration takes place on the rhyming beat in the final line of stanza 45:

45–12 (*PE* 540) Þe *d*ay watz al apassed *d*ate. [axxa]

The final lines of stanzas 13 and 17 contain four and three alliterating beats, respectively. If three alliterating beats per line are considered a requirement, the following lines fulfill both the alliteration and rhyme requirements:

13–12 (*PE* 156) Þat *m*eued my *m*ynde ay *m*ore and *m*ore. [aaaa]
17–12 (*PE* 204) With *p*recios *p*erlez al vmbe*p*yȝte. [aaxa]

The percentage of the lines without alliteration is slightly larger in stanza-final lines than in other lines. The final line of stanza 35 exemplifies such an occasion in which the line reflects no alliteration:

35–12 (*PE* 420) Is rote and grounde of alle my blysse.' [xxxx]

If Osberg's definition of alliterative verse, quoted earlier in this chapter, is presumed, the percentage of the stanza-final lines that satisfy the requirements of both alliteration on three beats and rhyme is small–less than nineteen percent. This proves how challenging it is to end the stanza with the same word five or six times and simultaneously fulfill the two metrical requirements, alliteration and rhyme.[16] The metrical framework of *PE* is multilayered and tight: rigid slots of beats and offbeats, alliteration, refrain words, and rhyme. In some lines, the poet fulfills all the requirements, but in other lines he has to ignore one or two. He is enthusiastic about expressing his zest for rhyme, but occasionally abandons alliteration in this *alliterative* poem.[17]

Three more peculiarities must be pointed out before presenting the conclusion on how the end rhyme operates in *PE*. First, it is a common rule to use completely different sounds for *a*, *b*, and *c* rhymes in a contrastive way between lines. But, the *b* and *c* rhymes of stanzas 78 and 83 end in a similar way:

78–1 (*PE* 925), 78–3 (*PE* 927), 78–5 (*PE* 929), 78–7 (*PE* 931):
mele, *fele*, *juele*, *gele*
78–2 (*PE* 926), 78–4 (*PE* 928), 78–6 (*PE* 930), 78–8 (*PE* 932), 78–9 (*PE* 933), 78–11 (*PE* 935): *r**oute***, *d**oute***, *þer**oute***, *ab**oute***, *l**oute***, *st**oute***
78–10 (*PE* 934), 78–12 (*PE* 936):
*g**ote***, *m**ote***
83–1 (*PE* 985), 83–3 (*PE* 987), 83–5 (*PE* 989), 83–7 (*PE* 991):
syȝt, *dyȝt*, *bryȝt*, *pyȝt*
83–2 (*PE* 986), 83–4 (*PE* 988), 83–6 (*PE* 990), 83–8 (*PE* 992), 83–9 (*PE* 993), 83–11 (*PE* 995): *ren**oun***, *ad**oun***, *br**oun***, *b**oun***, *ten**oun***, *t**oun***
83–10 (*PE* 994), 83–12 (*PE* 996):
*st**on***, *J**ohn***

Five consecutive lines underlined in the above examples, the *b* and *c* rhymes from the eighth line through the twelfth line, rhyme on different vowels but on the same consonant. Furthermore, the *a* and *b* rhymes of stanzas 60 and 89 end with the same consonant. In these two stanzas,[18] the first nine lines of the stanza end in a similar manner:

60–1 (*PE* 709), 60–3 (*PE* 711), 60–5 (*PE* 713), 60–7 (*PE* 715):
*r**ede**, are**þede**, ȝ**ede**, b**ede***
60–2 (*PE* 710), 60–4 (*PE* 712), 60–6 (*PE* 714), 60–8 (*PE* 716), 60–9 (*PE* 717),
60–11 (*PE* 719): *aw**ayed**, br**ayde**, pr**ayed**, rest**ayed**, s**ayde**, ar**ayed***
60–10 (*PE* 718), 60–12 (*PE* 720):
tyȝt, ryȝt
89–1 (*PE* 1057), 89–3 (*PE* 1059), 89–5 (*PE* 1061), 89–7 (*PE* 1063):
*sw**ete**, str**ete**, ȝ**ete**, m**ete***
89–2 (*PE* 1058), 89–4 (*PE* 1060), 89–6 (*PE* 1062), 89–8 (*PE* 1064),
89–9 (*PE* 1065), 89–11 (*PE* 1067):
*fl**et**, gl**et**, s**et**, ref**et**, ȝ**et**, res**et***
89–10 (*PE* 1066), 89–12 (*PE* 1068):
lone, mone

Alliterative verse is essentially the verse of repetition. The poet introduces another cycle of repetition in *PE*; namely the repetition of the same word endings in addition to the repetition of the word beginnings.

Another metrical device to note is the lack of the link between the twelfth and thirteenth clusters. This interruption is striking because the link never fails to appear in other places, which may suggest the idea of numerical symbolism (Røstvig 328–29). These lines (*PE* 720 and *PE* 721) appear in different editions as follows:

Andrew and Waldron	(*PE* 720)	Þe innocent is ay saf by **ryȝt**.
	(*PE* 721)	'**Ryȝt** con calle to Hym Hys mylde,
Morris	(*PE* 720)	Þe innocent is ay saf by **ryȝt**.
	(*PE* 721)	**Ihesuc** con calle to hym hys mylde
Cawley	(*PE* 720)	The innocent is ay saf by **ryght**.
	(*PE* 721)	'**Jesus** con calle to hym hys mylde,
Vantuono (*Pearl*)	(*PE* 720)	Þe innocent is ay saf by **riȝt**.
	(*PE* 721)	"**Ihecu** con calle to hym hys mylde,

The readings by Cawley, Morris, and Vantuono (*Pearl*) reflect the manuscript

(Gollancz), even though the word, *ryȝt*, is expected to appear preferably at the beginning of *PE* 721. Andrew and Waldron assert that this unfulfilled refrain word rule is a scribal substitution for explicitness, and they explain their emendation by stating, "the name *Jesus* has been used twice in the preceding stanza; the poet could therefore reasonably expect the reader to make the identification" (88). But as Finch admits, "it is certainly a bold intrusion into the text we have inherited. It is just as possible, after all, that the poet, rather than the scribe, is responsible for the break in the concatenation and that such emendation is overly scrupulous" (350).

One plausible explanation for this possible corruption in refrain words is that the refrain word may be neglected at the beginning of the stanza if a proper name appears in the first line (Medary 249). Even if the poet is aware of such a convention, *PE* 721 is the only occasion in *PE*. No definite clue is available regarding whether or not replacing the initial word with *riȝt* in *PE* 721 is permissible, but at least the original line presents a significant deviation in the repetition of the same word. As McGalliard maintains, "it is extremely unlikely that so careful a craftsman as the *Pearl* poet would violate the rules of the pattern as he understood them" (288). The absence of the refrain word in *PE* 721, as well as the surplus stanza in cluster 15, will prove a worthy topic for further investigation.[19]

5.6 Multiple Constraints in the Meter of *Pearl*

This chapter has observed how complicated and complete the rhyme of *PE* is. Lines, stanzas, and clusters are unified by end-rhyme, particularly by the *c* rhyme of the refrain word. At the same time, each line is governed by alliteration if it is not as regular as rhyme. Donner comments ("Word Play" 167):

> The morphological semantic dualism of the first link word pairing announce [sic] the poet's zest for word play; it establishes the importance he will assign to lexical affiliations, both formal and referential, throughout the poem. Word ties that call attention to themselves so blatantly at the poem's opening alert the reader to the attention they will demand until its conclusion.

Diagram 5.1 identifies the strict metrical constraints the rhyme and the refrain word create; about twenty-seven percent of the beats (thirteen out of forty-eight beats of a stanza or sixty-five out of 240 beats of a cluster) are not metrically free even if alliteration is not taken into account. Between each cluster of *PE*, there is a strong tension between the horizontal or internal constraint of alliteration and the vertical or external constraint of rhyme, which produces a dual enchaining among lines. In particular, the *c* rhyme that recurs conspicuously in every twelve lines plays an important role in ensuring homogeneity among the members of each metrical unit.

Diagram 5.2 illustrates the rhyme structure among the 240 beats in a cluster within the web of the *c* rhyme. The rhymes, *a*, *a'*, *a"*, *a'"*, etc., signify different rhyme sounds while the same *c* rhyme is maintained in the tenth and twelfth lines of all the five or six stanzas in a cluster. The symbol *B* is a beat without any rhyme constraint, but the *B* positions are under the confines of alliteration. The initial line of a cluster has to hold the refrain word of the previous cluster, which is indicated by the highlighted *B*. The capital *C* is where the refrain word typically appears. The refrain word may appear in places other than the first beat position of the stanza-initial line, but this diagram tentatively assumes it to be in the first beat position.

The stanza of *G* is not based on a fixed number of lines, but the rhymed five lines (the bob and the wheel) mark the stanza conclusion. *PE*, on the other hand, is composed in a fixed twelve-line stanza, and the repetition of the refrain word announces the end of a stanza and the beginning of another one. The refrain word, thus, "produces an effect of both pause and continuity between stanzas, which is one of the most charming external traits of the poem" (Medary 264). The verse line of *PE* is considerably shorter than that of other alliterative poems, which limits the number of words within the line. The circular design of *PE* is unique, demanding multiple poetic senses within the framework of such a short line. Utilizing his skills not only in meanings (Wilson, "Word Play") but also in forms (Milroy), the poet must have extended his craftsmanship as a versifier in *PE*. He highlights unity by means of a rhyme that cyclically rotates within the stanza and then within the cluster. This unity, nonetheless, is achieved at the expense of alliteration–alliteration that is already less regular than in other alliterative poems.

Diagram 5.1. Rhyming Syllables in *PE*

NB: The hyphen in front of the rhyming syllable(s) has been omitted due to limited space. Varying spellings that involve the final -*e* only are printed in bold face. The variations that include more than the final -*e* are underlined in addition to being in bold face. The Arabic number listed to the left of each horizontal row represents the line number within the cluster. The Arabic number at the top of each vertical row represents the cluster number.

	1	2	3	4	5	6	7	8	9	10	11	12	13	14	15	16	17	18	19	20
1	aye	ace	alez	**os**	**yʒt**	**ayse**	elle	we	ede	**aw**	yche	aue	ylde	**ene**	**echche**	alle	**yde**	**yʒe**	**ys**	ere
2	**ere**	euen	aynez	alle	ayned	yʒe	orde	**our**	**aye**	**eyny**	**arde**	**ente**	**ynne**	**ot**	yf	**one**	eued	atez	oun	**alte**
3	aye	ace	alez	**os**	**yʒte**	**oyse**	elle	we	ede	**owe**	yche	aue	ylde	**eene**	**eche**	alle	**yde**	**ye**	**yse**	ere
4	**ere**	euen	aynez	alle	ayned	yʒe	orde	**our**	**ay**	**ené**	**arde**	**ent**	**inne**	**ot**	yf	**one**	eued	atez	oun	**alte**
5	aye	ace	alez	**ose**	**yʒte**	**ayse**	elle	we	ede	**awe**	yche	aue	ylde	**ene**	**eche**	alle	**yde**	**ye**	**essse**	ere
6	**ere**	euen	aynez	alle	ayned	yʒe	orde	**our**	**ay**	**eny**	**arde**	**ent**	**ynne**	**ot**	yf	**on**	eued	atez	oun	**alte**
7	aye	ace	alez	**os**	**yʒte**	**ays**	elle	we	ede	**owe**	yche	aue	ylde	**ene**	**eche**	alle	**yed**	**ye**	**yse**	ere
8	**ure**	euen	aynez	alle	ayned	yʒe	orde	**our**	**ay**	**eny**	**arde**	**ente**	**ynne**	**ot**	yf	**one**	eued	atez	oun	**alte**
9	ere	euen	aynez	alle	ayned	yʒe	orde	**our**	**ay**	**eny**	**ard**	**ente**	**ynne**	**ot**	yf	**one**	eued	atez	oun	**alt**
10	ot	**ent**	ore	yʒt	er	**eme**	ysse	**y**	ate	ore	oghe	**yʒt**	**es**	em	esse	ote	**on**	one	**yte**	aye
11	ere	euen	aynez	alle	ayned	yʒe	orde	**or**	**ay**	**eny**	**arde**	**ente**	**ynne**	**oppe**	yf	**one**	eued	atez	oun	**alt**
12	ot	**ente**	ore	yʒt	er	**em**	ysse	**ye**	ate	ore	oghe	**yʒte**	**ez**	em	esse	ote	**ohn**	one	**yt**	aye
13	ange	ydez	yse	**ys**	**ente**	**ayly**	ope	**aye**	esse	o	ate	**as**	ere	elle	**yng**	ele	yʒt	ede	**ere**	**onc**
14	ele	ynde	ade	**ene**	**aye**	eue	on	**ace**	**yʒte**	ete	ere	**ylle**	**od**	**e**	**este**	oute	oun	**yʒt**	**asse**	**ayd**
15	ange	ydez	yse	**ys**	**ent**	**ayly**	ope	**ay**	esse	o	ate	**ace**	ere	elle	**ynge**	ele	yʒt	ede	**ere**	**onk**
16	ele	Ynde	ade	**ene**	**ay**	eue	on	**ace**	**yʒt**	ete	ere	**ylle**	**ode**	**e**	**este**	oute	oun	**yʒt**	**asse**	**ayed**
17	ange	ydez	yse	**ys**	**ente**	**ayle**	ope	**ay**	esse	o	ate	**ace**	ere	elle	**ynge**	ele	yʒt	ede	**ere**	**onc**
18	ele	ynde	ade	**ene**	**aye**	eue	on	**ace**	**yʒt**	ete	ere	**ylle**	**ode**	**é**	**este**	oute	oun	**yʒt**	**asse**	**ayde**
19	ange	ydez	yse	**yse**	**ente**	**ayl**	ope	**ay**	esse	o	ate	**ace**	ere	elle	**yng**	ele	yʒt	ede	**er**	**onk**
20	ele	ynde	ade	**en**	**aye**	eue	on	**ace**	**yʒte**	ete	ere	**ylle**	**ode**	**ye**	**est**	oute	oun	**yʒte**	**asse**	**ayde**
21	ele	ynde	ade	**ene**	**ay**	eue	on	**atz**	**yʒt**	ete	ere	**ille**	**ode**	**e**	**est**	oute	oun	**yʒte**	**as**	**ayd**
22	**ot**	**ente**	ore	yʒte	**ere**	eme	ysse	**y**	ate	ore	**oghe**	yʒt	es	em	es	ote	**on**	one	yt	**ay**
23	ele	ynde	ade	**ene**	**aye**	eue	on	**ace**	**yʒt**	ete	ere	**ylle**	**ode**	**y**	**este**	oute	oun	**yʒte**	**as**	**ayd**
24	**otte**	**ent**	ore	yʒte	**er**	eme	ysse	**ye**	ate	ore	**oʒe**	yʒt	es	em	es	ote	**ohn**	one	yt	**aye**
25	ede	ere	are	**yrle**	ose	ete	**ent**	yue	yne	**yfte**	**ent**	**ayn**	ure	ayn	ande	onde	emme	ete	oched	eme
26	**unne**	ete	onde	on	ef	yne	ate	yng	**os**	ykez	**yne**	yle	**ys**	olde	**o**	**akk**	ale	et	elle	**oun**
27	ede	ere	are	**erle**	ose	ete	**ente**	yue	yne	**yfte**	**ente**	**ayne**	ure	ayn	ande	onde	emme	ete	oched	eme
28	**unne**	ete	onde	on	ef	yne	ate	yng	**os**	ykez	**yne**	yle	**ys**	olde	**o**	**ake**	ale	et	elle	**one**
29	ede	ere	are	**erle**	ose	ete	**ente**	yue	yne	**yfte**	**ente**	**ayn**	ure	ayn	ande	onde	emme	ete	oched	eme
30	**unne**	ete	onde	on	ef	yne	ate	yng	**otz**	ykez	**yne**	yle	**ys**	olde	**o**	**ake**	ale	et	elle	**oun**
31	ede	ere	are	**erle**	ose	ete	**ente**	yue	yne	**yft**	**ente**	**ayn**	ure	ayn	ande	onde	emme	ete	oched	eme
32	**onne**	ete	onde	on	ef	yne	ate	yng	**os**	ykez	**yne**	yle	**éz**	olde	**o**	**ake**	ale	et	elle	**oun**
33	**onne**	ete	onde	on	ef	yne	ate	yng	**otz**	ykez	**ine**	yle	**ys**	olde	**oo**	**ake**	ale	et	elle	**oun**

	1	2	3	4	5	6	7	8	9	10	11	12	13	14	15	16	17	18	19	20
34	ot	ent	ore	yȝte	er	eme	ysse	yȝe	ate	ore	ow	yȝte	ez	em	esse	ote	on	one	yte	ay
35	onne	ete	onde	on	ef	yne	ate	yng	os	ykez	yne	yle	ys	olde	o	ake	ale	et	elle	oun
36	otte	ent	ore	yȝte	er	eme	ysse	ye	ate	ore	oghe	yȝte	ez	em	es	oote	ohn	one	yt	aye
37	oun	yse	aunt	emme	este	esse	yde	oule	onne	inne	ete	ome	ete	ye	arpe	ene	yt	yȝte	ise	ente
38	ene	erez	ere	ure	awez	o	ere	yst	oȝt	om	yt	it	é	on	ere	es	ent	ym	ent	euen
39	oun	yse	aunt	emme	este	esse	yde	aule	unne	ynne	ete	ome	ete	ye	arpe	ene	yt	yȝt	yse	ent
40	ene	erez	ere	ure	awez	o	ere	yste	oȝt	ome	yte	yet	é	on	ere	es	ent	ym	ent	yuen
41	oun	yse	aunt	emme	este	esse	yde	awle	onne	ynne	ete	om	ete	ye	arpe	ene	yȝt	yȝt	ys	ent
42	ene	erez	ere	ure	awez	o	ere	yste	oȝt	ome	yt	yed	é	on	er	ese	ent	ym	ent	yuen
43	oun	yse	aunt	emme	este	esse	yde	awle	unne	ynne	ete	ome	ete	yȝe	arpe	ene	yt	yȝt	yse	ente
44	ene	erez	ere	ure	awez	o	ere	yste	oȝte	um	yt	yed	e	on	ere	es	ente	ym	ente	yuen
45	ene	erez	ere	ure	awez	o	ere	yste	oȝte	om	yt	yed	é	on	ere	es	ent	ym	ent	iuen
46	ot	ent	ore	yȝt	er	eme	esse	yȝe	ate	ore	oghe	yȝt	ese	em	es	ote	on	one	yt	aye
47	ene	erez	ere	ure	awez	o	ere	yste	oȝte	om	yt	yed	é	on	ere	es	ent	ym	ent	yuen
48	ot	ent	ore	yȝt	er	eme	ysse	ye	ate	ore	oghe	yȝte	ez	em	es	ote	ohn	one	yt	aye
49	ennd	epe	ace	yse	ene	yte	ede	eue	onge	ert	elle	ede	ambe	ete	oynt	ylde	are	ayle	ene	aȝte
50	aȝt	yȝt	onte	ore	e	ype	age	ong	oun	able	ounde	ayed	yf	are	we	or	ayre	ure	ade	yin
51	enned	epe	ace	ece	ene	yte	ede	eue	onge	ert	elle	ede	ambe	ete	oynt	ylde	are	aly	ene	aȝte
52	aȝt	yȝt	onte	ore	e	ype	age	-	oun	able	ounde	ayde	yf	are	we	or	ayre	ure	ade	yin
53	enned	epe	ace	ece	ene	yte	ede	eue	onge	erte	elle	ede	ambe	ete	oynte	ylde	are	ayle	ene	aȝte
54	aȝt	yȝt	unt	ore	e	ype	age	onge	oun	able	ounde	ayed	yf	are	ue	or	ayre	ure	ade	yin
55	enned	epe	ace	yce	ene	yte	ede	eue	onge	erte	elle	ede	ambe	ete	oynt	ylde	are	ayle	ene	aȝte
56	aȝte	yȝt	unt	ore	e	ype	age	onge	oun	able	ounde	ayed	yf	are	we	or	ayre	ure	ade	yn
57	aȝt	yȝt	ount	ore	é	ype	age	onge	oun	able	ounde	ayde	yf	are	we	or	ayre	ure	ade	yn
58	ot	ente	ore	yȝte	ere	eme	ysse	yye	ate	ore	oȝ	yȝt	es	eme	esse	ote	on	one	yt	aye
59	aȝte	yȝt	ount	ore	e	ype	age	onge	oun	able	ounde	ayed	yf	are	we	our	ayre	ure	ade	yne
60	ot	ent	ore	yȝte	er	eme	ysse	é	ate	ore	ogh	yȝt	ez	em	es	ote	ohn	one	yt	ay
61															onc					
62															ose					
63															onc					
64															ose					
65															ong					
66															ose					
67															onc					
68															ose					
69															ose					
70															esse					
71															ose					
72															ese					

Diagram 5.2. The Cluster Structure of *PE*

Line #	B_1	B_2	B_3	B_4	Line #	B_1	B_2	B_3	B_4
1	B	B	B	a	37	C	B	B	a’’’
2	B	B	B	b	38	B	B	B	b’’’
3	B	B	B	a	39	B	B	B	a’’’
4	B	B	B	b	40	B	B	B	b’’’
5	B	B	B	a	41	B	B	B	a’’’
6	B	B	B	b	42	B	B	B	b’’’
7	B	B	B	a	43	B	B	B	a’’’
8	B	B	B	b	44	B	B	B	b’’’
9	B	B	B	b	45	B	B	B	b’’’
10	B	B	B	c	46	B	B	B	c
11	B	B	B	b	47	B	B	B	b’’’
12	B	B	B	C	48	B	B	B	C
13	C	B	B	a’	49	C	B	B	a’’’’
14	B	B	B	b’	50	B	B	B	b’’’’
15	B	B	B	a’	51	B	B	B	a’’’’
16	B	B	B	b’	52	B	B	B	b’’’’
17	B	B	B	a’	53	B	B	B	a’’’’
18	B	B	B	b’	54	B	B	B	b’’’’
19	B	B	B	a’	55	B	B	B	a’’’’
20	B	B	B	b’	56	B	B	B	b’’’’
21	B	B	B	b’	57	B	B	B	b’’’’
22	B	B	B	c	58	B	B	B	c
23	B	B	B	b’	59	B	B	B	b’’’’
24	B	B	B	C	60	B	B	B	C
25	C	B	B	a”		- - - - cluster boundary - - - -			
26	B	B	B	b”	61	C	B	B	a’’’’
27	B	B	B	a”	62	-	-	-	-
28	B	B	B	b”	63	-	-	-	-
29	B	B	B	a”	-				
30	B	B	B	b”	-				
31	B	B	B	a”	-				
32	B	B	B	b”					
33	B	B	B	b”					
34	B	B	B	c					
35	B	B	B	b”					
36	B	B	B	C					

Notes

1 Various terms have been used for the refrain word, including *concatenatio* (Røstvig 329), *key word* (Gardner 85), *link word* (Donner, "Grammatical" 322; Milroy 195), *linking word* (McGalliard 279), and *refrain word* (Andrew and Waldron 49).

2 Line 472 is missing, which makes the total line number 1,211.

3 The second stanza is used here because the first one is not in a complete rhyme; namely the second syllable of *synglure* in *PE* 8 is meant to rhyme with *clere* in *PE* 2, *pere* in *PE* 4, *were* in *PE* 6, and *daungere* in *PE* 11. Gollancz considers the word *synglure* a scribal error and emends it as *syng[u]l[e]re* (12). After this emendation, the first stanza holds a complete rhyme. Since this combination of *-ure* and *-ere* is not observed in other places, Gollancz's emendation can be considered reasonable. It is noteworthy, however, that the scribe made an error in the very first stanza of the poem if emendation is at all necessary for *PE* 8. As to the imperfect rhyme and scribal emendation, see Stanley "Rhymes," especially 35–38.

4 Occasional appearances of the line with only two alliterating beats have been recognized by other scholars. See Gardner 85 and Stanley, "*Pearl*" 160.

5 Andrew and Waldron, following Gollancz, emend the rhyming word of *PE* 702 as *cryed* whereas Vantuono reads it as *tryed*. Vantuono's reading creates identical rhyme between *PE* 702 and *PE* 707. There are only three occasions of identical rhyme in *Pearl*: *clere* in *PE* 735 and *PE* 737, *wale* in *PE* 1000 and *PE* 1007, and *wasse* in *PE* 1108 and *PE* 1112. Vantuono's emendation (*Pearl*) may not fully reflect the poet's intention since the poet is successful in achieving rhyme with different lexical items except for these three places.

6 Stanzas 82–86 form the seventeenth cluster. The *c* rhyme appears in the tenth and twelfth lines of each stanza, thus uniting these five stanzas.

7 One may conclude from this that the phonetic value of the word final *-e* had already been lost and that all the *-e*'s were never realized as a syllable. Since the idea about whether or not the word final *-e* could have formed a syllable affects the metrical structure of the entire line, any conclusion should be made through a careful investigation. The crucial fact is that the line endings could have been read in the same way despite the presence or absence of the final *-e*. As to the various types of *-e*'s, see Cable, *Tradition* 66–84.

8 Gollancz (12) emends the word *spennd* in *PE* 49 as *spenn[e]d*.

9 Rhyme proper is the rhyme in which the final vowel and consonant remain the same, as seen in examples of *great* and *bait*. Assonance is the rhyme on vowels as seen in *great* and *fail* whereas consonance maintains the same final consonant as in *great* and *meat*. As to various types of sound parallelism, see Fraser 63.

10 In this stanza, the poet makes a distinction between words that end with an *-e* and those that end without an *-e*. This may prove that the final *-e* was pronounced in order to differentiate it from a single consonant. The reader certainly could have used different pronunciation for these two groups, yet in actual performances these lines could have been read in the same manner despite the presence or absence of a final *-e*. To take into account several alternatives in actual reading seems to solve the problems that arise from the assumption that there should be only one authoritative reading. In Jakobson's terms, the reader could have applied several delivery designs to one verse design. See Chapter One and Jakobson, "Closing."

11 In the 1993 edition of *Princeton Encyclopedia of Poetry and Poetics*, Clark and Whiteall's

definition is replaced by Brogan's definition. The four distinctions in rhyme by Clark and Whiteall still provide useful classification.

12 *PE* 612, *PE* 624, and *PE* 636 are identical except for the spelling of the refrain word *innoghe*. *PE* 648 and *PE* 660 are composed of similar but not identical words as the first three examples.

13 McGalliard asserts that the refrain at the end of the stanza is not a mere dangling but produces cumulative emphasis to reinforce the significance of the refrain word. See McGalliard, especially 282.

14 This combination of *-ot* and *-oppe* (*blot* in *PE* 782, *not* in *PE* 784, *flot* in *PE* 786, *knot* in *PE* 788, *clot* in line *PE* 789, and *hyl-coppe* in *PE* 791) is the only occasion of inexact rhyme. This rhyme has been traditionally called assonance, in which a different consonant follows the rhyming vowel. In all the other places, *PE* maintains complete rhyme. See Diagram 5.1 for the list of all the rhymes.

15 OE includes Old English, Anglian, West Saxon, Old Anglian; OF includes Old French, Anglo-French, and Anglo-Norman; ON signifies Old Norse; Others include Latin, Dutch, Middle Dutch, Norwegian, Swedish, Icelandic, Medieval Latin, and Greek.

16 Because of the employment of both alliteration and rhyme in the same poem, the poet needs to consider multiple metrical constraints. Stanley explains the process of development from alliterative verse to rhyming verse as follows:

> The influence on English of Medieval Latin and, later, of Old French rhyming verse had the result that English versifiers could not escape rhymes and increasingly made use of rhymes instead of alliteration. ("Rhymes" 37)

The rhyme is not found in the other three poems of the same manuscript except for the bob and wheel of *G*. *PE* may be a result of the poet's innovative desire to create verse that rhymes in every line.

17 Contrary to Thomas's claim that *PE* is not an alliterative poem, Northup argues that it is "prevailingly alliterative" (338). Northup's calculation of stressed syllables that carry alliteration suggests thirty-two percent of the lines in *PE* without alliteration, which he believes as enough to make the poem alliterative. *PE* is composed in alliterative measure, though alliteration is "neither carefully sought after nor avoided" (Northup 340).

18 Stanza 89 may be an example to suggest that the poet regards words with the final *-e* and words without one having different metrical values. Since the poet avoids identical rhyme in *PE*, he must have expected that these two groups of rhyming words would be pronounced differently.

19 As Røstvig asserts, "in this carefully wrought poem such a sudden absence of overlapping must be deliberate" (328). Røstvig interprets the significance of numbers twelve and eight. If *PE* contains a considerable amount of number symbolism (Kean), Røstvig's assertion may be valid.

Chapter 6

Alliteration Techniques in Four Alliterative Poems in the MS Cotton Nero A. x

This chapter examines alliteration devices of the poems of the MS Cotton Nero A. x., namely *Pearl* (*PE*) *Cleanness* (*C*), *Patience* (*PT*), and *Sir Gawain and the Green Knight* (*G*). The first section explains various techniques in alliteration that reinforce the base pattern: excessive alliteration in all the stressed syllables of a line, additional alliteration by a liaison, alliteration in unstressed syllables, two sets of alliteration within a single line, and an identical alliterating sound stretching over several consecutive lines. These metrical phenomena prove that alliteration is not limited to the first three stressed syllables of the line but may appear in various places within the line often in an excessive manner. The second section explains possible combinations of consonants and consonant clusters in alliteration. It is one of the peculiarities of ME alliterative verse that different consonant clusters may alliterate with each other as long as the same consonant initiates them. About thirty-five percent of the lines of the four poems alliterate not in the identical consonant or consonant cluster but in combination of consonants and consonant clusters or in different consonant clusters. The third section reveals *secondary* alliteration in which the same sound is repeated in other than stem-initial positions. This subtle recurrence of the same sound offers a unique auditory equity among the syllables that are not considered related if a stem-initiating consonant only is taken into account. The term *secondary alliteration* will be used for the alliteration subtly reflected in other than stem-initiating consonants in order to differentiate it from *primary alliteration* discussed in the first and second sections. The explicit primary alliteration and the less conspicuous secondary alliteration prove that alliteration in the four poems is carefully manifested in all possible ways and achieves a highly-wrought effect and cohesion. Acknowledging secondary alliteration will increase the number of the *alliterating* syllables, especially in *PE* whose alliteration is less rigid than that of the other three poems. These phenomena prove that alliteration in ME alliterative verse is a complex system of sound reiteration in order to form aural homogeneity among the members of the metrical unit.

Alliteration of ME alliterative verse at a quick glance seems less systematic than that of OE verse, first due to less regular alliteration itself and second due to the freer treatment of stressed and unstressed syllables. As Waldron asserts, "it was the rhythmical flexibility and adaptability of the alliterative metre that enabled it to survive the syntactical changes between OE and ME" (*Gawain* 26). Flexibility and adaptability, nonetheless, imply that a larger number of complex variations and special deviations became permissible in order to adapt to various changes in alliterative meter. This chapter reveals various alliteration devices that are used in multiple ways in order to bring the intricate, elaborate enchaining of verbal echo.

Once again, the general rule of alliteration in ME alliterative verse is that the first three out of the four stressed syllables in the line alliterate. The line may be divided into two half-lines by a metrical pause called caesura. Each half-line contains two stressed syllables; however, there can be another stressed syllable, particularly in the first half-line, which may or may not alliterate. The first alliterating syllable in the second half-line plays a decisive role in establishing alliteration (Duggan, "Final *-e*") while the non-alliterating stressed syllable in the line-final position signals line closure. Thus, the basic alliteration pattern can be described as [aa/ax] for the four-beat line and [aaa/ax] or [xaa/ax] for the five-beat line.

6.1 Excessive Alliteration

The following lines represent the base alliteration pattern. Initial sounds that carry alliteration are italicized:

PE 811	For *s*ynne He *s*et Hym*s*elf in vayn,	[aaax]
C 1416	And *b*ougounz *b*usch *b*atered so þikke.	[aaax]
PT 81	Þis is a *m*eruayl *m*essage a *m*an for to preche	[aaax]
G 606	Þat watz *st*apled *st*ifly and *st*offed wythinne.	[aaax]

Several variations may be used in addition to this base pattern. First, all stressed syllables may alliterate:

PE 978	Bot *l*urked by *l*auncez so *l*ufly *l*eued,	[aaaa]
C 611	And as to *G*od þe *g*oodmon *g*os Hem a*g*aynez	[aaaa]
PT 88	And *l*yȝtly when I am *l*est He *l*etes me a*l*one.'	[aaaa]
G 437	And as *s*adly þe *s*egge hym in his *s*adel *s*ette	[aaaa]

Consecutive lines, each having alliteration in all stressed syllables, are found in *G* 2077–83. As pointed out by T. Turville-Petre, metrical tension in these lines is intense (*Revival* 131):

G 2077	Þay *b*oȝen bi *b*onkkez þer *b*oȝez ar *b*are;	[aaaa]
G 2078	Þay *cl*omben bi *cl*yffez þer *cl*engez þe *c*olde.	[aaaa]
G 2079	Þe *h*euen watz vp*h*alt, bot *v*gly þer*v*nder.	[aaaa]
G 2080	*M*ist *m*uged on þe *m*or, *m*alt on þe *m*ountez;	[aaaaa]
G 2081	Vch *h*ille hade a *h*atte, a myst-*h*akel *h*uge.	[aaaa]
G 2082	*Br*okez *b*yled and *br*eke bi *b*onkkez a*b*oute,	[aaaaa]
G 2083	*Sch*yre *sch*aterande on *sch*orez, þer þay doun *sch*owued.	[aaaa]

Alliteration does not necessarily appear in the first syllable of a word; the second syllable of a word may alliterate if stress falls on it. The following lines contain a word or two whose second syllable alliterates, which is underlined:

PE 686	<u>A*pro*che</u> he schal þat *pr*oper *p*yle–	[axaa]
C 959	Al <u>bi*r*olled</u> wyth þe *r*ayn, *r*ostted and brenned,	[aaax]
PT 169	Þenne <u>bi*sp*eke</u> þe *sp*akest, <u>di*sp*ayred</u> wel nere:	[aaax]
G 2248	*B*usk no more <u>de*b*ate</u> þen I þe *b*ede þenne	[aaax]

Another intricacy in sound correspondence involving alliteration is found in lines in which alliterating stressed syllables merge through a liaison of two adjacent syllables. Duggan and Turville-Petre name this *elision alliteration* (xix):

PE 233	Ho watz me *n*erre þe<u>*n a*unte</u> or *n*ece:	[xaaa]
G 356	Bot for as *m*uch as ȝe ar <u>*myn* e</u>m I a<u>*m* o</u>nly to prayse;	[aaax]
G 962	Þe twey<u>*ne y*</u>ȝen and þe *n*ase, þe *n*aked lyppez,	[aaax]

Alliteration may be found in an unstressed syllable in addition to stressed syllables. In the following examples, alliteration in unstressed syllables is also italicized:[1]

PE 190	*S*o *sm*oþe, *s*o *sm*al, *s*o *s*eme *sl*yȝt,	[aaaa]
C 1597	*A*nd *h*atz *a* *h*aþel *i*n þy *h*olde, *a*s *I* *h*af *h*erde *o*fte,	[aaaa]
PT 93	'Oure *S*yre *s*yttes,' he *s*ays, 'on *s*ege *s*o hyȝe	[aaax]
G 96	Oþer *s*um *s*egg hym bi*s*oȝt of *s*um *s*iker knyȝt	[aaax]

In these lines, the alliterating sound appears more than once as a constituent of unstressed syllables. When unstressed syllables alliterate in OE verse, Creed calls it *incidental alliteration* in contrast to *significant alliteration* that falls on stressed syllables (50). Yet such lines often appear in ME alliterative verse, for instance in *G*, which leads to the idea of the poet's deliberate intention. *PE* also presents many instances of alliteration in unstressed syllables, but in contrast to *G*, *PE* does not always maintain rigid alliteration in stressed syllables as Chapters Two, Three, and Four have explained. Alliteration in unstressed syllables in *PE* has a tendency of compensating weak alliteration in stressed syllables.

When the unstressed syllable that initiates the line carries the alliterating sound, this weak syllable plays a role in predicting the alliteration recurring in the stressed syllables that follow it. This has been often treated as a stressed syllable because of alliteration, which results in a reading that recognizes five stressed syllables per line instead of four:

PE 773	*O*uer *a*lle *o*þer so *h*yȝ þou clambe	[aaax] or [aaaax]
C 996	*F*or two *f*autes þat þe *f*ol watz *f*ounde in mistrauþe:	[aaax] or [aaaax]
PT 388	*B*oþe *b*urnes and *b*estes, *b*urdez and childer,	[aaax] or [aaaax]
G 50	*W*ith all þe *w*ele of þe *w*orlde þay *w*oned þer samen,	[aaax] or [aaaax]

One of the controversial issues in the study of ME verse is whether stress in certain word categories such as conjunctions and prepositions may be realized as metrical beats due to its alliterating initial sound.[2] The above examples prove that extra alliteration that such syllables carry emphasizes the homogeneity among the syllables of the line.

The identical alliterating sound sometimes continues over two or more consecutive lines, for example:

G 670 He *sp*erred þe *st*ed with þe *sp*urez and *spr*ong on his way
G 671 So *st*if þat þe *st*on-fyr *str*oke out þerafter.
G 672 Al þat *s*eȝ þat *s*emly *s*yked in hert
G 673 And *s*ayde *s*oþly al *s*ame *s*egges til oþer,

This repetition of the same alliterating sound over successive lines, called *running alliteration* (Schmidt, *Clerkly* 55) or *identical alliteration* (Oakden, *Alliterative* 233), does not occur often in all four poems, but is found occasionally in *G*.[3]

Another technique in excessive alliteration is found in lines that consist of two different sets of alliteration:

PE 363	If *r*apely I *r*aue, *sp*ornande in *sp*elle:	[aabb]
C 1720	*M*ade of *st*okkes and *st*onez þat neuer *st*yry *m*oȝt.	[abbba]
PT 213	He *o*ssed hym by vn*n*ynges þat þay *v*nder*n*omen	[abab]
G 335	And wyth a *c*ountenaunce *dr*yȝe he *dr*oȝ doun his *c*ote,	[abba]

Different terms have been used to designate two sets of alliteration in a line.[4] The term *double alliteration* may be the first choice to signify these (Waldron, *Gawain* 26), but this term has been somewhat confused among scholars of OE. Some (Bliss 12; Le Page 435) use it to designate alliteration in both stressed syllables within the first half-line while others (Kendall 7; Russom, *Old English Meter* 84) recognize double alliteration both in the first half-line and in the second half. In order to prevent confusion with the terms for OE versification, the term *duple alliteration* will be used in the present research to denote two sets of alliteration in a single verse line. Duple alliteration is specifically unique to *G*, appearing in about more than ten percent of its long alliterative lines.[5] Yet duple alliteration is not frequently found in the other three poems; the percentage of lines with duple alliteration is about seven in *PE*, and less than one in both *C* and *PT*.[6]

In OE verse, alliteration occurs in the identical consonant or the identical consonant cluster (Cassidy and Ringler 277). This practice is employed in ME alliterative verse as well, and the repetition of the same consonant cluster strengthens the link among the alliterating syllables:

PE 385	'In *bl*ysse I se þe *bl*yþely *bl*ent,	[axaa]
C 755	And *sp*are *sp*akly of *sp*yt in *sp*ace of My þewez,	[aaaax]
PT 186	*Sl*ypped vpon a *sl*oumbe-selepe, and *sl*oberande he routes.[7]	[aaax]

G 1339 Siþen *br*itned þay þe *br*est and *br*ayden hit in twynne. [aaax]

Table 6.1 summarizes alliteration that uses the identical consonant or consonant cluster throughout the line. Though variations of the same consonant such as *b*, *bl*, and *br* are listed together, this table intends to explain that each of these variations appears in all alliterating syllables but not in combination with other variations that start with the same sound:

Table 6.1. Consonants and Consonant Clusters Used for Exact Alliteration (*PE*, *C*, *PT*, *G*)[8]

PE (1,211 lines)	*C* (1,812 lines)	*PT* (531 lines)	*G* (2,025 lines)
b/bl/br	b/bl/br	b	b/br
c/ch/cl	c/ch/cl	c/ch	c/ch/cl
d	d/ dr	d	d/dr
f/ fl	f	f	f
g/gl/gr	g/gl/gr	g/gl/gr	g/gl/gr
ȝ	ȝ	-	ȝ
h	h	h	h
h & vowels	h & vowels	h & vowels	h & vowels
j	j	j	j
k	k	-	k/ kn
l	l	l	l
m	m	m	m
n	n	n	n
p/pl	p/pl/pr	p/pl/pr	p/pl/pr
q	q	q	q
r	r	r	r
s/sch/sl/sp	s/sc/sch/scr/sk	s/sc/sch/sl	s/sch/sl/sm
st/str/sw	sm/sp/st/str/sw	sp/st/str/sw	sn/sp/st/sw
t/tr	t	t/tr	t/tr
þ/þr	þ/þr	þ/þr	þ/þr
v	v	v	v
w/wr	w	w	w
-	-	-	y
vowels	vowels	vowels	vowels

Table 6.1 reveals that the consonant clusters that start with *b*, *c*, *d*, *f*, *g*, *p*, *s*, *t*, *þ*, and *w* are variable. Since each poem consists of a different number of lines,

generalizations should not be made instantaneously. It is evident, however, that consonant clusters that start with *s* are numerous in all four poems, and that *PT*, despite its short length (531 lines), has almost the same number of variants as the other three.

6.2 Possible Combinations of Consonants and Consonant Clusters

Each consonant cluster, such as *st*, *sp*, and *sc* (*sk*), is meant to alliterate only with itself in OE alliterative verse (Adams 37). This type of alliteration continued through ME alliterative poetry, as seen in Table 6.1. Alliteration in ME verse, however, may take place in a group of different consonant clusters; namely, consonants such as *c*, *f*, *g*, *p*, *s* and *t* are more likely to be combined with other consonants. Examples in which different consonant clusters alliterate are as follows:

PE 863	Vchonez *bl*ysse is *br*eme and *b*este,	[xaaa]
C 995	In a *st*onen *st*atue þat *s*alt *s*auor habbes,	[aaaax]
PT 429	Þe *s*oun of oure *S*ouerayn þen *sw*ey in his ere,	[aaax]
G 1536	*Gr*et is þe *g*ode *gl*e, and *g*omen to me huge,	[aaaax]

Table 6.2 lists possible combinations among different consonant clusters. The number indicates the occurrences of the combination in each poem:

Table 6.2. Variable Alliteration Combinations of Different Consonant Clusters (*PE*, *C*, *PT*, *G*)

	PE (1,211 lines)	*C* (1,812 liens)	*PT* (531 lines)	*G* (2,025 lines)
b/bl/br	45	99	26	125
c/k/q/cl/kl/cn/kn/cr/kr/xc	39	135	22	154
d/dr/dw	12	43	11	41
f/fl/fn/fr/ph/v	34	87	12	76

g/gl/gr/3/j/jh	48	51	19	87
h/hw	-	-	-	2
p/pl/pr	42	51	22	36
s/c/z/ch/sc/sk sck/scl/xc/sch schr/scr/skr skw/sl/sm/sn sp/spl/spr/xp st/str/sw	68	92	25	79
t/tr/tw/þ	14	29	10	40
þ/th/þr/þw	4	15	5	12
w/v/u/q/hw wh/wl/wr	32	52	30	50
Total	338 (27.9%)	654 (36.1%)	182 (34.3%)	702 (34.7%)

About thirty-five percent of the lines of *C*, *PT*, and *G* alliterate in combination of different consonant clusters. The relatively low percentage of *PE* reflects that its alliteration is not always regular. The variations with *c* and *s* are numerous while *b*, *f*, *g*, *p*, *t*, and *w* have a smaller number of variations. In order to supply different words for alliteration, the poet exerts his talent in a variety of words that start with the /k/ and /s/ sounds.

6.3 *Primary* and *Secondary* Alliteration within the Verse Line

The four poems sometimes contain a repetition of consonants, which is different from the repetition of word-initial sounds. This raises the question of whether or not such an unusual repetition is deliberate. The term *secondary alliteration* will be used hereafter to distinguish such a repetition from *primary alliteration*, which has been discussed in the first and second sections of this chapter. The words, *primary* and *secondary*, may not be the best terms, but secondary alliteration within the verse line can be tentatively classified into the following four categories.

The first category is found in lines whose fourth stressed syllable partly reflects primary alliteration. In this type, the second constituent of the consonant cluster that is used in primary alliteration reappears as the second constituent of the fourth unalliterating consonant cluster. In other words, the fourth unalliterating syllable is a consonant cluster whose second constituent is the non-initial constituent of the primary alliterating consonant cluster. If the symbol *A* is used for primary alliteration, *b* for secondary alliteration, and *x* for any unalliterating consonant, this pattern can be described as *A-A-Ab-xb*. In the following examples, primary alliteration is italicized while secondary alliteration is underlined:

PE 331 What seruez tresor bot *g*arez men *gr*ete,
C 310 A *c*ofer *cl*osed of tres, *cl*anlych planed.
PT 395 Al schal *cr*ye, for*cl*emmed, with alle oure *cl*ere strenþe;
G 337 Þen any *b*urne vpon *b*ench hade *br*oȝt hym to drynk

The repetition of the second constituent of the consonant cluster of primary alliteration is not very conspicuous, but it creates a certain bond among metrical beats.

The second category of secondary alliteration is found in lines whose fourth unalliterating stressed syllable begins with two consonants, the second of which is the sound of primary alliteration (*A-A-A-xA*):

PE 160 Mony *r*yal *r*ay con fro hit *r*ere.
C 1025 For *l*ay þeron a *l*ump of *l*ed, and hit on *l*oft fletez,
PT 188 Þer *R*agnel in his *r*akentes hym *r*ere of his dremes!
G 39 *R*ekenly of þe *R*ounde Table alle þo *r*ich breþer–

The third category is found in lines whose fourth stressed syllable starts with the second constituent of primary alliteration (*Ab-Ab-Ab-b*):

PE 111 *Sw*angeande *sw*ete þe water con *sw*epe,
C 1524 Neuer *st*euen hem a*st*el, so *st*oken is hor tonge.
PT 101 Then he *tr*on on þo *tr*es, and þay her *tr*amme ruchen,
G 1219 And de*pr*ece your *pr*ysoun and *pr*ay hym to ryse,

The fourth category is a type of alliteration in which two constituents of a consonant cluster are split between other stressed syllables (*A-Ab-A-b*). The sounds in boldface in the following examples are not considered alliterating if primary alliteration only is taken into consideration:

PE 103 Þe *f*yrre in þe *fr*yth, þe *f*eier con ryse
C 982 Ones ho *bl*uschet to þe *b*urȝe, *b*ot *b*od ho no lenger
PT 457 Þenne watz þe *g*ome so *gl*ad of his *g*ay logge,
G 523 He *dr*yues wyth *dr*oȝt þe *d*ust for to ryse,

Table 6.3 presents the occurrences of secondary alliteration in the four poems:

Table 6.3. Occurrences of Secondary Alliteration within the Verse Line (*PE*, *C*, *PT*, *G*)

	PE (1,211 lines)	*C* (1,812 liens)	*PT* (531 lines)	*G* (2,025 lines)
Category 1	25	31	6	38
Category 2	28	15	3	24
Category 3	21	3	5	6
Category 4	20	24	9	31
Total	94 (7.8%)	73 (4.0%)	23 (4.3%)	99 (4.9%)

Table 6.3 reveals that secondary alliteration in *PE* occurs more frequently than in the other three poems. This suggests that *PE*, though it does not achieve the basic alliteration in every line, supplies in a subtle manner as many alliterating syllables as possible. If secondary alliteration is recognized in a syllable that is not part of primary alliteration as seen in the following examples, it serves to link the *unalliterating* sound with primary alliteration:

PE 193 Perlez *p*yȝte of ryal *pr*ys [aaxa][9]
PE 268 And *b*usyez þe a*b*oute a raysoun *br*ef; [aaxa]

Acknowledging secondary alliteration enables the following lines to have another alliterating syllable as well:

PE 236 Enclynande *l*owe in wommon *l*ore, [xaxa]

PE 331 What seruez tresor bot *g*arez men *g*rete, [xxaa]

Finally, lines that have no alliterating syllables become somewhat alliterative if secondary alliteration is taken into account:

PE 280 My grete dystresse þou al todrawez. [xxxx]
PE 461 Ryȝt so is vch a Krysten sawle [xxxx]

The above lines are bound among their metrical beats by means of the repetition of *r*, especially if *r* is trilled.[10] By means of secondary alliteration, thus, an echo of primary alliteration is heard in the *unalliterating* syllable.

Secondary alliteration entails an interesting metrical phenomenon. Two constituents of a consonant cluster individually appear in other stressed syllables:

PE 785 Þe Lambes vyuez in *bl*ysse we *b*ene, [xxaa]
PE 813 For vus He lette Hym *fl*yȝe and *f*olde, [xxaa]

Fraser acknowledges Celtic influences in this type of alliteration while agreeing with his Welsh colleagues who consider it rather "crude and inept" (64). In looking for clues about this metrical phenomenon, I was led to the Welsh custom of *cynghanedd*, which is a complex system of sound correspondences (Lloyd and Brogan). Historically speaking, cynghanedd was highly developed in Welsh by the fourteenth century while the composition date of the poems of the *Pearl* manuscript is generally agreed to have been the last quarter of the fourteenth century. Comments by Vantuono (*Gawain* 230) and Osberg (*Gawain* xi) on Celtic influences on ME alliterative poems also support the possibility of contact with Celtic verse making.

Celtic influences are clearly detected in the linking of ME alliterative verse. Each stanza in *PE*, for instance, starts and ends with the identical refrain word.[11] Medary notes that stanza linking in English usually occurs in Northern poetry (245, 270) and that it is always accompanied by alliteration (263). This linking is found in a structure that is larger than a stanza; *PE*, *PT*, and *G* begin and end with an almost identical line:

PE 1 Perle plesaunte, to prynces paye
PE 1212 Ande precious perlez vnto His pay.

PT 1	Pacience is a poynt, þaȝ hit displese ofte.
PT 531	Þat pacience is a nobel poynt, þaȝ hit displese ofte.
G 1	Siþen þe sege and þe assaut watz sesed at Troye,
G 2525	After þe segge and þe asaute watz sesed at Troye,[12]

G presents two more cases of linking in the poem as a whole. One is the reference to Felix Brutus in *G* 13 and *G* 2524, and the other is the statement about King Arthur and the *aunter* in *G* 27 and *G* 2522. As A. Brown asserts, "the habit of beginning and ending a poem with the same word or words is Celtic and cannot be traced in early French or Latin poetry" (275).[13] Careful investigations must be made as to whether ME alliterative poets were familiar with Celtic conventions in verse making, but Huntsman-Mc, assuming Celtic influences in ME alliterative verse, contends that the alliterative poets of the West Midlands, who were often bilingual between Welsh and English, used a prosodic convention replicated from the ancient Celtic patterns. As Huntsman-Mc comments, "the prosodic complexity found in ME alliterative verse cannot reflect a spontaneous reinvention of a system that had taken the Celts many centuries to refine; instead it proves that their English-speaking creators knew, at least second-hand, the poetic traditions of their Welsh neighbors" (179).[14] When analyzing the Arthurian legend, knowledge of French materials is indispensable as Benson claims (110). However, it was quite possible for Celtic customs and forms to be absorbed into French or English traditions. Perhaps a cosmopolitan notion may be incorporated in the analysis of ME alliterative poems in order to acknowledge the wide-spread popularity of the Arthurian legend in many linguistic communities in the British isles as well as in the continent.[15]

It may not have been the poet's intention to knowingly imitate Celtic verse forms in ME alliterative verse. Yet it is difficult to assume that the instances of secondary alliteration in the poems analyzed in this chapter are never deliberate. Though secondary alliteration may be incidental, these lines attract not only the eye but also the ear if recited aloud. The poet probably smiled with satisfaction when he created these lines with secondary alliteration, adding his own modifications in contrast to the homogeneity of alliterative verse and proving his poetic potential. Secondary alliteration allows for a greater number of *alliterating* syllables in *PE* whereas it distributes alliteration in an excessive manner in *G*. If secondary alliteration is taken into account, *PE*, which contains a significant number of lines without (primary) alliteration, becomes even more "prevailingly alliterative" (Northup 338). The number of alliterating syllables changes as shown in Table 6.4 if secondary alliteration is counted:

Table 6.4. Increase of Alliterating Syllables via Secondary Alliteration (*PE*)

Increase of number of alliterating syllables per line if secondary alliteration is taken into account	Number of lines
0 → 2	30
0 → 3	1
2 → 3	32
2 → 4	6
3 → 4	11
Total	80

In total, eighty lines become more alliterative in *PE* via secondary alliteration, which is about 6.6% of the entire lines. Alliteration in *PE* is subtly achieved as a fragile decoration in other than normal metrical beats, and accordingly, the poet was justly proud of his poetic maneuvers as he "prefers elaboration to simplicity" (Benson 128).

Further investigation of secondary alliteration in other ME alliterative poems may suggest new aspects of controversial issues. In other words, compiling data on secondary alliteration in ME alliterative poems may reveal marked tendencies in certain poems or poets[16] and prove that alliteration is not a simple ornamental device. It may be at least assumed that alliteration in fourteenth-century alliterative verse, tolerating much more freedom, merges into a complex system, which is not a simple sound repetition like "rum, ram, ruf" (Chaucer).[17] Secondary alliteration could be positively utilized while prosodic complexities are far more intricate than have previously been considered. Alliteration in fourteenth-century alliterative verse, in this sense, is a metrical device that can structurally link the verse line within the prescribed metrical unit and add extra aural effect by sound repetition.

Notes

1 I do not imply that all alliterating syllables should receive stress. To say the least, the recurrence of the same sound in unstressed syllables, in addition to stressed syllables, creates special unity in rhythm.

2 Alliterating conjunctions and prepositions at the beginning of the line have been treated differently from scholar to scholar. Diverse arguments on how many metrical beats are realized in the following *G* line will be discussed in Chapter Thirteen:
G 1 Siþen þe sege and þe assaut watz sesed at Troye,
As discussed in Chapter Two, I assert that the ME alliterative line is flexible enough to produce four *or* five stressed syllables in a line according to the metrical necessity and stylistic variations. In other words, stress placement on an alliterating unstressed syllable is optional, depending upon the reader's choice in reading.

3 Running alliteration is observed in the following places of *G*. The alliteration sound appears between parentheses:
(i) Running alliteration in two adjacent lines (116 places in total):
3–4 (t), 20–21 (b), 26–27 (h & vowels), 39–40 (r), 87–88 (l), 110–11 (s), 141–42 (m), 184–85 (h & vowels), 213–14 (s), 235–36 (g), 270–71 (s), 303–04 (r), 325–26 (g), 331–32 (s), 394–95 (s), 398–99 (w), 418–19 (l), 424–25 (s), 516–17 (s), 540–41 (l), 556–57 (c), 577–78 (c), 583–84 (g), 592–93 (h), 597–98 (g), 609–10 (b), 651–52 (f), 682–83 (c), 694–95 (f), 716–17 (f), 720–21 (w), 724–25 (d), 768–69 (p), 788–89 (h), 822–23 (s), 852–53 (b), 854–55 (c), 888–89 (s), 892–93 (s), 908–09 (l), 920–21 (g), 948–49 (h & vowels), 952–53 (r), 974–75 (c), 1036–37 (g), 1039–40 (c), 1041–42 (b), 1162–63 (b), 1194–95 (l), 1198–99 (s), 1216–17 (b), 1250–51 (l), 1264–65 (f), 1269–70 (w), 1291–92 (s), 1294–95 (f), 1312–13 (m), 1330–31 (s), 1343–44 (r), 1345–46 (h & vowels), 1358–59 (f), 1374–75 (f), 1386–87 (w), 1436–37 (b), 1445–46 (h), 1481–82 (w), 1483–84 (c), 1492–93 (d), 1508–09 (w), 1514–15 (t), 1535–36 (g), 1540–41 (t), 1560–61 (l), 1563–64 (b), 1612–13 (h), 1614–15 (s), 1658–59 (s), 1675–76 (l), 1690–91 (m), 1727–28 (r), 1796–97 (s), 1825–26 (s), 1833–34 (b), 1846–47 (s), 1879–80 (s), 1882–83 (s), 1893–94 (l), 1898–99 (r), 1939–40 (ch), 1952–53 (m), 1962–63 (h), 1983–84 (m), 2006–07 (l), 2056–57 (h & vowels), 2060–61 (s), 2093–94 (s), 2118–19 (g), 2149–50 (g), 2178–79 (b), 2250–51 (g), 2259–60 (g), 2263–64 (d), 2265–66 (g), 2267–68 (s), 2287–88 (h & vowels), 2296–97 (h & vowels), 2319–20 (b), 2358–59 (w), 2379–80 (c), 2392–93 (p), 2395–96 (g), 2460–61 (g), 2466–67 (h & vowels), 2485–86 (b), 2514–15 (l), 2523–24 (b)
(ii) Running alliteration in three consecutive lines (ten places):
242–44 (s), 640–42 (f), 742–44 (h & vowels), 911–13 (p), 1438–40 (s), 1489–91 (c), 1609–11 (b), 2069–71 (b), 2312–14 (s), 2462–64 (h & vowels)
(iii) Running alliteration in four consecutive lines (one place):
670–73 (s)
Spearing, quoting lines from *The Alliterative Morte Arthure* (*MA*), considers the identical alliteration over several lines as "ostentatious virtuosity" (*Readings* 141). However, his statement, "neither Langland nor the *Gawain*-poet ever indulges in comparable displays" (*Readings* 141), contradicts these lines above if running alliteration of *G* is not as frequent as in *MA*. Chapters Ten and Eleven will discuss identical alliteration in ME alliterative verse in general and that specifically in *MA*, respectively.

4 For instance, [abba] is called *crossed alliteration* (Creed 50; Le Page 435) or *cross alliteration* (Kendall 7, 222). Osberg (*Gawain* xiv) uses the term *crossed alliteration* in a broader sense for [ab/ba] or [aa/bb]. Schmidt (*Clerkly* 274) calls the patterns [aaa/bb], [ab/ab], and [ab/ba] *double clustered*, *crossed*, and *chiastic* alliteration, respectively. Bliss calls the [ab/ab] pattern

extra alliteration, but he applies this term to occasions in which another set of alliteration coincidentally occurs (12). Northup's terms, *double* for [aabb], *transverse* for [abab], and *introverted* for [abba], may be the most adequate for ME alliterative verse if such details are needed for an argument of alliteration.

5 The percentage of duple alliteration in *G* possibly differs according to how one reads the line. Lines definitely in duple alliteration are about five percent of its long alliterative lines. The following line exemplifies such an occasion:

G 1223 'Ȝe schal not *r*ise of your *b*edde. I *r*ych yow *b*etter: [abab]

There are a significant number of lines in *G* that can produce duple alliteration if they are considered to contain five stressed syllables. The poet's intention is quite deliberate in such lines:

G 477 '*N*ow sir, *h*eng vp þin *a*x, þat hatz i*nn*ogh *h*ewen.' [abbab]

G 542 *M*ony *j*oylez for þat *j*entyle *j*apez þer *m*aden. [abbba]

In this way, the number of lines with duple alliteration increases if such lines are included.

6 As the lists of metrical complexity of the four poems presented in Chapters Two, Three, and Four indicate, two sets of alliteration are observed as a deviated form of the meter. Because *PE* does not always maintain alliteration as expected, lines with two sets of alliteration are not included in the list for it. In *C* and *PT*, lines with duple alliteration (designated as two sets of alliteration in the metrical complexity lists) are toward the end of the list, which implies that such lines may be perceived as a special case in these two poems. *G*, on the other hand, includes several types of duple alliteration, as shown in its metrical complexity list.

7 The word *selepe* appears to be the exact alliteration in *sl* to the eye, but actually it is not. The poet must have taken advantage of such visual illusion in this line.

8 Line 472 of *PE* is missing, which makes a total of 1,211 lines for data collection. Lines of *G* are alliterative long lines only; the rhymed bob and wheel are not included.

9 Square brackets present the primary alliteration only. In this line, all of the stressed syllables are connected with one another because the third one starts with the second constituent of a consonant cluster that appears in the fourth stressed syllable.

10 According to Vantuono, the ME *r* is "strongly trilled" whereas the OE *r* is "sounded as it is today in Modern English, but in initial position it may have been trilled" (*Texts* 8, 87). The trilled *r* must have overwhelmingly emphasized the recurrence of the same sound.

11 The following are the beginning and the end of the five initial stanzas of *PE* that form the first cluster. Each stanza of *PE* consists of twelve lines:

PE 1 Perle plesaunte, to prynces paye
PE 12 Of þat pryuy perle withouten **spot**.
PE 13 Syþen in þat **spote** hit fro me sprange,
PE 24 My priuy perle withouten **spotte**.
PE 25 Þat **spot** of spysez mot nedez sprede,
PE 36 Of þat precios perle wythouten **spotte**.
PE 37 To þat **spot** þat I in speche expoun
PE 48 My precious perle wythouten **spot**.
PE 49 Bifore þat **spot** my honde I spennd
PE 60 On þat precios perle withouten **spot**.

PE 61 Fro **spot** my spyryt þer sprang in space;
See Chapters Four and Five for the refrain word and the cluster structure in detail.

12 This is the last long alliterative line of *G*. Five rhymed lines (the bob and the wheel) directly follow this line to conclude the entire poem.

13 For an example of this verse form in Irish poetry, refer to Hyde 414. Also see Dunn and Brogan.

14 Donaldson contends that the poet obtained the plot of *G* from a French poet, or he may have "heard it recited in English–perhaps even in Welsh–in his own country" ("View Points" 98). Fox claims that the Gawain poet lived in southeast Cheshire or in northeast Staffordshire, which is near north Wales (5). If that is the case, chances are likely that the poet did encounter various verse forms that were different from his own tradition.

15 Arthur, who lived in the sixth century, became a legend when his name became famous beyond his country of origin, Ireland and Wales. Zesmer explains the process in which the Arthurian legend was spread as follows (96):

> After his literary fame crossed the Channel into France, Arthur returned to his own land as a literary hero at the beginning of the thirteenth century–for the first time in an English version, Layamon's *Brut*. Later in the thirteenth century he recrossed into Germany and soon established himself as the common literary property of much of the Western world.

16 Elaboration in alliteration to create recursive network of sound repetition has been proved in various ME alliterative poems, for instance, by Vaughan on *MA*, by Peters and Green on *Piers Plowman*, and by Burrow on *St Erkenwald*. Examining alliteration not only on the word-initial sounds but also on the entire phonological make-up of the line will supply evidence to reinforce the poetic significance of alliteration that has been argued by Blake ("Rhythmical"), Lawton ("Introduction"), Matonis ("Poetry"), and Oakden (*Alliterative*).

17 But trusteth wel, I am a Southren man,
I kan nat geeste 'rum, ram, ruf,' by lettre, (*The Canterbury Tales* X. 42–43)

Chapter 7

Langland's Alliteration Techniques in *Piers Plowman*

William Langland's *Piers Plowman* (*PP*) uses different rules of alliterative meter from the other poems that were popular in the fourteenth century. *PP*, extant in three texts-A, B, and C, is known as one of the major works of ME alliterative verse along with the poems of the MS. Cotton Nero A. x., that Chapters Two to Six have considered, but its meter is different from that of other ME alliterative poems. This chapter illuminates various alliteration techniques that Langland uses in *PP*, and argues that the poet uses his own sense and creates his own style of sound repetition in alliterative meter. Alliteration may be excessive even in unstressed syllables while it is obscure elsewhere, which creates a distinct contrast to other poems. Identical alliteration in consecutive lines also reflects the poet's innovative challenges, but the frequent appearance of lines in Latin interrupts alliterative meter. In other words, alliteration in *PP* is intense in some lines, but may be obscure or missing in others.

The unique points of Langland's meter include the special use of lines with five beats, the significant role of metrically subordinated stress, alliteration in weak stress especially in the second half-line, and the compensation of weak alliteration in places other than metrical beats. The first section of this chapter observes significant points within the verse line of *PP* whereas the second section considers the sound network that alliteration creates over several consecutive lines. The horizontal sound repetition within the verse line and the vertical sound repetition beyond the line unit create special aural effects in *PP*. Alliteration may be extreme in such lines, but it is often obscured in other lines, which gives an impression that the meter deviates from the alliteration norm. As explained in previous chapters, vigorous efforts have been made in defining ME alliterative meter as well as in describing the alliteration of various poems (Burrow; Cable, *Tradition*; Lawton, “Unity”; Matonis, “Poetry”; Oakden, *Alliterative*; Sapora). The alliteration of *PP* has not yet been comprehensively studied. Like the other poets, Langland is not always obedient to the base pattern of alliterative meter. Certain poems such as *The Alliterative Morte Arthure* (*MA*) and *Sir Gawain and the Green Knight* (*G*) are known to use excessive alliteration in multiple ways. The meter of *PP*, however, does not seem to be as rigid as the meters of other poems because its alliteration is subtle and sometimes disappears. Metrical phenomena in *PP* still arouse interests because Langland’s innovative challenges are certainly detected through a careful examination.

7.1 Alliteration within the Verse Line

The first passage of the B-Text illuminates how alliteration appears in the base pattern and how it deviates from it. Sounds that carry alliteration are italicized. The line number is identified as *PPB* P.1, signifying the first line of the Prologue of the B-Text. Lines in the regular pattern are marked as [aaax]. Lines that do not hold the basic pattern are not specially marked here:

PPB P.1	In a *s*omer *s*eson, whan *s*ofte was þe *s*onne,	
PPB P.2	I*sh*oop me into *shr*oudes as I a *sh*eep were,	[aaax]
PPB P.3	In *h*abite as an *h*eremite vn*h*oly of werkes,	[aaax]
PPB P.4	*W*ente *w*ide in þis *w*orld *w*ondres to here.	
PPB P.5	Ac on a *M*ay *m*orwenynge on *M*aluerne Hilles	[aaax]
PPB P.6	Me bi*f*el a *f*erly, of *f*airye me þoȝte.	[aaax]
PPB P.7	I was *w*ery [of] *w*andred and *w*ente me to reste	[aaax]
PPB P.8	Vnder a *br*ood *b*ank by a *b*ournes syde;	[aaax]
PPB P.9	And as I *l*ay and *l*enede and *l*oked on þe watres,	[aaax]
PPB P.10	I *sl*ombred into a *sl*epyng, it *sw*eyed so murye.	[aaax]
PPB P.11	Thanne gan [*me*] to *m*eten a *m*erueillous sweuene–	
PPB P.12	That I *w*as in a *w*ildernesse, *w*iste I neuere where.	
PPB P.13	As I bi*h*eeld into þe *e*est an *h*eiȝ to þe sonne,	[aaax]
PPB P.14	I seiȝ a *t*our on a *t*oft *tr*ieliche ymaked,	
PPB P.15	A *d*eep *d*ale byneþe, a *d*ongeon þerinne,	[aaax]
PPB P.16	Wiþ *d*epe *d*iches and *d*erke and *dr*edfulle of siȝte.	
PPB P.17	A *f*air *f*eeld ful of *f*olk *f*ond I þer bitwene–	

PPB P.18	Of alle *m*anere of *m*en, þe *m*eene and þe riche,	[aaax]
PPB P.19	*W*erchynge and *w*andrynge as þe *w*orld askeþ.	[aaax]

As demonstrated above, the base pattern constantly appears. However, lines whose alliteration patterns are not indicated, such as *PPB* P.4, *PPB* P.11, and *PPB* P.12, provoke different deviations from the norm. *PPB* P.1, for instance, alliterates in all of the beats, initiating the entire poem with a significant repetition of the same /s/ sound and emphasizing alliterative rhythm. The repetition of /s/ is further reinforced in *PPB* P.2 since the alliteration occurs in /ʃ /. In OE alliterative verse, the same consonant cluster only may alliterate. This practice continues in ME alliterative verse as well, though it is no longer the only rule for alliterating consonant clusters. The repetition of the same consonant cluster strengthens the link among the alliterating syllables. The following are the examples used in Chapter Six:

PE 385	'In *bl*ysse I se þe *bl*yþely *bl*ent,	[axaa]
C 755	And *sp*are *sp*akly of *sp*yt in *sp*ace of My þewez,	[aaaax]
PT 186	*Sl*ypped vpon a *sl*oumbe-selepe, and *sl*oberande he routes.	[aaax]
G 1339	Siþen *br*itned þay þe *br*est and *br*ayden hit in twynne.	[aaax]

In ME alliterative verse, however, this constraint can be ignored, and alliteration can occur among the clusters that are initiated by the same consonant. In other words, alliteration can be realized in a consonant cluster and a single consonant, as observed in *PPB* P.8, *PPB* P.10, *PPB* P.14, and *PPB* P.16. Examples from the four poems examined in Chapter Six, in which a consonant cluster alliterates with other clusters and a single consonant, are as follows:

PE 863	Vchonez *bl*ysse is *br*eme and *b*este,	[xaaa]
C 995	In a *st*onen *st*atue þat *s*alt *s*auor habbes,	[aaaax]
PT 429	Þe *s*oun of oure *S*ouerayn þen *sw*ey in his ere,	[aaax]
G 1536	*Gr*et is þe *g*ode *gl*e, and *g*omen to me huge,	[aaaax]

The line may contain five beats as seen in *PPB* P.4. Since the first four beats alliterate, a reading that realizes five beats with the [aaaax] alliteration pattern may be legitimate. *PPB* P.16 and *PPB* P.17 may be in the same pattern because they both contain four syllables that may be stressed and start with the same

/d/ and /f/, respectively. Five-beat readings are legitimate in *PP* as in other ME alliterative poems, but *PPB* P.16 and *PPB* P.17 can also be read in four-beat meter if the reader wishes to maintain the four-beat meter in successive lines. This flexibility in the number of beats per line is one of the special points of ME alliterative meter, which is applicable to *PP* as well.

Monosyllabic adjectives[1] are considered metrically subordinated to the noun that follows them. These short adjectives could be unstressed in recitation, as explained in Chapter Two. Since the adjectives, *depe* in *PPB* P.16 and *fair* in *PPB* P.17, are short and do not add significant meaning, they may be realized as a weak syllable in reading. The following scansions demonstrate two possible readings. The places where metrical beats may fall are indicated with an accent mark:

PPB P.16-a	Wiþ *d*epe *d*íches and *d*érke and *dr*édfulle of síȝte.	[aaax]
PPB P.16-b	Wiþ *d*épe *d*íches and *d*érke and *dr*édfulle of síȝte.	[aaaax]
PPB P.17-a	A *f*air *f*éeld ful of *f*ólk *f*ónd I þer bitwéne–	[aaax]
PPB P.17-b	A *f*áir *f*éeld ful of *f*ólk *f*ónd I þer bitwéne–	[aaaax]

In both *PPB* P.16 and *PPB* P.17, the two adjectives satisfy the alliteration requirement, and the two readings result in the alliteration patterns that are quite common. There are occasions, however, in which the adjective does not satisfy the alliteration requirement, which suggests that the four-beat reading may be favorable. For example, *alle* in *PPB* P.18 is not likely to receive metrical stress, even though it may do so in other lines:

PPB P.18	Of alle *m*anere of *m*en, þe *m*eene and þe riche,	[aaax]

It should be noted that there are many instances in which short adjectives are more likely to be stressed and alliterate. The same adjective *depe* in *PPB* P.15, for example, should not be treated as metrically subordinated stress because the line will not have the minimum number of beats and because the word *bynepe*, the only word left for another metrical beat, is not a very good candidate to receive metrical stress. Another example is *grete* in line 20 of Passus III of the A-Text. Metrically subordinated stress will not be realized in *grete*:

PPA III.20	Of here *g*rete *g*oodnesse, and *g*af hem ichone	[aaax]

The significant point regarding the role of short adjectives in alliterative meter is that they can be either stressed or unstressed, depending upon the metrical context and the reader's preference. It is this flexibility that has made English verse unique since the ME period (Halle and Keyser, *English Stress* 101–09). The collocation of an alliterating adjective and a non-alliterating noun raises the question as to which plays a more decisive role, alliteration or metrical subordination, in determining the positions of metrical beats. Such a syntactic unit is common in *PP* as observed in other ME alliterative poems.

Another point of interest regarding the meter of *PP* is that weak stress may be realized as metrical beats because of alliteration. *Me* in *PPB* P.11 and *was* in *PPB* P.12 do not appear to be alliterating beats. Since there are no other legitimate candidates in these lines that can be stressed and may alliterate, these words, usually unstressed, may be considered to alliterate so that the line can form the basic [aaax] pattern:

PPB P.11	Thanne gan [*m*e] to *m*eten a *m*erueillous sweuene–	[aaax]
PPB P.12	That I *w*as in a *w*ildernesse, *w*iste I neuere where.	[aaax]

In other ME alliterative poems, such words as *me* and *was* are not likely to act as metrical beats, especially if the line contains excessive alliteration. In *MA* and *G*, for example, it is not very necessary for the reader to wonder where alliteration falls within the line because the verse line usually contains syllables that will form more than four metrical beats. In *PP*, on the other hand, special emphasis should be placed on certain words for the sake of alliteration.

Lines that are flexible between four-beat and five-beat readings are observed also in *PP*:

PE 773	Ouer *a*lle *o*þer so *h*yȝ þou clambe	[aaax] or [aaaax]
C 996	*F*or two *f*autes þat þe *f*ol watz *f*ounde in mistrauþe:	[aaax] or [aaaax]
PT 388	Boþe *b*urnes and *b*estes, *b*urdez and childer,	[aaax] or [aaaax]
G 50	*W*ith all þe *w*ele of þe *w*orlde þay *w*oned þer samen,	[aaax] or [aaaax]

An interesting phenomenon occurs in *PP* regarding alliterating weak syllables. That is, the unstressed syllable at the beginning of the second half-line alliterates while no alliterating beats are found in the second half-line. In such a condition, the role that this alliterating weak syllable plays is different from the unalliterating weak stress. In the following examples, the second half-line does not have any alliterating syllables except for the initial prepositions and conjunctions such as *for*, *by*, and *but*. This phenomenon, not frequent in other poems, is notable in *PP*:

PPA I.56	Þanne I *fr*aynide hire *f*aire, *f*or Him þat hire made,
PPB I.58	Thanne I *fr*ayned hire *f*aire, *f*or Hym þat hire made,
PPC I.54	Y *fr*aynede her *f*ayr tho, *f*or Hym þat here made,
PPA II.92	Ȝe shuln a*b*igge *b*oþe, *b*e God þat me made!
PPB II.128	Ye shul a*b*iggen it *b*oþe, *b*y God þat me made!
PPC II.141	Ȝe shall a*b*yggen hit *b*othe, *b*ut ȝe amende þe sonner.

The reading that does not realize a metrical beat in *for*, *by*, or *but* results in the alliteration pattern [aaxx]. Since this pattern is not impossible in *PP*, the reader may interpret the alliteration pattern in that way. Stressing these weak syllables will inevitably produce the line with five beats, which again is possible in all the ME alliterative poems. Langland does not fully satisfy the alliteration requirement in these lines, but tries to echo it in parts other than legitimate metrical beats. Words, such as *by*, *for*, *siþen*, and *with*, are often used at the beginning of the second half-line in order to reflect the alliteration of the entire line. In the following examples, the C-Text amends alliteration in a more regular way, though the other two texts do not have any alliterating beats in the second half except for the word *so*:

PPA V.22	Ac I shal *s*eiȝe as I *s*aiȝ, *s*o me God helpe,	[aaxx] or [aaaxx]
PPB V.22	Ac I shal *s*eye as I *s*auȝ, *s*o me God helpe,	[aaxx] or [aaaxx]
PPC V.124	Ac Y shal *s*ey as Y *s*ayh, *sl*epynge as hit were,	[aaax]

7.2 Alliteration in Consecutive Lines

Section One has focused on alliteration within the verse line because an analysis of meter begins with the examination of the verse line. While investigating various ME alliterative poems, I have found that sound repetition often prevails over several consecutive lines in *PP*, as well as in other poems. The identical alliterating sound sometimes continues over two or more consecutive lines, as seen in *PPB* P.15 and *PPB* P.16 in the initial passage of the Prologue. The consecutive alliteration was first noted by Oakden while various scholars have acknowledged excessive sound repetition over consecutive lines, especially in *MA* (Hamel; Oakden, *Alliterative*; Vaughan). The duality in sound repetition, namely the horizontal sound repetition within the line and the vertical sound repetition beyond the line, intensifies the repetitive mode of alliterative meter.

Below are several examples of consecutive alliteration in *PP*. The alliteration is italicized within the line, and given between slashes after each line when necessary. The sound that is used in vertical alliteration will be underlined in other examples later:

PPA III.205	Takiþ *m*ede of here *m*aistris, as þei *m*owe accorde.	/m/
PPA III.206	*B*eggeris for here *b*idding *b*iddiþ *m*en *m*ede;	/b/ & /m/?
PPA III.207	*M*ynstralis for here *m*erþe *m*ede þei asken.	/m/
PPA III.208	Þe Kyng haþ *m*ede of his *m*en to *m*ake pes in londe.	/m/

PPA III.206 above seems to interrupt the consecutive alliteration, but it contains the consecutive alliteration sound in *men* and *mede* if not as the main alliteration sound. The sound weaving over several consecutive lines creates another type of sound repetition beyond the line unit. Alliteration in consecutive lines may be classified into the following five types:

Type 1 Consecutive alliteration over several lines
Type 2 Same alliteration in every other line
Type 3 The final beat of a line predicting the alliteration of the line that immediately follows it
Type 4 The final beat of a line reflecting the alliteration of the previous line
Type 5 The same sound initiating the final beats of two consecutive lines

Type 1 Consecutive alliteration over several lines:
The same alliteration takes place in consecutive lines in this type. Consecutive alliteration can extend to three, four, or even more lines. If consecutive alliteration recurs, it produces a significant sound effect. The following passage contains two occasions of consecutive alliteration in the same /p/ sound, which creates continued repetition:

PPA V.12	And *p*reyede þe *p*eple haue *p*ite on hemselue,	/p/

PPA V.13	And *pr*ouide þat þise *p*estilences was for *p*ur synne,	/p/
PPA V.14	And þe *s*outhwest wynd on *S*atirday at eue	
PPA V.15	Was a*p*ertly for *pr*ide and for no *p*oynt ellis.	/p/
PPA V.16	*P*iries and *pl*umtres wern *p*uffid to þe erþe	/p/

Identical alliteration in consecutive lines, along with the alliterating pattern within a given line, extends the homogeneity of sound over a group of lines. Sound repetition beyond the line highlights the alliterating words in a larger framework and intensifies the expected rhythm. The "percussive effect" of alliterative verse (Prior 13) is notable in such a cluster of lines, which reveals the aesthetic effect the poet achieves by using alliterative meter.

Type 2 Same alliteration in every other line:
In this type of vertical alliteration, alliteration does not occur in the line that immediately follows, but occurs a line later. This does not give a clear sense of continuity as the first type does, but the echo of the same sound remains in close vicinity:

PPA V.233	And wiþ þe *r*esidue and þe *r*emenaunt, be þe *R*oode of Chestre,	/r/
PPA V.234	I will *s*eke treuþe er I *s*e Rome!'	
PPA V.235	*R*obert þe *r*obbour on *R*eddite lokide,	/r/
PPB II.81	To *b*akbite and to *b*osten and *b*ere fals witnesse,	/b/
PPB II.82	To *sc*orne and to *sc*olde and *scl*aundre to make,	
PPB II.83	Vn*b*uxome and *b*olde to *br*eke þe ten hestes.	/b/

The same alliteration in every other line occurs three times in the following passage:

PPB I.132	Mowe be *s*iker þat hire *s*oule shul wende to heuene,	/s/
PPB I.133	Ther *Tr*euþe is in *Tr*initee and *tr*oneþ hem alle.	/t/
PPB I.134	Forþi I *s*eye, as I *s*eyde er, by *s*iȝte of þise textes–	/s/
PPB I.135	Whan alle *tr*esors arn *tr*ied, *Tr*uþe is þe beste.	/t/
PPB I.136	*L*ereþ it þ[u]s *l*ewed men, for *l*ettred it knoweþ–	
PPB I.137	That *Tr*euþe is *tr*esor þe *tr*ieste on erþe.'	/t/

The sense of repetition increases when the same sound initiates the unalliterating line-final beats as seen in lines below. *PPB* III.298 and *PPB* III.300 alliterate on /l/ and both of them end with a stressed syllable that starts with /r/:

PPB III.298	And ouer *l*ordes *l*awes [*l*ord]eþ þe reaumes.	/l/
PPB III.299	Ac *k*ynde loue shal *c*ome ȝit and *C*onscience togideres	
PPB III.300	And make of *l*awe a *l*aborer; swich *l*oue shal arise	/l/

Type 3 The final beat of a line predicting the alliteration of the line that immediately follows it:
In ME alliterative verse, the final unalliterating beat often predicts the alliteration of the line that immediately follows it. In other words, the stressed syllable that does not play any role in alliteration in the line to which it belongs, in fact, ties it to its follower. The following is such an example of two adjacent lines:

PPA V.220	And *b*eet þiself on þe *br*est, and *b*idde Hym of grace,	
PPA V.221	For is no *g*ilt here so *gr*et þat His *g*oodnesse nis more'.	/g/

The final beat of *PPB* II.158 and that of *PPB* II.159 predict the alliteration of *PPB* II.160:

PPB II.158	Thanne was *F*alsnesse *f*ayn and *F*auel as bliþe,	
PPB II.159	And feten *s*omone alle þe *s*egges in *sh*ires aboute,	
PPB II.160	And *b*ad hem alle be *b*own, *b*eggers and oþere,	/b/

Prediction occurs three times in a row among the following four lines:

PPB II.195	I wolde be *wr*oken of þo *wr*ecches þat *w*ercheþ so *i*lle,	
PPB II.196	And doon hem *h*ange by þe *h*als and *a*lle þat hem maynteneþ.	/h/ & vowels
PPB II.197	Shal neuere *m*an of þis *m*olde *m*eynprise þe leeste,	/m/
PPB II.198	But riȝt as þe *l*awe *l*oke[þ], *l*at falle on hem alle!'	/l/

The following lines also contain three cases of prediction, which are underlined:

PPA II.31	I may no *l*engere *l*ette, *L*ord I þe bekenne–	
PPA II.32	And be*c*ome a good man, for any *c*oueitise, I rede.'	/k/

PPA II.33	Alle þe *r*iche *r*etenaunce þat *r*egniþ wiþ False	/r/
PPA II.34	Were *b*eden to þe *br*idale on *b*oþe two sides.	
PPA II.35	Sire *S*ymonye is of*s*ent to a*s*ele þe chartres	/s/

Type 4 The final beat of a line reflecting the alliteration of the previous line: This is an opposing phenomenon to Type 3. The final beat of a line echoes the alliteration of the previous line, as seen in the following lines:

PPC I.24	And *dr*ynke þat *d*oth the good–ac *dr*ynke nat out of tyme.	/d/
PPC I.25	*L*o, *L*oot in his *l*yue, thorw *l*ikerous drynke,	

The /s/ alliteration in line 151 of Passus V of the A-Text is echoed twice in a row in the line-final beats of the two lines that follow it:

PPA V.151	And *s*iþen I wile be *sh*riuen, and *s*ynne no more.’	/s/
PPA V.152	‘I haue *g*ood ale, *g*ossib,’ quaþ heo; ‘*Gl*otoun, wilt þou assaie?’	
PPA V.153	‘*H*ast þou,’ quaþ *h*e, ‘any *h*ote spices?’	

Type 4 occurs three times in succession in the following passage:

PPB I.195	Manye *c*uratours *k*epen hem *cl*ene of hire bodies;	/k/
PPB I.196	Thei ben a*c*ombred wiþ *c*oueitise, þei *k*onne noȝt out *cr*epe,	
PPB I.197	So *h*arde haþ *a*uarice y*h*asped hem togideres.	/h/ & vowels
PPB I.198	And þat is no *tr*uþe of þe *Tr*inite, but *tr*icherie of helle,	
PPB I.199	And *l*ernynge to *l*ewed men þe *l*atter to deele.	/l/
PPB I.200	For [þise ben *w*ordes] *wr*iten in þe [Euaungelie]:	

Type 5 The same sound initiating the final beats of two consecutive lines: This phenomenon may not be considered an alliteration, but a certain sense of repetition pervades when the final beats of two consecutive lines start with the same sound. The following two lines alliterate on different sounds, but contain the same /b/ in their final beat:

PPC V.145	And be *st*ewardus of ȝoure *st*edes til ȝe be *st*ewed bettere.
PPC V.146	‘*Gr*egory þe *gr*ete clerk *g*art wryte in bokes

In the following passage, each line alliterates on a different sound, but the final beat of each line starts with the same /s/ sound:

PPA V.58	*E*nuye wiþ *h*euy *h*erte *a*skide aftir shrifte
PPA V.59	And *c*arfulliche his *c*ope [*c*omsiþ] he to shewe.
PPA V.60	He was as *p*ale as a *p*elet, in þe *p*alesie he semide;
PPA V.61	He was *cl*oþid in a *c*aurymaury–I *c*ouþe it nouȝt descryue–
PPA V.62	A *k*ertil and a *c*ourtepy, a *kn*yf be his side;
PPA V.63	Of a *fr*eris *fr*okke were þe *f*oresleuys.
PPA V.64	As a *l*ek þat hadde *l*eyn *l*onge in þe sonne,

Lines in which these five types are combined present a complex sound network. For instance, consecutive lines remain in the same alliteration sound while their final beats start with the same sound. This is the combination of Type 1 and Type 5. The repetition is emphasized in all the metrical beats:

PPB I.207	Whan alle *tr*esors ben *tr*ied, *tr*euþe is þe beste.	/t/
PPB I.208	'Now haue I *t*old þee what *tr*uþe is–þat no *tr*esor is bettre–	/t/

Another combination is the one in which the final beat of a line predicts the alliteration of the line that follows while the alliteration of the first line is reflected in the final beat of the second line. In other words, Type 3 and Type 4 are combined within two consecutive lines:

PPA IV.30	And *r*ombide forþ wiþ *R*esoun *r*iȝt to þe Kinge.	/r/
PPA IV.31	*C*urteisliche þe *K*ing þanne *c*om aȝen Resoun,	/k/

Two consecutive lines alliterating in all stressed syllables are also a result of the combination of Types 3 and 4:

PPA IV.79	'*B*etere is þat *b*oote *b*ale adoun *br*inge	/b/
PPA IV.80	Þanne *b*ale be *b*et, and *b*ote neuere þe *b*etere!'	/b/

Combination of Types 3 and 4 among three lines is commonly found. In the following lines, the alliteration of *PPA* III.113 is predicted in *PPA* III.112 while the alliteration of *PPA* III.113 is echoed in the final beat of *PPA* III.114.

Furthermore, the alliteration of *PPA* III.113 is repeated again in the line-final beat of *PPA* III.114:

PPA III.112	She *m*akiþ *m*en *m*ysdo *m*anye score tymes.	/m/
PPA III.113	In *t*rist of hire *t*resour she *t*eniþ ful manye;	/t/
PPA III.114	*W*yues and *w*ydewis *w*antonnesse she techiþ,	

The sound repetition is more conspicuous when Type 4 is followed by Type 3, as seen in the following lines of *PPA*. Since *PPA* I.122 and *PPA* I.124 alliterate on the same /t/, Type 2 is also found here:

PPA I.122	Þere *T*reuþe is in *T*rinite and *t*roniþ hem alle.	/t/
PPA I.123	Forþi I *s*eye as I *s*eide er, be *s*iȝte of þise textis–	
PPA I.124	Whanne alle *t*resours arn *t*riȝed, *T*reuþe is þe beste.	/t/

Several combinations of different types increase sound effects that each line already has from its own alliteration. In the following passage of *PPB*, /m/ and /l/ are interwoven. These two sounds in beats are underlined:

PPB II.31	And haþ yeuen me *M*ercy to *m*arie wiþ myselue;	/m/
PPB II.32	And what *m*an be *m*erciful and *l*eelly me *l*oue	/m/ & /l/
PPB II.33	Shal be my *l*ord and I his *l*eef in þe *h*eiȝe *h*euene;	/l/ & /h/
PPB II.34	And what *m*an takeþ *M*ede, myn heed dar I legge	/m/
PPB II.35	That he shal *l*ese for hire *l*oue a *l*ippe of Caritatis.	/l/
PPB II.36	'How *c*onstrueþ Dauid þe *K*yng of men þat [*c*acch]eþ Mede,	/k/ & /m/
PPB II.37	And *m*en of þis *m*oolde þat *m*ayntenep truþe,	/m/

7.3 Idiosyncrasies of Langland's Alliteration

Two points are special about vertical alliteration of *PP*. The first is the frequent alliteration on the combination of /h/ and vowels. Many lines contain vertical alliteration using this combination, though examples that alliterate on more distinctive consonants have been given in the previous section. The most frequent sound pattern used in vertical alliteration of *PP*, however, is the one that involves /h/ and vowels. The role that these weak sounds play in alliterative meter is crucial.

The second point is the disruption of vertical alliteration by lines in the Latin language. Certain Latin lines may appear alliterative, but most of them do not alliterate. This interrupts the alliterative rhythm, highlighting a completely different prosody that Latin lines introduce. Lines in Latin separate the passage that precedes them and the passage that follows them, which eliminates the possibility of vertical alliteration. This may help prevent boredom if such an interpretation justifies the use of lines in Latin in alliterative meter.

Alliterative verse is essentially an extreme mode of reiteration; the recurrence of the same sound is redundant if "redundancy is a characteristic of all verse" (Burrow 128). As Cureton asserts, "linguistic rhythms are best defined as recursive hierarchies of prominence" ("Rhythm" 105). The five types of vertical alliteration may not be the primary requirement of ME alliterative verse, but certainly contributes to a recursive hierarchy of beats within a larger metrical unit. The frequency of lines that utilize the five types of vertical alliteration and their mixture suggests the poets' deliberate intention to create excessive sound repetition. One element that distinguishes *PP* from the other ME alliterative poems is the clear contrast between the part that employs alliteration in an overt manner and the part in which alliteration is obscure or even disappears.

Notes

1 Adjectives such as *longe*, *gude*, and *riche* can be both monosyllabic and disyllabic. Adjectives that are considered here are those that can be read in one syllable if the final *-e* is considered silent.

Chapter 8

Excessive Sound Repetition in Three Minor ME Alliterative Poems Composed in the Thirteen-Line Stanza

Certain ME alliterative poems employ a special stanza format along with end rhyme. This chapter considers three such poems composed in the thirteen-line stanza. These poems use rhyme in addition to alliteration, which considerably complicates the meter. Chapters Four and Five have observed that the meter of *Pearl* (*PE*) is different from that of the other poems because it utilizes both alliteration and rhyme. The authors of the thirteen-line stanza poems compose their work in a framework that is even more rigid than that of *PE*: fixed rhyme, excessive alliteration, several constraints in the line-final metrical beat, and the inflexible stanza structure. They must also have an abundant stock of vocabulary in order to fulfill the multiple metrical constraints. Clashing of two stressed syllables in a row and consecutive monosyllabic words are frequently observed. These techniques reinforce the repetitious rhythm, creating a clear contrast to ordinary speech rhythm.

The three ME alliterative poems in the thirteen-line stanza examined in this chapter are *A Pistel of Susan* (*PS*), *Somer Soneday* (*SS*), and *The Three Dead Kings* (*K*). The repetitive mode of ME alliterative verse is attested in search for their metrical template. The thirteen-line stanza is the most favored framework among ME alliterative poems if they employ any stanza form (T. Turville-Petre, "Summer Sunday"). The number of poems written in this stanza form proves how popular it was for alliterative poets. Examples are found in both England and Scotland from the late fourteenth century to the late sixteenth century.[1] Alliterative meter itself is repetitious. End-rhyme complicates the verse line structure even more, and creates an inundate amount of sound repetition.

8.1 Alliteration and Rhyme in the Thirteen-Line Stanza

The following is the sixth stanza of *PS* that exemplifies the stanza structure and the relationship between alliteration and rhyme. The rhyme is underlined whereas its overall pattern appears immediately after each line. Metrical beat positions are indicated by a stress mark, and the alliteration pattern follows in brackets:

PS 66	In þe séson of sómere with Síbell and Jáne	*a*	[aaax]
PS 67	Heo gréiþed hire til hire gárdin þat gró wed so gréne,	*b*	[aaaa]
PS 68	Þer lýndes and lórers were lént vpon láne,	*a*	[aaaa]
PS 69	Þe sáuyne and sýpres, sélcouþ to séne,	*b*	[aaaa]
PS 70	Þe pálme and þe póplere, þe pírie, þe pláne,	*a*	[aaaa]
PS 71	Þe júnipere jéntel, jónyng bitwéne,	*b*	[aaax]
PS 72	Þe róse rágged on rýs, ríchest in ráne,	*a*	[aaaaa]
PS 73	Iþéuwed with þéþorn thríuand to séne,	*b*	[aaax]
PS 74	So tíht.	*c*	
PS 75	Þer wéore pópejayes prést,	*d*	[xaa]
PS 76	Níhtyngáles vppon nést,	*d*	[axa]
PS 77	Blíþe bríddes o þe bést,	*d*	[aaa]
PS 78	In blóssoms so bríht.	*c*	[aa]

The first eight lines rhyme in the *abababab* pattern while the remaining five lines rhyme in *cdddc*. The first eight lines, commonly called long alliterative lines, contain four metrical beats. The final several lines are called the wheel while the very short line consisting of one metrical beat is called the bob. *Sir Gawain and the Green Knight* (*G*) has the one-line bob and the four-line wheel at the end of each stanza, though the number of long alliterative lines is not fixed. The first three lines of the wheel in the above stanza of *PS*, namely *PS* 75, *PS* 76, and *PS* 77, contain three stressed syllables and may alliterate. The final line consists of two metrical beats. If the subscript number is used to represent the number of metrical beats per verse line, the overall structure of the stanza can be summarized as $abababab_4c_1ddd_3c_2$. *PS* and *SS* are composed in this metrical template.

This complex meter has several unique points. First, the long alliterative lines may contain excessive alliteration. Five out of eight lines in the sixth stanza of *PS*, namely *PS* 67, *PS* 68, *PS* 69, *PS* 70, and *PS* 72, alliterate in all metrical beats. This is a common phenomenon in *K* as well. *SS* favors immoderate alliteration, and almost all the lines in it alliterate in every metrical beat. The following is the long alliterative lines of the third stanza of *SS*:

SS 27	So pássede I þe pás príuely to pléye	/p/	[aaaa]
SS 28	And férde forþ in þat fríth fólk for to fýnde,	/f/	[aaaa]
SS 29	Láwly lónge I lústnede and vnder lówe láy,	/l/	[aaaaa]
SS 30	Þat I ne hérde hond, hórn, húnte, hért ne hýnde.	/h/	[aaaaa]
SS 31	So wýde I wálkede þat I wax wéry of þe wéy;	/w/	[aaaa]
SS 32	Þanne lés I my láyk and lénede vnder lýnde,	/l/	[aaaa]
SS 33	And als I sát beside I sáy, sóþ for to séy,	/s/	[aaaa]
SS 34	A wífman wiþ a wónder whel wéue with þe wýnde,	/w/	[aaaa]

In recitation, the repetition of the same alliteration sound tires one's mouth. If all beats alliterate in every line, the line may feel like a tongue twister. The poets who employ this complex framework enthusiastically present an array of words whose first sound is identical. Their success as alliterative poets largely depends on their ability to find a group of words alliterating on the same sound and rhyming with words in adjacent lines.

End-rhyme also demands rich vocabulary since each line has to end with the identical combination of a vowel and a consonant or consonant cluster. Though alliteration may sometimes deviate and the line may not hold alliteration in all the possible positions, end-rhyme never fails to appear at the end of each line. The verse line, in which rhyme is a crucial device, is not the original verse form that the English language favored. The stress-timed nature of Germanic languages is fully utilized in alliterative meter but not necessarily in end-rhyme (Freeborn 146). For certain ME alliterative poets, alliteration is not enough as foregrounding rhythm. Adding rhyme to alliteration is an innovation used to introduce foreign elements. In *PS*, *SS*, and *K*, each stanza never fails to contain end-rhyme in every line, but slight variations exist, as observed in the following six groups:

(i) The final *-e* is sometimes absent in rhyme:
riche-liche-dich-sich (*PS* 1, *PS* 3, *PS* 5, *PS* 7)
playe-aye-day-say (*PS* 28, *PS* 30, *PS* 32, *PS* 34)

coupe-ȝoupe-mouþ-souþ (*PS* 249, *PS* 251, *PS* 253, *PS* 255)
come-kyngdom (*SS* 79, *SS* 80)
beholde-bolde-itolde-wold (*K* 14, *K* 16, *K* 18, *K* 20)
wyn-myn-inne-kyn (*K* 27, *K* 29, *K* 31, *K* 33)
wane-man-an-can (*K* 28, *K* 30, *K* 32, *K* 34)
fewe-ischeue-lew-bewe (*K* 40, *K* 42, *K* 44, *K* 46)
fow-chow-loue-blow (*K* 41, *K* 43, *K* 45, *K* 47)
iwys-kysse-amys (*K* 100, *K* 102, *K* 103)
masse-was-allas (*K* 139, *K* 141, *K* 142)

(ii) Different spellings are used for the same rhyme group:
eyre-feire-mayre-piere (*PS* 15, *PS* 17, *PS* 19, *PS* 21)
play-awai-say-Kai (*PS* 53, *PS* 55, *PS* 57, *PS* 59)
wyre-fyre-schire (*PS* 192, *PS* 193, *PS* 194)
arayed-reneyed-leyed-paied (*PS* 196, *PS* 198, *PS* 200, *PS* 202)
tyne-prine-fine-dine (*PS* 340, *PS* 342, *PS* 344, *PS* 346)
pleye-lay-wey-sey (*SS* 27, *SS* 29, *SS* 31, *SS* 33)
mayn-seyn (*SS* 61, *SS* 65)
gay-wey-lay-may (*SS* 67, *SS* 69, *SS* 71, *SS* 73)
kyng-sweting-ring (*SS* 96, *SS* 97, *SS* 98)
roune-howne-adoun-toun (*SS* 108, *SS* 110, *SS* 112, *SS* 114)
wyn-myn-inne-kyn (*K* 27, *K* 29, *K* 31, *K* 33)
beholdis-coldis-woldis-foldus (*K* 79, *K* 81, *K* 83, *K* 85)
heldis-kelddus-weldus-feldus (*K* 80, *K* 82, *K* 84, *K* 86)
fynden-lynden-byndon-wyndon (*K* 92, *K* 94, *K* 96, *K* 98)
fondon-Londen-bondon-wondon (K 93, *K* 95, *K* 97, *K* 99)

(iii) The length of vowels is sometimes ignored:
rede-weede (*PS* 22, *PS* 26)
nere-rere-here-peere (*PS* 27, *PS* 29, *PS* 31, *PS* 33)
lees-pres (*PS* 113, *PS* 117)
feete-swete-mete (*PS* 257, *PS* 258, *PS* 259)
foode-blode-stode (*PS* 283, *PS* 284, *PS* 285)
sere-apere-steere-vnclere (*PS* 300, *PS* 302, *PS* 304, *PS* 306)
seene-bideene-bene (*PS* 309, *PS* 310, *PS* 311)
hende-weende-strende-leende (*PS* 119, *PS* 121, *PS* 123, *PS* 125)
feere-lorere (*PS* 139, *PS* 143)
keuercheue-preue-greue-lecue (*PS* 158, *PS* 160, *PS* 162, *PS* 164)

knes-glees-tres-lees (*PS* 352, *PS* 354, *PS* 356, *PS* 358)

(iv) Different consonants are used:

siht-miht-hiht-briȝt (*PS* 313, *PS* 315, *PS* 317, *PS* 319)
fewe-ischeue-lew-bewe (*K* 40, *K* 42, *K* 44, *K* 46)
fow-chow-loue-blow (*K* 41, *K* 43, *K* 45, *K* 47)

(v) A single consonant is equivalent to two consonants:

Juwesse-fresse-sese-chese (*PS* 41, *PS* 43, *PS* 45, *PS* 47)
heldis-kelddus-weldus-feldus (*K* 80, *K* 82, *K* 84, *K* 86)
iwys-kysse-amys (*K* 100, *K* 102, *K* 103)
masse-was-allas (*K* 139, *K* 141, *K* 142)

(vi) End-rhyme is not quite achieved:

hored-rored-Lord-acorde (*PS* 339, *PS* 341, *PS* 343, *PS* 345)
flyȝtte-sitte (*SS* 85, *SS* 86)
knyth-myȝth (*SS* 100, *SS* 102)
sout-browth-rout-nawth (*SS* 109, *SS* 111, *SS* 113, *SS* 115)

The sound weaving in *K* is the most remarkable among the three poems analyzed here. Its rhyme pattern is *abababab*$_4$*cdccd*$_3$, which is slightly different from that of *PS* and *SS*. The *K* poet expresses a craving for excessive alliteration as the other two do. Especially striking is his sound play in alliteration. The thirteen lines, not only fulfilling the rhyme requirement, alliterate in the pattern of *aabbccddddxee* throughout the entire poem. The first eight lines usually contain four metrical beats, and a pair of lines alliterate on the same sound. The last five lines usually contain three metrical beats with consecutive alliteration in the seventh, eighth, ninth, and tenth lines, and another consecutive alliteration appears in the twelfth and thirteenth lines. The fifth stanza of *K* exemplifies the complex sound repetition that alliteration and rhyme create within the thirteen lines:

		alliteration	rhyme
K 53	The furst kyng he had care, his hert ourcast,	/k/=*a*	*a*
K 54	Fore he knew þe cros of þe cloþ þat couerd þe cyst;	/k/=*a*	*b*
K 55	Forþ wold not his fole bot fnyrtyd ful fast,	/f/=*b*	*a*
K 56	His fayre fawkun fore ferd he fel to his fyst:	/f/=*b*	*b*
K 57	'Now al my gladchip is gone, I grue and am agast	/g/=*c*	*a*
K 58	Of þre gostis ful grym þat gare me be gryst,	/g/=*c*	*b*
K 59	Fore oft haue I walkon be wodys and be wast,	/w/=*d*	*a*

K 60	Bot was me neuer so wo in þis word þat Y wyst.	/w/=*d*	*b*
K 61	So wo was me neuer I wene,	/w/=*d*	*c*
K 62	My wit is away oþer wane;	/w/=*d*	*d*
K 63	Certis sone hit wil be sene	x	*c*
K 64	Our tounyng wil turne vs to tene,	/t/=*e*	*c*
K 65	Fore tytle I trow we bene tane.'	/t/=*e*	*d*

Each line is connected with its neighboring lines by means of alliteration and rhyme.

Another distinctive point of *K* is that the two alternating rhyme sounds, designated as *a/b* and *c/d* in scansion, are in an unusual similarity. Table 8.1 below is the list of rhyme sounds in all the stanzas of *K*:

Table 8.1. Rhyme Patterns in *K*

Stanza #	*a/b*	*c/d*
1	*-yȝt / -oȝt*	*-ow / -ew*
2	*-olde /-elde*	*-are / -ere*
3	*-yn / -an*	*-yst / -est*
4	*-ew / -ow*	*-yde / -ede*
5	*-ast / -yst*	*-ene / -ane*
6	*-yȝt / -aȝt*	*-ow / -ew*
7	*-oldis / -eldis*	*-are / -ore*
8	*-yndon / -ondon*	*-ys / -as*
9	*-ere / -are*	*-yus / -eus*
10	*-ene / -yne*	*-ome / -yme*
11	*-yde / -ade*	*-asse / -osse*

The alternating rhyme sounds are similar with each other and intricately interwoven. They are identical except for their initial vowel. In the first stanza, for instance, repetition of analogous syllables, such as *-yȝt* and *-oȝt* in the first eight lines, produces strong unity among the eight lines concerned, and the remaining five lines are in another unity under the repetition of *-ow* and *-ew*. The alliteration is in a complex pattern, which suggests that the poet needs to consider several requirements within the verse line. Since rhyme includes the syllable nucleus but alliteration does not, the rhythmic foregrounding by the consonance in rhyme presents an unusual sense of unity among the thirteen lines. As Fabb asserts, the inclusion of the syllable nucleus "gives rhyme a greater acoustic prominence and hence enables it to stay in memory for longer" (*Linguistics* 122).

Neither *PS* nor *SS* employs this perplexing rhyme, but the complex rhyme sometimes results in a repetition of the same rhyme sound. For instance, the *a* and *d* rhyme sounds are identical in the seventeenth stanza of *PS*, which are underlined below:

PS 209 ‘Þorwout þe pomeri we passed us to play,
PS 210 Of preiere and of penaunce was vre purpose.
PS 211 Heo com with two maidens dressed þat day,
PS 212 In riche robes arayed, red as þe rose.
PS 213 Wylyliche heo wyled hir wenches away
PS 214 And comaunded hem kenely þe ȝates to close.
PS 215 Heo eode to a ȝong mon in a valay;
PS 216 Þe semblaunt of Susan wolde no mon suppose,
PS 217 For soþ!
PS 218 Be þis cause þat we say,
PS 219 Heo wyled hir wenches away;
PS 220 Þis word we witnesse for ay,
PS 221 Wiþ tonge and wiþ toþ.

Seven out of thirteen lines rhyme on -*ay* in this stanza, which is another piece of evidence that the poet is eager to show his potential in verbal play.

8.2 Distinctive Features Due to Rigid Alliteration and Rhyme

One significant feature that the complex meters of the three poems in the thirteen-line stanza present is the level stress that the line end frequently receives due to alliteration and rhyme. For instance, the following lines end with a single word that receives stress in two places:

PS 16 Lóuelich and lílie-whit, of þat lýnáge,
PS 41 Al for géntrise and jóye of þat Júwésse,
PS 136 And vnder this lórere bén vr lémmóne?
PS 161 Þo seid þes lóselles alóude to þe ládí:
PS 163 And léyn with þi lémon in avóutrí,
PS 210 Of préiere and of pénaunce was vre púrpóse.

PS 250	'I wís I wráþþed þe neuere, at my wítánd,
SS 92	He léyde his lég opon líþ at his líkýng,
SS 94	He wénde al þe wórld were at his wéldýng

T. Turville-Petre explains that level stress occurs when a final disyllabic word alliterates on the first syllable and rhymes on the second (*Poetry* 121). There are no such occasions in *K*, but the line-final position is a common place for two stressed syllables in a row in *K*, as well as in *PS* and *SS*:

K 2	I saw a brýmlyche bóre to a báy bróȝt,
K 45	Hadyn lóst þe lýp and þe lýuer seþyn þai were láyd lóue.
K 82	So doþ þe knýf ore þe kýe þat þe knóc kélddus
K 84[2]	Oure Lórd wyss vs þe redé wáy þat al þe wórd wéldus!
K 105	That oþer bódy bégan a ful brým bére:

ME alliterative poems tend to place two stressed syllables without any intervening unstressed syllable at the line end. In other words, two metrical beats and an implied offbeat between them can be a device to signal the line end. Table 8.2 compares occurrences of the implied offbeat in various ME alliterative poems. The positions of metrical beats within the line are numbered from zero to four as B_0 to B_4. The number of lines analyzed from each poem is between parentheses:

Table 8.2. Occurrences of the Implied Offbeat in Various ME Alliterative Poems[3] (Twelve Poems)

		Between B_0 and B_1	Between B_1 and B_2	Between B_2 and B_3	Between B_3 and B_4
A	(1,000 lines)	12	30	40	132
AG	(661 lines)	1	2	6	19
C	(1,000 lines)	34	45	61	117
E	(352 lines)	5	7	15	29
G	(900 lines)	34	26	58	102
J	(1,000 lines)	28	35	78	158
MA	(1,009 lines)	5	8	10	39
PE	(1,211 lines)	0	17	11	29
PPB	(1,000 lines)	18	34	42	65
PT	(531 lines)	15	9	24	65
T	(1,000 lines)	2	0	30	165
W	(503 lines)	1	2	6	24

The three poems written in the thirteen-line stanza contain the implied offbeat in each position as listed in Table 8.3:

Table 8.3. Occurrences of the Implied Offbeat in the Thirteen-Line Stanza Poems (*PS*, *SS*, *K*)

	Between B_0 and B_1	Between B_1 and B_2	Between B_2 and B_3	Between B_3 and B_4
PS (364 lines)	1	5	14	21
SS (133 lines)	0	1	4	5
K (143 lines)	1	2	5	6

Table 8.3 supports the idea that clashing of two stressed syllables is more likely to occur toward the line end in ME alliterative poems. Because of an absence of any unstressed syllables before the final beat, the rhythm of the line slows down toward the end of the line. This slow tempo is reinforced even more by rhyme. Quoting Hogg and McCully, Cable contends that zero syllables, which are realized as pauses in actual speech or equated with lengthening phenomena, are not desirable except for the phrase-final position ("Clashing" 21). The two metrical beats without any offbeat in between inevitably emphasize the alliteration and the rhyme at the line conclusion. They serve as a domain-end marker by lengthening the boundary between them (McCully, "Domain-End" 46).

The final unique point of the thirteen-line stanza poems is that line-final words tend to be monosyllabic. In the fifth stanza of *PS*, for example, most of the words that form metrical beats and alliterate line-initially and line-medially are polysyllabic. Words that include metrical beats are underlined while the metrical beats in monosyllabic words are in boldface:

PS 53 Whon þeos perlous prestes perceyued hire **play**,
PS 54 Þo **þouȝte** þe wrecches to bewile þat worly in **wone**;
PS 55 Heore wittes wel waiwordes þei wrethen awai
PS 56 And turned fro his teching þat **teeld** is in **trone**;
PS 57 For **siht** of here souerayn, soþli to say,
PS 58 Heore hor heuedes fro heuene þei **hid** apon **one**.
PS 59 Þei **cauȝt** for heor couetyse þe cursyng of **Kai**,
PS 60 For riȝtwys jugement recordet þei **none**,
PS 61 Þey **two**.
PS 62 Euery **day** bi **day**

PS 63	In þe pomeri þei **play**,
PS 64	Whiles þei mihte Susan assay
PS 65	To worchen hire **wo**.

Out of thirty-one metrical beats that do not fall in the line-final position, only six are monosyllabic (*þouȝte*, *teeld*, *siht*, *hid*, *cauȝt*, *day*). On the contrary, eleven out of thirteen line-final words are monosyllabic. This is because stress must be placed in the line-final syllable for the sake of rhyme. The percentage of polysyllabic words at the line end is about twenty-two percent in *PS*, seventeen in *SS*, and twenty in *K*. In other words, around eighty percent of the lines end with a monosyllabic word in the three poems. This exhibits an interesting complementary distribution between monosyllabic words and polysyllabic words according to the place where they appear.

8.3 Mobile Stress via Two Different Stress Systems

Keyser asserts that two stress systems were in operation in the English language during the inundation of French words after the Norman Conquest (354–55). The poet could have switched between the native Germanic stress assignment and the newly adapted Romance pattern, depending upon how the line should end. As discussed in Chapter Five, the etymological make-up of line-terminal words in *PE* and *G* summarized in Table 5.1 proves that words of a certain origin tend to appear in a certain metrical position.[4] In other words, Romance polysyllabic words are favored line-initially and line-medially, but the line-final position tends to contain OE origin words that are typically monosyllabic. The poets who composed their works in the thirteen-line stanza were also aware of mobile stress in words, and took advantage of the two stress rules, Romance and Germanic, so that the stress would fall in a desired manner at the line closure.

A question arises as to why ME poets are so enthusiastic in pursuing this complex form of word play. The metrical template that they use in order to link the lines within the stanza is so demanding and challenging that they manipulate abundant vocabulary and technical skills to fulfill it. They have to supply words that accomplish both the sequential alternation between stressed and unstressed syllables within the line and the sequential alternation between alliteration and rhyme within the stanza. The tension that the metrical foreground creates against the ordinary language is strong and intense.

Furniss and Bath assert that the ultimate goal of verbal art is to defamiliarize ordinary language. Along with extraordinary figurative language and different viewpoints, poetic art utilizes various devices to reorganize sounds and produce an unfamiliar form. Furniss and Bath comment, "The pronunciation should be made difficult through the 'roughing' effects achieved by the repetition of identical sounds (rhyme, alliteration, and so on), and poetic rhythm should avoid the potentially lulling effect of regular prose rhythms by 'disordering' rhythm" (86). The repetitious rhythm of ME alliterative meter along with the end-rhyme is an extreme case of defamiliarized language. The thirteen-line stanza poems achieve a deliberate form of defamiliarized language within their rigid meters.

Notes

1 Examples are *Dispute Between Mary and the Cross* (two different versions, one in Vernon MS. fol. 315b, col. 3 and another in Royal MS. 18 A 10, leaf 126b.) and *The Quatrefoil of Love*. All these three are composed in the rhyme pattern of *abababab cdddc*. Among fifty-five poems by John Audelay extant in a unique manuscript, Douce 302, Bodleian Library, nine are written in the thirteen-line stanza with the following rhyme patterns:

#1	*ababbabacdddc*
#2	*ababbcbcdeeed*
#3	*ababbcbcdeeed*
#11	*ababbcbcdeeed*
#15	*ababbcbcdeeed*
#16	*ababbcbcdeeed*
#18	*ababbcbcdeeed*
#54	*ababababcdccd*
#55	*ababbcbcdeeed*

Oakden (*Alliterative*) offers a detailed explanation on the stanza in ME alliterative verse in Chapter 10 while T. Turville-Petre's appendix is a comprehensive list of the poems and dramas composed in the thirteen-line stanza in England and Scotland ("Summer Sunday" 12–14).

2 The accent mark over the final syllable of the word *redé* is original in the text, and is not meant for a metrical beat.

3 The full names of the poems analyzed in Table 8.2 are *The Wars of Alexander*, *The Parlement of the Thre Ages*, *Cleanness*, *Saint Erkenwald*, *Sir Gawain and the Green Knight*, *The Siege of Jerusalem*, *The Alliterative Morte Arthure*, *Pearl*, *Piers Plowman* (B-Text), *Patience*, *The Destruction of Troy*, and *Wynnere and Wastoure*.

4 Line-terminal words in the two poems are classified in Table 5.1 into four groups according to their origin: Old English, Old French, Old Norse, and Others. See Chapter Five, especially Section Four.

Chapter 9

Revisiting Oakden's Insights into ME Alliterative Verse

Oakden's book on the Alliterative Revival, *Alliterative Poetry in Middle English: The Dialectal and Metrical Survey*, is one of the monumental works for the study of ME alliterative verse because it established a unique approach based on philological studies. Reexamining his statements through the knowledge of modern metrical studies not only provides evidence to support his ideas but also illuminates issues that he did not acknowledge. The present chapter first reviews the role of alliterative meter in the English poetic tradition. Then it introduces various alliteration techniques in ME alliterative verse, and finally offers a response to Oakden's observations. Oakden's overall conclusion about ME alliterative meter is that "it was the desire for ornament that led these poets to overcrowd their lines with alliterating sounds," which eventually made the long line "a mere jingle of sounds" (*Alliterative* 244). Despite the ornamental features, ME alliterative verse is not superfluous repetition because it tolerates much freedom, merging into a complex sound network.

After eighty years of publication, Oakden's book still offers insights about ME alliterative verse. Modern knowledge of linguistics has made crucial contributions to the study of meter, and has revealed what differentiates poetic language from ordinary speech (Fabb; Freeborn; Furniss and Bath). Yet Oakden's philological approach illuminates certain critical ideas that modern linguists may overlook. Cable emphasizes the importance of revising Oakden because alliterative verse is "a most positivistic tradition that is still manifested in most studies of Old and Middle English phonology and meter" (*Tradition* 1–2).[1] Reviewing Oakden's ideas on ME alliterative meter will illuminate why the alliterative tradition is favored throughout the history of the English language, as well as why that tradition received a strong favor in the fourteenth century.

9.1 Reduplication in English Verse and Alliteration in OE Verse

Alliterative meter is a repetitive mode of composition that utilizes reduplication of the same stem-initial sounds. Ordinary speech also may be repetitive, which sometimes creates a sense of word play. The following phrases are modern examples of alliteration (Meredith 45–47, 95–98):

> *A*lcoholics *A*nonymous, *B*est *B*uy, *Cl*ean *C*ut, *C*ozy *C*orner, *D*onald *D*uck, *F*ickle *F*inger of *F*ate, *Fr*equent *Fl*yer, *G*ood *Gr*ief, *J*ust *J*oking, *M*ickey *M*ouse, *N*o *N*onsense, *Pr*oof *P*ositive, *Q*uite a *Q*uandary, *S*esame *Str*eet, *St*erling *S*ilver, *Sw*eet *S*ixteen, *U*niversity of *U*tah, *Y*ale *Y*uppie

Modern speakers may sense certain amusement in these phrases, but not many will consider *Clean Cut* or *Lots of Luck* artistic, let alone poetic. A question arises as to what makes repetitious language artistic or eventually poetic in the case of English alliterative verse.

The English language has favored alliterative meter since the time of Anglo-Saxons. Alliterative meter is one of the Germanic traditions that the language still cherishes despite the later introduction of romance meter (Cable, *Tradition* 132–53; Cochrane 10). In the first eleven lines of *Beowulf*, for example, the old Germanic meter establishes a rigid metrical framework. Alliteration is italicized:

Hwæt, wē *g*ārdena   in *g*ēardagum,
*þ*ēodcyninga   *þ*rym gefrūnon,
*h*ū ðā *æ*þelingas   *e*llen fremedon!
Oft *Sc*yld *Sc*ēfing   *sc*eaþena þrēatum,
*m*onegum *m*ǣgþum   *m*eodosetla oftēah,
*e*gsode *e*orl[as],   syððan *ǣ*rest wearð
*f*ēasceaft *f*unden;   hē þæs *fr*ōfre gebād,
*w*ēox under *w*olcnum   *w*eorðmyndum þāh,
*o*ð þæt him *ǣ*ghwylc   *y*mbsittendra
*o*fer *h*ronrāde   *h*ȳran scolde,
*g*omban *g*yldan;   þæt wæs *g*ōd cyning!   (Klaeber's edition)

The verse line of OE alliterative meter typically contains four stressed syllables per line, each half-line alliterating in their first beat. It is purely accentual and reflects Germanic rhythm. Alliteration adds linguistic vigor and offers a strong sense of vitality, especially in describing heroic deeds and violent actions (T. Turville-Petre, *Poetry* 1).

Reduplication is a universal feature to any language in creating a sense of word play. Examples include *yum-yum*, *tum-tum*, *cous-cous*, and *bon-bon*. End rhyme, such as *helter-skelter*, *super-duper*, *nitty-gritty*, or *hodge-podge*, can be another source of word play, but repeating the same sound at the beginning of words, or more precisely at the beginning of stems, is a more archaic tradition of the English language. The phrase *veni, vidi, vici* by Julius Caesar, though not in English, may owe its popularity to its alliterative make-up. The preference of alliteration may come from primary desire in language use. Babies' first words tend to be repetitious as seen in *mama*, *dada*, and *papa*. According to *The Oxford English Dictionary*, the word *mammal*, originally denoting "breast" in Latin, may come from an onomatopoetic expression. Linguists have argued that reduplication often occurs in the so-called primitive languages (Barber, Beal, and Shaw 26–27; Cochrane 10). Children's rhymes are rich in such expressions. Examples are *Humpty-Dumpty* and *Peter Piper and his Pickled Peppers*. The following nursery rhymes utilize both alliteration and end rhyme, which creates solid repetitive rhythm:

Star light, star bright,
First star I see tonight,
I wish I may, I wish I might,
Have the wish I wish tonight.

Jack and Jill went up the hill
To fetch a pail of water.
Jack fell down and broke his crown,
And Jill came tumbling after.

Up Jack got and down he trot
As fast as he could caper;
And went to bed and covered his head

In vinegar and brown paper.

When Jill came in how she did grin
To see Jack's paper plaster;
Mother vexed, did whip her next,
For causing Jack's disaster

Reduplication in this manner presents an unusual form of verbal play by means of everyday language. It reminds one of barbarian, illiterate, uncultured, or pagan traditions. In spite of these negative connotations, it is pleasant to the ear and easy to notice (Bloomfield and Dunn 1–6).

9.2 Innovations in ME Alliterative Verse

The flourish of alliterative meter in the OE period seems to have ceased because no significant work is extant between OE poetry and the revival that took place in the fourteenth century. The old popular meter probably survived in minor works and in folk traditions, but not much evidence is available except for Laȝamon's *Brut*. The sudden flourish of alliterative meter in the West Midlands in the fourteenth century seems to suggest a competition to innovate different metrical devices among poets whose language had undergone significant changes from the time of the Anglo-Saxons. Utilizing the varying stress rules affected by the romance rules and loan words from various sources, these ME poets enthusiastically composed in alliterative meter.

The base meter of ME alliterative poems consists of four or five beats per verse line, as already seen in previous chapters. The first three beats usually alliterate. The following lines from the major poems exemplify the base meter. The alliteration pattern is given between brackets:

A 1458	And *b*odword to þe *b*ischop *b*roȝt of his come,	[aaax]
AG 72	I *ch*ese to the *ch*awylls *ch*efe to be-gynn,	[aaax]
C 1416	And *b*ougounz *b*usch *b*atered so þikke.	[aaax]
E 23	So he hom *d*edifiet and *d*yght all to *d*ere halowes	[aaax]
G 606	Þat watz *st*apled *st*ifly and *st*offed wythinne.	[aaax]
J 905	Þan *fl*owe þat *fr*eke *fr*endles alone,	[aaax]
MA 3994	*K*aughte it vpe *k*yndly with his *cl*ene handis,	[aaax]

PE 811	For *s*ynne He *s*et Hym*s*elf in vayn,	[aaax]
PPA II.97	She miȝte *k*isse þe *K*ing for *c*osyn and heo wolde.	[aaax]
PPB III.315	'Shal neiþer *k*yng ne *kn*yght, *c*onstable ne meire	[aaax]
PT 81	Þis is a *m*eruayl *m*essage a *m*an for to preche	[aaax]
T 2792	To *p*as with a *p*ower to þaire *pl*ayne londys,	[aaax]
W 439	Forthi, *W*ynnere, with *wr*onge thou *w*astes thi tyme;	[aaax]

The ME verse line may sometimes deviate. Alliteration may appear in more places than the base meter predetermines. *The Satire against the Blacksmiths*, which consists of only twenty-two lines and is composed between the years 1300 and 1325, is an extreme example of excessive alliteration. All metrical beats may alliterate in certain lines while other lines contain two sets of alliteration:[2]

*S*warte *s*mekyd *s*methes *s*materyd wyth *s*moke
*D*ryue me to *d*eth wyth *d*en of here *d*yntes.
Swech *n*oys on *n*yghtes *n*e herd men *n*euer:
What *k*nauene *c*ry and *c*lateryng of *k*nockes!
The *c*ammede *k*ongons *c*ryen after '*c*ol, *c*ol!'
And *b*lowen here *b*elllewys, that al here *b*rayn *b*restes:
'*H*uf, *p*uf!' seith that *o*n; '*h*af, *p*af!' that *o*ther.
Thei *sp*yttyn and *sp*raulyn and *sp*ellyn many *sp*elles;
Thei *g*nauen and *g*nacchen, thei *g*ronys togydere,
And *h*oldyn *h*em *h*ote wyth *h*ere *h*ard *h*amers.
*Of a b*ole-*h*yde *b*en *h*ere *b*arm-fellys;
Here *sch*ankes ben *sch*akeled *f*or the *f*ere-*fl*underys;
*H*euy *h*amerys thei *h*an, that *h*ard ben *h*andled,
*St*ark *st*rokes thei *st*ryken on a *st*elyd *st*okke:
*L*us, *b*us! *l*as, *d*as! *r*owtyn be *r*owe.
Swech *d*olful a *d*reme the *d*euyl it to*d*ryue!
The mayster *l*ongith a *l*ityl, and *l*ascheth a *l*esse,
*T*wyneth hem *t*weyn, and *t*owchith a *t*reble:
*T*ik, *t*ak! *h*ic, *h*ac! *t*iket, *t*aket! *t*yk, *t*ak!
*L*us, bus! *l*us, das! swych *l*yf thei *l*edyn
Alle *c*lothemerys: *C*ryst hem gyue sorwe!
*M*ay no *m*an for brenwaterys on nyght han hys rest!

Oakden uses this poem in order to suggest that alliteration, which used to be structural, is now ornamental and losing its artistic value to convey the poetic sense (*Alliterative* 149–50). Still, the vivid sound pattern of the poem indisputably reflects the noise that the blacksmiths make, which proves the power of alliterative meter.

A brief review on linguistic changes that the English language underwent regarding aesthetic use proves useful in consideration of metrical devices of ME alliterative poems. By the latter half of the fourteenth century when most of the ME alliterative poems were composed, Romance languages had influenced the vocabulary and rhythm of the English vernacular. Since alliterative meter demands abundant stock of words that start with the same sound, poets had to have a vast knowledge of variations in words and their prosodic nature.

One significant difference that ME meter exhibits against its OE counterpart is that the number of beats per line is more flexible. Four-beat lines are typical in OE, but five-beat lines are frequent in ME alliterative verse, as discussed in Chapters Two and Three. Four-beat meter is a simple and strong rhythmic pattern, and creates a special sense of unusual language because of its rigid template as seen in nursery rhymes. On the other hand, five-beat meter, which cannot be divided into even halves, creates tension against the rigid four-beat pattern and provides more speech-like lines. Thus, five-beat meter is not observed in popular verse such as nursery rhymes and folk jingles because these forms prefer salient rhythm. Attridge uses the following two examples in order to explain the difference between four-beat meter and five-beat meter (*Rhythms* 159). The places for metrical beats are indicated by the accent mark:

a: Had Í the stóre in yóunder móuntain
Where góld and sílver are hád for cóunting,
I cóuld not cóunt for the thóught of thée,
My éyes so fúll I cóuld not sée.
b: Had Í the stóre in the cáve of yóunder móuntain
Where précious góld and sílver are hád for cóunting,
I would nót be áble to cóunt for the thóught of thée,
My éyes so fúll I would scárcely be áble to sée.

The rhythmic sway of the 4 × 4 structure in *a* sets a rigid metrical framework while the five-beat line in *b* reflects the rhythm of the spoken language. The number five cannot be divided into equal parts. The verse line that is flexible between four and five beats allowed ME poets to produce different types of alliteration. As explained in Chapter Seven, William Langland, a resident not of the West Midlands but of the capital, employed alliterative meter because he was aware that the meter reminds people, especially peasants, of old days and because he knew that he could express his potential in his language by means of that meter.

In Section One of Chapter Six, various alliteration patterns have been observed. Similar phenomena in alliteration are reviewed here in order to reconfirm different types of sound repetition around the alliterating syllables. Since Chapter Six has used examples from *Pearl* (*PE*), *Cleanness* (*C*), *Patience* (*PT*), and *Sir Gawain and the Green Knight* (*G*), examples are quoted from other poems that consist of a considerable number of lines: *The Wars of Alexander* (*A*), *The Parlement of the Thre Ages* (*AG*), *The Siege of Jerusalem* (*J*), *The Alliterative Morte Arthure* (*MA*), and *The Destruction of Troy* (*T*). The following lines are examples in which all metrical beats alliterate:

A 134	Vn-*w*etandly to any *w*ee þat *w*ont in his *w*anes.	[aaaa]
AG 295	Bot *m*any *m*odyere than I, *m*en one this *m*olde,	[aaaa]
J 1234	And *w*yten her *w*o þe *w*ronge þat þey *w*roȝte	[aaaa]
MA 568	In at the *p*ortes of *P*avye schall no *p*rynce *p*asse,	[aaaa]
T 1240	But *st*ert vp *st*ithly, *st*raght out a *sw*erde	[aaaa]

In the ME line, another alliterating beat is added to the OE alliteration pattern *ax/ax*, which results in the *aa/ax* pattern. The above lines alliterate in all the metrical beats, which is sometimes found in ME alliterative verse.

OE alliteration occurs in a single consonant or a single consonant cluster. This occurs in ME alliterative verse as well, which strengthens the link among the alliterating words within the line:

A 1106	Þou sall be *dr*enchid of a *dr*inke a *dr*aȝte of vnsele,
AG 638	E*ccl*esiastes the *cl*erke de*cl*ares in his booke
J 502	Ne to *tr*ete of no *tr*ewe for *tr*ibute þat he askeþ;
MA 1799	That all *bl*endez with *bl*ode thare his *bl*anke rynnez–
T 1011	He *sp*ed hym vnto *sp*art, *sp*arit he noght,

Each consonant cluster, such as *dr*, *cl*, *tr*, *bl*, and *sp* in the above examples, may alliterate only with itself in OE alliterative verse. In ME alliterative poetry, however, alliteration in a group of different consonant clusters is common. As a result, the alliteration has gained certain flexibility:

A 1099	Þe *pr*ophecy, or þou *p*as of all my *pl*ayn werdis,
AG 156	His *b*erde and *br*owes were *bl*anchede full whitte,
J 78	And he [hem] *fr*aynes, how *f*er þe *fl*ode hadde y*f*erked.
MA 1692	'Sir *K*yng' sais sir *Cl*egys 'full *kn*yghttly þow askez;
T 1626	With *fl*oures and *fr*esshe bowes *f*ecchyng of somer:

The identical alliteration sometimes continues over a group of lines. Three consecutive lines alliterate in /s/ below:

AG 500	That he *sw*iftely his *sw*erde scholde *sw*ynge in the mere,
AG 501	And whatt *s*elcouthes he *s*ee the *s*othe scholde he telle.
AG 502	And Sir Wawayne [*st*art] *sw*ith to the *sw*erde and *sw*ange it in the mere,

The alliteration on /b/ prevails in the following passage of *J*:

J 657	*Br*enten and *b*eten doun þat *b*ilde was wel þycke,
J 658	*Br*osten þe *br*itages and þe *br*ode toures.
J 659	By þat was many *b*old *b*urne þe *b*urwe to assayle,
J 660	Þe hole *b*atail *b*oun, a-*b*oute þe *br*ode walles,
J 661	Þat wer *b*yg and *br*ode and *b*ycchet to wynne,
J 662	Wonder heye to byholde, with holwe diches vnder,
J 663	Heye *b*onked a-*b*ou[t]e, vpon *b*oþe sydes,
J 664	Riȝt wicked to wynne, bot ȝif wyles helpe.
J 665	*B*ow-men atte *b*onke *b*enden her ger,

Two different sets of alliteration are also common:

A 425	With a *r*ede *g*olde *r*ynge on þis a*r*ay *gr*ayuyn;	[abaab]
AG 191	Thi *br*ydell of *br*ent *g*olde wolde *b*ullokes the *g*ete;	[aabab]
J 1228	*J*erusalem, þe *J*ewen *t*oun, and þe *j*oly *t*emple!"	[aabab]
MA 1971	To sir *L*eo be *c*omen with all his *l*ele *kn*yghtez,	[abab]
T 430	The *gr*et *t*empull *t*op *t*erned to *gr*ound.	[abbba]

Elision alliteration, alliteration merged through a liaison of two adjacent syllables, is observed in almost all ME alliterative poems, though its occurrences are not many:

PE 233	Ho watz me *n*erre þe*n a*unte or *n*ece:	[xaaa]
A 364	*N*owþire my*ne a*wen ne na *n*othire god lat þe *n*oȝt spare,	[aaaax]
A 582	And *n*orisch him as *n*amely as he my*ne a*wyn warre,	[aaax]
A 1829	*T*akis þam with him to his *t*ent and þam a*t e*se makis.	[aaax]
G 962	Þe twey*ne y*ȝen and þe *n*ase, þe *n*aked lyppez,	[aaax]
MA 130	It es *l*efull ti*ll* vs his *l*ikynge till wyrche;	[aaax]

The unstressed syllable that initiates the line may echo the alliteration of the line. The following lines may be read in five beats if the line-initial word is considered to form a metrical beat due to its initial sound. The two possible alliteration patterns are [aaax] and [aaaax] for all five examples:

A 104	E*m*ang þe *m*ultitude of *m*en quare *m*ane ere togeder,
AG 266	And *s*ayde, '*S*irres, by my *s*oule, *s*ottes bene ȝe bothe.
J 740	*B*oþe *bl*owyng on *b*ent and on þe *b*urwe walles.
MA 1336	And *s*ythen *s*eke in by *S*ayne with *s*olace þeraftere,
T 473	*B*othe to *b*urde and to *b*ede *bl*essid were I:

These examples suggest that the extra alliteration found in various parts in the verse line increases the homogeneity among the syllables of the line. Oakden acknowledges this phenomenon. Realizing that it is not found in OE verse, he interprets it as alliteration not only for the ear but also for the eye (*Alliterative* 159).

9.3 Multiple Forms of Repetitions in ME Alliterative Verse

A subtle form of alliteration occurs in a repetition of consonants that do not fall in the word-initial position. In Chapter Six, I have used the term *secondary alliteration* for this, making a distinction from *primary alliteration* observed in metrical beats. Several examples are given below for each of the four categories. The sounds in secondary alliteration are underlined:[3]

(i) *A-A-Ab-xb*

PE 331 What seruez tresor bot *g*arez men *g*rete,
C 310 A *c*ofer *cl*osed of tres, *cl*anlych planed.
PT 395 Al schal *c*rye, for*cl*emmed, with alle oure *cl*ere strenþe;
G 337 Þen any *b*urne vpon *b*ench hade *b*roȝt hym to drynk

(ii) *A-A-A-xA*

PE 160 Mony *r*yal *r*ay con fro hit *r*ere.
C 1025 For *l*ay þeron a *l*ump of *l*ed, and hit on *l*oft fletez,
PT 188 Þer *R*agnel in his *r*akentes hym *r*ere of his dremes!
G 39 *R*ekenly of þe *R*ounde Table alle þo *r*ich breþer–

(iii) *Ab-Ab-Ab-b*

PE 111 *Sw*angeande *sw*ete þe water con *sw*epe,
C 1524 Neuer *st*euen hem a*st*el, so *st*oken is hor tonge.
PT 101 Then he *tr*on on þo *tr*es, and þay her *tr*amme ruchen,
G 1219 And de*pr*ece your *pr*ysoun and *pr*ay hym to ryse,

(iv) *A-Ab-A-b*

PE 103 Þe *f*yrre in þe *fr*yth, þe *f*eier con ryse
C 982 Ones ho *bl*uschet to þe *b*urȝe, *b*ot *b*od ho no lenger
PT 457 Þenne watz þe *g*ome so *gl*ad of his *g*ay logge,
G 523 He *dr*yues wyth *dr*oȝt þe *d*ust for to ryse,
PE 785 Þe Lambes vyuez in *bl*ysse we *b*ene, [xxaa]
PE 813 For vus He lette Hym *fl*yȝe and *f*olde, [xxaa]

Stanza linking is often found as seen in all the 101 stanzas of *Pearl* (*PE*). As seen in Chapter Five, the first and the last lines of the twelve-line stanzas of *PE* contain similar words or phrases. For instance, the word *spot* appears in all the stanza-initial and stanza-final lines except for the initial line of the first stanza. Furthermore, the stanza-final lines, lines 12, 24, 36, 48, and 60, end with the same phrase *perle wythouten spotte*:

PE 1 Perle plesaunte, to prynces paye
PE 12 Of þat pryuy perle withouten *spot*.

PE 13 Syþen in þat *spote* hit fro me sprange,
PE 24 My priuy perle withouten *spotte.*

PE 25 Þat *spot* of spysez mot nedez sprede,
PE 36 Of þat precios perle wythouten *spotte.*

PE 37 To þat *spot* þat I in speche expoun
PE 48 My precious perle wythouten *spot.*

PE 49 Bifore þat *spot* my honde I spennd
PE 60 On þat precios perle withouten *spot.*

PE 61 Fro *spot* my spyryt þer sprang in space;

All other clusters, consisting of five stanzas each, use this repetition.[4] In addition to this stanza linking, the whole verse structure can be cyclic as seen in the first and final lines of *PE*, *PT*, and *G*. The first and last lines of the poem echo with each other, as observed in Chapter Six:

PE 1 Perle plesaunte, to prynces paye
PE 1212 Ande precious perlez vnto His pay.

PT 1 Pacience is a poynt, þaȝ hit displese ofte.
PT 531 Þat pacience is a nobel poynt, þaȝ hit displese ofte.

G 1 Siþen þe sege and þe assaut watz sesed at Troye,
G 2525 After þe segge and þe asaute watz sesed at Troye,

Sound repetition, not in such a grand scale but in close vicinity, can be observed in alliteration stretching over more than a single line. In Chapter Seven, five types have been explained regarding the repetition of the same consonant in places other than primary alliteration in consecutive lines. This may be called vertical alliteration in comparison to the alliteration within the verse line:[5]

Type 1 Consecutive alliteration over several lines:
G 670 He *sp*erred þe *st*ed with þe *sp*urez and *spr*ong on his way /s/

G 671 So *st*if þat þe *st*on-fyr *str*oke out þerafter. /s/
G 672 Al þat *s*eȝ þat *s*emly *s*yked in hert /s/
G 673 And *s*ayde *s*oþly al *s*ame *s*egges til oþer, /s/

Type 2 Same alliteration in every other line:
W 370 Thurgh the *p*oure *pl*enté of corne that the *p*eple sowes, /p/
W 371 That God will *gr*aunte of his *gr*ace to *gr*owe on the erthe,
W 372 Ay to a*pp*aire the *p*ris, and it *p*asse nott to hye, /p/

Type 3 The final beat of a line predicting the alliteration of the line that immediately follows it:
AG 616 And Sir *S*ampsone hym-*s*elfe, full *s*auage of his dedys,
AG 617 And *D*alyda his *d*erelynge, now *d*ethe has þam bo[th]e. /d/

Type 4 The final beat of a line reflecting the alliteration of the previous line:
T 822 Whan he was *w*are of þe *w*egh, *w*elcomed hym faire, /w/
T 823 And *sp*ird at hym *sp*ecially what his *sp*ede were. /s/
T 824 Than *J*ason vn*i*oynid to the *g*entill speche:–

Type 5 The same sound initiating the final beats of consecutive lines:
J 1222 Ouer þe *c*yte wer *s*eyn *s*undrede tymes;
J 1223 A *c*alf aȝen *k*ynde *c*alued in þe temple
J 1224 And *e*ued an *e*we-lombe at [þe] *o*ffryng-tyme.

These five types may be combined in order to create a further complex sound network:

Type 1 and Type 5:
J 130 With two *f*isches he *f*edde and *f*if ber loues, /f/
J 131 Þat eche *fr*eke hadde his *f*ulle, and ȝit *f*erre leued /f/

Type 3 and Type 4:
PPA IV.30 And *r*ombide forþ wiþ *R*esoun *r*iȝt to þe Kinge. /r/
PPA IV.31 *C*urteisliche þe *K*ing þanne *c*om aȝen Resoun, /k/

E 313 Til he *t*oke hym a *t*ome and to þe *t*oumbe lokyd, /t/

E 314	To þe *l*iche þer hit *l*ay, with *l*auande teres.	/l/

The following passage of *Piers Plowman* B-Text (*PPB*) has been examined in Chapter Seven. The lines contain /m/ and /l/ in various metrical positions, creating different vertical alliteration types. More examples will be given in Chapter Ten:

PPB II.31	And haþ yeuen me *M*ercy to *m*arie wiþ myselue;	/m/
PPB II.32	And what *m*an be *m*erciful and *l*eelly me *l*oue	/m/ & /l/
PPB II.33	Shal be my *l*ord and I his *l*eef in þe *h*eiȝe *h*euene;	/l/ & /h/
PPB II.34	And what *m*an takeþ *M*ede, myn heed dar I legge	/m/
PPB II.35	That he shal *l*ese for hire *l*oue a *l*ippe of Caritatis.	/l/
PPB II.36	'How *c*onstrueþ Dauid þe *K*yng of *m*en þat [*c*acch]eþ *M*ede,	/k/ & /m/
PPB II.37	And *m*en of þis *m*oolde þat *m*ayntenеþ truþe,	/m/

9.4 Oakden's Insights into ME Alliterative Verse

As seen in the examples quoted above, alliteration in ME verse is much more variable than in the OE counterpart. These varieties verify Oakden's observations. The first point of discussion is the following statement:

> About 1350 there is in the west a renaissance, a new outburst of feeling, a new interest in poetry. Doubtless the inspiration had spread from the south and east. The French material stirred the hearts of poets and imaginative poetry found a new home in the west-midlands. As before, poets turned to French for their subjects and often contented themselves with free adaptations of French romances. . . . But time and distance had weakened the French influence, and the new school of poets did not catch, as the southern poets did, the form and spirit of their models. (*Alliterative* 86)

Oakden makes another observation regarding the vocabulary used in ME alliterative verse:

> . . . a distinctive alliterative vocabulary has come into being, derived largely from traditional sources, but not exclusively so. In particular, older poetic

> senses of native words and specialised senses of French words are markedly present, as are words of obscure origin. These words circulated among the various alliterative writers, partly through a common tradition and partly through imitation, but they never gained the same popularity among non-alliterative writers, except occasionally in the north.
> (*Alliterative* 180–81)

The rich stock of vocabulary that ME alliterative poets use proves that they were familiar with different ways of composing poems. They must have also been aware of what was popular in London. Poets of the royal court or those in London did not use alliterative meter except for Langland. On the other hand, poets in the West Midlands intended their work not for people in the capital but for those who would enjoy the archaic rhythm deeply implanted in their language.

Oakden's response to the question of sound reduplication and redundancy appears in the following two passages:

> Again, in the rhythmical lyrical prose in late OE and early ME, alliteration was an important feature, yet nevertheless not structural but purely ornamental. Alliterative prose must have been exceedingly popular in ME, and it was natural that poets, when writing in French forms, should not hesitate to add alliteration of the stressed syllables. (*Alliterative* 233)

> It was the desire for ornament that led these poets to overcrowd their lines with alliterating sounds, and to employ so many metrical devices. In its last stages the long line is a mere jingle of sounds. Possibly the northern and western schools of alliterative poets were rivals. We have already made a detailed comparison of the two, and have suggested that the intrinsic difference lies in the fact that the northern school made light of tradition, whereas the western school was faithful to it, in so far as the actual knowledge of it had survived. The two schools flourished and both passed away. Alliteration, once structural, had become more and more ornamental, until finally the verse became chaotic and ceased to be a worthy vehicle of what little poetic inspiration survived. (*Alliterative* 244–45)

Whether or not repetition is an artistic virtue is open to discussion. Certain scholars of ME alliterative meter have often been annoyed with its repetitious language, which led them to a conclusion that these redundant phrases are simply tags (Krishna, "Parataxis" 74–75). ME alliterative lines observed in this chapter, however, suggest that the recurring metrical structures are neither redundant nor meaningless. The frequency of lines that utilize different types of alliteration within the verse line and beyond it suggests the poets' deliberate intention to pursue this meter as their artistic mode. The complex form of sound repetition was such a challenging task that they had to manipulate abundant vocabulary and technical skills to fulfill these requirements, and apparently they took this challenge with professional pride. The tension that the poets create against the ordinary language is remarkable. Alliteration in the fourteenth-century alliterative verse, in this sense, is a metrical device that could structurally link the verse line within the prescribed metrical unit and add extra aural effect by sound repetition. In spite of the ornamental features, ME alliterative verse is not superfluous repetition because it tolerates much freedom and merges into a complex sound network. Its artistic significance is clear compared to the phrase *rum, ram, ruf* (Chaucer, *The Canterbury Tales* X. 42) or modern jingles such as *American Automobile Association* and *Coca-Cola*. It is full of innovations that the old tradition did not attain (Dunn and Byrnes 28) and what modern jingles have not achieved.

Notes

1 As to various approaches from Oakden to modern scholars, see Chism, Chapter One.
2 The poem is quoted from Sisam.
3 Examples include those used in Chapter Six.
4 See Dunn and Byrnes 30–33 for a detailed explanation of alliterative stanzas.
5 Chapter Ten will discuss consecutive alliteration in detail.

Chapter 10

Consecutive Alliteration in ME Alliterative Verse: Sound Repetition over the Verse Line

The study of alliterative meter has largely focused on alliteration within the verse line because such analyses dramatize distinctive features of its repetitious meter. Limited research, however, has been made regarding the sound repetition beyond the line unit. Through analyses of major and minor ME alliterative poems, I have found that sound repetition often prevails over several consecutive lines of ME alliterative verse. This chapter reveals how the vertical sound repetitions unite consecutive lines. After classifying vertical alliteration in consecutive lines into five types, the chapter will explain that lines that contain one or more occasions of these types increase repetitive mode in addition to the alliteration within the line.

Sound repetition has been considered a crucial feature of linguistic rhythms as insightful investigations on prosody and verse rhythm were made in the field of modern linguistics (Attridge, *Rhythms*, *Poetic Rhythm*; Couper-Kuhlen, *Introduction*, *Rhythm*; Cureton, *Rhythmic Phrasing*; Hayes, *Metrical Theory*, *Metrical Stress Theory*). Studies on medieval English meters are no exception in utilizing this modern approach. More and more scholars consider ME alliterative meter not as a mere ornamentation but as a systematic manipulation in linking the constituents within the prescribed metrical framework and in placing emphasis on important words (Burrow and Turville-Petre; Lawton, "Introduction"; Matonis, "Poetry"; Sapora; T. Turville-Petre, *Revival*). Since ME alliterative meter reflects various changes that occurred to the English language from the days of the Anglo-Saxons, the alliteration within the verse line is complex enough to attract scholarly attention (Cable, *Tradition*, "Grammar"; Duggan, "Final *-e*"; Spearing, *Readings*; Waldron, *Gawain*).

The appearance of the same alliteration sound in adjacent lines, if not fully discussed, has been pointed out in different terms such as *identical alliteration* (Oakden, *Alliterative* 233), *grouped alliteration* (Hamel 32), *running alliteration* (Schmidt, *Clerky* 55), or *consecutive alliteration* (Vaughan 2). Oakden noted this phenomenon eighty years ago (*Alliterative* 221–22). Not many scholars, however, have investigated the metrical effect of consecutive alliteration in detail. The only exception is *The Alliterative Morte Arthure* (*MA*) that uses alliteration in an excessive manner within and beyond the verse line (Hamel; Vaughan). The use of the same sound over several consecutive lines is frequently observed in other ME alliterative poems, which suggests that the duality in sound repetition, namely the horizontal sound repetition within the line and the vertical sound repetition beyond the line, is a common feature of ME alliterative verse. The terms, *vertical alliteration*, *identical alliteration*, and *consecutive alliteration*, will be used interchangeably to denote identical alliteration in consecutive lines.

10.1 Five Types of Consecutive Alliteration

The following twelve poems, the major works in the ME alliterative tradition, have been analyzed. This list differs from the one presented in Chapter One because minor poems are not included for the present analysis:

Excerpts from *The Wars of Alexander* (*A*)	2,005 lines
The Parlement of the Thre Ages (*AG*)	661 lines
Cleanness (*C*)	1,812 lines
Saint Erkenwald (*E*)	352 lines
Sir Gawain and the Green Knight (*G*)[1]	2,530 lines
The Siege of Jerusalem (*J*)	1,334 lines
The Alliterative Morte Arthure (*MA*)	4,345 lines
Excerpts from *Piers Plowman,* A-Text (*PPA*)	1,180 lines
Excerpts from *Piers Plowman,* B-Text (*PPB*)	1,030 lines
Patience (*PT*)	531 lines
Excerpts from *The Destruction of Troy* (*T*)	3,531 lines
Wynnere and Wastoure (*W*)	503 lines

The typical verse line of ME alliterative meter consists of four beats, three of which frequently alliterate.[2] The following *T* lines exemplify how alliteration occurs in ME alliterative lines. The alliteration is italicized within the line and shown between slashes after it:

T 1609 Of *f*ilth and of *f*eum, throughe *fl*etyng by nethe. /f/[3]
T 1610 In En*s*ample of this *C*ite, *s*othely to telle, /s/
T 1611 *R*ome on a *R*iuer *r*ially was set, /r/

Consecutive alliteration is not observed in these lines, but the same alliteration can be extended over two or more lines. For instance, the following passages from various poems use the same alliteration sound in successive lines:

T 874 And me *c*omford of thy *c*oursse, *k*epe I no more." /k/
T 875 When the *kn*ight was *c*omyn into þe *cl*iffe ferre, /k/

W 400 For to *s*ave to your *s*ones: bot the *sch*ame es your ownn. /s/
W 401 Nedeles *s*ave ye the *s*oyle, for *s*ell it ye thynken. /s/
AG 339 Then *gr*athede he hym to *G*adres the *g*ates full righte, /g/
AG 340 And there Sir *G*[adyfer]e þe *g*ude the *G*aderayns assemblet, /g/

J 585 *B*ounden þe *b*ischup on *b*ycchyd wyse, /b/
J 586 Þat þe *bl*ode out *b*arst eche *b*and vnder, /b/
J 587 And *br*oȝten [to] þe [*b*erfraye] alle [þo] *b*ew clerkes /b/

PPB P.114 And þanne *c*am *K*ynde Wit and *cl*erkes he made, /k/
PPB P.115 For to *c*ounseillen þe *K*yng and þe *C*ommune saue. /k/
PPB P.116 The *K*yng and *Kn*yȝthod and *Cl*ergie boþe /k/
PPB P.117 *C*asten þat þe *C*ommune sholde hem [*c*ommunes] fynde. /k/
PPB P.118 The *C*ommune *c*ontreued of *K*ynde Wit *cr*aftes, /k/

Sound repetition beyond the line unit is not limited to the use of the same alliteration sound in adjacent lines. The same alliteration sound can occur in every other line while the unalliterating line-final beat may reflect the alliteration of the previous or subsequent line. In Chapters Seven and Nine, these phenomena within successive lines have been classified into the following five types. This chapter presents more examples from the twelve poems in order to reconfirm that repetitions in consecutive lines in ME alliterative verse seem deliberate:

Type 1	Consecutive alliteration over several lines
Type 2	Same alliteration in every other line
Type 3	The final beat of a line predicting the alliteration of the line that immediately follows it
Type 4	The final beat of a line reflecting the alliteration of the previous line
Type 5	The same sound initiating the final beats of two consecutive lines

The five types of vertical alliteration are explained below with examples. The lines highlight the complex aural network among consecutive lines.

Type 1 Consecutive alliteration over several lines:
Type 1 is the most overt use of consecutive alliteration since two or more adjacent lines alliterate on the same sound. When it occurs to two lines, O'Loughlin calls it *couplet alliteration* (157). Consecutive alliteration is not limited to the two adjacent lines, but can be extended. Examples of consecutive alliteration in two, three, and four lines are given below:

PT 530	Forþy *p*enaunce and *p*ayne to*p*reue hit in syȝt	/p/
PT 531	Þat *p*acience is a nobel *p*oynt, þaȝ hit des*pl*ese ofte.	/p/

W 248	When thou haste *w*altered and *w*ent and *w*akede alle the nyghte,	/w/
W 249	And iche a *w*y in this *w*erlde that *w*onnes the abowte,	/w/
W 250	And hase *w*erpede thy *w*yde howses full of *w*olle sakkes–	/w/

G 670	He *sp*erred þe *st*ed with þe *sp*urez and *spr*ong on his way	/s/
G 671	So *st*if þat þe *st*on-fyr *str*oke out þerafter.	/s/
G 672	Al þat *s*eȝ þat *s*emly *s*yked in hert	/s/
G 673	And *s*ayde *s*oþly al *s*ame *s*egges til oþer,	/s/

If consecutive alliterations alternate in different sounds, they produce a significant sound effect. The passage from *MA* 3840 to *MA* 3855 contains several cases of consecutive alliteration in a different number of lines:

MA 3840	Þan he *m*oues to sir *M*odrede a*m*ange all his knyghttes	/m/
MA 3841	And *m*ett hym in þe *m*yde-schelde and *m*allis hym thorowe;	/m/
MA 3842	Bot the *sch*alke for the *sch*arpe, he *sch*ownttes a littill.	/s/

MA 3843	He *sch*are hym one þe *sch*orte rybbys a *sch*aftmonde large;	/s/
MA 3844	The *sch*afte *sch*oderede and *sch*otte in the *sch*ire beryn,	/s/
MA 3845	Þat þe *sch*adande blode ouer his *sch*anke rynnys	/s/
MA 3846	And *sch*ewede on his *sch*ynbawde þat was *sch*ire burneste.	/s/
MA 3847[4]	And so they *sch*yfte and *sch*ove; he *sch*otte to þe erthe–	/s/
MA 3848	With þe *l*ussche of þe *l*aunce he *l*yghte one hys schuldyrs	/l/
MA 3849	Ane akere *l*enghe one a *l*aunde, full *l*othely wondide!	/l/
MA 3850	Than Gawayne *g*yrde to þe *g*ome and one þe *gr*offe fallis–	/g/
MA 3851	Alls his *gr*efe was *gr*aythede, his *gr*ace was no bettyre!–	/g/
MA 3852	He *sch*okkes owtte a *sch*orte knyfe *sch*ethede with *s*iluere	/s/
MA 3853	And *sch*olde haue *sl*ottede hym in, bot no *sl*ytte happenede:	/s/
MA 3854	His hand *sl*eppid and *sl*ode o *sl*ante one þe mayles,	/s/
MA 3855	And þe toþer *sl*ely *sl*ynges hym vndire.	/s/

Consecutive alliteration is extremely conspicuous in *MA*. There are 1,271 occurrences, and the number of lines involved differs in each case. A total of 3,277 lines uses the same alliteration sound as in the previous or subsequent line. This means that more than seventy-five percent of all the lines of *MA* remains in the same alliteration as their adjacent lines.[5] Identical alliteration in consecutive lines, along with the alliterating pattern within a given line, reinforces the homogeneity among them. It highlights the alliterating words in a larger sound network, and intensifies the repetitious effect of alliterative meter.

The following passages exemplify extended cases of identical alliteration in ten and eleven lines of *MA*, respectively. The first passage alliterates on /k/ while the second one alliterates on /f/. These are the most extreme cases of consecutive alliteration in all poems analyzed here:

MA 3509	'Me awghte to *kn*owe þe *k*ynge; he es my *k*ydde lorde,	/k/
MA 3510	And I, *c*alde in his *c*ourte a *kn*yghte of his chambire.	/k/
MA 3511	Sir *Cr*addoke was I *c*allide in his *c*ourte riche,	/k/
MA 3512	*K*epare of *K*arlyon vndir the *k*ynge selfen.	/k/
MA 3513	Nowe am I *c*achede owtt of *k*yth with *k*are at my herte,	/k/
MA 3514	And that *c*astell es *c*awghte with vn*c*owthe ledys!'	/k/
MA 3515	Than the *c*omliche *k*ynge *k*aughte hym in armes,	/k/
MA 3516	*K*este of his *k*etill-hatte and *k*yssede hym full sone,	/k/
MA 3517	Saide 'Wel*c*om, sir *Cr*addoke, so *Cr*iste mott me helpe!	/k/

MA 3518 Dere *c*osyn of *k*ynde, thow *c*oldis myn herte– /k/

MA 2755 *Fl*orennt and *Fl*oridas with *fy*ve score knyghttez; /f/
MA 2756 *F*olewede in þe *f*oreste and on þe way *f*owndys, /f/
MA 2757 *Fl*yngande a *f*aste trott, and on þe *f*olke dryffes. /f/
MA 2758 Than *f*olewes *f*ast to oure *f*olke wele a *fy*ve hundreth /f/
MA 2759 Of *fr*eke men to þe *fy*rthe appon *fr*esche horses– /f/
MA 2760 One sir *F*eraunt be*f*ore apon a *f*ayre stede, /f/
MA 2761 Was *f*osterde in *F*amacoste; the *f*ende was his *f*adyre. /f/
MA 2762 He *fl*enges to sir *Fl*orent and pristly he kryes, /f/
MA 2763 'Why *fl*ees thow, *f*alls knyghte? Þe *f*ende hafe þi saule!' /f/
MA 2764 Thane sir *Fl*orent was *f*ayne and in *f*ewter castys; /f/
MA 2765 One *F*awuell of *Fr*yselande to *F*eraunt he rydys /f/

Such a large group of lines that alliterate on the identical sound inevitably exaggerates one specific sound and creates strong unity among its constituents. Consecutive alliteration increases the "percussive effect" (Prior 13) of alliterative verse.

Type 2 Same alliteration in every other line:
In this type of vertical alliteration, alliteration does not occur in the line that immediately follows, but occurs a line later. This does not give a clear sense of continuity as Type 1 does, but the echo of a specific sound remains within close vicinity:

W 370 Thurgh the *p*oure *pl*enté of corne that the *p*eple sowes, /p/
W 371 That *G*od will *gr*aunte of his *gr*ace to *gr*owe on the erthe,
W 372 Ay to a*pp*aire the *pr*is, and it *p*asse nott to hye, /p/

Alliteration on /l/ occurs in every other line four times from *G* 1780 to *G* 1786:

G 1780 Ȝif ȝe *l*uf not þat *l*yf þat ȝe *l*ye nexte, /l/
G 1781 Bifore alle þe *w*yȝez in þe *w*orlde *w*ounded in hert,
G 1782 Bot if ȝe haf a *l*emman, a *l*euer, þat yow *l*ykez better, /l/
G 1783 And *f*olden *f*ayth to þat *fre*, *f*estned so harde
G 1784 Þat yow *l*ausen ne *l*yst–and þat I *l*eue nouþe! /l/

G 1785 And þat ȝe *t*elle me þat now *tr*wly I pray yow;
G 1786 For alle þe *l*ufez vpon *l*yue, *l*ayne not þe soþe /l/

The same alliteration in every other line three or four times in a row is found in all the poems analyzed here, even though different poems exhibit different frequencies. *PT, MA,* and *J* contain a significant number of examples of this type.

The sense of repetition increases when the same sound initiates the unalliterating line-final beats of the two lines concerned of Type 2. In other words, the two lines can alliterate on the same sound and have the same sound in their unalliterating line-final beat. For instance, *AG* 138 and *AG* 140 alliterate on the same /g/ while their line-final beats start with the same /m/:

AG 138 In a *g*olyone of *gr*aye *g*irde in the <u>m</u>yddes, /g/
AG 139 And iche *b*agge in his *b*osome *b*ettir than othere.
AG 140 One his *g*olde and his *g*ude *gr*etly he <u>m</u>ousede, /g/

In the following passage of *PPB*, the /m/ sound prevails:

PPB III.216 And *m*edeþ *m*en hemseluen to *m*ayntene hir lawes; /m/
PPB III.217 *S*eruauntȝ for hire *s*eruyce, we *s*eeþ wel þe *s*oþe,
PPB III.218 Taken *m*ede of hir *m*aistres, as þei *m*owe acorde. /m/
PPB III.219 *B*eggeres for hir *b*iddynge *b*idden *m*en *m*ede; /b/ & /m/
PPB III.220 *M*ynstrales for hir *m*yrþe *m*ede þei aske. /m/
PPB III.221 The Kyng haþ *m*ede of his *m*en to *m*ake pees in londe. /m/
PPB III.222 *M*en þat [*k*enne *cl*erkes] *cr*auen of hem *m*ede. /k/ & /m/
PPB III.223 *P*reestes þat *pr*echen þe *p*eple to goode
PPB III.224 Asken *m*ede and *m*assepens and hire *m*ete [alse]. /m/
PPB III.225 Alle *k*ynne *cr*afty *m*en *cr*auen *m*ede for hir prentis; /k/ & /m/
PPB III.226 *M*archaundise and *m*ede *m*ote nede go togideres: /m/

PPB III.219, *PPB* III.222, and *PPB* III.225 may not necessarily alliterate on /m/, but /m/ in words such as *men* and *mede* plays the role of linking the adjacent lines. Lines that do not seem to be involved in consecutive alliteration can be part of alliteration that continues vertically.

Type 3 The final beat of a line predicting the alliteration of the line that immediately follows it:
In ME alliterative verse, the final unalliterating beat frequently predicts the alliteration of the line that immediately follows it. In other words, the final beat that does not play any role in the alliteration of the line to which it belongs, in fact, links it to the line that follows. Below is an example from *AG*. The initial sound of the line-final beat involved in this type of consecutive alliteration is underlined:

AG 616 And Sir *S*ampsone hym-*s*elfe, full *s*auage of his dedys,
AG 617 And *D*alyda his *d*erelynge, now *d*ethe has þam bo[th]e. /d/

The final beats of *C* 697 and *C* 698 predict the alliteration of *C* 699:

C 697 I *c*ompast hem a *k*ynde *cr*afte and *k*ende hit hem derne,
C 698 And *a*med hit in Myn *o*rdenaunce *o*ddely dere,
C 699 And *d*yȝt *dr*wry þerinne, *d*oole alþer-swettest, /d/

The same phenomenon is observed in *G* 1062-*G* 1065. The final beats of the first three lines predict the /w/ alliteration of *G* 1065. In other words, the alliteration is announced three times before it appears in *G* 1065:

G 1062 And of þat ilk *N*w Ȝere bot *n*eked *n*ow wontez,
G 1063 And I wolde *l*oke on þat *l*ede, if God me *l*et wolde,
G 1064 *Gl*adloker, bi *G*oddez Sun, þen any *g*od welde!
G 1065 Forþi, i*w*ysse, bi ȝowre *w*ylle, *w*ende me bihoues; /w/

The final beat of *E* 313 predicts the consecutive alliteration in *E* 314-*E* 316. This phenomenon in which the sound of consecutive alliteration is announced just prior to the consecutive alliteration group appears as frequently as the one observed above in *G*:

E 313 Til he *t*oke hym a *t*ome and to þe *t*oumbe lokyd,
E 314 To þe *l*iche þer hit *l*ay, with *l*auande teres. /l/
E 315 'Oure *L*ord *l*ene', quod þat *l*ede, 'þat þou *l*yfe hades, /l/
E 316 By Goddes *l*eue, as *l*onge as I myȝt *l*acche water, /l/

Prediction occurs three times in a row in different alliteration sounds among the following four lines of *PPB*:

PPB II.195	I wolde be *wr*oken of þo *wr*ecches þat *w*ercheþ so ille,	
PPB II.196	And doon hem *h*ange by þe *h*als and *a*lle þat hem mayntenеþ.	/h/ & vowels[6]
PPB II.197	Shal neuere *m*an of þis *m*olde *m*eynprise þe leeste,	/m/
PPB II.198	But riȝt as þe *l*awe *l*oke[þ], *l*at falle on hem alle!	/l/

Prediction occurs twice in a row in *G* 1479-*G* 1480 in a more complex manner. The final beat of *G* 1479 predicts the alliteration of *G* 1480 while the final beat of that line predicts the consecutive alliteration of *G* 1481-*G* 1482:

G 1479	*S*ettez hir *s*ofly by his *s*yde and *sw*yþely ho laȝez	
G 1480	And wyth a *l*uflych *l*oke ho *l*ayde hym þyse wordez:	/l/
G 1481	'Sir, ȝif ȝe be *W*awen, *w*onder me þynkkez,	/w/
G 1482	*W*yȝe þat is so *w*el *wr*ast al*w*ay to god	/w/

Three cases of prediction occur in a row in the following lines of *PPA*:

PPA II.31	I may no *l*engere *l*ette, *L*ord I þe bekenne–	
PPA II.32	And be*c*ome a good man, for any *c*oueitise, I rede.'	/k/
PPA II.33	Alle þe *r*iche *r*etenaunce þat *r*egniþ wiþ False	/r/
PPA II.34	Were *b*eden to þe *br*idale on *b*oþe two sides.	
PPA II.35	Sire *S*ymonye is of*s*ent to a*s*ele þe chartres	/s/

Type 4 The final beat of a line reflecting the alliteration of the previous line: This is a phenomenon opposite to Type 3. The final beat of a line echoes the alliteration of the previous line, as seen in *J* 878 below. The initial sound of the line-final beat that belongs to this type is underlined:

J 877	For þer as *f*ayleþ þe *f*ode þer is *f*eynt strengþe,	/f/
J 878	And þer as *h*unger is *h*ote, *h*ertes ben feble."	

The /b/ alliteration in *A* 105 is echoed in the line-final beats of the three lines that immediately follow it:

A 105	Bot þer a*b*oute as þai ere *b*lend with *b*ignes of will.	/b/
A 106	If þai be *f*olke bot a *f*a oft tydis þam þe better.	
A 107	Or elis *w*ate þou noȝt *w*ele þe *w*itles berne,	
A 108	How it is *c*omonly *c*arped in *c*ontries a-boute,	

Type 4 occurs twice in *T* 822-*T* 824. The final beat of *T* 823 and that of *T* 824 echo the alliteration of their predecessor, /w/ and /s/, respectively:

T 822	Whan he was *w*are of þe *w*egh, *w*elcomed hym faire,	/w/
T 823	And *sp*ird at hym *sp*ecially what his *sp*ede were.	/s/
T 824	Than *J*ason vn*i*oynid to the *g*entill speche:–	

Type 4 does not create a metrical link as strongly as Type 3 does. Yet its frequency is too significant to be dismissed from consecutive alliteration patterns.

Type 5 The same sound initiating the final beats of two consecutive lines: This phenomenon is not considered alliteration, but a certain sense of repetition pervades when the final beats of two consecutive lines start with the same sound. The following three lines of *J* alliterate on different sounds, but contain the same /t/ sound in their final beat, which is underlined:

J 1222	Ouer þe *c*yte wer *s*eyn *s*undrede tymes;	/s/
J 1223	A *c*alf aȝen *k*ynde *c*alued in þe temple	/k/
J 1224	And *e*ued an *e*we-lombe at [þe] *o*ffryng-tyme.	vowels

The repetition is emphasized when two consecutive lines alliterate on the identical sound and their final beats start with the same sound, as seen in the following lines:

AG 440	And *c*onquerede *k*ynges and *k*yngdomes twelue,	/k/
AG 441	And was a *c*onqueroure full *k*ene and moste *k*yd in his tyme.	/k/

G 418	A *l*ittel *l*ut with þe hede, þe *l*ere he discouerez;	/l/
G 419	His *l*onge *l*ouelych *l*okkez he *l*ayd ouer his croun,	/l/

In the following passage, every two lines alliterate on the same sound and contain the same sound in their final beat:

G 2263	Hade hit *dr*yuen a*d*oun as *dr*eȝ as he atled,	/d/
G 2264	Þer hade ben *d*ed of his *d*ynt þat *d*oȝty watz euer.	/d/
G 2265	Bot *G*awayn on þat *g*iserne *gl*yfte hym bysyde,	/g/
G 2266	As hit com *gl*ydande adoun on *gl*ode hym to schende,	/g/
G 2267	And *schr*anke a lytel with þe *sch*ulderes for þe *sch*arp yrne.	/s/
G 2268	Þat oþer *sch*alk wyth a *sch*unt þe *sch*ene wythhaldez	/s/

In the following passage of *PPA*, each line alliterates on a different sound, but the final beats of all lines start with the same /s/ sound:

PPA V.58	*E*nuye wiþ *h*euy *h*erte *a*skide aftir shrifte	/h/ & vowels
PPA V.59	And *c*arfulliche his *c*ope [*c*omsiþ] he to shewe.	/k/
PPA V.60	He was as *p*ale as a *p*elet, in þe *p*alesie he semide;	/p/
PPA V.61	He was *cl*oþid in a *c*aurymaury–I *c*ouþe it nouȝt descryue–	/k/
PPA V.62	A *k*ertil and a *c*ourtepy, a *kn*yf be his side;	/k/
PPA V.63	Of a *fr*eris *fr*okke were þe *f*oresleuys.	/f/
PPA V.64	As a *l*ek þat hadde *l*eyn *l*onge in þe sonne,	/l/

10.2 Combination of Different Types of Consecutive Alliteration

Consecutive lines may show complex sound network when different types of consecutive alliteration are involved in the same group of lines. For instance, the same alliteration may recur after a cluster of consecutive alliteration. This can be found in lines 549–557 of *C* which remain in the consecutive alliteration of /s/. Skipping *C* 554 and *C* 556, the same /s/ alliteration returns in *C* 555 and *C* 557. This passage, thus, is the combination of Type 1 and Type 2:

C 549	For is no *s*egge vnder *s*unne so *s*eme of his craftez,	/s/
C 550	If he be *s*ulped in *s*ynne, þat *s*yttez vnclene;	/s/
C 551	On *sp*ec of a *sp*ote may *sp*ede to mysse	/s/
C 552	Of þe *s*yȝte of þe *S*ouerayn þat *s*yttez so hyȝe;	/s/
C 553	For þat *sch*ewe me *sch*ale in þo *sch*yre howsez,	/s/

C 554	As þe *b*eryl *b*ornyst *b*yhouez be clene,	
C 555	Þat is *s*ounde on vche a *s*yde and no *s*em habes–	/s/
C 556	Withouten *m*askle oþer *m*ote, as *m*argerye-perle.	
C 557	Syþen þe *S*ouerayn in *s*ete so *s*ore forþoȝt	/s/

In the following example, consecutive lines stay in the same alliteration while their final beats start with the same sound. This is the combination of Type 1 and Type 5:

J 130	With two *f*isches he *f*edde and *f*if ber loues,	/f/
J 131	Þat eche *f*reke hadde his *f*ulle, and ȝit *f*erre leued	/f/

Combination of Type 3 and Type 4 in two adjacent lines is found in the following lines of *PPA* and *G*. The final beat predicts the alliteration of the line that follows while the alliteration of the first line is reflected in the final beat of the second line. In other words, the alliterating sound and the line-final unalliterating sound of a particular line are reversed in the line that follows it:

PPA IV.30	And *r*ombide forþ wiþ *R*esoun *r*iȝt to þe Kinge.	/r/
PPA IV.31	*C*urteisliche þe *K*ing þanne *c*om aȝen Resoun,	/k/

G 1704	And he *f*yskez hem by*f*ore; þay *f*ounden hym sone.	/f/
G 1705	And quen þay *s*eghe hym with *s*yȝt þay *s*ued hym fast,	/s/

Reversing takes place in the following two lines from a passage from *E* used earlier to explain Type 3. Types 3 and 4 are combined:

E 313	Til he *t*oke hym a *t*ome and to þe *t*oumbe lokyd,	/t/
E 314	To þe *l*iche þer hit *l*ay, with *l*auande teres.	/l/

Two consecutive lines alliterating in all stressed syllables, including the line-final beat, present another case in which Types 3 and 4 are combined:

PPA IV.79	'*B*etere is þat *b*oote *b*ale adoun *br*inge	/b/
PPA IV.80	Þanne *b*ale be *b*et, and *b*ote neuere þe *b*etere!'	/b/

Combining Types 3 and 4 in three consecutive lines is a common phenomenon. In the following lines of *A*, the alliteration of *A* 579 is predicted in *A* 578 and echoed in the line-final beat of *A* 580. In other words, Type 3 is followed by Type 4:

A 578 It be *c*onsayued of my *k*ynde ne *c*ome of my-selfe.
A 579 I *s*aȝe so, in þe *s*ame tyme he *s*euyrd fra þi wambe, /s/
A 580 Þe *e*rd and all þe *e*lementis so *e*girly schontid.

The sound repetition is more conspicuous when Type 4 is followed by Type 3, as seen in the following lines of *PPA*. Since *PPA* I.122 and *PPA* I.124 alliterate on the same /t/ sound, Type 2 is also involved:

PPA I.122 Þere *Tr*euþe is in *Tr*inite and *tr*oniþ hem alle. /t/
PPA I.123 Forþi I *s*eye as I *s*eide er, be *s*iȝte of þise textis–
PPA I.124 Whanne alle *tr*esours arn *tr*iȝed. *Tr*euþe is þe beste. /t/

Combining different types may generate complex forms of sound repetition. For instance, the sound /s/ constantly appears in the following passage of *G*. The /s/ sound in beats is underlined while the alliteration within each line is italicized:

G 2312 Bot *sn*yrt hym on þat on *s*yde, þat *s*euered þe hyde. /s/
G 2313 Þe *sch*arp *schr*ank to þe flesche þurȝ þe *sch*yre grece, /s/
G 2314 Þat þe *sch*ene blod ouer his *sch*ulderes *sch*ot to þe erþe. /s/
G 2315 And quen þe *b*urne seȝ þe *bl*ode *bl*enk on þe snawe,
G 2316 He *spr*it forth *sp*enne-fote more þen a *sp*ere lenþe, /s/
G 2317 Hent *h*eterly his *h*elme and on his *h*ed cast,
G 2318 *Sch*ot with his *sch*ulderez his fayre *sch*elde vnder, /s/
G 2319 *Br*aydez out a *br*yȝt sworde and *br*emely he spekez–

In the following passage of *PPB*, /m/ and /l/ are interwoven, as already shown in Chapter Seven. These two sounds in beats are underlined:

PPB II.31 And haþ yeuen me *M*ercy to *m*arie wiþ myselue; /m/
PPB II.32 And what *m*an be *m*erciful and *l*eelly me *l*oue /m/ & /l/
PPB II.33 Shal be my *l*ord and I his *l*eef in þe *h*eiȝe *h*euene; /l/ & /h/

PPB II.34 And what *m*an takeþ *M*ede, myn heed dar I legge /m/
PPB II.35 That he shal *l*ese for hire *l*oue a *l*ippe of Caritatis. /l/
PPB II.36 'How *c*onstrueþ Dauid þe *K*yng of *m*en þat [*c*acch]eþ *M*ede, /k/ & /m/
PPB II.37 And *m*en of þis *m*oolde þat *m*ayntene þ truþe, /m/

The following passage demonstrates how different types of vertical sound repetition appear in the initial lines of *PT*. Types of vertical alliteration that each line has are given in parentheses:

PT 1 *P*acience is a *p*oynt, þaȝ hit dis*pl*ese ofte. (Type 3) (Type 5)
PT 2 When *h*euy *h*erttes ben *h*urt wyth *h*eþyng oþer elles, (Type 5)
PT 3 *S*uffraunce may a*sw*agen hem and þe *sw*elme leþe, (Type 2)
PT 4 For ho *qu*elles vche a *qu*ed and *qu*enches malyce;
PT 5 For quoso *s*uffer cowþe *s*yt, *s*ele wolde folȝe, (Type 2)
PT 6 And quo for *þ*ro may noȝt *þ*ole, þe *þ*ikker he sufferes. (Type 2) (Type 4) (Type 5)
PT 7 Þen is *b*etter to a*b*yde þe *b*ur vmbestoundes (Type 5)
PT 8 Þen ay *þ*row forth my *þ*ro, þaȝ me *þ*ynk ylle. (Type 2) (Type 3)
PT 9 I *h*erde on a *h*alyday, at a *h*yȝe masse, (Type 2) (Type 3)
PT 10 How *M*athew *m*elede þat his *M*ayster His *m*eyny con teche.
PT 11 Aȝt *h*appes *H*e hem *h*yȝt and *v*cheon a mede, (Type 2) (Type 4)
PT 12 *S*underlupes, for hit di*ss*ert, vpon a *s*er wyse:
PT 13 Thay arn *h*appen þat *h*an in *h*ert pouerté, (Type 1) (Type 2)
PT 14 For *h*ores is þe *h*euen-ryche to *h*olde for *e*uer; (Type 1) (Type 3) (Types 4)
PT 15 Þay ar *h*appen *a*lso þat *h*aunte mekenesse, (Type 1) (Type 2)
PT 16 For þay schal *w*elde þis *w*orlde and alle her *w*ylle haue; (Type 3) (Types 4)
PT 17 Thay ar *h*appen *a*lso þat for her *h*arme wepes, (Type 2) (Type 4)

PT 13, *PT* 14, and *PT* 15 remain in consecutive alliteration (Type 1). *PT* 3 and *PT* 5 alliterate on /s/ while *PT* 6 and *PT* 8 alliterate on / θ / (Type 2). Type 2 on /h/ and vowels is found three times between *PT* 9 and *PT* 11, *PT* 11 and *PT* 13, and *PT* 15 and *PT* 17. The final beats of *PT* 8 and *PT* 9 predict the alliteration of *PT* 9 and *PT* 10, respectively (Type 3). The final beat of *PT* 11 reflects the /m/

alliteration of *PT* 10 while the final beat of *PT* 16 echoes the alliteration on /h/ and vowels in the three previous lines, *PT* 13-*PT* 15 (Type 4). The final beats of *PT* 6 and *PT* 7 start with the same /s/ sound (Type 5). *PT* 14 contains the alliteration on /h/ and vowels in all the metrical beats, which is at the same time the alliteration of its predecessor and follower (Types 3 and 4). The alliterating sound and the unalliterating sound in metrical beats of *PT* 16 are reversed in *PT* 17 (Types 3 and 4). The final beat of *PT* 16 echoes the alliteration of *PT* 15, which is another case of Type 4. It is revealing that most of these seventeen lines are involved in the sound reiteration that works beyond the line unit.

The following passage from *AG* offers another example of the combination of different types:

AG 90 And þe *h*ede and the *h*aulse *h*omelyde in sondree. (Type 2) (Type 5)
AG 91 Þe *f*ete of the *f*ourche I *f*este thurgh the sydis, (Type 5)
AG 92 And *h*euede alle in-to ane *h*ole and *h*idde it with ferne, (Type 1) (Type 2) (Type 4)
AG 93 With *h*ethe and with *h*oremosse *h*ilde it about, (Type 2)
AG 94 Þat no *f*ostere of the *f*ee scholde *f*ynde it ther-aftir; (Type 3) (Types 4)
AG 95 *H*id the *h*ornes and the *h*ede in ane *h*ologhe *o*ke, (Type 1) (Type 2) (Type 3) (Type 5)
AG 96 Þat no *h*unte scholde it *h*ent ne *h*aue it in sighte. (Type 1)
AG 97 I *f*oundede *f*aste there-fro for *f*erde to be wryghede,
AG 98 And *s*ett me oute one a *s*yde to *s*ee how it cheuede, (Type 2)
AG 99 To *w*ayte it frome *w*ylde swyne that *w*yse bene of nesse.
AG 100 And als I *s*atte in my *s*ette the *s*one was so warme, (Type 1) (Type 2) (Type 4) (Type 5)
AG 101 And I for *sl*epeles was *sl*ome, and *sl*omerde a while; (Type 1) (Type 2) (Type 5)
AG 102 And there me *dr*emed, in that *d*owte, a full *dr*eghe sweuynn, (Type 3) (Types 4)
AG 103 And whate I *s*eghe in my *s*aule the *s*othe I schall telle. (Type 2)

Every line except for *AG* 97 and *AG* 99 contains one or more types of vertical alliteration. *AG* 95, *AG* 100 and *AG* 101 are especially notable because they contain multiple types.[7]

Before a summary of the frequency and mixture of the five types in each poem, two brief comments may be made regarding vertical alliteration. The first is the frequent appearance of alliteration on the combination of /h/ and vowels. Many lines contain vertical alliteration in this combination. In this chapter, I have tried to quote examples that alliterate on more distinctive consonants such as /p/, /t/, /k/, /b/, /d/, /g/, /f/, and /s/, but the most frequent sound pattern observed in vertical alliteration is the one that uses /h/ and vowels. The role that these weak sounds play is significant.

The second point to note is the disruption of vertical alliteration by lines partly or fully consisting of Latin words in *PP*. Certain lines in Latin may alliterate, but the alliteration is not in a regular pattern. The following lines, for example, consist of English and Latin:

PPB I.52 "'*Reddite Cesari*," quod God, "þat *Cesari* bifalleþ,
PPB I.53 *Et que sunt Dei Deo*, or ellis ye don ille."

If the entire line is in Latin, it may not alliterate at all:

PPA III.228 *In quorum manibus iniquitates sunt; dextera eorum repleta est muneribus.*

These lines interrupt the alliterative rhythm, switching to a completely different prosody that Latin lines bring in. Since a line in Latin does not usually contain vertical sound repetition, it separates itself from the passage that precedes or follows it. This may help prevent boredom if such an interpretation justifies the role that lines in Latin may play in alliterative meter.

10.3 Frequencies of Five Types in the Major Twelve Poems

Table 10.1 summarizes the frequencies of vertical alliteration in each type. Because of the different size of the corpora and for ease of comparison, the percentage of each type is provided instead of the actual number of lines. For instance, 15.9% of the lines of *A* contain Type1 while 13.2% of them contain Type 2. Not all lines are under consecutive alliteration. The five types are not exclusive with each other, and may be combined in a single line. The total percentages for each poem, thus, is not one hundred:

Table 10.1. Percentages of the Five Types of Consecutive Alliteration (Twelve Poems)

	Type 1	Type 2	Type 3	Type 4	Type 5	Total % of lines in cons. a.
A	15.9 %	13.2 %	16.7 %	19.4 %	11.8 %	77.0 %
AG	15.4 %	12.9 %	19.7 %	16.2 %	19.7 %	83.9 %
C	14.7 %	11.5 %	15.2 %	13.3 %	12.7 %	67.4 %
E	13.6 %	7.4 %	14.5 %	11.6 %	14.8 %	61.9 %
G	13.7 %	6.2 %	10.9 %	10.1 %	8.5 %	49.4 %
J	13.6 %	15.3 %	15.0 %	11.4 %	14.2 %	69.5 %
MA	75.4 %	14.5 %	18.5 %	10.0 %	15.3 %	133.5 %
PPA	16.2 %	14.7 %	17.7 %	14.8 %	13.1 %	76.5 %
PPB	18.9 %	14.7 %	14.8 %	10.6 %	12.8 %	71.8 %
PT	15.4 %	15.4 %	14.1 %	18.8 %	14.9 %	78.6 %
T	6.3 %	10.6 %	13.1 %	13.3 %	16.4 %	59.7 %
W	16.1 %	9.9 %	15.5 %	11.3 %	17.3 %	70.1 %

The extreme frequency of Type 1 in *MA* is distinct. It is also noticeable that the five types are almost evenly observed in approximately fifteen percent of the lines in each poem. *G* does not use vertical alliteration as frequently as the other poems do, which reflects fewer occurrences of vertical alliteration in the bob and wheel part. On the other hand, the consistent appearance of vertical alliteration in both *PPA* and *PPB* is prominent. Lines in Latin may interrupt vertical alliteration in *PP*, which suggests that alliterative lines in *PP* employ vertical alliteration more frequently than other poems so that the poem can keep these frequency rates around the fifteen percent level.

The fifteen percent frequency of each type may not be strong evidence to prove that ME alliterative verse uses vertical alliteration as a metrical norm. When combined in two or three consecutive lines, however, vertical alliteration links the adjacent lines in a distinctive manner. Table 10.2 presents the percentages of the total occurrences of the five types in the left column. Since one line may contain more than one type, the actual percentage of the lines that remain in vertical alliteration is given in the right column:

Table 10.2. Total Percentages of Consecutive Alliteration, Single and Combined (Twelve Poems)

	Simple addition of five types from Table 10.1	Actual percentage of lines affected by one or more types
A	77.0%	56.1%
AG	83.8%	56.6%
C	67.7%	51.6%
E	61.9%	49.4%
G	49.4%	40.9%
J	69.4%	52.0%
MA	133.5%	75.9%
PPA	76.6%	55.5%
PPB	71.7%	52.5%
PT	78.7%	58.4%
T	59.7%	46.8%
W	70.2%	55.5%

The total percentage exceeds one hundred for *MA* due to its frequent use of Type 1. *MA* exhibits the highest degree of vertical alliteration in actual occurrences as well, but the other poems also show a steady percentage of single and combined occurrences of vertical alliteration. About half of the entire lines are linked with their predecessor or follower by means of the repetition of the same sound in addition to alliteration.

The five types of vertical alliteration create certain unity over a group of lines. Analyzing other ME alliterative poems regarding the use of vertical alliteration may offer new insights into the innovations that ME alliterative poets challenged, and may also reveal points to observe between those who employ vertical alliteration occasionally and those who do not. The next chapter will examine the first type, the *MA* poet who utilizes consecutive alliteration in an excessive manner in his work.

Notes

1 The bob and wheel are included because they sometimes contain consecutive alliteration.

2 A general explanation on ME alliterative meter is found, for instance, in Andrew and Waldron 47.

3 Unlike OE alliterative verse, different consonant clusters may alliterate in ME verse as long

as the same sound initiates them. In this line, /f/ and /fl/ are supposed to alliterate with each other. Another example is /s/, /sp/, /st/, and /str/ in *G* 670 and *G* 671 shown under Type 1. Since the continuation of the initial sound over consecutive lines is important for consecutive alliteration, the alliteration on different consonant clusters will be simply marked by their initial sound.

4 As seen in *MA* 3852-*MA* 3855, /ʃ/ and /s/ may alliterate with each other. Six consecutive lines alliterate on /ʃ/ from *MA* 3842 to *MA* 3847, which creates a strong sense of percussion.

5 For a detailed analysis of the identical alliteration of *MA*, see Chapters Eleven and Twelve.

6 Vowels and /h/ are considered to alliterate with each other.

7 There are many examples of passages in which various types are combined. Some examples include: *A* 497-*A* 502, *A* 899-*A* 904, *AG* 462-*AG* 476, *C* 547-*C* 560, *C* 595-*C* 604, *E* 311-*E* 320, *G* 1131-*G* 1142, *G* 2457-*G* 2467, *J* 392-*J* 396, *J* 416-*J* 424, *MA* 94-*MA* 113, *MA* 623-*MA* 655, *PPA* I.105-*PPA* I.124, *PPA* V.11-*PPA* V.20, *PPB* II.26-*PPB* II.37, *PPB* III.271-*PPB* III.279, *PT* 23-*PT* 40, *PT* 227-*PT* 238, *T* 183-*T* 196, *T* 917-*T* 926, and *W* 260-*W* 269.

Chapter 11

Recurring Alliteration in Consecutive Lines in *The Alliterative Morte Arthure*

One of the metrical peculiarities that distinguish *The Alliterative Morte Arthure* (*MA*) from the other poems in the fourteenth-century alliterative movement is that it has the same alliterating sound continuing over several consecutive lines. As explained in Chapter Ten, this is called by means of different terms: *identical alliteration, grouped alliteration, running alliteration*, and *consecutive alliteration*. The use of the same alliteration sound in consecutive lines has been used especially to ascribe a line to the *MA* poet. Vaughan explains identical alliteration as follows (3):

> Most readers of the *Morte Arthure* have remarked the poet's habit of extending a single alliterating sound over two or more consecutive lines. . . . Few commentators, however, have gone beyond remarking this as a distinctive feature of the poet's alliterative style; none has analyzed fully the incidence of such consecutive alliteration in the poem, being content to regard it as a "conscious device" of English alliterative poetry.

Vaughan argues that this phenomenon is not a mere ornament but a structural norm of the poem. About three-quarters (75.4%)[1] of *MA* lines alliterate on the same sound with their predecessor or follower, which produces a considerable quantity of sound repetition beyond the line, as well as within it. This chapter examines identical alliteration of *MA* in order to explore the aural homogeneity that the repetition of the same sound creates among consecutive lines. The goal is to reconfirm that the metrical phenomena described in the previous chapter are most pronounced in its voluminous lines of *MA*.

11.1 Consecutive Alliteration in *The Alliterative Morte Arthure*

Table 11.1 quantifies the occurrence of identical alliteration for each alliterating sound in the 4,345 lines of *MA*. Note that the total number in the right-hand column is not the total number of occurrences but the total number of lines that alliterate on that particular sound. Letters between slashes signify the phonetic value of the alliteration sound while letters in italics indicate the orthographic representation of alliteration:

Table 11.1. Sounds Used in Identical Alliteration and Their Frequencies (*MA*)

Allit. sound \ Lines	2	3	4	5	6	7	8	9	10	11	Total
/b/	71	7	13	2	2	-	-	-	-	-	237
/k/	104	18	27	2	6	1	1	-	1	-	441
ch	29	4	3	-	-	-	-	-	-	-	82
/d/	46	5	7	-	-	-	-	-	-	-	135
/f/	81	8	23	-	6	-	-	-	2	1	345
/g/	40	3	12	1	1	-	-	-	-	-	148
j	4	-	-	-	-	-	-	-	-	-	8
j/g	7	2	-	-	-	-	-	1	-	-	29
g/ȝ	1	-	1	-	-	-	-	-	-	-	6
/h/	20	2	-	-	-	-	-	-	-	-	46
vowels	67	10	15	-	3	1	-	-	-	-	249
/l/	62	5	15	-	-	-	-	-	-	-	199
/m/	37	4	3	-	-	-	-	-	-	-	98
/n/	2	-	-	-	-	-	-	-	-	-	4
/p/	44	3	9	-	-	-	-	-	-	-	133
q/ȝ/qwh/w	1	-	-	-	-	-	-	-	-	-	2
/r/	75	5	14	1	4	-	1	-	-	-	258
/s/	116	15	34	2	7	-	1	1	-	-	482
/t/	38	3	3	-	-	-	-	-	-	-	97
th	4	-	-	-	-	-	-	-	-	-	8
/v/	8	-	2	-	3	-	-	-	-	-	42
v/w	4	-	-	-	-	-	-	-	-	-	8
/w/	54	10	12	3	1	1	-	-	-	-	214
w/qw/wh/ȝ	6	-	-	-	-	-	-	-	-	-	12
Total	921	104	193	11	33	3	3	2	3	1	1,274/3,283

Table 11.1 reveals that there are 1,274 occurrences of identical alliteration in a varying number of lines and that a total of 3,283 lines[2] alliterates with the

previous or subsequent line by using the identical sound. Certain sounds are favored for identical alliteration: the group with initial /b/ such as *b*, *bl*, and *br*; the group that starts with an initial /k/ sound such as *c*, *k*, *cl*, *cr*, and *kn*; the /f/ group such as *f*, *fl*, and *fr*; /l/; /r/; and /w/. Consecutive alliteration in the mixture of vowels and /h/ is also frequent. Especially remarkable is the group containing the sound /s/ which includes fourteen variants; namely *s*, *sc*, *sch*, *schr*, *sh*, *sk*, *sl*, *sm*, *sn*, *sp*, *spr*, *st*, *str*, and *sw*. A high proportion of the total number of lines alliterates using /s/ sounds if single alliteration that does not extend over one line is also taken into account.[3] The sound /n/ is rarely used for identical alliteration, and the /t/ group is relatively infrequent.

Identical alliteration that occurs in two consecutive lines is the most frequent. Identical alliteration in three, four,[4] five, and six lines is also common while the most extreme example occurs in a group of eleven lines. In the following passage from *MA* 3080 to *MA* 3097, identical alliterations in two consecutive lines alternate nine times:[5]

MA 3080	Thare his *g*alays ware *gr*aythede, a full *gr*et nombyre,	/g/
MA 3081	All *gl*eterand as *gl*ase vndire *gr*ene hyllys,	/g/
MA 3082	With *c*abanes *c*ouerede for *k*ynges anoyntede,	/k/
MA 3083	With *cl*othes of *cl*ere golde, for *kn*yghtez and oþer;	/k/
MA 3084	Sone *st*owede theire *st*uffe and *st*ablede þeire horses,	/s/
MA 3085	*Str*ekes *str*eke ouer þe *str*em into þe *str*ayte londez.	/s/
MA 3086	Now he *m*oues his *m*yghte with *m*yrthes of herte	/m/
MA 3087	Ouere *m*owntes so hye þase *m*eruailous wayes,	/m/
MA 3088	*G*osse in by *G*oddarde; the *g*arett he wynnys,	/g/
MA 3089	*Gr*aythes the *g*arnison *gr*isely wondes!	/g/
MA 3090	When he was passede the *h*eghte, than the kyng *h*ouys	/h/
MA 3091	With his *h*ole bataylle, be*h*aldande abowte,	/h/
MA 3092	*L*ukande one *L*umbarddye, and one *l*owde melys,	/l/
MA 3093	'In ȝone *l*ykande *l*onde *l*orde be I thynke!'	/l/
MA 3094	Thane they *c*ayre to *C*ombe with *k*yngez anoyntede,	/k/
MA 3095	That was *k*yde of þe *c*oste *k*ay of alle oþer.	/k/
MA 3096	Sir *Fl*orent and sir *Fl*oridas þan *f*owndes before	/f/
MA 3097	With *fr*eke men of *Fr*aunce, well a *f*yve hundreth;	/f/

The general principle of ME alliterative meter, as explained several times in the previous chapters, is that alliteration occurs three times if the line consists of four metrical beats. The unalliterating final stressed syllable does not exhibit much metrical prominence, but plays a role in signaling the line conclusion. Identical alliteration in consecutive lines, in addition to the alliterating pattern within a given line, extends the homogeneity of sound beyond it.

The following passages exemplify extended cases of identical alliteration in ten and eleven lines, employing the /k/ and /f/ sounds, respectively:

MA 3509	'Me awghte to *kn*owe þe *k*ynge; he es my *k*ydde lorde,	/k/
MA 3510	And I, *c*alde in his *c*ourte a *kn*yghte of his chambire.	/k/
MA 3511	Sir *Cr*addoke was I *c*allide in his *c*ourte riche,	/k/
MA 3512	*K*epare of *K*arlyon vndir the *k*ynge selfen.	/k/
MA 3513	Nowe am I *c*achede owtt of *k*yth with *k*are at my herte,	/k/
MA 3514	And that *c*astell es *c*awghte with vn*c*owthe ledys!'	/k/
MA 3515	Than the *c*omliche *k*ynge *k*aughte hym in armes,	/k/
MA 3516	*K*este of his *k*etill-hatte and *k*yssede hym full sone,	/k/
MA 3517	Saide 'Wel*c*om, sir *Cr*addoke, so *Cr*iste mott me helpe!	/k/
MA 3518	Dere *c*osyn of *k*ynde, thow *c*oldis myn herte–	/k/

MA 2755	*Fl*orennt and *Fl*oridas with *f*yve score knyghttez;	/f/
MA 2756	*F*olewede in þe *f*oreste and on þe way *f*owndys,	/f/
MA 2757	*Fl*yngande a *f*aste trott, and on þe *f*olke dryffes.	/f/
MA 2758	Than *f*olewes *f*ast to oure *f*olke wele a *f*yve hundreth	/f/
MA 2759	Of *fr*eke men to þe *f*yrthe appon *fr*esche horses–	/f/
MA 2760	One sir *F*eraunt be*f*ore apon a *f*ayre stede,	/f/
MA 2761	Was *f*osterde in *F*amacoste; the *f*ende was his *f*adyre.	/f/
MA 2762	He *fl*enges to sir *Fl*orent and pristly he kryes,	/f/
MA 2763	'Why *fl*ees thow, *f*alls knyghte? Þe *f*ende hafe þi saule!'	/f/
MA 2764	Thane sir *Fl*orent was *f*ayne and in *f*ewter castys;	/f/
MA 2765	One *F*awuell of *Fr*yselande to *F*eraunt he rydys	/f/

Such a large cluster of lines that alliterate on the identical sound inevitably emphasizes the same sound, and creates a strong sound unity among its constituents. This percussive rhythm raises the question as to what aesthetic effects the poet intends to achieve.

Different groups of identical alliteration in different numbers of lines appear in succession in *MA*. For instance, there are only five lines[6] between *MA* 1446 and *MA* 1687 that do not have identical alliteration:

1446–47–48 (/l/); 1449–50 (/b/); 1451–52 (/f/); 1453–54–55–56 (/r/); 1457–58 (/s/); 1459–60 (/l/); 1461–62–63 (/g/); 1464–65–66–67 (/sw/);[7] 1468–69–70–71 (/g/); 1472–73–74–75 (/r/); 1476–77–78–79 (/p/); 1480–81 (/w/); 1482–83–84–85–86–87 (/b/); 1488–89 (/s/); 1491–92–93 (/s/); 1494–95–96–97 (/f/); 1498–99 (*vowels*); 1500–01 (/s/); 1502–03 (*ȝ*); 1504–05 (/d/); 1506–07 (/s/); 1508–09 (/r/); 1511–12–13–14 (/k/); 1515–16–17–18 (/l/); 1519–20–21–22 (/p/); 1523–24–25–26–27–28–29–30 (/r/); 1532–33–34 (/m/); 1535–36–37–38 (/f/); 1539–40–41–42 (*ch*); 1543–44–45–46 (/p/); 1547–48–49–50 (/s/); 1551–52 (*ch*); 1553–54 (/r/); 1555–56–57–58 (/s/); 1559–60 (/k/); 1561–62 (/sk/); 1563–64 (/d/); 1565–66 (/k/); 1567–68–69–70 (/t/); 1571–72–73–74–75–76–77–78 (/s/); 1579–80–81–82 (/k/); 1583–84 (/p/); 1585–86 (/k/); 1587–88 (/m/); 1589–90 (/k/); 1591–92–93–94–95–96 (*vowels*); 1597–98–99–1600 (/l/); 1601–02–03–04 (/k/); 1605–06 (/b/); 1607–08 (/r/); 1609–10–11–12 (/p/); 1613–14–15–16 (/w/); 1617–18 (/b/); 1619–20 (*ch*); 1621–22–23–24 (*vowels*); 1625–26–27–28 (/s/); 1629–30 (/tr/); 1631–32 (/p/); 1633–34 (/b/); 1635–36 (/p/); 1637–38–39–40 (/k/); 1641–42–43–44 (/s/); 1645–46–47–48 (/h/); 1649–50–51–52–53–54 (/k/); 1655–56 (/r/); 1659–60–61–62–63–64 (*vowels*); 1665–66–67–68–69–70 (/r/); 1671–72 (/k/); 1673–74 (*vowels*); 1675–76–77–78–79–80 (/r/); 1681–82 (/k/); 1683–84 (/tr/); 1685–86–87 (/s/).

In these 242 lines, there are thirty-five occasions of identical alliteration in two lines, five occasions in three lines, twenty-five occasions in four lines, six occasions in six lines, and two occasions in eight lines.

Sounds such as /l/, /m/, /n/, and /r/ can alliterate only with themselves while other sounds allow variations of consonant clusters. In particular, consonant clusters of /f/ and /s/ play a significant role in supplying variations in alliterating syllables, as seen in Table 11.1.[8] In the glossary of Hamel's edition, there are 356 entries for *f* and 572 entries for *s*, including proper names. These are remarkably numerous when compared to those for *c*, *d*, or *p*. "An important consideration . . . was the need to create a large stock of alliterating words" (Lester 102) for alliterative poets, and the *MA* poet utilized his knowledge and borrowed many words of foreign origin. Hamel notes, "The *Morte Arthure* poet stands out not because he fundamentally was different from his contemporaries but because he carried the tendency of borrowing to an extreme" (Hamel 33). The numerous words that start with /f/ and /s/ are a significant aid in maintaining identical alliteration. Though words that start with /b/ and /t/ are not infrequent in the glossary, these sounds are not common in identical alliteration.

11.2 Amalgamated Sound Repetition via Consecutive Alliteration

Identical alliteration achieves various metrical effects other than reinforcing the repetition of the same sound. *MA* lines may not alliterate in the first three metrical beats or may not have enough lexical items initiated by the same sound. Alliteration of the surrounding lines helps identify the alliterative pattern of such lines if they remain in identical alliteration. It even seems that alliteration does not need to be consistent in each line of the group. For instance, alliteration is weak in the following lines:

MA 1440	Wyth fyue hundrethe men appon faire stedes;
MA 2720	'Ʒondyr es a companye of clene men of armes,
MA 3855	And þe toþer slely slynges hym vndire.

The alliterating syllables in the above lines are not as easy to locate as those of other lines. If the neighboring lines accompany them, the locating task becomes easier:

MA 1440	Wyth *f*yue hundrethe men appon *f*aire stedes;	/f/
MA 1441	*Fr*aynez *f*aste at oure *f*olke *fr*eschely þareaftyre,	/f/
MA 1442	Ʒif þer *fr*endez ware *f*erre þat on þe *f*elde *f*oundide.	/f/
MA 2718	With a *cl*aryone *cl*ere thire *kn*yghtez to gedyre,	/k/
MA 2719	*C*allys to *c*oncell and of this *c*ase tellys:	/k/
MA 2720	'Ʒondyr es a *c*ompanye of *cl*ene men of armes,	/k/
MA 2721	The *k*eneste in *c*ontek þat vndir *Cr*iste lenges;	/k/
MA 3852	He *sch*okkes owtte a *sch*orte knyfe *sch*ethede with *s*iluere	/s/
MA 3853	And *sch*olde haue *sl*ottede hym in, bot no *sl*ytte happenede:	/s/
MA 3854	His hand *sl*eppid and *sl*ode o *sl*ante one þe mayles,	/s/

MA 3855 And þe toþer *sl*ely *sl*ynges hym vndire. /s/

MA 1440, in which alliteration is weak, initiates the first identical alliteration group whereas *MA* 3855 with weak alliteration concludes another group.[9] The line with weak alliteration in the second group, *MA* 2720, appears in the middle. Weak alliteration can be easily complemented in groups in which such a line appears in the middle or at the end because the preceding lines establish the alliterating sound prior to the line with weak alliteration. The first group, in which the line with weak alliteration initiates the identical alliteration group, may be problematic. This arrangement of weak alliteration at the beginning of the identical group, nonetheless, is most frequent. Among approximately 170 occasions of weak alliteration that appear in lines of identical alliteration, 52.1% of such occasions occur at the beginning of the group, 25.7% in the middle, and 22.2% at the end. The *MA* poet seems to have intended metrical blurring in these cases by deviating from the typical pattern, but he immediately amends the alliteration in lines that follow.

Some lines reciprocally complement their weak alliteration:

MA 3477 The kyng, *l*ordelye, hym selfe of *l*angage of Rome /l/
MA 3478 (Of *L*atin corroumppede all) full *l*ouely hym menys: /l/

MA 4064 In *s*euen grett batailles *s*emliche arrayede– /s/
MA 4065 *S*exty thowsande men, the *s*yghte was full hugge!– /s/

Only two syllables alliterate in the above four lines, and the word *sexty* in *MA* 4065 is not as strong a candidate for alliteration as other lexical items are. The prevalence of identical alliteration throughout the poem suggests that these lines are also read with the expectation of consecutive alliteration. The italicized syllables in the above lines naturally become conspicuous due to the metrical expectation of the same alliteration over consecutive lines. Another occasion in which weak alliteration is compromised by identical alliteration is found in *MA* 2042. This line seems to contain no alliteration:

MA 2042 Do dresse we therefore and byde we no langere,

However, the line that follows it offers a clue about the alliteration:

MA 2042 Do *dr*esse we tharefore and byde we no langere, ?
MA 2043 Fore *dr*edlesse withowttyn *d*owtte the *d*aye schall be ourez.' /d/

Without identical alliteration, *MA* 2042 would disturb the rhythmic regularity, but even a line without definite alliteration sustains the alliterative rhythm by echoing the alliteration of the adjacent lines. Hamel, quoting several passages of this *parallel alliteration*, asserts that these lines exemplify the poet's inclination to create new metrical bonds among lines (18–22).

A brief comment should be made concerning the possible scribal intervention in alliteration. Editors of the ME alliterative texts must decide on how to handle possible changes and errors made by the scribe. They may assume either that the scribe intervened in order to make the alliteration conform to the regular pattern, or that the scribe may have maintained the irregular alliteration of the poet's original. Some of the lines that have been used as examples in this chapter may conform to normal alliterative patterns if certain words are replaced. This is indicated with an asterisk in the following examples:

MA 1440 Wyth *f*yue hundrethe men appon *f*aire stedes;
MA 1440 Wyth *f*yue hundrethe *fr*ekes* appon *f*aire stedes;

MA 4065 *S*exty thowsande men, the *s*yghte was full hugge!–
MA 4065 *S*exty thowsande *s*eggez,* the *s*yghte was full hugge!–

Duggan, Hamel, and T. Turville-Petre all acknowledge the likelihood of scribal corruption. As Duggan asserts, "irregularity in alliterative patterning is a certain indication of scribal corruption and is true for most of the other alliterative poems" ("Patterning" 102). But as Hamel states, "there is little evidence of scribal rationalization, normalization of alliterative patterns, or other sorts of editorial tampering" in the work of Thornton and his predecessors (4)[10]. Reference to the various editions[11] will offer sufficient clues about the metrical expectations that the poet had in mind, though it is imperative to be aware of possible intervention by the scribe.

A significant number of *MA* lines reflect the alliteration of the previous line:

MA 1337 En*s*egge all þa *c*etese be þe *s*alte *st*randez, /s/
MA 1338 And seyn *r*yde in by *R*one þat *r*ynnez so faire /r/

MA 1374	Þane *pr*esez a *pr*eker in, full *pr*oudely arayede,	/p/
MA 1375	That beres all of *p*ourpour *p*alyde with syluer.	/p/
MA 1376	*B*yggly on a *br*oune stede he profers full large;	/b/
MA 1377	He was a *p*aynyme of *P*erse þat þus hym persuede.	/p/

MA 1419	To þe *S*enatour Petyr a *s*andesmane es commyn	/s/
MA 1420	And *s*aide 'Sir, *s*ekyrly ȝour *s*eggez are supprysside!'	/s/
MA 1421	Than ten thowsande men he *s*emblede at ones,	?
MA 1422	And *s*ett *s*odanly on oure *s*eggez by þe *s*alte *str*andez.	/s/

MA 1338 alliterates on /r/, but its unstressed syllables reflect the alliteration of the previous line, /s/. *MA* 1376 is another example. Its first half-line alliterates on /b/, but the identical alliteration that continues from *MA* 1374 inevitably emphasizes the initial sound of the word *profers*. Alliteration does not stand out in *MA* 1421 either, but in this metrical context, in which /s/ is repeated over several lines, the word *semblede* would be treated as an alliterating word, and stress would shift to the second syllable of the word *thowsánd* in order to supply a syllable that looks alliterating.[12]

Another piece of evidence of deliberate sound repetition is observed in a line that predicts the alliteration of the subsequent lines instead of fulfilling the alliteration requirement within itself:

MA 1066	Thow has *m*arters *m*ade and broghte oute of lyfe	/m/
MA 1067	Þat here are *br*ochede on *b*ente and *br*ittenede with thi handez,	/b/
MA 1068	I sall *m*erke þe thy *m*ede, as þou has *m*yche serfede,	/m/
MA 1069	Thurghe *m*yghte of Seynt *M*ighell þat þis *m*onte ȝemes–	/m/

MA 1567	I ȝif the for thy *t*ythandez *T*olouse þe riche–	/t/[13]
MA 1568	The *t*oll and þe *t*achementez, *t*auernez and oþer,	/t/
MA 1569	Þe *t*own and þe *t*enementez, with *t*owrez so hye,	/t/
MA 1570	That *t*owchez to þe *t*emporaltee, whills my *t*ym lastez.	/t/

MA 2073	Now *b*uskez sir Launcelot and *br*aydez full euen	/b/
MA 2074	To sir *L*ucius the *l*orde, and *l*othelye hym hyttez;	/l/

Even though *MA* 1066, *MA* 1567, and *MA* 2073 have only two alliterating syllables, they have a stressed syllable that alliterates with that of the subsequent line. Because of the successive use of the same letter and the same sound, the weak alliteration in these lines does not obscure the alliterative meter.

A similar phenomenon is observed in a line that repeats the same letter in other than the word-initial position:

MA 1511	'Thow sall hafe *c*ondycyon as þe *k*ynge lykes	/k/
MA 1512	When thow *c*omes to þe *k*yth there the *c*ourte haldez,	/k/
MA 1513	In *c*aase his *c*oncell bee to *k*epe the no langere,	/k/
MA 1514	To be *k*illyde at his *c*ommandment his *kn*yghttez before.'	/k/

MA 1511 has only two alliterating syllables as italicized, but the orthographic convention of using the letter *c* for the /ʃ/ sound gives the impression that the syllable -*cyone* alliterates with both *c* and *k* within the same line. This may be called eye alliteration. In the same manner, words that start with *w*- in the following lines behave as if they alliterated with *sw*-:

MA 812	'Has mad me full wery. Ȝe tell me my swefen,
MA 931	Þat whate [for] *sw*owynge of watyre and *s*yngynge of byrdez,

Another example of pseudo-alliteration is found in a line in which the second constituent of the alliterating consonant cluster appears close to the other alliterating sound:

MA 4002	Ne neuer *f*owle see *f*ellide þat *fl*ieghes with wenge,	/f/

In this line, alliteration occurs in word-initial /f/ and /fl/. The words *fowle* and *fellide* contain /l/ in their second syllable, which is not a constituent of the alliteration. This /l/, however, stays close enough to the alliterating syllables so that *fowle* and *fellide* appear to conform to the subsequent alliterating word *flieghes* that starts with /fl/.

MA 4152	He sall *f*erkke be*f*ore and I sall come aftyre.

MA 4152 above alliterates in two words *ferkke* and *before*. The /f/ sound in the final word *aftyre* gives the impression that it complements the weak alliteration of this line because the line contains only two alliterating syllables and because *before* is not a very strong candidate for a metrical beat.

Two different sets of alliteration may cross in two consecutive lines:

MA 1601	Bot in þe *c*lere *d*aweynge þe *d*ere *k*ynge hym selfen	/d/ and /k/
MA 1602	*C*omaundyd sir *C*adore with his dere *kn*yghttes,	/k/

MA 2939	That *s*odanly in defawte for*s*akes theire lorde!'	/s/
MA 2940	The *d*uke [*dr*essys] in his schelde and *dr*eches no lengere,	/d/

The /k/ and /d/ sounds coexist in *MA* 1601 and *MA* 1602 while /s/ and /d/ are repeated both in *MA* 2939 and in *MA* 2940.

The following two lines alliterate on the same sound. In addition, the same sound initiates their unalliterating final metrical beats, which produces the same sound pattern in two consecutive lines:

MA 3142	Bothe *p*urpur and *p*alle and *pr*ecious stonys,	/p/
MA 3143	*P*alfrayes for any *pr*ynce and *pr*ouede stedes,	/p/

MA 3228	Forthy *r*awnsakes *r*edyly and *r*ede me my swefennys.	/r/
MA 3229	And I sall *r*edily and *r*yghte *r*ehersen the sothe.	/r/

The poet seems to have used identical alliteration not only in a single group of lines but also over several different groups. The alliterating sound for the subsequent group of lines is sometimes announced before the sequence starts. As stated earlier, an identical /f/ alliteration is repeated in eleven consecutive lines from *MA* 2755 to *MA* 2765. The subsequent two lines, *MA* 2766 and *MA* 2767, alliterate on /r/, which is the sound of the final stressed syllable of *MA* 2765:

MA 2765	One *F*awuell of *Fr*yselande to *F*eraunt he rydys	/f/
MA 2766	And *r*aghte in þe *r*eyne on þe stede *r*yche,	/r/
MA 2767	And *r*ydes towarde the *r*owte; *r*estes he no lengere.	/r/

This prediction of the same alliteration sound appearing in a subsequent group of lines is also observed in *MA* 2271:

MA 2270	*R*omaynes þe *r*ycheste and *r*yall kynges,	/r/
MA 2271	Braste with *r*anke stele theire *r*ybbys in sondyre,	/r/
MA 2272	*Br*aynes fore*br*usten thurghe *b*urneste helmes,	/b/
MA 2273	With *br*andez for*br*ittenede one *br*ede in þe laundez,	/b/

The word *braste* does not play any role in alliteration in *MA* 2271. However, it is the same sound found in the identical alliteration of the subsequent lines. Similarly, the word *rydes* in *MA* 2783 predicts the alliteration that follows it:

MA 2783	*F*oloes his *f*ole *f*otte, whene he *f*urthe rydes.	/f/
MA 2784	Than *r*ydes a *r*enke to *r*eschewe þat byerne,	/r/
MA 2785	Þat was *R*aynalde of þe *R*odes and *r*ebell to Criste–	/r/

Another peculiar point regarding identical alliteration is that it may occasionally skip one or two lines:

MA 2774	He has bene *f*raistede on *f*elde in *f*yftene rewmes–	/f/
MA 2775	He *f*onde neuer no *f*reke myghte *f*eghte with hym one.	/f/
MA 2776	Thow schall *d*ye for his *d*ede with my *d*erfe wapen,	/d/
MA 2777	And all þe *d*oughtty for *d*ule þat in ȝone *d*ale houes!'	/d/
MA 2778	'*F*y!' sais sir *Fl*oridas, 'thow *fl*eryande wryche!	/f/
MA 2779	Thow wenes for to *fl*ay vs, *fl*oke-mowthede schrewe!'	/f/
(*MA* 2780	Bot Floridas with a swerde, as he by glenttys,	?)
MA 2780	Bot *Fl*oridas with a swerde, as he by *fl*yngis,	/f/
MA 2781	All þe *fl*esche of þe *fl*anke he *fl*appes in sondyre,	/f/
MA 2782	That all þe *f*ilthe of þe *f*reke and *f*ele of þe guttes	/f/
MA 2783	*F*oloes his *f*ole *f*otte, whene he *f*urthe rydes.	/f/

Alliteration on /f/ in the above passage is interrupted twice in *MA* 2776–*MA* 2777 and possibly in *MA* 2780.[14] The following passage contains the sound /k/ in a deliberate manner:

MA 673	Thow has *cl*enly þe *c*ure that to my *c*oroune langez,	/k/
MA 674	Of all my *w*er[l]dez *w*ele and my *w*eyffe eke;	/w/
MA 675	Luke þowe *k*epe the so *cl*ere there be no *c*ause fonden	/k/
MA 676	When I to *c*ontré *c*ome, if *Cr*yste will it thole;	/k/

MA 677	And thow haue *g*race *g*udly to *g*ouerne thy seluen,	/g/
MA 678	I sall *c*oroune þe, *kn*yghte, *k*yng with my handez.'	/k/
MA 679	Þan sir *M*odrede full *m*yldly *m*eles hym seluen,	/m/
MA 680	*Kn*elyd to þe *C*onquerour and *c*arpes þise wordez:	/k/

Identical alliteration is observed only in *MA* 675 and *MA* 676 in this passage, but the /k/ alliteration alternates with the other sounds of /w/, /g/, and /m/. This type of recurrence reinforces the metrical homogeneity among these lines in a subtle manner, but aural unity can be clearly detected in them. Different types of identical alliteration alternate in a somewhat systematic manner in the following passage as well:

MA 3150	Into *T*uskane he *t*ournez, when þus wele *t*ymede,	/t/
MA 3151	*T*akes *t*ownnes full *t*yte with *t*owrres full heghe;	/t/
MA 3152	*W*alles he *w*elte down, *w*ondyd knyghtez,	/w/
MA 3153	*T*owrres he *t*urnes and *t*urmentez þe pople;	/t/
MA 3154	*Wr*oghte *w*edewes full *wl*onke, *wr*otherayle synges,	/w/
MA 3155	Ofte *w*ery and *w*epe and *wr*yngen theire handis,	/w/
MA 3156	And all he *w*astys with *w*erre thare he a*w*aye rydez–	/w/
MA 3157	Thaire *w*elthes and theire *w*onny[n]ges *w*andrethe he *wr*oghte!	/w/
MA 3158	Thus they *spr*yngen and *spr*ede and *sp*aris bot lyttill,	/s/
MA 3159	*Sp*oylles di*sp*etouslye and *sp*illis theire vynes,	/s/
MA 3160	*Sp*endis vn*sp*arely þat *sp*arede was lange;	/s/
MA 3161	*Sp*edis them to *Sp*olett with *sp*eris inewe.	/s/
MA 3162	Fro *Sp*ayne into *Spr*uyslande, the worde of hym *spr*ynges	/s/
MA 3163	And *sp*ekynngs of his *sp*encis– di*ssp*ite es full hugge!	/s/
MA 3164	Towarde *V*iterbe this *v*alyant a*v*ires the reynes;	/v/
MA 3165	A*v*issely in þat *v*ale he *v*etailles his biernez	/v/
MA 3166	With *v*ernage and oþer *w*yne and *v*enyson baken,	/v/ & /w/
MA 3167	And one the *V*icounte *l*ondes he *v*isez to *l*enge.	/v/ & /l/
MA 3168	*V*ertely the a*v*awmwarde *v*oydez theire horsez	/v/
MA 3169	In the *v*erteuous *v*ale, the *v*ines imangez.	/v/
MA 3170	Thare *s*uggeournes this *s*ouerayne with *s*olace in herte,	/s/
MA 3171	To *s*ee when the *s*enatours *s*ent any wordes;	/s/

Despite the varying numbers of lines that show identical alliteration, the group as a whole forms an alliteration stream of /t/-/w/-/s/-/v/-/s/.

11.3 The *MA* Poet's Deliberation in Consecutive Alliteration

In alliterative verse, which is essentially an unusual form of speech rhythm, identical alliteration further forms a marked sound repetition woven not only among syllables within the line but also across a group of lines. Its onomatopoetic effects are prominent. Some of the examples that have been quoted in the previous sections may be accidental,[15] but the frequency of lines with elaborate sound repetition in successive lines strongly suggests a conscious intention on the part of the poet. There have been diverse opinions as to whether this is aesthetically appealing or otherwise:

> *The Alliterative Morte Arthure* has always been notorious for its repetitious language, a point that has in fact caused critics some unease. J. P. Oakden, for example, long ago singled out for censure the poem's particularly repetitious second half-lines, condemning them as empty "tags."
>
> (Krishna, "Parataxis" 74–75, emphasis original)

Whether or not this complex craft of repetition can be considered an artistic virtue is open to discussion. Extended alliteration in this deliberate fashion is especially unique to *MA*.[16] The *MA* poet exploits extended repetition, generating internal unity formed by alliteration within the line and external unity formed by identical alliteration over a group of lines. The cumulative evidence that this chapter and Chapter Ten have offered proves that, even if scribal intervention may have reduced the number of occurrences of irregular alliteration, it is clear that the *MA* poet achieves a form of peculiar verbal play by means of his extraordinary patterns of sound repetition.

Notes

1 This percentage is high compared to those of other alliterative poems. According to Vaughan, other poems show the following percentages: Dunbar's *Tretis of the Twa Mariit Wemen and the Wedow* (65 percent), *Rauf Coilyear* (20 percent), *The Awntyrs of Arthur* (35 percent), and *St. John the Evangelist* (56 percent). The overall preponderance of identical alliteration in alliterative poems is around ten to fifteen percent as discussed in Chapter

Ten.

2 Eight of these lines consist of two sets of alliteration, which makes the number of the lines that hold identical alliteration 3,275. The percentage 75.4 is calculated from this number divided by 4,345.

3 Alliteration on /s/ occurs in 149 single lines, which makes the total number of the lines alliterating on /s/ 631. This is approximately fifteen percent of the entire poem.

4 Identical alliteration in even numbers of lines is dominant. Together with the numerous occurrences of identical alliteration in two lines, this may support the contention that the poet structured the poem in the four-line strophe. See Day 245 and 248, Duggan, "Strophic" 224–28, Duggan and Turville-Petre xvii-xxiv, and Vaughan 7.

5 There are two other occasions in *MA* in which nine pairs of identical alliteration are observed: from *MA* 874 through *MA* 891 and from *MA* 3440 through *MA* 3457. These alternations of alliteration in two consecutive lines reinforce their metrical unity.

6 *MA* 1490 and *MA* 1510 alliterate on vowels, *MA* 1531 alliterates on /k/, *MA* 1657 has no alliteration, and *MA* 1658 alliterates on *j*.

7 Lines in *MA* often alliterate on the identical consonant cluster. The repetition of the same consonant cluster, /sw/, strongly binds these four lines.

8 The *MA* poet utilizes medial parts of words for alliteration, especially for alliteration on /s/. In the following lines, for instance, the morphological boundary or word boundary is ignored so that regular alliteration is achieved:

MA 813	Ore I mon *sw*elte as *sw*ythe, a*s w*ysse me oure Lorde!'	/s/
MA 1641	Di*sc*oueres now *s*ekerly *skr*ogges and oþer,	/s/
MA 3101	*Sk*ailande di*sc*ouerours, *sk*yftes theire horses;	/s/
MA 3103	Di*sk*oueres for *sk*ulkers, that they no *sk*athe lymppen.	/s/
MA 3789	*S*odaynly in di*sch*ayte by tha *s*alte *str*andes.	/s/

9 The word *fyue* is not a very strong candidate for alliteration by itself. However, when combined with numbers such as *hundred* or *thousand*, the numerals that precede them are marked as stressed and carry alliteration. Such examples are found in *MA* 930, *MA* 2160, and *MA* 3705. Other alliterative poems also contain such lines: lines 1166 and 1319 of *The Wars of Alexander* and lines 9530 and 13540 of *The Destruction of Troy*.

10 As for a counter argument of this claim, see Duggan, "Scribal" 215–17.

11 T. Turville-Petre divides the edited *MA* texts into two groups according to the editors' view on emendation. Deliberate emendation is made by Björkman while Brock and Krishna (and also Hamel) are rather cautious in this respect. See T. Turville-Petre, "Emendation" 302.

12 Alliteration is not always achieved in a regular manner if numerals such as *thousand* and *hundred* appear in the line. This may be due to the lack of synonyms that signify these numbers. In order to fulfill the alliteration requirement, the line should always have words that start with *th*- or *h*- whenever these numerals are mentioned.

13 Brock's and Krishna's editions read this line as follows:

MA 1567 I ȝif the for thy thy ȝandez Tolouse the riche,

Hamel assumes that *MA* 1567 alliterates on *t*, but according to Brock's and Krishna's reading, the line alliterates on yogh and the unalliterating word *Tolouse* predicts the identical alliteration that starts in the subsequent line. This device to assign an unalliterating stressed syllable to predict the alliteration of the subsequent line is so common that the reading by Brock and Krishna is reasonable as far as the alliteration is concerned.

14 Though Hamel considers that *MA* 2780 alliterates on /f/, other editions read the final word as *glenttys*. This reading, as shown in parentheses, interrupts the /f/ alliteration.

15 *Accidental alliteration*, which signifies the alliteration not intended by the poet, is already found in OE alliterative verse. See Hutcheson, "Accidental" 1.

16 Intricate alliteration is observed in other poems, which has been discussed in Chapter Six. In *Sir Gawain and the Green Knight*, for example, alliteration occasionally appears in unstressed syllables in addition to stressed ones, in all of the stressed syllables, and in two sets within a line. *The Wars of Alexander* (*A*) begins in a deceiving way because the first twenty-two lines except for *A* 19 are in identical alliteration: *A* 1, *A 2*, *A* 3 on /f/, *A* 4, *A* 5, *A* 6, *A* 7 on /l/, *A* 8, *A* 9, *A* 10 on /k/, *A* 11, *A* 12, *A* 13, *A* 14 on /w/, *A* 15, *A* 16, *A* 17, *A* 18 on vowels, and *A* 20, *A 21*, *A* 22 on /r/. After *A* 22, however, identical alliteration is infrequent.

Chapter 12

The Repetition of the Sound *r* in *The Alliterative Morte Arthure*: Overt and Covert Repetitions in Successive Lines

The meter of *The Alliterative Morte Arthure* (*MA*) presents several unique points compared to other fourteenth-century alliterative poems. One of these peculiarities is the excessive amount of sound repetition. The complex system of resonance contributes toward different realizations of the meter in the line as well as toward rhythmic homogeneity among different groups of lines. This chapter argues that deliberate sound repetition, particularly the repetition of *r*, plays an important role in creating unity among successive lines. First, the extended alliteration over a group of lines will be observed on /r/. As discussed in the previous chapter, identical alliteration sometimes reinforces the alliteration sound in the line that does not hold the common three alliterating metrical beats. The prediction of the *r* alliteration prior to the identical alliteration group will be clarified. Next, the chapter will reveal the repetition of *r* in other places than word-initial positions that may be divided into eight patterns. Finally, based on the idea of primary and secondary alliteration, the chapter will conclude that the recurrence of *r* in successive lines, in addition to alliteration in each of them, generates coherent rhythm beyond the line unit.

12.1 Identical Alliteration and Compensation of Weak Alliteration

Alliteration within a single line bears two functions: to unite the two half-lines and put extra prominence on stressed syllables (T. Turville-Petre, *Revival* 52). The verse line is the principal formal element that creates a verbal wit within alliterative meter. A single alliterating sound, however, stretches in *MA* over several consecutive lines. This phenomenon may be realized in various sounds and in various numbers of lines. For instance, the following passage includes four cases of identical alliteration in which the same alliteration occurs in successive lines:

MA 419	'Gret wele *L*ucius thi *l*orde and *l*ayne noghte þise wordes,	/l/
MA 420	Ife þow be *l*ygmane *l*ele; *l*ate hym wiet sone,	/l/
MA 421	I sall at *L*ammese take *l*eue and *l*oge at my *l*arge	/l/
MA 422	In de*l*itte in his *l*anndez wyth *l*ordes ynewe,	/l/
MA 423	*R*egne in my *r*ealtee and *r*yste when me lykes,	/r/
MA 424	Be þe *r*yuere of *R*oone halde my *R*ounde Table,	/r/
MA 425	*F*annge the *f*ermes in *f*aithe of all þa *f*aire rewmes	/f/
MA 426	For all þe *m*anace of hys *m*yghte and *m*awgree his eghne,	/m/
MA 427	And *m*erke sythen ouer the *m*ounttez into his *m*ayne londez,	/m/
MA 428	To *M*eloyne the *m*eruaylous and *m*yn doun the walles.	/m/
MA 429	In *L*orrayne ne in *L*umberdye *l*efe schall I nowthire	/l/
MA 430	Nokyn *l*ede appon *l*iffe þat þare his *l*awes ȝemes,	/l/

Table 11.1 presented in the previous chapter has indicated the number of identical alliteration in each alliterating sound in the 4,345 lines of *MA*.[1] This table demonstrates that identical alliteration most frequently occurs in two consecutive lines. Identical alliteration in a larger number of lines, such as three, four, five, and six, is also common while an extreme example is found in eleven consecutive lines from *MA* 2755 through *MA* 2765, as shown in Chapter Eleven. A considerable number of *MA* lines are under identical alliteration, which is one of the major points that discriminate it from other ME alliterative poems.

The following passage is another example in which two identical alliterations appear in a row: one on /f/ in ten successive lines and another on /s/ in eight successive lines:

MA 3300	'The *f*ourte was a *f*aire man and *f*orsesy in armes,	/f/
MA 3301	Þe *f*ayreste of *f*egure that *f*ourmede was euer.	/f/
MA 3302	"I was *fr*ekke in my *f*aithe" he said "whills I one *f*owlde regnede,	/f/
MA 3303	*F*amows in *f*erre londis and *fl*oure of all kynges;	/f/
MA 3304	Now es my *f*ace de*f*adide, and *f*oule es me hapnede,	/f/
MA 3305	For I am *f*allen fro *f*erre and *fr*endles byleuyde."	/f/

MA 3306	'The *f*ifte was a *f*air[r]e man þan *f*ele of þies oþer,	/f/
MA 3307	A *f*orsesy man and a *f*erse, with *f*omand lippis;	/f/
MA 3308	He *f*ongede *f*aste on þe *f*eleyghes and *f*alded [in] his armes,	/f/
MA 3309	Bot ȝit he *f*ailede and *f*ell a *f*yfty *f*ote large.	/f/
MA 3310	Bot ȝit he *spr*ange and *spr*ente and *spr*adde his armes,	/s/
MA 3311	And one þe *sp*ere-lenghe *sp*ekes he *sp*ekes þire wordes:	/s/
MA 3312	"I was in *S*urrye a *s*yr and *s*ett by myn one	/s/
MA 3313	As *s*ouerayne and *s*eyngnour of *s*ere kynges londis.	/s/
MA 3314	Now of my *s*olace, I am full *s*odanly fallen,	/s/
MA 3315	And for *s*ake of my *s*yn ȝone *s*ete es me rewede!"	/s/
MA 3316	'The *s*exte hade a *s*awtere *s*emliche bownden	/s/
MA 3317	With a *s*urepel of *s*ilke, *s*ewede full faire,	/s/

Consecutive alliteration on /r/ is found in various places in *MA*, though the number of lines involved differs in each case. The following three passages contain identical alliteration on /r/ in six lines:

MA 1665	The a*r*aye and þe *r*yalltez of þe *R*ounde Table	/r/
MA 1666	Es wyth *r*ankour *r*ehersede in *r*ewmes full many,	/r/
MA 1667	Of oure *r*enttez of *R*ome syche *r*euell he haldys;	/r/
MA 1668	He sall ȝife *r*esoun full *r*athe, ȝif vs *r*eghte happen,	/r/
MA 1669	That many sall *r*epente that in his *r*owtte *r*ydez,	/r/
MA 1670	For the *r*eklesse *r*oy so *r*ewlez hym selfen.'	/r/

MA 1675	The *r*enke so *r*eall þat *r*ewllez vs all,	/r/
MA 1676	The *r*yotous men and þe *r*yche of þe *R*ounde Table,	/r/
MA 1677	He has a*r*aysede his accownte and *r*edde all his *r*ollez;	/r/
MA 1678	For he wyll gyfe a *r*ekenyng that *r*ewe sall aftyre,	/r/
MA 1679	That all þe *r*yche sall *r*epente þat to *R*ome langez	/r/
MA 1680	Or þe *r*ereage be *r*equit of *r*entez þat he claymez.	/r/

MA 2790	Bot thane a *r*enke, sir *R*ichere of þe *R*ounde Table,	/r/
MA 2791	One a *r*yall stede *r*ydes hym aȝaynes;	/r/
MA 2792	Thorowe a *r*ownnde *r*ede schelde he *r*uschede hym sone,	/r/
MA 2793	That the *r*osselde spere to his herte *r*ynnes.	/r/
MA 2794	The *r*enke *r*elys abowte and *r*usches to þe erthe,	/r/

MA 2795	*R*oris full *r*uydlye, bot *r*ade he no more.	/r/

The above lines, which alliterate on the same word-initial sound *r*, emphasize aural unity beyond the line unit. The percussive effect of alliterative meter is powerful. Identical alliteration or consecutive alliteration[2] seems neither simply ornamental nor accidental because of its high frequency. About three-quarters, 75.4%,[3] of the *MA* lines alliterate on the same sound with their predecessor or follower, which produces an elaborate degree of sound repetition.

Identical alliteration in eight consecutive lines is the maximum occurrence for the sound *r*, which appears from *MA* 1523 through *MA* 1530:

MA 1523	Thare myghte men see *R*omaynez *r*ewfully wondyde,	/r/
MA 1524	Ouer*r*edyn with *r*enkes of the *R*ound Table;	/r/
MA 1525	In þe *r*aike of þe furthe they *r*itten þeire brenys,	/r/
MA 1526	Þat *r*ane all on *r*eede blode *r*edylye all ouer.	/r/
MA 1527	They *r*aughte in þe *r*erewarde full *r*yotus knyghtez,	/r/
MA 1528	For *r*aunsone of *r*ede golde and *r*eall stedys,	/r/
MA 1529	*R*adly *r*elayes and *r*estez theire horsez;	/r/
MA 1530	In *r*owtte to þe *r*yche kynge they *r*ade al at onez.	/r/

Alliteration on /r/ is not the most frequent sound in identical alliteration, as demonstrated in Table 11.1. The groups of the /s/ sound, /k/ sound, and /f/ sound more frequently appear than the /r/ group. A significant point that differentiates these /s/, /k/, and /f/ sounds from *r* is that they may take different forms of consonant cluster. The /s/ group is especially numerous including fourteen variants: single *s*, *sc*, *sch*, *schr*, *sh*, *sk*, *sl*, *sm*, *sn*, *sp*, *spr*, *st*, *str*, and *sw*. The /k/ group may be realized as single *c*, single *k*, single *q*, *cl*, *cr*, and *kl*. The sound /r/, on the contrary, cannot alter in different consonant clusters. The total number of 258 lines that alliterate on the single consonant /r/ proves how conspicuous this single sound is in the poem.[4]

Identical alliteration generates various metrical effects other than reinforcing the repetition of the word-initial sound. For instance, the common pattern to contain alliteration in three metrical beats within the line is not consistent, as seen in *MA* 1523 through *MA* 1530 above. Since ME alliterative meter generally intends rigid regularity in alliteration (Duggan, "Patterning," "Shape"), weak alliteration lessens the rhythmic unity. If alliteration is weak in a certain line of

MA, however, the surrounding lines may help identify the alliteration intended. This is especially so when the line remains in identical alliteration with the adjacent lines. *MA* 143, *MA* 144, and *MA* 345 contain only two alliterating syllables, but remain in identical alliteration:

MA 142	Sen I [was] *c*orounnde in *k*yth wyth *cr*ysum enoyntede,	/k/
MA 143	Was neuer *cr*eature to me þat *c*arpede so large!	
MA 144	Bot I sall tak *c*oncell at *k*ynges enoyntede,	

MA 344	Ȝife my *c*oncell a*cc*orde to *c*onquere ȝone landez,	/k/
MA 345	By þe *k*alendez of Juny we schall en*c*ountre ones	
MA 346	Wyth full *cr*euell *kn*yghtez, so *Cr*yste mot me helpe.	/k/

In these three-line groups, the surrounding lines, *MA* 142, *MA* 344, and *MA* 346, maintain the common alliteration pattern, which will inevitably mark the syllable that starts with *c* (/k/) in *MA* 143, *MA* 144, and *MA* 345. Namely, the lines that remain in identical alliteration with *MA* 143, *MA* 144, and *MA* 345 do not allow these lines to become metrically insignificant. Another example in which weak alliteration may be compensated within the identical alliteration link is *MA* 1357 below. The line looks alliterating on /f/, but the continuing /w/ alliteration will highlight *wondyrlyche*, and may compensate weak alliteration of the line. Also, this alliteration on /w/ is predicted in the line-final metrical beat of *MA* 1355, which further unites the four lines from *MA* 1356 to *MA* 1359:

MA 1355	And sterttes owtte to hys stede and with his stale wendes.	
MA 1356	Thurghe þe *w*acches þey *w*ente, thes *w*irchipfull knyghtez,	/w/
MA 1357	And fyndez in theire fare-*w*aye *w*ondyrlyche many;	
MA 1358	Ouer þe *w*atyre þey *w*ente by *w*yghtnesse of horses	/w/
MA 1359	And tuke *w*ynde as þey *w*alde by þe *w*odde hemmes.	/w/

O'Loughlin pays attention to this phenomenon, and asserts that alliteration does not need to be perfect in every line of the identical group (155). Alliteration can be lightened due to the insistent and heavy texture that identical alliteration creates. This suggests that a line in consecutive alliteration may have fewer alliterating syllables because other lines supply enough information about alliteration. The line whose alliteration is weak may appear at the beginning, in the middle, or at the end of the identical alliteration group. The arrangement of weak alliteration at the beginning of the identical group, nonetheless, is most frequent. Chapter Eleven has indicated that 52.1% of the lines whose alliteration is weak appear at the beginning of the group, 25.7% in the middle, and 22.2% at the end. The same alliteration sound can be weak in a certain line, and can be rigid in its adjacent lines. Hamel interprets this as a deliberate attempt to prevent monotony (19).

The alliteration of *MA* consists of various types of repetition over successive lines. As already observed, the unalliterating metrical beat sometimes predicts the alliteration of the subsequent lines. In the following groups, the final metrical beat of their first line, *MA* 623 and *MA* 1804, contains the alliteration sound that appears in the subsequent lines. The unalliterating line-final word announces the alliteration sound that will follow it. The consonant in the line-final metrical beat that announces the forthcoming alliteration is underlined:

MA 623	In the contré of Coloine castells enseggez	
MA 624	And *s*uggeournez þat *s*eson wyth *S*arazenes ynewe.	/s/

MA 1804	One sir Cador the kene with cruell wordez,	
MA 1805	'Thowe hase *w*yrchipe *w*onne and *w*ondyde knyghttez;	/w/
MA 1806	Thowe *w*enes fore thi *w*ightenez the *w*erlde es thy nowen.	/w/
MA 1807	I sall *w*ayte at thyne honnde, *w*y, be my trowthe;	/w/
MA 1808	I haue *w*arnede þe *w*ele, be*w*are ȝif the lykez.'	/w/

Prediction of the /r/ alliteration occurs in the initial line of the following passages:

MA 361	Þat borne es in his banere, of brighte golde ryche,	
MA 362	And *r*aas it from his *r*iche men and *r*yfe it in sondyre,	/r/
MA 363	Bot he be *r*edily *r*eschowede with *r*iotous knyghtez.	/r/

MA 2277	Sowdane ne Sarazene ne senatour of Rome.	
MA 2278	Thane *r*eleuis þe *r*enkes of the *R*ounde Table	/r/
MA 2279	Be þe *r*iche *r*euare that *r*ynnys so faire,	/r/

MA 2765	One Fawuell of Fryselande to Feraunt he rydys	
MA 2766	And *r*aghte in þe *r*eyne on þe stede *r*yche,	/r/
MA 2767	And *r*ydes towarde the *r*owte; *r*estes he no lengere.	/r/

MA 2911 Þat þe hiltede swerdes to þaire hertes r̲ynnys.
MA 2912 Than þe *r*enkes *r*enownde of þe *R*ownd Table /r/
MA 2913 *R*yffes and *r*uyssches down *r*enayede wreches, /r/

MA 919 And there hys knyghtes hym kepede, full clenlyche ar̲ayede.
MA 920 Than they *r*oode by þat *r*yuer þat *r*ynnyd so swythe, /r/
MA 921 Þare þe *r*yndez ouer*r*echez with *r*eall bowghez. /r/
MA 922 The *r*oo and þe *r*aynedere *r*eklesse thare ronnen /r/
MA 923 In *r*anez and in *r*osers to *r*yotte þam seluen. /r/

MA 3891 For sake of his sybb blode sygheande he r̲ydys.
MA 3892 When þat *r*enayede *r*enke *r*emembirde hym seluen /r/
MA 3893 Of [þe] *r*euerence and *r*yotes of þe *R*ownde Table, /r/
MA 3894 He *r*emyd and *r*epent hym of all his *r*ewthe werkes: /r/
MA 3895 *R*ode awaye with his *r*owte, *r*istys he no lengere, /r/
MA 3896 For *r*ade of oure *r*iche kynge, *r*yve þat he scholde. /r/

When the line-final metrical beat reflects the alliteration of subsequent lines, this implies that the syllable that does not participate in alliteration of a certain line, in fact, foretells the alliteration sound dominating the subsequent lines.

Weak alliteration may be compensated if the line remains in a group of identical alliteration, as seen in *MA* 387, *MA* 389, *MA* 391, *MA* 1428, *MA* 1456, and *MA* 2986 below:

MA 387 And I may se þe *R*omaynes þat are so *r*yche halden
MA 388 A*r*ayede in þeire *r*iotes on a *r*ounde felde, /r/
MA 389 I sall, at þe *r*euerence of þe *R*ounde Table,
MA 390 *R*yde thrughte all þe *r*owtte, *r*erewarde and oþer, /r/
MA 391 *R*edy wayes to make and *r*enkkes full rowme,
MA 392 *R*ynnande on *r*ede blode as my stede *r*uschez; /r/

MA 1427 The *R*omaynes *r*edyes them, a*rr*ayez þam better, /r/
MA 1428 And al to-*r*uscheez oure men withe theire *r*yste horsez–
MA 1429 A*r*estede of the *r*icheste of þe *R*ounde Table, /r/
MA 1430 Ouer*r*ydez oure *r*erewarde and grette *r*ewthe wyrkes. /r/

MA 1453	The *R*omaynes than *r*edyly a*rr*ayes them bettyre,	/r/
MA 1454	One *r*awe on a *r*owm felde *r*eghttez theire wapyns	/r/
MA 1455	By þe *r*yche *r*euare, and *r*ewles þe pople;	/r/
MA 1456	And with *r*eddour sir Boice es in a*r*este halden.	

MA 2983	And thane he *r*aykes to þe *r*owte and *r*uysches one helmys;	/r/
MA 2984	*R*iche hawberkes he *r*ente and *r*asede schyldes,	/r/
MA 2985	*R*ydes on a *r*awndoune and his *r*ayke holdes.	/r/
MA 2986	Thorowowte þe *r*erewarde he holdes [his] wayes	
MA 2987	And thare *r*aughte in the *r*eyne, this *r*yall þe *r*yche,	/r/
MA 2988	And *r*ydez in to þe *r*owte of þe *R*ownde Table.	/r/

In the following passage, *r* appears as the line-final metrical beat of *MA* 1606 and *MA* 1609. The two lines in between alliterate on /r/, which creates the /r/ network within these four lines:

MA 1606	Sir Bawdwyne, sir Bryane, and sir Bedwere þe ryche,	
MA 1607	Sir *R*aynalde and sir *R*ichere, *R*awlaunde childyre,	/r/
MA 1608	To *r*yde with þe *R*omaynes in *r*owtte wyth theire feres.	/r/
MA 1609	'Prekez now preualye to Parys the ryche	

12.2 Recurring *r* in Alliteration within the Line and over Consecutive Lines

In identical alliteration, *r* often plays a different role that other sounds do not. As mentioned earlier, *r* cannot initiate different consonant clusters, but it can be part of different consonant clusters as their second or third constituent. Namely, the sound *r* acts in a peculiar way in the English language because the same *r* can be a second or third constituent of different consonant clusters. For instance, *r* in the following lines recurs not as the word-initial sound but as a second or third constituent of a consonant cluster:

MA 561	*Str*yke þem doun in [þe] *str*ates and *str*uye them fore euere.	/str/
MA 1753	And than the *Br*etons *br*othely en*br*assez þeire scheldez,	/br/
MA 2357	'We hafe *tr*ystily *tr*ayuellede þis *tr*ibutte to feche:	/tr/

In these lines, *r* keeps repeating in the same consonant cluster. The consonant clusters that can include *r* in *MA* are: *br*, *cr*, *dr*, *fr*, *gr*, *kr*, *pr*, *schr*, *spr*, *str*, *thr*, *tr*, and *wr*. Combined with the alliteration on *r*, these clusters sustain the same *r* sound if not as a word-initial sound. For example, *r* constantly appears in the metrical beats in the passage that starts from *MA* 912. The letter *r* in metrical beats is underlined:

MA 912	His *gl*oues *g*aylyche *g*ilte and *gr*auen at þe hemmez	/g/
MA 913	With *gr*aynez and *g*obelets *gl*orious of hewe.	/g/
MA 914	He *br*acez a *br*ade schelde and his *br*ande aschez,	/b/
MA 915	*B*ounede hym a *br*oun stede and on þe *b*ente houys;	/b/
MA 916	He *st*erte till his *st*erepe and *str*idez on lofte,	/s/
MA 917	*Str*eynez hym *st*owttly and *st*erys hym faire,	/s/
MA 918	*Br*ochez þe *b*aye stede and to þe *b*uske rydez,	/b/
MA 919	And there hys *kn*yghtes hym *k*epede, full *cl*enlyche arayede.	/k/
MA 920	Than they *r*oode by þat *r*yuer þat *r*ynnyd so swythe,	/r/
MA 921	Þare þe *r*yndez ouer*r*echez with *r*eall bowghez.	/r/
MA 922	The *r*oo and þe *r*aynedere *r*eklesse thare *r*onnen	/r/
MA 923	In *r*anez and in *r*osers to *r*yotte þam seluen.	/r/
MA 924	The *fr*ithez ware *fl*oreschte with *fl*ourez full many,	/f/

Even though alliteration occurs in different sounds and in a different number of lines, *r* echoes throughout the above passage. The lines in which *r* participates in alliteration can be classified into the following five types and three sub-types:

Type A⁺ (The line alliterates on /r/ while the final unalliterating metrical beat starts with a consonant cluster that includes *r*.):

MA 1124	Thane he *r*omyede and *r*arede, and *r*uydly he strykez
MA 2881	That the *r*askaille was *r*ade and *r*ane to þe grefes
MA 4207	With *r*ynges and *r*elikkes, and þe *r*egale of Fraunce

This type contains words starting with *r* in all metrical beats. Other alliterative poems such as *Sir Gawain and the Green Knight* and *Piers Plowman* may alliterate on the same sound in all the metrical beats of the line, which makes a clear contrast to *MA*. In *MA*, it is not common for all metrical beats to alliterate within the line. The following *MA* line is one of the few examples in which all metrical beats alliterate on /r/:

MA 2987 And thare *r*aughte in the *r*eyne, this *r*yall þe *r*yche,

Despite his adherence to excessive alliteration, the *MA* poet leaves the line-final metrical beat alliteration free, and the maximum placement of *r* in all the four metrical beats is not to fill them with words starting with *r* but to use a consonant cluster that includes *r* for the final one.

Type A (Three out of four metrical beats alliterate on /r/ while the final unalliterating metrical beat does not include *r*.):

MA 17 Off the *r*yeall *r*enkys of the *R*ownnde Table,
MA 1529 *R*adly *r*elayes and *r*estez theire horsez;
MA 3601 By þe *r*oche with *r*opes he *r*ydes on ankkere

Type A is a typical realization of alliterative meter with first three metrical beats alliterating.

Type B (All the alliterating syllables contain the identical consonant cluster that includes *r* while the final unalliterating metrical beat starts with *r*.):

MA 1374 Þane *pr*esez a *pr*eker in, full *pr*oudely arayede,
MA 2566 *Br*istes þe rere*br*ace with the *br*onde ryche,
MA 3352 That the *kr*ispan[d]e *kr*oke to my *cr*ownne raughte,

Type B^{-} (The first three metrical beats alliterate on the identical consonant cluster that includes *r* while another consonant cluster that includes *r* initiates the final unalliterating metrical beat.):

MA 1471 Fore *gr*eefe of þe *gr*ett lorde so *gr*ymlye he strykez;
MA 2114 *Cr*aschede doun *cr*estez and *cr*uschede braynez,
MA 3657 *Br*awndeste *br*own stele, *br*aggede in trompes;

In Type B^{-}, all metrical beats include *r*, but this *r* is not the word-initial sound as seen in Type A^+.

Type C (Alliteration occurs on the identical consonant cluster that includes *r* while the final unalliterating metrical beat does not include *r*.):

MA 760 Hym *d*remyd of a *d*ragon *d*redfull to beholde,

MA 930 They *th*repide wyth the *th*rostills, *th*re hundreth at ones,

MA 1141 *W*rothely þai *w*rythyn and *w*rystill togederz,

Type D (One or two alliterating metrical beats include *r* while the final unalliterating metrical beat starts with *r*.):

MA 37 Gyan and Gothelande and Grece the ryche,

MA 1111 And with his *b*urlyche *b*rande a *b*ox he hym reches:

MA 4249 Thane *f*rescheliche þe *f*reke the *f*ente vpe rererys,

Type D^- (Two metrical beats of the line include *r* as a second or third constituent of different consonant clusters.):

MA 589 Iche *p*rynce with his *p*owere a*pp*ertlyche graythede.

MA 2079 The *st*ede and the *st*eryn mane *st*rykes to þe grownde,

MA 3567 Hym sall *t*orfere be*t*yde, þis *t*resone has wroghte,

Type E (One alliterating syllable of the line includes *r* as a second or third constituent of a consonant cluster.):

MA 535 Of *k*ynge or of *c*onquerour *c*rownede in erthe,

MA 536 Of *c*ountenaunce, of *c*orage, of *c*rewelle lates,

MA 537 The *c*omlyeste of *k*nyghtehode þat vndyre *C*ryste lyffes.

The echo of *r* is weak in Type E. Occurring in several consecutive lines, however, this type creates a subtle repetition of *r*, as seen in the above passage from *MA* 535 through *MA* 537. These five types of *r* alliteration can be summarized in Table 12.1. The capital letters A and B denote the initial consonant or consonants of a cluster while X denotes any unalliterating sound. The frequency of each type in *MA* appears in the right column. The dotted line divides these types into the ones that alliterate on *r* and those that alliterate on other sounds but include *r* as a constituent of a consonant cluster:

Table 12.1. Alliteration Types Involving *r* and Their Frequencies (*MA*)

Type A^{+}	r-r-r-Ar	19 lines
Type A	r-r-r-X	310 lines
Type B	Ar-Ar-Ar-r	9 lines
Type B^{-}	Ar-Ar-Ar-Br	9 lines
Type C	Ar-Ar-Ar-X	144 lines
Type D	A-Ar-A-r	54 lines
Type D^{-}	A-Ar-A-Br	37 lines
Type E	A-Ar-A-X	813 lines
Total		1,395 lines

A total of 1,395 lines remains in primary and secondary alliteration, which indicates that 32.1% of the entire 4,345 lines echo the *r* sound. Types A^{+} and A are traditionally considered alliteration. Types from B through E are not considered alliteration if the term refers only to the repetition of a stem-initial sound. The recurrence of *r*, however, creates special rhythm in *MA*. In the passage quoted earlier, *r* echoes from *MA* 912 through *MA* 919 before the alliteration on *r* occurs in four consecutive lines from *MA* 920 through *MA* 923. The consonant cluster that includes *r* can behave as a linking bridge between lines that primarily alliterate in different sounds. Another example in which *r* echoes in this way is from *MA* 1606 to *MA* 1611:

MA 1603	Sir *Cl*eremus, sir *Cl*eremonte, with *cl*ene men of armez,	
MA 1604	Sir *Cl*owdmur, sir *Cl*egis, to *c*onuaye theis lordez,	
MA 1605	Sir *B*oyce and sir *B*erell, with *b*aners displayede,	
MA 1606	Sir *B*awdwyne, sir *Br*yane, and sir *B*edwere þe ryche,	Type D
MA 1607	Sir Raynalde and sir Richere, Rawlaunde childyre,	Type A
MA 1608	To ryde with þe Romaynes in rowtte wyth theire feres.	Type A
MA 1609	‘*Pr*ekez now *pr*eualye to *P*arys the ryche	Type D
MA 1610	Wyth *P*etir the *pr*yssonere and his *pr*ice knyghttez;	Type C
MA 1611	Beteche þam þe *Pr*oueste in *pr*esens of lordez,	Type C

From *MA* 1603 through *MA* 1607, the word *sir* is repeated, though this syllable is realized unstressed in reading and the lines alliterate on sounds other than /s/. *MA* 1603 and *MA* 1604 alliterate on /k/ sounds while *MA* 1605 and *MA* 1606 alliterate on /b/ sounds. These four lines exemplify identical alliteration in two consecutive lines. The additional echo created by *sir* stands clearly, and in the next group of lines, namely from *MA* 1607 through *MA* 1611, *r* takes its turn to sustain the rhythmic homogeneity in different identical alliteration groups.

12.3 Primary and Secondary Alliteration

If Type A is termed *primary alliteration*, Types from B to E may be called *secondary* alliteration. This secondary alliteration may be considered *accidental* as Hutcheson argues ("Accidental" 4). He claims that the poet himself did not intend to employ secondary alliteration systematically and that the result is purely incidental. Hutcheson implies that accidental alliteration occurs in syllables that are unstressed. In the case of *MA*, however, secondary alliteration on *r* occurs in metrical beats, creating a strong percussive effect that Prior regards as the primary function of alliterative meter.

The language was still rhotic at the time when *MA* was composed. The letter *r* was pronounced in all occasions: word-initially, word medially, word-finally, before a vowel, before a pause, and before any consonant. The *r* sound must have been extremely emphasized in *MA* by its frequent appearance in metrical beats of primary and secondary alliterations. It does not seem purely incidental that Chaucer used the phrase *rum, ram, ruf* in *The Canterbury Tales* to describe alliterative meter cynically. It must be Chaucer's good ear to have *r* represent alliterative meter, but the meter is far more complex than mere ornamentation like *rum, ram, ruf*, as already seen several times. The *MA* poet tried to expand the alliterative device in order to add extra prominence beyond the prescribed metrical unit. Even if the poet did not intend to use secondary alliteration as a formal requirement of his meter, it is difficult to assume that the recurrence of *r* in metrical beats of thirty-two percent, or about one-third, of the whole lines is never deliberate.

Two other passages are analyzed below in order to examine how constantly *r* is heard. Vaughan uses binding lines to show the strophic patterns of *MA*. Following his method, I use this marking system on both sides of the lines in order to mark identical alliteration on the left side and secondary alliteration in *r* on the right side. The metrical network that the letter *r* produces in secondary alliteration divides the lines into groups that are different from identical alliteration groups.

/k/	*MA* 3212	will by þe *C*rosse-dayes en*c*roche þeis londez	Type C
/k/	*MA* 3213	And at þe *C*rystynmesse daye be *c*rownned theraftyre;	Type C
/r/	*MA* 3214	Ryngne in my *r*yalltés and holde my Rownde Table	Type A
/r/	*MA* 3215	Withe the *r*entes of Rome, as me beste lykes.	Type A
	MA 3216	Syne *g*raythe ouer þe *G*rette See with *g*ud men of armes	Type C
	MA 3217	To *r*euenge the Renke that on the Rode dyede.’	Type A
	MA 3218	Thane this *c*omlyche *k*ynge, as *c*ronycles tellys,	Type E
	MA 3219	*B*ownnys *b*rathely to *b*ede with a *bl*ythe herte;	Type E
/b/	*MA* 1407	Thane þe en*b*uschement of *B*retons *b*rake owte at ones	Type C
/b/	*MA* 1408	*B*rothely at *b*anere, and *B*edwere knyghtez	Type E
/r/	*MA* 1409	A*rr*estede of þe Romayns þat by þe fyrthe *r*ydez,	Type A
/r/	*MA* 1410	All þe *r*ealeste *r*enkes þat to Rome lengez.	Type A
vowels	*MA* 1411	Thay *i*che on þe *e*nmyse and *e*gerly strykkys,	
vowels	*MA* 1412	*E*rles of *I*nglande, and ‘*A*rthure!’ ascryes;	
/b/	*MA* 1413	Thrughe *b*renés and *b*ryghte scheldez *b*restez they thyrle,	Type C
/b/	*MA* 1414	*B*retons of the *b*oldeste, with theire *b*ryghte swerdez.	Type C
/r/	*MA* 1415	Thare was Romayns ouer*r*edyn and *r*uydly wondyde,	Type A
/r/	*MA* 1416	A*rr*estede as *r*ebawdez with *r*yotous knyghttez;	Type A
/r/	*MA* 1417	The Romaynes owte of a*r*aye *r*emouede at ones	Type A
/r/	*MA* 1418	And *r*ydes awaye in a *r*owtte– for *r*eddoure, it semys!	Type A
/s/	*MA* 1419	To þe *S*enatour Petyr a *s*andesmane es commyn	
/s/	*MA* 1420	And *s*aide ‘Sir, *s*ekyrly ȝour *s*eggez are supprysside!’	
/s/	*MA* 1421	Than ten thow*s*ande men he *s*emblede at ones,	
/s/	*MA* 1422	And *s*ett *s*odanly on oure *s*eggez by þe *s*alte *st*randez.	Type E
/b/	*MA* 1423	Than ware *B*retons a*b*aiste and greuede a lyttill;	Type D^{-}
/b/	*MA* 1424	Bot ȝit the *b*anerettez *b*olde and *b*achellers noble	
/b/	*MA* 1425	*B*rekes that *b*attaille with *b*restez of stedes;	Type C
/b/	*MA* 1426	Sir *B*oice and his *b*olde men myche *b*ale wyrkes.	
/r/	*MA* 1427	The Romaynes *r*edyes them, a*rr*ayez þam better,	Type A
/r/	*MA* 1428	And al to-*r*uscheez oure men withe theire *r*yste horsez–	

____Type A
/r/ *MA* 1429 Arestede of the richeste of þe Rounde Table,________Type A
/r/ *MA* 1430 Ouerrydez oure rerewarde and grette rewthe wyrkes._Type A
MA 1431 Thane the *Br*etons on þe *b*ente ha*b*yddez no lengere__Type E

Different webs among the lines can be seen through this marking. Reading the above passage aloud inevitably reveals the recurrence of *r*. In *MA*, primary alliteration is already heavy. Even without the idea of secondary alliteration, the *MA* lines are alliterative enough. Acknowledging secondary alliteration reveals another system that reinforces sound repetition. The *MA* poet was ambitious to use excessive repetition of the same sound more than required in alliterative meter, generating internal unity made by alliteration within the line and external unity made by identical alliteration and secondary alliteration over a group of lines. The result is an amazing and amusing form of verbal play in multiple sound repetitions.

Peters and Green, acknowledging enormous resonance of the letter *p* in *Piers Plowman*, conclude that the *p* words play a vital role in it. In *MA* on the other hand, the sound *r* achieves overt and covert metrical networks. The repetition of the sound *r* is not mere coincidence, but forms the rhythm in the sense of Cureton's definition. That is, the sound *r* creates the complex but coherent sensation of leveled hierarchies of resonance (Cureton, "Rhythm"). The *MA* poet, whether conscious or not, must have appreciated the complexity of consonant clusters of the English language that could be manipulated in order to create untraditional linkages in his verbal wit.

Notes

1 For a detailed analysis about the sounds used in identical alliteration and their frequencies, see Chapters Ten and Eleven.
2 See Chapter Ten for various terms proposed for this phenomenon.
3 This percentage is high compared to other alliterative poems since the average appearance of identical alliteration in others is around 10–15 percent. See Vaughan 3.
4 Alliteration on /r/ in a single line that does not remain in identical alliteration with the adjacent neighbor is observed in seventy-one lines, which makes the total number of lines alliterating on /r/ in *MA* 329. This comprises 7.6 percent of the entire lines.

Chapter 13

Tension between Alliteration and Speech Rhythm in the Meter of ME Alliterative Verse

In the scansion of ME alliterative verse, alliteration provides in most cases a clue about where to locate metrical beats. Editors of ME alliterative poems usually explain that the alliterative meter of the fourteenth century often consists of four beats within a verse line, three of which typically alliterate (Andrew and Waldron 47). The following lines of *Sir Gawain and the Green Knight* (*G*) exemplify the typical alliteration, which is marked by italics. The accent mark indicates where metrical beats fall while the alliteration sound appears between slashes:

G 137	On þe *m*óst on þe *m*ólde on *m*ésure hýghe;	/m/
G 138	Fro þe *sw*ýre to þe *sw*ánge so *sw*áre and so þík,	/s/
G 139	And his *l*ýndes and his *l*ýmes so *l*ónge and so gréte,	/l/

Not all lines, however, are as regular as these three examples. Reading the line strictly according to alliteration may result in an unnatural way of reading. For example, the following lines of *The Destruction of Troy* (*T*) suggest two or three ways of recitation. In the following scansion, which offers two alternatives in four-beat reading, alliteration is italicized while the overall pattern is shown in brackets after each line:

T 1568-a	Grete *p*ális of *p*ríse, *pl*énty of hóuses,	[aaax]
T 1568-b	Gréte *p*alis of *p*ríse, *pl*énty of hóuses,	[xaax]
T 1252-a	But a *g*rét nowmbur of *G*rékes *g*édrit hym ýmbe,	[aaax]
T 1252-b	But a *g*ret nówmbur of *G*rékes *g*édrit hym ýmbe,	[xaax]

The reading that conforms to alliteration, namely reading *a* in the above examples, will not put metrical stress on *grete* in *T* 1568, but will do so in *T* 1252, and this way of reading results in the regular [aaax] pattern. Yet a question arises as to whether the reading that puts metrical stress on *grete* in *T* 1568 and on *nowmbur* in *T* 1252, namely reading *b*, is totally erroneous. Claiming that reading *b* of *T* 1568 is not legitimate will contradict with reading *a* of *T* 1252. This implies that alliteration may not always be the primary determiner in placing metrical beats, and that other factors can intervene in order to justify two readings.

In the study of English prosody, it is known that English stress is affected by a relative relationship between syllables placed in linear order. In considering metrical stress, it is crucial to separate lexical stress from stress within a phrase, which is called *phrasal stress* or *postlexical stress pattern* (Fabb, *Linguistics* 25–50; Cureton, *Rhythmic Phrasing* 120–78). According to the natural rhythmic rule of English, stress is relatively weaker in the monosyllabic adjective than the noun that immediately follows it if the noun has its primary stress on its first syllable. Thus, stress is relatively weaker on the adjective of the phrase *rich men*, though both words receive stress when uttered slowly and carefully. Reading *b* of *T* 1568 and reading *a* of *T* 1252 above create tension against natural speech rhythm because the natural rhythm of the phrase does not coincide with the alliteration pattern. In other words, the linguistic make-up of a short adjective immediately followed by a stressed syllable of a noun can create tension against the metrical template. The reader may perceive the reading *b* of *T* 1568 and reading *a* of *T* 1252 as uneasy because of this tension, which leads to a slow performance and special emphasis on the adjective.

The present chapter is a cumulative study of the relationship between alliteration and natural speech rhythm in ME alliterative verse. The following ten poems will be used for this analysis:[1]

Excerpts from *The Wars of Alexander* (*A*)	2,000 lines
The Parlement of the Thre Ages (*AG*)	661 lines
Cleanness (*C*)	1,812 lines
Saint Erkenwald (*E*)	352 lines
Sir Gawain and the Green Knight (*G*)	2,530 lines
The Siege of Jerusalem (*J*)	1,334 lines
The Alliterative Morte Arthure (*MA*)	4,345 lines
Patience (*PT*)	531 lines

Excerpts from *The Destruction of Troy* (*T*)	2,000 lines
Wynnere and Wastoure (*W*)	503 lines

Using the corpus consisting of the above poems, this chapter reveals the tension that alliteration creates against natural speech rhythm in determining metrical beats.

13.1 Metrical Subordination Rule in ME Alliterative Verse

One metrical phenomenon that reflects the tension between alliteration and natural speech rhythm is the collocation of a short adjective and a noun, such as *grete palis* and *gret nowmbur*, as observed above. When alliteration is ignored and *nowmbur* receives metrical stress in *T* 1252 as in reading *b* below, rhythmic blurring occurs due to the deviation in alliteration:[2]

T 1252-a But a *g*rét nowmbur of *G*rékes *g*édrit hym ýmbe, [aaax]
T 1252-b But a *g*ret nówmbur of *G*rékes *g*édrit hym ýmbe, [xaax]

If metrical stress on *gret* is plausible for *T* 1252, the only reason to reject the same reading for *T* 1568 is that metrical stress on *grete* does not conform to alliteration:

T 1568-a Grete *p*ális of *p*ríse, *p*lénty of hóuses, [aaax]
T 1568-b Gréte *p*alis of *p*ríse, *p*lénty of hóuses, [xaax]

However, reading *b* may be favorable and legitimate because rhythmic blurring prevents boredom. Scholars such as Hamel acknowledge the deliberate blurring as an effective device to avoid monotony (Hamel 19).

To complicate the situation, scholars of ME alliterative meter have frequently acknowledged five beats per verse line. The following line from *G* is Burrow and T. Turville-Petre's example to show that the ME alliterative line can be read in either four-beat or five-beat meter:

G 159 Of *b*ryȝt golde, vpon silk *b*ordes *b*arred ful ryche, [aaax] or [axaax]

The lines from *T* examined earlier, thus, can be read in five-beat meter if the reader wishes to do so:[3]

*T*1568-c	Gréte *p*ális of *p*ríse, *pl*énty of hóuses,	[xaaax]
T 1252-c	But a *gr*ét nówmbur of *Gr*ékes *g*édrit hym ýmbe,	[axaax]

If both the adjective and the noun alliterate, the [aaaax] pattern will yield. This pattern reinforces the alliteration, and five-beat reading may be felt reasonable. The following are a few examples that contain the collocation of a short adjective and a noun both of which alliterate:

J 747	A <u>*g*rete *g*irdel</u> of *g*old with-out *g*er oþer	[aaaax] or [aaax]
PT 302	Þe <u>*b*ygge *b*orne</u> on his *b*ak and *b*ete on his sydes.	[aaaax] or [aaax]
A 1174	<u>*F*resch *f*olke</u> for þe *f*iȝt and *f*ode for his oste,	[aaaax] or [aaax]

Reading these lines in five-beat meter does not violate the alliteration rule, but rather reinforces it. The adjectives, *grete*, *bygge*, and *fresch* in these examples, may be realized unstressed if the meter demands only four beats per line. This suggests that natural speech rhythm may reduce stress from the short adjective.

The syntactic relationship between a short adjective and a noun is known to stay in metrical subordination. Since the publication of Chomsky and Halle's theory that assigns relative degrees of stress to a linear sequence of syllables, metrists have acknowledged the hierarchy in stress. This was first called the nuclear stress rule, which places relatively stronger stress on the rightmost constituent within a phrase (Chomsky and Halle; Cureton, *Rhythmic Phrasing*). More specifically in the study of metrical phonology, it is argued that stress is reduced from the first constituent of a syntactic unit of a short adjective and a noun (Attridge, *Rhythms* 230–39; Hanna, "Defining" 44; T. Turville-Petre, *Poetry* 6). A short adjective immediately followed by a noun whose first syllable is stressed becomes weak, and is realized unstressed due to its syntactic relationship with its follower. Attridge provides a thorough explanation on metrical subordination (*Rhythms* 230):

> It must be emphasised once more that subordination is not simply a matter of one syllable's being pronounced longer, louder, or at a higher pitch than another, but of a perceived relationship within the syntactic structure, ultimately related to habitual muscular actions but in a given case not necessarily manifested by physical means at all. This fact is crucial to an understanding of poetic rhythm.

Adjectives, such as *great*, *good*, *royal*, *deep*, *noble*, and *rich*, are common examples of metrically subordinated stress in ME alliterative poems. According to Couper-Kuhlen, English verse has utilized metrically subordinated stress since the time of the Anglo-Saxons (*Rhythm* 79–113). Metrically subordinated stress works ideally for the collocation in which the noun does alliterate but the adjective does not. The first example quoted earlier, *T* 1568, is such a case. Reducing stress from *grete* and realizing metrical stress in *palis* will produce the recitation that matches with natural speech rhythm and simultaneously satisfies the alliteration requirement in a most typical pattern:

T 1568-a	Grete *p*ális of *pr*íse, *pl*énty of hóuses,	[aaax]

A few more examples that satisfy both the rule of natural speech rhythm and the alliteration rule are given below:

C 1506	*St*ád in a ryche *st*ál, and *st*áred ful brýȝte;	[aaax]
J 1273	Riche *p*élour and *p*áne, *pr*ínces to wér,	[aaax]
E 236	For to *dr*ésse a wrang *d*óme, no *d*áy of my lýue.	[aaax]

The reading that does not acknowledge metrical stress in the adjective can be justified by means of its subordination to the noun that follows.

The same phenomenon is observed in the combination of a verb and its object, though such occasions are not as frequent as the collocation of an adjective and a noun. In this case, the verb is subordinated to its object and may lose its strong stress:

J 47	Caled *N*ero by *n*ame, þat hym to *n*oye wroȝt,	[aaax] or [xaaax]
W 303	Maken *d*ale aftir thi *d*aye, for thou *d*urste never.	[aaax] or [xaaax]
T 1526	Toke *c*ouncell in the *c*ase and his *c*are leuyt.	[aaax] or [xaaax]
C 99	Waytez *g*orstez and *g*reuez, if ani *g*omez lyggez;	[aaax] or [xaaax]

The alliteration patterns that conform to the common one yield if the verb is considered metrically subordinated to its object. The rule of metrical subordination of short adjectives and short verbs is often observed in many of the poems analyzed here. In summary, metrical subordination in ME alliterative verse, which reduces the stress from the first constituent and places metrical stress on the second, reflects the natural speech rhythm of the English language, and operates for the collocation of a short adjective and a noun and that of a short verb and its object.

Metrical subordination in certain lines, however, exhibits a different placement of alliteration from the common pattern. For instance, the adjective, but not the noun, alliterates in the following lines:

MA 944	*C*aughte of þe <u>colde wynde</u> to *c*omforthe hym seluen.
G 1179	And *G*awayn þe <u>god mon</u> in <u>gay bed</u> lygez,
A 1043	Of <u>*cl*ere gold</u> of þaire *k*ist and *c*oruns a hundrethe.
PT 294	<u>Þre dayes</u> and <u>*þ*re nyȝt</u>, ay *þ*enkande on Dryȝtyn,

The adjectives, *colde*, *god*, *gay*, and *clere*, as well as the numeral *þre*, do alliterate but the accompanying nouns do not. In the case of *PT* 294, it may be awkward not to place metrical stress on the word *þre* and read the line with the alliteration on *dayes* and *Dryȝtyn* only. It is difficult to apply the metrical subordination rule strictly in such a combination if regular alliteration is desired. But, this collocation of an *alliterating* adjective and an *unalliterating* noun is much more frequent than the collocation of an *unalliterating* adjective and an *alliterating* noun. More detailed observation will be made in the next section.

13.2 Compound Stress Rule in ME Alliterative Verse

If the metrical subordination rule is unable to explain why alliteration occurs not in the noun but in the adjective, another principle must be operating in order for the line to achieve regular alliteration. There are a significant number of lines that do not conform to natural speech rhythm. To consider alliteration as the most decisive factor in deciding metrical beats will be problematic because it is difficult to explain why the mismatch between the natural rhythm and the metrical beat is found so occasionally. One possible explanation is the Germanic compound stress rule postulated by Lass:

> **Compound Stress Rule**
> For any sequence $[_X A, B]$, where X is a lexical category (Noun, Verb, Adjective, Adverb), A is strong and B is weak. (*Old English* 90)

In Chapter Fifteen, I will argue that the compound stress rule operates in *MA* in a prevailing manner, and this phenomenon is common in many of ME alliterative poems.[4] I modify Lass's definition to postulate the following for ME alliterative meter:

Compound Stress Rule in ME Alliterative Meter

(i) For any sequence $[_X A, B]$, where X is a lexical category (Noun, Verb, Adjective, Adverb), assign metrical stress to the leftmost primary stressed vowel.

(ii) B usually acts as an unstressed element. If the meter demands another stressed syllable, it may recover its stress quality and be realized as a stressed syllable.

If the phrases, *colde wynde* of *MA* 944, *god mon* of *G* 1179, and *clere gold* of *A* 1043 quoted earlier, are assumed to act like a compound, stress can fall on the adjective, and the lexical stress of the noun can be reduced. In the following three consecutive lines of *AG*, the noun *knyghte* may not receive stress in order for the line to achieve alliteration in three metrical beats. The common alliteration [aaax] can be justified if the phrases, *trewe knyghte*, *noble knyghte*, and *prise knyghte*, are considered to act as a compound. If the noun receives metrical stress according to the metrical subordination rule, the [axax] pattern will yield. If five beats are acknowledged, the alliteration pattern will be [aaxax]. Three different readings, in short, are possible for these lines. All three readings are legitimate, even though each reader may have different preferences:

AG 326 Sir *Tr*oylus, a *tr*ewe knyghte þat *tr*istyly hade foghten,
[aaax], [axax] or [aaxax]

AG 327 *N*eptolemus, a *n*oble knyghte at *n*ede þat wolde noghte fayle,
[aaax], [axax] or [aaxax]

AG 328 *P*alamedes, a *p*rise knyghte, and *p*reued in armes,
[aaax], [axax] or [aaxax]

In order for these lines to maintain the regular [aaax] pattern, the underlined phrases must act like a compound. However, the reading that places metrical stress on nouns and uses the alliteration pattern of [axax] cannot be dismissed immediately because it follows the rule of metrical subordination. Reading these lines in five-meter is also a legitimate delivery instance.[5] The lines, in other words, are flexible enough to be read in three different ways, and the alliteration patterns that emerge from these delivery instances differ slightly.

Table 13.1 summarizes the percentages of the alliteration patterns found in the collocation of a short adjective and a noun in the ten poems analyzed. The pattern *ax* is the combination of an *alliterating* adjective and an *unalliterating* noun like *colde wynde* with alliteration on /k/, the pattern *xa* is the combination of an *unalliterating* adjective and an *alliterating* noun like *gret showres* with alliteration on /ʃ/, and the pattern *aa* is the combination of an *alliterating* adjective and an *alliterating* noun like *grete girdel*:

Table 13.1. Alliteration Patterns of a Short Adjective and a Noun (Ten Poems)

	ax	*xa*	*aa*	Total
A	64.8%	10.0%	25.2%	100.0%
AG	64.9%	9.6%	25.5%	100.0%
C	31.3%	19.9%	48.8%	100.0%
E	52.8%	16.7%	30.5%	100.0%
G	44.2%	21.5%	34.3%	100.0%
J	71.3%	17.7%	11.0%	100.0%
MA	68.4%	15.8%	15.8%	100.0%
PT	32.5%	27.3%	40.2%	100.0%
T	80.6%	9.7%	9.7%	100.0%
W	60.8%	16.2%	23.0%	100.0%

Table 13.1 reveals that the *ax* pattern is frequent in the collocation of a short adjective and a noun. *C* and *PT* favor the *aa* pattern. *G* also shows the similar tendency, though the *ax* pattern is more frequent in it. These three poems, *C*, *G*, and *PT*, tend to use alliteration in an excessive manner, and the frequent collocation pattern of *aa* may be a reflection of this tendency. The remaining poems exhibit a strong preference for the *ax* pattern. The tension that this metrical make-up creates against natural speech rhythm is high.[6] Reading the line with regular alliteration requires the natural rhythm to be deformed. This results in an artificial array of alliterating beats. The larger percentages of the *ax* and *aa* patterns than the *xa* pattern suggest that the compound stress rule is presumably more dominant than the metrical subordination rule in ME alliterative verse. Again, this is true if regular alliteration is desired all the time.

13.3 Mobile Stress and ME Alliterative Meter

T. Turville-Petre comments on the flexible stress placement in ME alliterative verse as follows:

> The conventional formulation for lines with extra alliteration is aaa/ax. This is accurate in so far as it is taken to represent the alliterative pattern alone. However, the alliterative pattern is only significant in its relation to the stress-pattern. The formulation aaa/ax is misleading in that it suggests that all the alliterating syllables bear metrical stress. To show that the first alliterating word, while possessing some weight and contributing to the sound and pace of the line, is not one of the four accents, the designation (a)aa/ax might be used. The bracketed element alliterates but is not equivalent to the stressed syllables. (T. Turville-Petre, *Revival* 55)

I have modified T. Turville-Petre's method and use brackets to mark the collocation of an adjective and a noun or the collocation of a verb and a noun. Either of the constituents in the brackets may be realized as a metrical beat and the remaining one may be realized as a metrical offbeat; choosing the alliterating syllable or the unalliterating syllable for a metrical beat will be at the discretion of each reader in each delivery instance. The reader also may put metrical stress on both of the constituents grouped by brackets. Examples used earlier are reanalyzed below by means of the brackets to indicate flexible placement of metrical beats. The reader may choose one of the constituents in the brackets as a metrical beat, or may put metrical stress on both of them:

T 1568	Grete *p*alis of *pr*ise, *pl*enty of houses,	[(xa)aax]
T 1252	But a *gr*et nowmbur of *Gr*ekes *g*edrit hym vmbe,	[(ax)aax]
G 159	Of *bry*ȝt golde, vpon silk *b*ordes *b*arred ful ryche,	[(ax)(xa)ax]
J 747	A *gr*ete *g*irdel of *g*old with-out *g*er oþer	[(aa)aax]
PT 302	Þe *b*ygge *b*orne on his *b*ak and *b*ete on his sydes.	[(aa)aax]
A 1174	*F*resch *f*olke for þe *f*iȝt and *f*ode for his oste,	[(aa)aax]
C 1506	*St*ad in a ryche *st*al, and *st*ared ful bryȝte;	[a(xa)ax]
J 1273	Riche *p*elour and *p*ane, *pr*inces to wer,	[(xa)aax]
E 236	For to *dr*esse a wrang *d*ome, no *d*ay of my lyue.	[a(xa)ax]

J 47	Caled *N*ero by *n*ame, þat hym to *n*oye wroȝt,	[(xa)aax]
W 303	Maken *d*ale aftir thi *d*aye, for thou *d*urste never.	[(xa)aax]
T 1526	Toke *c*ouncell in the *c*ase and his *c*are leuyt.	[(xa)aax]
C 99	Waytez *g*orstez and *g*reuez, if ani *g*omez lyggez;	[(xa)aax]
MA 944	*C*aughte of þe *c*olde wynde to *c*omforthe hym seluen.	[a(ax)ax]
G 1179	And *G*awayn þe *g*od mon in *g*ay bed lygez,	[a(ax)(ax)x]
A 1043	Of *cl*ere gold of þaire *k*ist and *c*oruns a hundrethe.	[(ax)aax]
PT 294	*Þ*re dayes and *þ*re nyȝt, ay *þ*enkande on Dryȝtyn,	[(ax)(ax)ax]
AG 326	Sir *T*roylus, a *t*rewe knyghte þat *t*ristyly hade foghten,	[a(ax)ax]
AG 327	*N*eptolemus, a *n*oble knyghte at *n*ede þat wolde noghte fayle,	[a(ax)ax]
AG 328	*P*alamedes, a *p*rise knyghte, and *p*reued in armes,	[a(ax)ax]

The collocation marked in brackets indicates that the meter is flexible enough to produce three different readings. If the alliterating constituent is considered to receive metrical stress, the line will form a common alliteration pattern. If the unalliterating constituent receives metrical stress, the pattern that contains a smaller number of alliterating beats will merge. For each case, a different stress rule, the metrical subordination rule or the compound stress rule, operates.

One of the unique features of the alliterative style of the fourteenth century is the variable number of stressed syllables per line. Several debates have occurred between various proponents concerning the number of metrical beats in a line; some, such as Borroff, Sapora, and Stillings, assume that four per line is the base while others like Gardner consider the base to be a five-beat meter. For example, both Gardner and Vantuono scan *G* 1 in five-beat meter (Gardner 87; Vantuono, *Gawain* 260):

G 1 Síþen þe sége and þe assáut watz sésed at Tróye,

Not all scholars, however, will accept Gardner's scansion because they consider the first syllable of *siþen* unstressed (Burrow and Turville-Petre 59). Borroff's term *extended lines* ("Reading") and Sapora's list of lines with five stressed syllables as a deviation presuppose that four-beat meter is the base. The conflicting results of these arguments lie in the assumption that the metrical scheme should be in one single form and that the line consisting of four beats is always the base. Lines with five beats, however, neither sound unmetrical nor disturb poetic rhythm. For instance, it will be difficult to read the following lines in strict four-beat meter:

PT 151 Þe *s*ayl *sw*eyed on þe *s*ee, þenne *s*uppe bihoued
PPB XI.347 *L*erned to *l*egge þe stikkes in whiche she *l*eyeþ and bredeþ.
W 121 He *br*ake a *br*aunche in his hande, and caughte it swythe,

As discussed in Chapter Two, my assertion regarding this issue is that the ME alliterative line is flexible enough to produce four *or* five beats according to metrical necessity and stylistic preferences. The underlying meter can generate four or five beats while the resulting alliteration may deviate from the norm or may be reinforced by another alliterating beat.

The crucial point is that metrical stress in certain circumstances is mobile. Yet this does not mean that metrical stress is not rule-governed. The poets left only certain lines with metrical flexibility in which readers may take advantage of different stress rules. If regular alliteration is the first priority in such lines, the line can conform to that way of reading. The same line may be read in a different manner if stress is reduced from the alliterating constituent. That reading may be unfavorable or sound distasteful, but such a reading is one of the possible choices.

In conclusion, the metrical subordination rule must be in operation in order for the line to be read in natural speech rhythm whereas the compound stress rule must operate in order to achieve common alliteration patterns. ME alliterative poets utilized flexibility in stress placement so that readers might take advantage of both alliteration and natural speech rhythm while maintaining the lines alliterative enough. This signifies that the mobility of English stress was already in effect in the fourteenth century. It also proves that rules governing beyond a group of words could take precedence over the stress rules within words for the sake of rhythmicality. A significant number of ME alliterative poets deliberately utilized various rules of prosody available to them in their time.

Notes

1 *Pearl* and *Piers Plowman* are not included since their metrical norms are different from these poems, as examined in Chapters Four, Five, and Seven.

2 Realizing metrical stress in the adjective that does not seem to alliterate sometimes results in a different alliteration pattern. In the following lines, for instance, putting metrical stress on a short adjective rather than on the noun it modifies produces two sets of alliteration:

T 405 Grét showres to shéde and shynýng agáyne, [abba]
T 430 The grét tempull tóp térned to gróund. [abba]

J 283 Ffrésch water and wýn wóunden yn fáste, [abba]

The same is true to the noun that does not look alliterating until the line-final metrical beat is known:

MA 3167 And one the Vícounte lóndes he vísez to lénge. [abab]

J 781 Þan wróþ as a wode bóre he wéndeþ his brídul: [abab]

3 Reading the line in five-beat meter often results in two stressed syllables in a row like *grét nówmbur*. Since English prosody shows a strong preference toward the regular alternation between stressed and unstressed syllables, this reading inevitably places extra emphasis on both of the words. Cable claims that even in the nonpoetic, ordinary form the English language tries to alleviate a stress clash. See Cable, "Clashing" 16–17.

4 Another definition of the CSR is made by Couper-Kuhlen (*Introduction* 28): "Compound Stress Rule . . . assigns primary stress to the *leftmost* primary stressed vowel in lexical categories (N, A, V), automatically reducing all other stresses by one [degree]" (italics original).

5 According to Jakobson, the *verse design* determines the meter of the verse line whereas the verse design allows variations called the *verse instance*. The *delivery design* and the *delivery instance* are not directly governed by the meter, but these two elements operate in the actual reading of the verse line. See Jakobson, "Closing" 350–77.

6 As to the tension between the natural rhythm and the metrical expectation, see Chapter Four of Furniss and Bath. Also insightful is the observation made by Kelly and Rubin.

Chapter 14

Metrical Constraints of the Line End of ME Alliterative Verse

The verse line of alliterative poems popular in the fourteenth century exhibits certain metrical peculiarities. One of them is the line end, which has more restrictions on syllables and stress than other parts of the line do. This chapter analyzes a corpus of major and minor poems of the ME alliterative movement, and argues that special prosodic rules are always in operation in the second half-line, particularly with the final metrical beat. These constraints may be summarized as follows:

1. The number of unstressed syllables is slightly larger in the first half-line than in the second, which enables the first half-line to formulate a relatively regular alternation between stressed and unstressed syllables.
2. The absence of unstressed syllables, which is found more frequently prior to the final metrical beat than at any other point of the line, suggests that ME alliterative meter tends to become slower toward the end.
3. The number of unstressed syllables at the line end presents a certain limitation. It tends to be less than one, which makes a clear contrast to the other offbeat positions that may contain various numbers of unstressed syllables.
4. The metrical beat at the line end does not alliterate. The absence of alliteration, especially in recitation, signals the line boundary.
5. Another metrical constraint can be added at the line end when the verse uses end-rhyme in addition to alliteration. Fulfilling both the alliteration requirement and the rhyme requirement complicates the meter and affects how the line ends.

All of these constraints result in the special rhythm of ME alliterative verse, creating a sound pattern that is overwhelmingly repetitious. Chapter Two has investigated the metrical template and its variations of the so-called Gawain poems: *Pearl* (*PE*), *Cleanness* (*CL*), *Patience* (*PT*), and *Sir Gawain and the Green Knight* (*G*). The present analysis uses larger data in order to reveal the metrical norm and constraints of the ME alliterative meter in general. A corpus consisting of the following major and minor ME alliterative poems is used for the present analysis:

Excerpts from *The Wars of Alexander* (*A*)	1,000 lines
The Parlement of the Thre Ages (*AG*)	661 lines
Excerpts from *Cleanness* (*C*)	1,000 lines
Dispute Between Mary and the Cross (*CR*)	900 lines
Saint Erkenwald (*E*)	352 lines
Excerpts from *Sir Gawain and the Green Knight* (*G*)	900 lines
Excerpts from *The Siege of Jerusalem* (*J*)	1,000 lines
The Three Dead Kings (*K*)	143 lines
Excerpts from *The Alliterative Morte Arthure* (*MA*)	1,009 lines
Pearl (*PE*)	1,211 lines
Excerpts from *Piers Plowman*, B-Text (*PPB*)	1,000 lines
A Pistel of Susan (*PS*)	364 lines
Patience (*PT*)	531 lines
Somer Soneday (*SS*)	133 lines
Excerpts from *The Destruction of Troy* (*T*)	1,000 lines
Wynnere and Wastoure (*W*)	503 lines

14.1 Beats, Offbeats, and the Final -*e* Revisited

As explained in Chapter Two, a scansion method proposed by Attridge is practical and beneficial in analyzing ME alliterative lines. Attridge's system has been adapted and simplified for the present analysis. *B* indicates the place of a metrical beat while a lowercase *o* indicates offbeats with a numeral that marks the actual number of unstressed syllables between metrical beats. The absence of any unstressed syllables, which is called the implied offbeat, is marked by the null symbol, *ø*, while the word final -*e* without any accompanying unstressed syllables is marked by the symbol °:

```
E 177        Then he turnes to þe toumbe and talkes to þe corce,
                 o2   B    o3      B    o2    B     o3     B  °

A 1305       And þan in batis and in bargis he bownes him swyth,
                 o3      B    o3      B    o2   B    o2     B

C 221        Fellen fro þe fyrmament fendez ful blake,
              B      o3     B   o2    B    o2     B °

PT 487       Bot now I se Þou art sette my solace to reue;
                  o3    B    o2    B   o2   B   o3    B °

G 3          Þe tulk þat þe trammes of tresoun þer wroȝt
              °  B    o2      B    o2    B    o2     B

J 675        Kesten at þe kernels and clustred toures,
              B    o3      B      o2     B   o   B  o

PPB I.143    For to louen þi Lord leuere þan þiselue,
               o2    B   o2   B  ø B      o4     B  °
```

One important point in analyzing medieval English verse is that a final *-e* may be elided either to a following vowel or to a sequence of *h* and a vowel. In *E* 177, for instance, the final *-e* of *toumbe* may be elided to the initial vowel of *and*, which results in a single offbeat rather than a double offbeat. Since elision does not affect the beat positions, the final *-e*'s are usually counted as separate syllables. Examples used later, such as *E* 89, *MA* 2, and *MA* 364, also contain a final *-e* prior to a vowel. The number of unstressed syllables that form an offbeat may slightly differ if elision is taken into consideration. However, recognizing a single offbeat or double offbeat depending on how the final *-e* is counted does not drastically affect the alternation between beats and offbeats. This method of scansion reveals the composition of unstressed syllables in an explicit manner, and metrical beats are easily found. Furthermore, the controversial final *-e*'s are separately marked since the unstable status of this syllable sometimes requires an explanation. The role of the final *-e* is considered in more detail later in this section.

The first significant point regarding the line end of ME alliterative verse is that the first half-line may contain more unstressed syllables and even an additional metrical beat. The following passage, namely the initial fourteen lines of *A*, in principle, can have the number of syllables in each half as demonstrated in brackets. The numbers within the brackets, such as [8–5], indicate that the first half-line of *A* 1 can have eight syllables while the maximum number of syllables is five for the second half. The number will be smaller if the elision is taken into account, but I have tentatively counted the word final *-e* as a separate syllable for the following fourteen lines:

A 1	When folk ere festid and fed fayn wald þai here	[8–5]
A 2	Sum farand þing efter fode to fayn þare her[t],	[8–5]
A 3	Or þai ware fourmed on fold or þaire fadirs oþer.	[8–7]
A 4	Sum is leue to lythe þe lesing of Sayntis,	[7–6]
A 5	Þat lete þer lifis be lorne for oure lordis sake;	[9–7]
A 6	And sum has langing of lufe lays to herken,	[8–4]
A 7	How ledis for þaire lemmans has langor endured.	[8–6]
A 8	Sum couettis and has comforth to carpe and to lestyn	[8–7]
A 9	Of curtaissy of knyȝthode of craftis of armys,	[8–6]
A 10	Of kyngis at has conquirid and ouer-comyn landis.	[8–7]
A 11	Sum of wirschip I-wis slike as þam wyse lattis,	[6–8]
A 12	And sum of wanton werkis þa þat ere wild-hedid;	[7–7]
A 13	Bot if þai wald on many wyse a wondire ware it els;	[9–8]
A 14	For as þaire wittis ere with-in so þer will folowis.	[10–6]

The first half-line contains more syllables than the second half except for *A* 11 and *A* 12. The number of unstressed syllables produces these differences since the number of metrical beats in each half-line is usually the same, namely two metrical beats per each half-line. Even though the difference in numbers is not always large, the larger number of unstressed syllables in the first half-line is one of the significant phenomena of ME alliterative verse. A clear contrast between the two half-lines regarding the number of syllables is found in the following examples. The maximum number of syllables that each half-line possibly contains appears between brackets:

A 219	As tite as Anec him amed out of his awyn kythe,	[9–7]

J 165 Þer is no gome [o]n þis [grounde] þat is grym wounded, [9–5]
T 1855 That he may menske hur with mariage þat ye mart haue, [10–5]
MA 364 I sall enforsse ȝowe in þe felde with fresche men of armes, [11–7]
PPB XVIII.298 And þus haþ he trolled forþ þise two and þritty wynter. [10–5]

Certain lines may have three metrical beats in the first half, but this is not very likely in the second half. Forcing four-beat meter onto lines containing five stressable syllables that may be legitimate candidates for metrical beats can produce unnatural rhythm. For example, the following lines are likely to be in five-beat meter since they contain three metrical beats that are clearly separated by offbeats in their first half:

```
C 1014   Þat foundered hatz so fayr a folk and þe folde sonkken.
           o   B        o4          B   o  B   o2       B  °  B   o

PT 151   Þe sayl sweyed on þe see, þenne suppe bihoued
           o  B  ø  B    o3     B    o2     B    o2  B o

E 15     He turnyd temples þat tyme þat temyd to þe deuell,
           o  B  o  B      o2     B   o2    B    o3     B o

MA 3680 Bruschese boldlye on burde brynyede knyghtes,
            B   o2   B     o2   B  °   B   o2   B   o

J 915    Hym-self he strykeþ myd þat staf: streȝt to þe hert,
           o   B   o   B      o3         B  ø  B    o2    B
```

Alliteration supports the idea of the five-beat line since all of the above lines alliterate in the [aaaax] pattern. The first half-line is, therefore, flexible enough to have a different number of beats and a different number of syllables for offbeats. The second half-line usually does not exhibit this flexibility.

The second significant point regarding ME alliterative verse is that the number of unstressed syllables in the line expresses certain tendencies according to the position where they appear. An implied offbeat, which designates no unstressed syllable between two metrical beats, tends to appear in a certain position within the line. Out of 503 lines of *W*, for instance, only nine implied offbeats occur in the line-medial positions whereas twenty-four lines hold an implied offbeat in the position prior to the final metrical beat. The following are two examples that contain an implied offbeat in a line-medial position:

```
W 220 If I schall deme yow this day, dothe me to here."
              o3       B      o3      B ø  B    o3     B °

W 488 When that es dronken and don, duell ther no lenger,
               o3        B    o2     B  ø  B      o2     B  o
```

The implied offbeat in the following two lines appears just prior to the final metrical beat:

```
W 210 Kayren up at the clyffe and one knees fallyn.
         B       o4         B       o4     B  ø B  o

W 302 Thi sone and thi sektours, ichone slees othere;
          o  B       o3    B        o4         B ø B  o2
```

This position, that is, in the middle of the second half-line or between the third beat and the fourth beat of the line, may contain a different number of unstressed syllables, but the implied offbeat appears frequently in this position. This is one of the reasons why the second half-line tends to have a smaller number of unstressed syllables than the first half-line. The following lines are a few more examples that contain an implied offbeat prior to the final metrical beat:

```
A 1603 Enclynes þam to þe conquirour and him on kneis gretis,
          o   B        o4      B          o5            B  ø  B o

PT 322 Þat I may lachche no lont, and Þou my lyf weldes.
              o3      B    o2    B          o3      B ø B  o
```

```
E 89    And als freshe hym þe face and the flesh nakyd
          o2       B     o3      B       o3     B  ø B o

MA 2¹   And the precyous prayere of Hys prys modyr
           o2      B     o2  B          o4    B ø B o

J 1196 And vp stondiþ for ston[es] or for steel gere.
           o2     B    o2      B      o3        B  ø  B °
```

Table 14.1 demonstrates the occurrences of the implied offbeat in the twelve poems analyzed. The table indicates the number of lines that contain no unstressed syllable in each metrical position. An additional metrical beat that is sometimes allowed in the first half-line is designated as B_0. The metrical beats in the line are numbered from B_0 to B_4. The number of lines examined in each poem is given in parentheses:

Table 14.1. Occurrences of the Implied Offbeat (Twelve Poems)

	Between B_0 and B_1	Between B_1 and B_2	Between B_2 and B_3	Between B_3 and B_4
A (1,000 lines)	12	30	40	132
AG (661 lines)	1	2	6	19
C (1,000 lines)	34	45	61	117
E (352 lines)	5	7	15	29
G (900 lines)	34	26	58	102
J (1,000 lines)	28	35	78	158
MA (1,009 lines)	5	8	10	39
PE (1,211 lines)	0	17	11	29
PPB (1,000 lines)	18	34	42	65
PT (531 lines)	15	9	24	65
T (1,000 lines)	2	0	30	165
W (503 lines)	1	2	6	24

Table 14.1 reveals the general tendency to place the implied offbeat toward the line end. Because of the absence of any unstressed syllables before the final metrical beat, the rhythm of the line significantly slows at the end of the line. Traditionally called *trochee*, two stressed syllables in succession have the effect of slowing the rhythm of the line whereas a succession of unstressed syllables produces a trotting rhythm.[2]

The metrical value of the word final -*e* is a matter of controversy in considering the phonological make-up of medieval English. What metrical value this weak syllable can have has not met any consensus yet. If the final *-e* is assumed to be already silent in the days of ME alliterative verse, the number of syllables per line becomes smaller and the line can be interrupted more frequently by a pause. The final *-e* without any accompanying vowel or combination of *h* and a vowel allows a certain tendency to appear in a particular position within the verse line.

One significant point regarding the final *-e* is that it can be elided either to the subsequent vowel or to the combination of *h* and a vowel. However, if there is only one final *-e* between metrical beats, it would naturally form an offbeat so that the alternation between beats and offbeats will be maintained. It can be silent if the reader prefers that way of reading. This metrical instability of the final *-e* is important for the study of alliterative meter since its interpretation will result in different verse instances.

There are fourteen occasions in *W* in which the final *-e* without any accompanying unstressed syllables appears in the middle of the line, and eighty-five occasions in which the single final *-e* appears prior to the final metrical beat. The following two lines contain a single final –*e* in a line-medial position, which is marked as °:

```
W 120 That any wy in this werlde wiste of his age.
          o3        B    o2      B   °  B        o3    B  °
```

```
W 498 For at the proude pales of Parys the riche
           o3          B   °  B      o2   B   o2       B   °
```

The following examples contain a single final –*e* prior to the final metrical beat:

```
W 17  Bot whoso sadly will see and the sothe telle,
           o3       B     o2     B       o2     B  °  B   °
```

```
W 271 Some hafe girdills of golde that more gude coste
           o4       B     o2      B          o4       B  °  B   °
```

If the final *-e* is assumed to be silent all the time, the line will have a smaller number of syllables, and the above *W* lines will contain an implied offbeat in the middle of the line where marked with °. Even if it is assumed to form an offbeat, the offbeat consisting of a single final -*e* is not as conspicuous as other unstressed syllables. The higher frequency of the single final –*e* toward the end of the line (fourteen as compared to eighty-five) supports the idea that the verse line tends to have a very few or no unstressed syllables at all in front of the final metrical beat.

A row of unstressed syllables has the opposite tendency. The offbeat consisting of more than three metrically unstressed syllables is commonly observed in all the poems analyzed. Table 14.2 illustrates the occurrences of such offbeats in the first hundred lines of each of the same twelve poems considered in Table 14.1. Since offbeats consisting of more than three unstressed syllables are frequent, the first hundred lines reflect how they appear in general:

Table 14.2. Occurrences of the Offbeat Consisting of More Than Three Unstressed Syllables (First One Hundred Lines of Twelve Poems)

	Before B_0	Between B_0 and B_1	Between B_1 and B_2	Between B_2 and B_3	Between B_3 and B_4
A	1	35	44	30	18
AG	0	22	24	11	20
C	1	21	13	10	1
E	3	26	22	22	5
G	1	21	4	10	4
J	0	19	16	20	6
MA	0	11	20	23	7
PE	0	0	0	0	0
PPB	0	9	23	24	14
PT	2	22	15	10	4
T	0	9	21	15	1
W	0	35	11	17	5

It is evident from Table 14.2 that the offbeat consisting of more than three unstressed syllables is less frequently observed between the third metrical beat and the fourth metrical beat, which makes a distinct contrast to the other positions. The table also proves that the trotting rhythm created by a group of unstressed syllables in succession initiates the ME alliterative line. The slow rhythm toward the end of the line, in addition to the non-alliterating beat in the line-final position, signals the line boundary.[3]

14.2 Three Patterns to Conclude the Verse Line

The metrical structure of the line conclusion has certain peculiarities. The verse line can end with a metrical beat (or a stressed syllable), a final -*e*, or an offbeat (a single unstressed syllable or possibly two unstressed syllables). Below are examples for each case; *T* 3054 ends with a metrical beat, *T* 1150 with a final -*e*, and *T* 745 with an offbeat:

```
T 3054 To telle of hir tethe þat tryetly were set,
        o  B      o3    B   o2     B      o2   B
```

```
T 1150 Pollux with his pupull pursu on the laste.
        B       o3      B o    B    o3     B  °
```

```
T 745  All þe course for to know, þat is to cum after:
         o2    B     o3      B      o3      B ø B  o
```

Certain lines end with more than two unstressed syllables as lines below demonstrate, but such lines are not many:[4]

```
C 1492 Expouned His speche spiritually to special prophetes.
       o  B     o2    B  °   B       o4     B  o    B   o2
```

```
G 1414 So þat þe mete and þe masse watz metely delyuered,
           o3     B    o3     B      o2  B    o3  B  o2
```

If the line ends with an offbeat, it is usually a single offbeat consisting of a single unstressed syllable, as seen in *T* 1150 above. An unstressed syllable plus a final -*e* can also appear, as seen in *A* 855 below. It is possible to read such an ending with a double offbeat, but I consider this combination in the line-final position as a single offbeat. This is because of the high frequency of a single offbeat at the line end:

```
A 855  And so þe wee in his wreth wrekis his modire,
           o3     B     o2    B  ø  B     o2  B o
```

The percentages of the line end patterns are summarized in Table 14.3:

Table 14.3. Three Patterns to Conclude the Verse Line (Twelve Poems)

	Lines that end with an offbeat	Lines that end with a final *-e*	Lines that end with a beat	Total
A	54.7%	29.7%	15.6%	100.0%
AG	43.4%	51.1%	5.5%	100.0%
C	44.2%	46.4%	9.4%	100.0%
E	50.0%	39.8%	10.2%	100.0%
G	42.0%	47.4%	10.6%	100.0%
J	42.7%	47.7%	9.6%	100.0%
MA	73.3%	24.0%	2.7%	100.0%
PE	7.4%	61.0%	31.6%	100.0%
PPB	45.2%	51.5%	3.3%	100.0%
PT	39.0%	52.7%	8.3%	100.0%
T	28.2%	44.8%	27.0%	100.0%
W	41.3%	51.3%	7.4%	100.0%

Lines that end with a metrical beat are not many in any of the poems while lines ending with an offbeat exhibit high percentages. An offbeat in the line-initial or line-medial position may consist of a varying number of unstressed syllables, but the line-final offbeat has a special restriction that does not allow so many unstressed syllables. The line-final offbeat typically consists of a single unstressed syllable, though a final *-e*, which can form another syllable, may accompany it. It has been argued that the final *-e* behaves differently at the line closure. As Tolkien and Gordon assert, the final *-e* is more likely to be realized as a separate syllable because of the line boundary (133). This instability of the final *-e* is one of the most difficult and important issues in formulating metrical rules for medieval English meter.

If the independent final *-e* is considered to form a single offbeat at the line boundary where a pause naturally falls, the line will end not with a metrical beat but with an unstressed syllable. If the combination of an unstressed syllable and a final *-e*, as seen at the end of *A* 855, is assumed to form a single offbeat, most of the lines that seem to end with two unstressed syllables will end with a single offbeat. The number of lines ending with a final *-e* and those ending with an offbeat, thus, will constitute more than ninety percent of each poem. The line that ends with a beat is justifiable, but as Cable claims, the ME alliterative line strongly favors an unstressed syllable at the end (*Tradition* 74). The ME alliterative poets may have considered a final unstressed syllable a metrical requirement. To say the least, the metrical structure of the line end proves that the final *-e* plays a different role at the line conclusion. Namely, its potential to form a syllable is a significant aid to satisfy the metrical expectations, and its realization as a separate syllable depends on the metrical context.

14.3 End Rhyme in Addition to Alliteration

The fourteenth-century alliterative line is not only flexible enough to form certain patterns of metrical beats and offbeats, but is also highly regulated in its placement of unstressed syllables. As discussed in the previous section, the two weak syllables, the implied offbeat and the single final *–e*, could have been a significant aid in creating a special meter of ME alliterative verse. Some of the ME alliterative poems may include another constraint at the end of the line, namely end-rhyme in addition to alliteration. *The Three Dead Kings* (*K*) is written in the thirteen-line stanza with end rhyme, which has been analyzed in Chapter Eight along with other thirteen-line stanza poems. The first eight lines rhyme in the pattern of *abababab* whereas the bob and wheel rhyme in *cdccd*. In this complex metrical structure, the poet needs to consider multiple metrical constraints at the line end.[5] The third stanza of *K* is given below in order to highlight these constraints. Alliteration appears between slashes while the rhyme sound is underlined within the line and shown after the alliteration sound:

K 27	When þai weren of þese wodys went at here wyn,	/w/	*-yn*
K 28	Þai fondyn wyndys ful wete and wederys ful wane,	/w/	*-ane*
K 29	Bot soche a myst vpo molde with mowþ as I ȝoue myn,	/m/	*-yn*
K 30	Of al here men and here mete þai mystyn vche man.	/m/	*-an*
K 31	'Al our awnters' quod one, 'þat we ar now inne,	vowels	*-inne*
K 32	I hope fore honor of erþ þat anguis be ous an.	/h/ & vowels	*-an*
K 33	Þaȝ we be kyngis ful clene and comen of ryche kyn,	/k/	*-yn*
K 34	Moche care vs is caȝt fore kraft þat I can.	/k/	*-an*
K 35	Can I mo no cownsel be Cryst,	/k/	*-yst*
K 36	Bot couerys and cachis sum rest;	/k/	*-est*
K 37	Be morne may mend þis myst,	/m/	*-yst*
K 38	Our Lord may delyuer vs with lyst,	/l/	*-yst*
K 39	Or lelé our lyuys ar lest.'	/l/	*-est*

The alliteration and the end-rhyme are woven in a dense manner within the stanza. The poet has to fulfill the alliteration pattern of *aabbccddddxff* and the end-rhyme pattern of *ababababcdccd* simultaneously. Another point to note regarding the line conclusion is that the line frequently alliterates in all metrical beats. The other two thirteen-line stanza poems that T. Turville-Petre includes in his anthology, *A Pistel of Susan* (*PS*) and *Somer Soneday* (*SS*), place alliteration even more rigidly in all the metrical beats including the line-final one.[6] In such lines that need to fulfill both the alliteration requirement and the end-rhyme requirement, the second half-line echoes the sound repetition within the line (alliteration) and the sound repetition beyond the line (end-rhyme). In order to provide the proper alliteration and rhyme, short words, usually monosyllabic or disyllabic words, are frequent at the end of the line. In other words, all the words that end the line in the above stanza can be monosyllabic if the word final *-e* of *wane* in *K* 28 and *inne* in *K* 31 is considered being silent. It is notable that many lines end with a monosyllabic word or a word that has a potential to be realized as monosyllable, when the meter demands both rhyme and alliteration within the same line.

When the implied offbeat appears prior to the final metrical beat that rhymes with other lines, the metrical impact is intense. The first metrical beat of the second half-line repeats the alliteration for the third time within the line, and after a pause created by the implied offbeat, the final metrical beat repeats the alliteration again and adds another sound repetition by means of end rhyme. There are a significant number of occasions in which the final two words receive stress without any intervening unstressed syllables in between. The first word of such a group alliterates with the preceding metrical beats within the same line whereas the second word adds the rhyming sound in addition to the alliteration. The absence of any offbeat between them inevitably emphasizes the two consecutive metrical beats. Below are a few examples from *SS* and *K*:[7]

```
SS 70 Wyterly him was wel whan þe whel wente,
                                  B  ø  B

SS 89 Caste kne ouer kne as a kyng kete,
                              B  ø  B
```

K 2   I saw a brymlyche bore to a bay broȝt,
B ø B

K 105 That oþer body began a ful brym bere:
B ø B

If the line-final word consists of more than one syllable, it may receive stress in two places. Lines from *PS* 131 through *PS* 138 exemplify a clear contrast between the final two beats as two separate words or one single word:

PS 131 Nou were þis domesmen derf drawen in derne
PS 132 Whiles þei seo þat ladi was laft al hire one,
PS 133 Forte heilse þat hende þei hiȝed ful ȝerne,
PS 134 With wordes þei worshipe þat worliche in wone:
PS 135 'Wolt þou, ladi, for loue on vre lay lerne,
PS 136 And vnder this lorere ben vr lemmone?
PS 137 Þe þarf wonde for no wiȝt vr willes to werne,
PS 138 For alle gomes þat scholde greue of gardin ar gone

The first syllable of *lemmone* that concludes *PS* 136 forms a metrical beat due to the alliteration on /l/. Its second syllable will receive metrical stress because the word rhymes with the words *one* in *PS* 132, *wone* in *PS* 134, and *gone* in *PS* 138. T. Turville-Petre explains this phenomenon as follows (*Poetry* 121):

> One common feature of these rhymed alliterative poems needs special comment: where a final disyllabic word alliterates on the first syllable and rhymes on the second, it receives level stress.

Thus, the final word of the following lines receives level stress without any unstressed syllables between the final two metrical beats:

PS 18 Þei lerned hire lettrure of heore langage,
B ø B

PS 210 Of preiere and of penaunce was vre purpose.
B ø B

```
SS 92   He leyde his leg opon liþ at his likyng,
                                         BøB

SS 94   He wende al þe world were at his weldyng
                                         B ø B
```

This chapter has observed that a monosyllabic word tends to appear at the end of the verse line if it requires both rhyme and alliteration. The polysyllabic words that conclude the lines above receive metrical stress in two places, which suggests that the sequence of two metrical beats without any intervening offbeat also plays a vital role in rhymed alliterative meter. Though polysyllabic, these words behave as if they were two separate words.

The places for implied offbeats in the three rhymed alliterative poems are summarized in Table 14.4:[8]

Table 14.4. Implied Offbeats in the Rhymed Alliterative Verse (Three Poems)

	Between B_0 and B_1	Between B_1 and B_2	Between B_2 and B_3	Between B_3 and B_4
PS	1	5	14	21
SS	0	1	4	5
K	1	2	5	6

The three poems that use end rhyme in addition to alliteration are no exception as to the placing of the implied offbeat toward the line end. The rhyme sound is significant enough to signal the line closure, but the poets mark the line conclusion even more securely by means of slower rhythm.

14.4 Defamiliarized Language of ME Alliterative Verse

In conclusion, the second half-line of ME alliterative verse is loaded with various metrical devices that reinforce sound repetition and clearly mark the line boundary. As Duggan contends, the first metrical beat of the second half-line plays an important role in signaling the alliteration of the entire line ("Shape"; "Final *-e*"). Furthermore, the other metrical constraints on the right edge of the line emphasize the recurrence of the same sound: the smaller number of unstressed syllables in the second half-line, the frequent placement of the implied offbeat prior to the final metrical beat, the unique way to conclude the line with an unstressed syllable, and additional alliteration and end rhyme on the final metrical beat. These phenomena raise the question as to why ME poets are so enthusiastic in pursuing this complex meter.

Furniss and Bath assert that the ultimate goal of verbal art is to defamiliarize ordinary language. By means of figurative language, poetic art utilizes various devices to reorganize sounds and produce an unfamiliar form. Furniss and Bath assert (86):

> The pronunciation should be made difficult through the 'roughing' effects achieved by the repetition of identical sounds (rhyme, alliteration, and so on), and poetic rhythm should avoid the potentially lulling effect of regular prose rhythms by 'disordering' rhythm.

ME alliterative meter can be an ultimate form of defamiliarized language. The right edge of the ME alliterative line, in particular, is a good example of defamiliarization in order to produce a dense sound repetition and an astonishing form of amusement.

Notes

1 The word *precyous* may consist of two syllables rather than three, which is a reasonable way of reading. Counting this word as either a two-syllable or three-syllable word, however, does not significantly change the metrical structure.

2 As to the special role that zero syllables or pauses play in English verse, see Chapter Two.

3 The implied offbeat and the offbeat consisting of more than three unstressed syllables have notable tendencies in OE alliterative verse as well. The implied offbeat may evenly occur among the three possible positions in the OE line, which is one of the major differences from ME alliterative verse. The rare appearance of multiple unstressed syllables prior to the last metrical beat of the OE line suggests that OE meter already avoided numerous unstressed syllables in succession in this position. For a detailed discussion on the offbeat and the line end patterns in OE alliterative verse, see Chapter Sixteen.

4 The line ends of these examples are scanned as double offbeats. Yet as modern pronunciation suggests, these words, *prophets* and *delivered*, have only one single unstressed syllable after the stressed one. Even in the occasion where the line could end with a double offbeat, its constituents are not the ones that have rigid quality to form two separate syllables.

5 See also Chapter Five for a discussion on a major alliterative poem that includes end rhyme, *Pearl*.

6 The rhyme schemes of the three poems are as follows:
PS: *ababababcdddc*
SS: *ababababcdddc*

K: *ababababcdccd*

See T. Turville-Petre, *Poetry* 148–49 for a detailed explanation on the use of rhyme in alliterative verse.

7 The final word that concludes these lines is in rhyme with the following words:

wente (*SS* 70): *sente* (66), *ibente* (68), *lente* (72)
kete (*SS* 89): *sete* (87), *hete* (91), *lete* (93)
broȝt (*K* 2): *roȝt* (4), *soȝt* (6), *noȝt* (8)
bere (*K* 105): *were* (107), *fere* (109), *lere* (111)

8 The bob and the wheel are not included; the long alliterative lines only are taken into account in Table 14.4.

Chapter 15

Alliteration and Metrical Subordination in *The Alliterative Morte Arthure*

This chapter analyzes the collocation of a short adjective and a noun in *The Alliterative Morte Arthure* (*MA*). As discussed in Chapter Thirteen, the rule of metrical subordination usually places stress on the noun and reduces that of the adjective when these lexical items stay within the same syntactic boundary. In *MA*, however, the adjective, but not the noun, alliterates, which may encourage readers to stress the adjective, but not the noun, due to the consistent alliteration throughout the poem. Stress seems to shift onto the adjective if alliteration is assumed to be more important, and the stressed syllable of the noun is reduced to a weak syllable. The common alliteration in the first three metrical beats within the line is achieved accordingly. The *MA* poet presumably considered this type of collocation as a strong link, and treated it according to the Germanic compound stress rule, but not according to the metrical subordination rule. By means of the compound stress rule, the collocation of an adjective and a noun may be considered as a pseudo-compound that can have stress in its initial constituent. The line, thus, may be interpreted as realizing a metrical beat in the adjective. Variations in stress placement in such a collocation suggest that the stress rule within words was already subordinated in the fourteenth century to a rule that operates beyond them.

Alliterative verse utilizes repetition of the identical stem-initial sound within a line to create a certain rhythm. It was a favored form of verse in OE, and flourished once again in the ME period. One of the unique features of the alliterative style of the fourteenth century is the variable number of metrical beats per line, as already seen in Chapters Two, Six, and Thirteen. Various discussions have been made concerning the number of stressed syllables per line. For instance, as seen in the first line of *Sir Gawain and the Green Knight* (*G*) in Chapter Thirteen, the line may be considered to consist of five metrical beats. Similar lines are also observed in *MA*. It seems natural to read the following lines in five-beat, because the line-initial word alliterates:

G 1 Síþen þe sége and þe assaáut watz sésed at Tróye,
MA 159 Sýthin síttandly in sále séruyde ther áftyr,
MA 1785 Becáuse he kíllyde þis kéne, Críste hafe þi sáule!
MA 2669 Wíth this wórtheliche wýe, that wóndyd was sóre;

If the initial words of the above lines are considered not to form a metrical beat though alliterating, the line will be in four-beat meter with the [aaax] pattern. The ME alliterative line is flexible enough to produce four *or* five metrical beats in a line according to metrical necessity and stylistic variations; namely, the underlying meter is capable of generating four or five metrical beats, and the resulting lines are both metrical.

The present chapter analyzes *MA*, one of the masterpieces of the alliterative movement of the fourteenth century, and argues that the collocation of a short adjective and a noun plays a unique role in sustaining alliteration. As discussed in Chapter Thirteen, this collocation is frequently found in lines that have the potential to be read both in four-beat and five-beat. Thus, such flexible lines are chosen for the present analysis.

15.1 Flexible Lines between Four-Beat and Five-Beat

The first thirteen lines of the poem represent the base meter, though deviations occur in certain lines. Alliteration is noted in the line with italics while the overall alliteration pattern is provided within square brackets:

MA 1 Now *gr*ett *gl*orious *G*odde thurgh *gr*ace of Hym seluen [aaax] or [aaaax]
MA 2 And the *pr*ecyous *pr*ayere of His *pr*ys modyr [aaax]
MA 3 *Sch*elde vs fro *sch*amesdede and *s*ynfull werkes [aaax]
MA 4 And *gy*ffe vs *gr*ace to *gy*e and *g*ouerne vs here [aaaax]
MA 5 In this *wr*echyde *w*erlde thorowe *v*ert[u]ous lywynge, [aaax]
MA 6 That we may *k*ayre til Hys *c*ourte, the *k*yngdom of hevyne, [aaax]

MA 7	When oure *s*aules schall parte and *s*undyre fra the body,	[axax]
MA 8	Ewyre to *b*elde and to *b*yde in *bl*ysse wyth Hym seluen;	[aaax]
MA 9	And *w*ysse me to *w*erpe owte som *w*orde at this tym	[aaax]
MA 10	That nothyre *v*oyde be ne *v*ayne, bot *w*yrchip till Hym selvyn,	[aaax]
MA 11	*Pl*esande and *pr*ofitabill to the *p*ople þat them heres.	[aaax]
MA 12	Ȝe that *l*iste has to *l*yth or *l*uffes for to here	[aaax]
MA 13	Off elders of alde tym and of theire awke dedys,	?

Except for *MA* 1, *MA* 4, and *MA* 7, the lines clearly consist of four metrical beats, the first three of which alliterate. *MA* 7 is an example of weak alliteration whereas *MA* 4 indicates that the line may have five metrical beats. *MA* 1 has alternatives of alliteration because it may be read in two ways:

MA 1	Now *gr*ett *gl*órious *G*ódde thurgh *gr*áce of Hym séluen	[aaax]

The above scansion treats the adjective *grett* as unstressed. It is known that monosyllabic adjectives[1] are considered metrically subordinated to the following word, and can be unstressed in reading (Attridge, *Rhythms* 230–39). Since the adjective *glorious* is longer and its second syllable cannot be reduced to a schwa, this word will receive more force of stress than *grett*. The same line can be read in five-beat, as seen in the second scansion:

MA 1	Now *gr*étt *gl*órious *G*ódde thurgh *gr*áce of Hym séluen	[aaaax]

This scansion places stress on the word *grett*, and reads the line in five-beat because this word alliterates. The alliterating initial sound of the adjective *grett* satisfies the alliteration requirement in both four-beat and five-beat readings. These metrically flexible lines, thus, allow two or more different variations in reading. The significant point regarding monosyllabic or disyllabic adjectives is that they can be either stressed or unstressed, depending on the metrical context and readers' preference. It is this flexibility that has made English verse unique since the time of Middle English (Halle and Keyser, *English Stress* 101–09).

MA 13 is not as simple as *MA* 1. It is flexible enough to be read in four-beat or five-beat, but different alliteration patterns yield in a four-beat reading depending on where metrical beats are located. The line is scanned in five-beat as follows:

MA 13 Off *é*lders of *á*lde tým and of theire *á*wke dédys, [aaxax]

The alliteration pattern [aaxax] is not impossible in *MA*, as seen in *MA* 834 quoted below. If the four-beat reading is strictly applied in the same manner as that used for *MA* 1, *MA* 13 is scanned as follows:

MA 13 Off *é*lders of *a*lde tým and of theire *á*wke dédys, [axax]

However, readers may be tempted to read it as [aaax], placing greater stress on the alliterating adjective *alde* (old) than on its unalliterating follower:

MA 13 Off *é*lders of *á*lde tym and of theire *á*wke dédys, [aaax]

Though it contradicts the rule of metrical subordination, this reading may immediately come to the readers' minds due to the succession of [aaax] lines in the poem. The collocation of an alliterating adjective and a non-alliterating noun raises the question as to which plays a more decisive role, alliteration or metrical subordination, in determining the positions of metrical beats.

The following lines confirm that the line may consist of five metrical beats. Applying a five-beat reading to flexible lines such as *MA* 1 and *MA* 13 is justifiable and metrical because the following lines can only be read in five-beat. They also reveal that alliteration patterns may vary:

MA 834 The *c*omely *c*oste of Normandye they *c*achen full euen, [aaxax]
MA 992 And *t*ake *t*rew for a *t*ym to better may worthe.' [aaaxx]
MA 1012 And sent his *b*erde to that *b*olde wyth his *b*este *b*erynes. [xaaaa]
MA 1116 The kyng *ch*aungez his fote, e*sch*ewes a lyttill– [xaxax]
MA 1438 Be*s*oughte Gode of *s*ocure, *s*ende whene Hym lykyde. [axaax]
MA 2083 To-day sall my name be *l*aide and my *l*ife aftyre, [xxaax]
MA 2097 With *fl*onez *fl*eterede þay *fl*itt full *f*rescly þer *f*rekez, [aaaaa]
MA 2248 The *n*akyde *sw*erde at þe *n*ese *n*oyes hym *s*are– [abaab]
MA 2350 Ne to aske *t*rybut ne *t*axe be nakyn *t*ytle [xaaxa]
MA 2561 With þe *l*yghte of þe *s*onne men myghte *s*ee his *l*yuere! [abxba]
MA 3414 The fyfte was *J*osue, þat *j*oly mane of armes, [xaaxx]
MA 3615 *Dr*esses *dr*omowndes and *dr*agges, and *dr*awen vpe stonys. [aaaax][2]
MA 3980 And *l*eue siche *cl*amoure, for *Cr*istes *l*ufe of heuen!' [abbax]

MA 4312 The kyng *s*ees be a*s*aye þat *s*ownde bese he neuer, [xaaax]
MA 4324 I fore*g*yffe all *g*reffe, for Cristez lufe of heuen; [aaxxx]
MA 4332 Throly belles thay *r*ynge and *r*equiem syngys; [xxaax]

The above examples indicate that a line of *MA* can have five metrical beats, even though many of the lines contain four metrical beats as seen in the first thirteen lines. Between lines that are definitely five-beat and lines that are definitely four-beat lie flexible lines that may be read in both four-beat and five-beat.

The collocation of an adjective and a noun can play a distinct role in English verse. Attridge explains that the two words remain in stress subordination:

> Subordination is a reflection of syntactic relations, and holds between stresses within a single syntactic unit; thus the stressed syllable of an adjective is usually subordinate to the stressed syllable of a following noun, and the same is true of the relation between a verb and a noun functioning as its object. (*Rhythms* 230)

The collocation of an adjective and a noun is one of the unique points of alliterative verse (T. Turville-Petre, *Revival* 89).[3] There are many instances of such a syntactic unit in *MA*. These instances reveal a striking similarity as to their metrical make-up; namely, it is usually the adjective, but not the noun, that alliterates. *MA* 1369 is such an example; the collocation is underlined:

MA 1369 He *gr*yppes hym a <u>*gr*ete spere</u> and *gr*aythely hym hittez;

If the line is read in five-beat, the alliteration pattern is [aaxax]. A four-beat reading produces the alliteration pattern [axax] if metrical subordination is assumed in order for the adjective *grete* to be realized as unstressed. The [axax] reading with an alliterating weak syllable, however, may give a strange sense since the majority of the lines are in the [aaax] pattern. Lines with this collocation of an adjective and a noun suggest that the poet intended to place metrical stress on the adjective and demote the stress from the noun that holds a syntactic link with the adjective.

15.2 Patterns in Flexible Readings between Four-Beat and Five-Beat

Flexible lines between four-beat and five-beat may be grouped into the following nine types according to the two alliteration patterns resulting from the two readings. There are five types of flexible lines in which the [aaax] alliteration will emerge in the four-beat reading if the adjective, but not the noun, forms a metrical beat:

(i) [aaaax] ⟷ [aaax]

The potential syllable for the fifth metrical beat alliterates in this group as in the following lines. The resulting alliteration in the four-beat reading is the same in this group regardless of whether the adjective or the noun receives stress:[4]

MA 837 The *fl*oure and þe *f*aire *f*olke of *f*yftene rewmez.
MA 1057 *R*aykez towarde þe *r*enke *r*eghte with a *r*uyde will,
MA 1103 Fro þe *f*ace to þe *f*ote was *f*yfe *f*adom lange.
MA 4240 That *d*erfe *d*ynt was his *d*ede; and *d*ole was þe more

The adjectives, *derfe* (strong), *faire* (fair), and *fyfe* (five), can be monosyllabic. They alliterate with the other stressed syllables in the line, and so do the nouns to which they are subordinated. The collocation of an adjective plus a noun is found in the first two metrical beat positions in *MA* 4240, the second and third positions in *MA* 837, the third and fourth positions in *MA* 1103, and the final two positions in *MA* 1057. Out of thirty-five lines that include the collocation of an *alliterating* adjective and an *alliterating* noun, nineteen contain this collocation in their first and second metrical beat positions, twelve lines in their second and third positions, three in their third and fourth positions, and one in its final two positions. In other words, this type of collocation more frequently appears in the first half-line than in the second one. If the link between the metrically subordinated adjective and the noun is underlined as well in the alliteration pattern, the above lines can be reanalyzed as follows:

MA 837 The *fl*oure and þe *f*aire *f*olke of *f*yftene rewmez. [aaaax]
MA 1057 *R*aykez towarde þe *r*enke *r*eghte with a *r*uyde will, [aaaax]

MA 1103 Fro þe *f*ace to þe *f*ote was *f*yfe *f*adom lange. [aaaax]
MA 4240 That *d*erfe *d*ynt was his *d*ede; and *d*ole was þe more [aaaax]

If the four-beat reading is applied, these lines have the alliteration pattern [aaax] regardless of whether the adjective or the noun forms a metrical beat.

(ii) [axaax] ⟷ [aaax]
In this group, an alliterating adjective precedes a noun that does not alliterate, and its place is limited to the first two stressed positions within the line. The collocation is again underlined:

MA 1391 Than a *r*yche man of *R*ome *r*elyede to his byerns: [axaax]
MA 3629 The *b*olde kynge es in a *b*arge and a*b*owtte rowes, [axaax]

There are about twenty such lines in *MA*. If the rule of metrical subordination directly operates, the alliteration pattern will be [xaax]. The recurrence of [aaax] may encourage readers to use the same alliteration pattern in these lines by acknowledging stronger stress on the adjective.

(iii) [aaxax] ⟷ [aaax]
There are about 120 occasions in *MA* in which the five-beat line with the alliteration pattern [aaxax] can also be read in four-beat. The collocation of a metrically subordinated adjective and a noun falls in the second and third metrical beat positions in *MA* 722, *MA* 1056, and *MA* 1526 whereas it appears in the third and fourth metrical beat positions in *MA* 1289:

MA 722 *G*arneschit on þe *g*rene felde and *g*raythelyche arayede: [aaxax]
MA 1056 *B*raundesch[t]e his *b*ryghte swerde by þe *b*ryghte hiltez, [aaxax]
MA 1289 *P*ensels and *p*omell of ryche *p*rynce armez, [aaxax]
MA 1526 Þat *r*ane all on *r*eede blode *r*edylye all ouer. [aaxax]

In *MA* 1289, the metrically subordinated stress of *ryche* is likely to be realized as unstressed in a four-beat reading because the word does not alliterate. However, the adjectives that appear in the other three examples above are legitimate candidates to receive stress due to their alliterating initial syllable, resulting in the [aaax] pattern in the four-beat reading.

(iv) [aaaxx] ⟷ [aaax]

Thirty lines whose alliteration pattern is [aaaxx] can also be read with four metrical beats:

MA 2013	Bothe the *cl*ewez and þe *cl*yfez, with *cl*ene men of armez;	[aaaxx]
MA 3858	And thus sir *G*awayne es *g*onn, the *g*ude man of armes,	[aaaxx]
MA 3998	'To *M*essie and to *M*arie, the *m*ylde Qwenne of heuenn,	[aaaxx]

The collocation occupies the third and fourth metrical beat positions in the five-beat reading. If the rule of metrical subordination operates, the alliteration pattern in the four-beat reading will be [aaxx]. If the stress of the head noun is demoted, however, the alliteration pattern will be [aaax].

(v) [axaax] ⟷ [aaax]

MA 1537	*F*yfty thosannde on *f*elde of *f*erse men of armez	[axaax] / [aaax]

Two different subordinated adjectives appear in this line. Both of the adjectives, *fyfty* and *ferse* (fierce), alliterate whereas their head nouns, *thosaunde* and *men,* do not. If the adjectives form a metrical beat in a four-beat reading, the alliteration pattern will remain consistent in [aaax]. If a different four-beat reading is employed, the line can be read as follows, and different alliteration patterns will emerge:

MA 1537	*F*yfty thósannde on *f*élde of *f*erse mén of ármez	[xxxx]
MA 1537	*F*yfty thósannde on *f*élde of *f*érse men of ármez	[xaax]
MA 1537	*F*ýfty thosannde on *f*élde of *f*erse mén of ármez	[aaxx]

The following four groups provide another piece of evidence that the stress of a noun can be demoted for the sake of alliteration if it is preceded by an alliterating adjective. Alliteration in these examples is already weak in the five-beat reading, but alliterating syllables all remain as metrical beats in the four-beat reading. The collocation is underlined:

(vi) [axaxx] ⟷ [axax]

MA 1120 That he *h*illid þe swerde *h*alfe a fote large.

(vii) [axxax] ⟷ [axax]
MA 1440 Wyth *f*yue hundrethe men appon *f*aire stedes;
MA 4065 *S*exty thowsande men, the *s*yghte was full hugge!–

(viii) [aaxxa] ⟷ [aaxa]
MA 2240 The *r*yall *r*annke stele to his herte *r*ynnys,
MA 2560 Who *l*ukes to þe *l*efte syde when his horse *l*aunches,

All the metrical beats alliterate in the following two groups if the alliterating adjective forms a metrical beat in the four-beat reading:

(ix) [aaxaa] ⟷ [aaaa]
MA 1077 For *gr*efe of þe *g*ude kynge þat hym with *gr*ame *gr*etez.
MA 3606 *H*atches with *h*aythen men *h*illyd ware thare*v*ndyre;

[aaxaa] ⟷ [aaaa]
MA 1104 Thane *st*ertez he vp *st*urdely on two *st*yffe *sch*ankez

A phenomenon worthy of note in *MA* is the metrical subordination between the verb and its object. If the verb is not considered to form a metrical beat because it is subordinated to its object, the alliteration pattern is all [aaax] in the four-beat reading of the following lines:

MA 1219 To make a *k*yrke on þe *cr*agg ther the *c*orse lengez [xaaax]/[aaax]
MA 1365 Come *f*orþermaste on a *f*reson in *f*lawmande wedes; [xaaax]/[aaax]
MA 3406 Take *k*epe ȝitte of oþer *k*ynges, and *k*aste in thyne herte, [xaaax]/[aaax]

These examples suggest that it is unquestionable that the rule of metrical subordination operates for the collocation of a verb and a noun. Namely, it is the noun that alliterates in the pair of a verb and a noun, which satisfies the alliteration requirement without shifting the stress. The combination of an adjective and a noun, on the other hand, displays an opposing tendency. These different operations of stress rules can only be explained by the dominance of alliteration.

15.3 Rules to Realize Mobile Stress in Certain Collocations

A possible explanation as to why the rule of metrical subordination is not applicable in the case of an adjective followed by a non-alliterating noun may be found in compound words. The following lines in two readings reveal the relationship between a compound and alliteration:

MA 694	At *l*ordez, at *l*egemen þat *l*eues hym byhynden,	[aaxax]/[aaax]
MA 2116	*Ch*oppede thurghe *ch*eualers on *ch*alke-whytte stedez;	[aaaxx]/[aaax]
MA 2287	*M*oyllez *m*ylke-whitte and *m*eruayllous bestez.	[aaxax]/[aaax]
MA 3265	The *sp*ace of a *sp*ere-lenghe *spr*ingande full faire;	[aaxax]/[aaax]
MA 4244	*Sw*appes of þe *sw*erde hande als he by glentes.	[aaxxx]/[aaxx]

If the first constituent of the compound receives stress, common alliteration is maintained except for *MA* 4244. This implies that the poet treated a compound as having more force of stress on the first constituent than the second one.

The compound stress rule (CSR) was already in use in OE (Halle and Keyser, *English Stress* 87–97). Lass (*Old English* 88–89) explains the CSR as "a reiteration of the Germanic Stress Rule" that places stress on the first syllable of the word. In Chapter Thirteen, I have proposed the compound stress rule for ME alliterative verse as follows:

Compound Stress Rule in ME Alliterative Meter

(i) For any sequence [$_{X}$A, B], where X is a lexical category (Noun, Verb, Adjective, Adverb), assign metrical stress to the leftmost primary stressed vowel.

(ii) B usually acts as an unstressed element. If the meter demands another stressed syllable, it may recover its stress quality and be realized as a stressed syllable.

This rule has been in effect from OE to Modern English (Giegerich, *English Phonology* 254–58; Halle and Keyser, *English Stress* 95). Lass comments that noun and adjective compounds are common in OE, which reflects a Germanic feature that derives from the Indo-European antiquity (*Old English* 195–98).

As Fudge claims, the CSR places the main stress at the beginning of the combination. Penultimate or antepenultimate stress is a general tendency for separate words, as well as words in succession (134–36). The *MA* poet intended to apply the same stress rule to a compound of an adjective and a noun. Seemingly, he perceived the combination of an adjective and a noun as a compound in a broader sense, allowing stress to shift onto the adjective so that regular alliteration could be achieved. This assumption is further validated by lines that contain two sets of alliteration:

MA 797 Ne *w*are it fore þe *w*ylde *f*yre þat he hym *w*yth de*f*endez.
[aabab] /[aaax]/[abab]
MA 2542 *L*aggen with *l*onge *sp*eres one *l*yarde *steeds*, [aabab]/[aaax]/[abab]
MA 2711 With [the] *cl*ere *w*atire a *kn*yghte *cl*ensis theire *w*ondes,
[abaab]/[aaax]/[abba]
MA 4236 The *f*elone with þe *f*yn *sw*erde *f*reschely he *str*ykes;
[aabab]/[aaax]/[abab]
MA 4237 The *f*elettes of þe *f*errere *s*yde he *fl*assches in *s*ondyre
[aabab]/[aaax]/[abab]

Two different four-beat readings are possible for the above lines. If metrical subordination does not operate and the adjective receives more stress than its follower, the consistent alliteration [aaax] results. However, if the noun receives stronger stress than the adjective it subordinates, two sets of alliteration in a line, which are possible in ME alliterative poems, are formed.

One of the features unique to *MA* is that consecutive lines often alliterate in the same sound, as discussed in Chapters Ten and Eleven. A considerable number of lines, about three-fourths of the entire poem, contain identical alliteration to their predecessor or follower. Identical alliteration commonly takes place in two lines, but can stretch out over eight, nine, ten, or even eleven lines. The following passage quoted in Chapter Ten explains identical alliteration that appears in eleven consecutive lines:

MA 2755 *Fl*orennt and *Fl*oridas with *f*yve score knyghttez;
MA 2756 *F*olewede in þe *f*oreste and on þe way *f*owndys, [aaxa]
MA 2757 *Fl*yngande a *f*aste trott, and on þe *f*olke dryffes.
MA 2758 Than *f*olewes *f*ast to oure *f*olke wele a *f*yve hundreth
MA 2759 Of *f*reke men to þe *f*yrthe appon *f*resche horses–

MA 2760	One sir *F*eraunt be*f*ore apon a *f*ayre stede,	[aaax]
MA 2761	Was *f*osterde in *F*amacoste; the *f*ende was his *f*adyre.	[aaaa]
MA 2762	He *fl*enges to sir *Fl*orent and pristly he kryes,	[aaxx]
MA 2763	'Why *fl*ees thow, *f*alls knyghte? Þe *f*ende hafe þi saule!'	
MA 2764	Thane sir *Fl*orent was *f*ayne and in *f*ewter castys;	[aaax]
MA 2765	One *F*awuell of *Fr*yselande to *F*eraunt he rydys	[aaax]

Several occasions of the collocation of an adjective and a noun are observed in this passage, which is underlined. The phrases, such as *faste trott* (fast trot), *freke mene* (bold men), and *falls knyghte* (false knight), exemplify the collocation in which the adjective alliterates but the noun does not. If the rule of metrical subordination is strictly applied, the reading and the alliteration will be as follows:

MA 2757	*Fl*ýngande a *f*aste trótt, and on þe *f*őlke drýffes.	[axax]
MA 2759	Of *fr*eke mén to þe *f*ýrthe appon *fr*ésche hórses–	[xaax]
MA 2763	'Why *fl*ées thow, *f*alls knýghte? Þe *f*énde hafe þi sáule!'	[axax]

The above readings are justifiable since lines whose alliteration pattern is [axax] or [xaax] do appear in *MA*. However, in this particular metrical context in which the identical /f/ sound recurs among eleven consecutive lines, the reading that values alliteration rather than metrical subordination may sound natural:

MA 2757	*Fl*ýngande a *f*áste trott, and on þe *f*őlke drýffes.	[aaax]
MA 2759	Of *fr*éke men to þe *f*ýrthe appon *fr*ésche hórses–	[aaax]
MA 2763	'Why *fl*ées thow, *f*álls knyghte? Þe *f*énde hafe þi sáule!'	[aaax]

Taking these possible variations into consideration does not necessarily imply that stress should always fall on the adjective of the adjective and noun collocation. The crucial point is that when an adjective accompanies a noun, either may be stressed. The poet left the line flexible enough for readers to take advantage of different stress rules. If alliteration is the first priority, metrical subordination does not operate and the common [aaax] pattern will result. Yet the line may be read in a different manner if the metrical subordination rule reduces stress of the alliterating adjective. On such an occasion rhythmic blurring occurs because the alliteration becomes weak, but this is not an inaccurate method of reading. Rhythmic blurring prevents boredom, and English poets have been utilizing variable realizations of verse lines. The English language of the fourteenth century underwent various changes while the traditional stress rules could remain dominant in certain metrical contexts. This signifies that the flexibility of English stress was already in effect in the fourteenth century and that rules governing beyond a group of words could take precedence over the stress rules within words for the sake of rhythmicality.

Notes

1 According to Attridge, metrically subordinated stress functions in monosyllabic adjectives and verbs (*Rhythms* 230–32). The term *monosyllabic* needs to be defined differently for ME because of the word-final *-e*. Since the issue of the final *-e* concerning its possibility to form a syllable remains unsettled, adjectives such as *longe*, *gude*, and *riche* can be both monosyllabic and disyllabic. Adjectives that are considered in this chapter include those that *can* be read in one syllable if the final *-e* is considered silent.

2 A significant number of lines are in this alliteration pattern. This indicates that the poet considers alliteration so important that he often tries to distribute it more frequently than expected.

3 ME alliterative verse repeats an identical or similar set of words, which is often called a formula (Finlayson, "Formulaic" 373). Scholars such as Finlayson, Johnson, Krishna ("Parataxis"), and Waldron ("Technique") assert that the stock of formulae supports the idea of oral composition in alliterative verse. Johnson considers the structure of "FUNCTION-WORD ADJECTIVE knight" as a formula in which the adjective varies according to the alliteration requirement. The structure of FUNCTION-WORD ADJECTIVE NOUN in general can be a syntactic formula in *MA*.

4 *MA* 1057 is different from *MA* 837, *MA* 1103, and *MA* 4240 because the collocation occupies the final two positions of the five-beat reading. If the metrical subordination reduces stress of *ruyde*, the alliteration in the four-beat reading will be [aaax]. Since the line-final stressed syllable is rarely demoted, the rule of metrical subordination must operate in this case in order to secure stress on *will*, and the alliterating adjective is not realized as a metrical beat in the four-beat reading.

Chapter 16

The Line End and Its Significance in OE Alliterative Meter and ME Alliterative Meter

It has been a common practice in the study of alliterative meter to divide the verse line into two halves and to examine the metrical structure of each half-line (Osberg, *Gawain* xiii). When reading the poem aloud, however, the entire line is a main unit that organizes stressed and unstressed syllables into a specific rhythm. This chapter compares alliterative meters of OE and ME, focusing on different structures of the line end. ME alliterative meter systematically marks the line conclusion by means of several different metrical devices that are not employed in OE alliterative meter. One such device, the uneven distribution of unstressed syllables within the line, suggests that ME alliterative meter tends to be quick at the beginning of the line and slower toward the end. This tendency is not found in OE verse; unstressed syllables almost evenly appear in all possible positions of the OE alliterative line. Furthermore, the two meters significantly differ in the number of syllables in each line. The ME line, usually containing more syllables than the OE line, is capable of formulating a more regular alternation of stressed and unstressed syllables.

The poems that have been analyzed for the present analysis and their number of lines are as follows. Hyper-metrical lines and corrupt or missing lines are excluded:

OE:[1]

Excerpts from *Beowulf* (*B*)	302 lines
The Battle of Maldon (*M*)	324 lines
The Dream of the Rood (*R*)	119 lines
The Seafarer (*S*)	123 lines

The Wanderer (*WA*) 114 lines
The Wife's Lament (*WL*) 52 lines

ME:

Excerpts from *The Wars of Alexander* (*A*) 2,000 lines
Excerpts from *Cleanness* (*C*) 1,000 lines
Saint Erkenwald (*E*) 352 lines
The long alliterative lines of *Sir Gawain and the Green Knight* (*G*) 2,025 lines
The Siege of Jerusalem (*J*) 1,334 lines
Excerpts from *The Morte Arthure* (*MA*) 2,171 lines
Pearl (*PE*) 1,211 lines
Patience (*PT*) 531 lines

16.1 The Scansion Method and Issues in Defining the Meter

This section reviews the scansion method based on Attridge's, and proposes that the method is also effective in analyzing OE verse. Various issues in the study of early English meter are also reconsidered. Locating beats (*B*) in metrically stressed syllables and offbeats (*o*) in metrically unstressed syllables provides a consistent and coherent system to reveal the metrical framework.[2] The number of offbeats between beats is also important in determining the meter, which is marked by numerals. For instance, OE lines are scanned as follows:[3]

```
R 15   wædum geweorþod    wynnum scinan,
         B   o2   B    o    B   o    B o

S 121 Þær is lif gelong    in lufan Dryhtnes,
           o2   B   o B     o   B o    B   o
```

The metrical value of the word final *-e* is a matter of controversy in scanning medieval English verse. Different scholars have treated this weak but important syllable in different ways. Some believe that it was always silent whereas others claim that it could have formed an unstressed syllable. No convincing evidence is available for either side. For the present analysis, I have counted the word final *-e* in OE verse as a single syllable, but considered the ME final *-e* to have varied metrical values, as explained in Chapters One and Two. The final *-e* in the ME line could be silent *or* form a syllable, depending upon its position within the line and its relationship with the adjacent syllables.

To acknowledge the varying quality of the final *-e* means that this minor syllable may be utilized in verse reading as an optional aid to avoid the clashing of stress. For instance, compare the phrases *riche tounnes* in *J* 303 and *rich rises* in *J* 790 below and consider the effect of the final *-e* between stressed syllables in a context where there are no other unstressed syllables. In order to highlight the point of this argument, the scansion of the concerned part is given instead of the full scansion:

```
J 303 Was noȝt bot roryng and r[ut]h in alle þe riche tounnes,
                                                     B  º  B
```

```
J 790 Rich rises hem fro; þe Romayns byholden,
      B  ø  B
```

When a final *-e* is directly preceded and followed by metrical beats, as in *J* 303, it seems natural for the *-e* to be realized as an unstressed syllable. It would be difficult to utter two beats without an intervening offbeat when a final *-e*, a potential candidate for an offbeat, exists between them. The final *-e* at the end of the line is treated as a separate syllable. This is because the puff of air is easily attached when the final consonant is released at the line boundary (Conner 36). On the contrary, when there is no vowel between two metrical beats, as in *J* 790, the successive beats result. Though it has been traditionally called a trochee, the implied offbeat, no unstressed syllable between consecutive beats, is marked with the symbol *ø* in scansion. *G* 39 exemplifies another occasion of the implied offbeat:

```
G 39 Rekenly of þe Rounde Table alle þo rich breþer-
                                        B  ø  B
```

Assigning stress to the ME line is a more complicated task than doing so to the OE line because the ME language was already syllabo-tonic and not as purely accentual as Anglo-Saxon (Stillings). Especially in verse reading, an unstressed *-e* could have been realized as silent or as an independent syllable in order to maintain the regular alternation between beats and offbeats as well as a consistent number of unstressed syllables for an offbeat.[4] This seems to be a more rational argument than the idea that the final *-e* was always silent (Borroff, *Gawain* 187). However, as Cable argues, "to say that final *-e* was preserved in poetic texts is not, of course, to say that it was preserved in every instance in the spoken language" (Cable, *Tradition* 80, "Standards" 53).

As discussed in Chapters One and Two, the present analysis assumes that the phonetic value of the final *-e* and other inflectional suffixes is determined by their relationship with surrounding syllables and by their position in the line. The number of unstressed syllables between stressed ones in ME alliterative verse is usually considered not to be of metrical significance. Clarifying the value and function of these syllables, however, will be meaningful because the offbeat of ME verse exhibits more regularity than the OE offbeat. This potential syllable for an offbeat is marked with the symbol ^{o} in scansion.

Another confirmation has to be made as to the number of metrical beats per line. The OE base meter usually consists of four positions for metrical beats while the ME base meter four or five. Since ME alliterative lines sometimes consist of five metrical beats, the first metrical beat position is treated as an optional element, as postulated in Chapter Two. These metrical beats are numbered from B_0 to B_4; the four-beat line does not fulfill the optional slot in the line-initial position. The following are postulated as the base meters of OE and ME verse:

$$\text{OE Verse} \rightarrow B_1\ B_2\ B_3\ B_4$$
$$\text{ME Verse} \rightarrow (B_0)\ B_1\ B_2\ B_3\ B_4$$

The position number for each metrical beat will not be shown in the analysis but simply indicated as *B*.

Various numbers of unstressed syllables may form an offbeat. The following *MA* lines exemplify how the ME line is scanned and how the offbeat is counted:

```
MA 2 And the precyous prayere of Hys prys modyr
        o2     B  o     B      o3      B ø B o

MA 3 Schelde vs fro schamesdede and synfull werkes
        B      o2      B      o2     B    /  B  o
```

```
MA 4   And gyffe vs grace to gye and gouerne vs here
       o    B    o     B     o  B    o    B    o2     B º

MA 5   In this wrechyde werlde thorowe vert[u]ous lywynge,
         o2        B   o     B         o2       B      o     B   o
```

The number of unstressed syllables for the offbeat presents certain tendencies according to the position in the line.

16.2 Line-Endings of OE and ME Alliterative Verses

Four types are observed regarding the line conclusion of the OE verse:

(i) Lines ending with a beat:

```
M 274   gearo and geornful,     gylpwordum spræc
          B    o2     B     o      B    o2         B

R 71    stodon on staþole;     stefn up gewat
          B    o2     B   o2      B    o2     B
```

(ii) Lines ending with a final -*e*:

```
WA 100 wapen wælgifru,     wyrd seo mære,
         B o    B  o2         B     o   B º

S 4     bitre breostceare     gebiden hæbbe,
          B  °   B          o3     B o    B  º
```

(iii) Lines ending with a single offbeat:

```
M 218   wæs min ealda fæder     Ealhelm haten,
          o2     B    o  B o      B    o    B o
```

WL 34 leofe lifgende, leger weardiaþ,
B º B o2 B o B o

(iv) Lines ending with a double offbeat:

B 1321 Hroþgar maþelode, helm Scyldinga
B o B o3 B ø B o2

WA 97 Stondeþ nu on laste leofre duguþe
B o3 B º B º B o2

The number of unstressed syllables at the line end is usually less than two. This makes a contrast to the other offbeat positions, especially to the offbeat at the half-line boundary that may contain up to seven syllables.[5] Furthermore, the number of lines that end with a double offbeat is not very large, as seen later in Table 16.1. The OE line, in other words, tends to end with either a metrical beat or a single offbeat, even though a double offbeat may be an alternative. As observed in Section Two of Chapter Fourteen, the ME verse line ends with one of the following patterns. The line that ends with a double offbeat is rather rare, so such examples are not provided. ME line endings are limited to these three patterns:

(i) Lines ending with a beat:

PE 811 For synne He set Hymself in vayn,
o B o B o B o B

G 96 Oþer sum segg hym bisoȝt of sum siker knyȝt
o2 B o2 B o2 B o B

(ii) Lines ending with a final-*e*:

C 1416 And bougounz busch batered so þikke.
o B o B ø B o2 B º

PT 81 Þis is a meruayl message a man for to preche
o3 B o B o2 B o2 B º

(iii) Lines ending with a single offbeat:

```
C 959  Al birolled wyth þe rayn, rostted and brenned,
          o2  B       o3       B  ø B      o2      B  o

PT 188 Þer Ragnel in his rakentes hym rere of his dremes!
         o   B     o2       B    o3      B      o2      B o
```

The percentages of the OE line-end patterns are summarized in Table 16.1:

Table 16.1. Patterns in OE Line-Endings (Six Poems)

	B	*-e*	o	o2	o3 etc.	Total
B	28.9%	18.2%	41.3%	10.7%	0.9%	100.0%
M	22.2%	21.9%	46.3%	8.7%	0.9%	100.0%
R	40.3%	19.3%	31.1%	9.3%	0%	100.0%
S	25.2%	16.3%	44.7%	13.0%	0.8%	100.0%
WA	18.4%	32.5%	44.7%	4.4%	0%	100.0%
WL	24.5%	22.7%	39.6%	13.2%	0%	100.0%

In Chapter Fourteen, Table 14.3 has presented the percentages of the three common patterns, which is rearranged according to the categories used in Table 16.1:

Table 14.3. Three Patterns to Conclude the Verse Line (Twelve Poems)

	B	*-e*	o	Total
A	15.6%	29.7%	54.7%	100.0%
AG	5.5%	51.1%	43.4%	100.0%
C	9.4%	46.4%	44.2%	100.0%
E	10.2%	39.8%	50.0%	100.0%
G	10.6%	47.4%	42.0%	100.0%
J	9.6%	47.7%	42.7%	100.0%
MA	2.7%	24.0%	73.3%	100.0%
PE	31.6%	61.0%	7.4%	100.0%
PPB	3.3%	51.5%	45.2%	100.0%
PT	8.3%	52.7%	39.0%	100.0%
T	27.0%	44.8%	28.2%	100.0%
W	7.4%	51.3%	41.3%	100.0%

The number of lines that end with a metrical beat is greater in OE verse whereas only about ten percent of the ME lines end with a metrical beat in most of the poems. The number of lines that end with a final -*e* increases notably in ME verse. Lines ending with a single offbeat do not show a significant change from OE to ME except for *PE*. If the final -*e* is assumed to form an unstressed syllable and provide a single offbeat at the line closure, many ME lines will end not with a beat but with an unstressed syllable. The number of OE lines that end with a final -*e* or a single offbeat suggests that the OE line tends to have a single offbeat at the line closure. Yet the line that ends with a beat is reasonable in OE meter.

Also discussed in Chapter Fourteen is the distribution of unstressed syllables prior to the final metrical beat. This position, namely in the middle of the second half-line or between the third metrical beat and the fourth one, may contain from zero to three unstressed syllables in the ME line. This has been presented in Table 14.1, which is quoted again below. The table indicates the number of lines that do not contain any unstressed syllable in each possible metrical position in the ME line:

Table 14.1. Occurrences of the Implied Offbeat (Twelve Poems)

	Between B_0 and B_1	Between B_1 and B_2	Between B_2 and B_3	Between B_3 and B_4
A (1,000 lines)	12	30	40	132
AG (661 lines)	1	2	6	19
C (1,000 lines)	34	45	61	117
E (352 lines)	5	7	15	29
G (900 lines)	34	26	58	102
J (1,000 lines)	28	35	78	158
MA (1,009 lines)	5	8	10	39
PE (1,211 lines)	0	17	11	29
PPB (1,000 lines)	18	34	42	65
PT (531 lines)	15	9	24	65
T (1,000 lines)	2	0	30	165
W (503 lines)	1	2	6	24

Although more than a thousand lines of *MA* and the entire lines of *PE* have been examined, these two poems tend not to contain many implied offbeats. This means that the clashing of stressed syllables is not likely in these two poems. The single offbeat, or at least the final -*e* that may form a syllable, is strongly favored in every possible offbeat position in *MA* and *PE*. Yet among these scarce occurrences of the implied offbeat, the line-final position is a common place in *MA* and *PE*. The other poems clearly indicate a strong preference for placing the implied offbeat toward the line end. Because of the absence of any unstressed syllables before the final metrical beat, the rhythm of the line significantly slows at the end of the line. The successive stressed syllables without an intervening unstressed syllable slow the rhythm whereas unstressed syllables in a row quicken it.

Table 14.2 has revealed that the triple offbeat displays a contrastive tendency, which is quoted below. The table presents occurrences of the triple offbeat in the first hundred lines of each of the twelve ME poems. Since triple offbeats are more frequent than implied offbeats, the first hundred lines will suffice to describe the general tendency:

Table 14.2. Occurrences of the Offbeat Consisting of More Than Three Unstressed Syllables (First One Hundred Lines of Twelve Poems)

	Before B_0	Between B_0 and B_1	Between B_1 and B_2	Between B_2 and B_3	Between B_3 and B_4
A	1	35	44	30	18
AG	0	22	24	11	20
C	1	21	13	10	1
E	3	26	22	22	5
G	1	21	4	10	4
J	0	19	16	20	6
MA	0	11	20	23	7
PE	0	0	0	0	0
PPB	0	9	23	24	14
PT	2	22	15	10	4
T	0	9	21	15	1
W	0	35	11	17	5

The implied offbeat occurs more frequently toward the end of the line than in the line-initial position whereas the triple offbeat tends to appear at the beginning of the line. Namely, the triple offbeat does not commonly appear between the third metrical beat and the fourth one, displaying a clear contrast to the likely position for the implied offbeat. The slow rhythm toward the end of the line, in addition to the non-alliterating beat in the line-final position, plays a role in signaling the line boundary of ME alliterative verse.

Tables 16.2 and 16.3 summarize the number of occasions in which implied offbeat and a group of unstressed syllables occur in OE verse. All of the analyzed lines are taken into account for both of the tables. The OE offbeat may consist of up to seven unstressed syllables; an offbeat consisting of between three and seven unstressed syllables is taken into account instead of the triple offbeat only:

Table 16.2. Occurrences of the Implied Offbeat in OE Verse

	Between B_1 and B_2	Between B_2 and B_3	Between B_3 and B_4
B	43	44	58
M	37	52	32
R	6	7	14
S	18	10	15
WA	22	24	16
WL	11	6	9

Table 16.3. Occurrences of a Group of Unstressed Syllables in OE Verse

	Before B_0	Between B_0 and B_1	Between B_1 and B_2	Between B_2 and B_3	Between B_3 and B_4
B	15	51	108	17	2
M	14	70	103	18	3
R	9	27	46	6	0
S	14	21	43	10	0
WA	13	11	32	10	0
WL	4	5	17	6	0

The implied offbeat evenly occurs among the three possible positions in the OE line. The ME line, on the contrary, uses this device of the implied offbeat to slow the rhythm deliberately at the line conclusion. The rare appearance of multiple unstressed syllables prior to the final metrical beat of the OE line, however, suggests that this position avoids numerous unstressed syllables in succession. This tendency is reinforced even more in ME verse. The OE lines, especially lines of *M* and *B*, contain many occasions of multiple unstressed syllables in the middle. Thus, the initial tempo of the OE line is not necessarily as quick as that of the ME line.

16.3 Major Differences between OE and ME Alliterative Lines

ME alliterative verse marks the half-line boundary, but the syntactic boundary tends to fall at the end of the verse line rather than in the middle. If the syntactic boundary, which demands a metrical pause, does not exist between the two half-lines, the rhythm will not be interrupted in the middle of the line. Unlike its ME counterpart, OE meter does not utilize a device to slow down toward the end of the line because a group of unstressed syllables is common in its middle. The following two groups illuminate differences between the half-line boundary of OE verse and that of ME verse:

OE:

```
M 41   on flot feran,   and eow friþes healdan.
        o  B ø B        o3         B o   B   o

R 85   hlifre under heofenum,     and ic hælan mæg
          B    o3     B          o4        B o   B

S 122  hyht in heofonum.    þæs sy þam Halgan þonc,
         B    o  B          o5            B  o   B
```

ME:

```
MA 2   And the precyous prayere of His prys modyr
          o2      B   o    B      o3      B ø B o

A 1291 Þat he had sett in þe see þe cite with-out,
            o3      B    o2    B   o  B °  B   o

C 649  And þenne schal Saré consayue and a sun bere,
                o3      B o2    B      o2   B ø B º

G 1430 Bitwene a flosche in þat fryth and a foo cragge.
            o3     B     o2       B     o2   B ø  B  º
```

PT 430 Þat vpbraydes þis burne vpon a breme wyse:
o2 B o2 B o3 B o̲ B o̲

E 262 Þat hit thar ryne no rote ne no ronke wormes;
o3 B o B o2 B o̲ B o

The ME lines above reveal that the middle of the line is not marked with a special metrical device; the distribution of the offbeat does not differ according to the position in the line except for the line-final one.

Another unique point about the line closure is found in Borroff's observation that the weak form is preferred in the line-final position, as opposed to the strong form in other places (Borroff, *Gawain* 188 and 270). For instance, the form *rysed* is preferred at the end of the line, but the form *ros* is used medially. Cable also recognizes that in lines of *C* monosyllabic words such as *courte*, *prys*, *duk*, and *fry* do not appear at the end of the second half-line, though they do appear at the end of the first half-line (Cable, "Standards"). The poets of ME alliterative verse seem to be selective about the word that falls at the end of the line so that the metrical expectation may not be violated and that the line boundary may not be blurred.

A third difference between the OE line and the ME line is that the latter tends to contain a larger number of syllables. The following are the initial ten lines of *S* and *J*. The number of syllables that *could* be vocalized in each line is shown between parentheses:

OE:

S 1	Mæg ic be me sylfum	soþgied wrecan,	(10)
S 2	siþas secgan,	hu ic geswincdagum	(10)
S 3	earfoþhwile	oft þrowade,	(8)
S 4	bitre breostceare	gebiden hæbbe,	(10)
S 5	gecunnad in ceole	cearselda fela,	(11)
S 6	atol yþa gewealc.	þær mec oft bigeat	(11)
S 7	nearo nihtwaco	æt nacan stefnan,	(10)
S 8	Þonne he be clifum cnossaþ.	Calde geþrungen	(13)
S 9	wæron mine fet,	forste gebunden,	(10)
S 10	caldum clommum,	þær þa ceare seofedun	(11)

ME:

J 1	In Tiberyus tyme, þe trewe emperour,	(12)
J 2	Sir Sesar hym sulf seysed in Rome,	(10)
J 3	Whyle Pylat was prouost vnder þat prince riche	(14)
J 4	And ȝewen iustice also, in Judeus londis.	(13)
J 5	Herodes vnder his emperie, as heritage wolde,	(16)
J 6	Kyng of Galile ycalled, whan þat Crist deyed.	(13)
J 7	Þey Sesar sakles wer, þat oft synne hatide,	(13)
J 8	Þrow Pylat pyned he was and put on þe rode;	(13)
J 9	A pyler pyȝt was doun vpon þe playn erþe,	(12)
J 10	His body bonden þer to, beten with scourgis;	(12)

The ME line tends to contain more syllables than the OE line does. A sharp contrast is found in the following short OE lines and long ME lines. Again, the number of possible syllables appears in parentheses:

OE:

B 759	æfenspræce,	uplang astod	(8)
B 1335	þurh hæstne had	heardum clammum,	(8)
R 93	ælmihtig God	for ealle menn	(8)
WL 24	is nu swa hit	næfre wære,	(8)

ME:

A 219	As tite as Anec him amed out of his awyn kythe,	(16)
A 591	And fede we þis othire, þat folke quen we ere fay worthid,	(18)
G 1445	Þise oþer halowed 'Hyghe!' ful hyȝe, and 'Hay! Hay!' cryed,	(16)
MA 276	Myne ancestres ware emperours and aughte it þem seluen–	(17)
MA 364	I sall enforsse ȝowe in þe felde with fresche men of armes,	(18)

In the above ME lines, the number of syllables can be twice as many as in OE verse. The first half-line of OE verse creates a clear boundary while the ME first half-line merges into the second half due to the similar composition of the offbeat between the two half-lines. This is aided by words like conjunctions, prepositions, and determiners since these words are capable of acting as a bridge between the final metrical beat of the first half-line and the first metrical beat of the second half-line. Furthermore, the English stress rule that underwent radical changes from OE to ME plays a decisive role. The Germanic stress rule that places stress on the first syllable of a word had been altered by the fourteenth century and the Romance stress system that stresses the medial or final syllable of a word could have coexisted with the Germanic rule (Halle and Keyser, "Chaucer," *English Stress*). The ME line, which contains a larger number of unstressed syllables and can move stress to the end of a word, therefore, is capable of creating more regular alternation between beats and offbeats. The heavy stress on the beats of the OE line, on the contrary, is inevitably emphasized by the scarcity of unstressed syllables and the irregular number of unstressed syllables. In sum, the ME line forms a smooth flow of rhythm whereas the OE line creates four conspicuous metrical bumps that can be further grouped into two separate units.

One obvious difference between OE meter and ME meter is that OE meter has more varieties in line conclusions while ME meter strongly prefers ending the line with a single offbeat. If the line-final *-e* is considered to form a syllable, the number of lines that have an unstressed syllable at the end is close to ninety percent in most of the ME verse analyzed here except for *PE*. A line-final unstressed syllable may be considered a metrical requirement of ME alliterative verse. This tendency is not very strong in OE verse. The fourteenth-century alliterative line is more regulated in its distribution of unstressed syllables than the OE verse line.

In conclusion, both OE meter and ME meter utilize the recurrence of word-initial sounds, called alliteration. Yet the alliterative meter that became popular in the West Midlands in the fourteenth century was not a *revival* of the exact OE alliterative meter. Nor was it an alliterative *survival* as claimed by scholars who believe that the alliterative tradition never ceased in English verse making (Everett; Lawton, "Introduction"; Moorman). Assuming the tradition of composing in alliterative meter was broken after the time of Anglo-Saxon poetry may support Huntsman-Mc's idea, *renewal*, or Pearsall's term, *reflourishing* (Huntsman-Mc; Pearsall, "Origins"). As Osberg comments, "Whether the form of the alliterative line was preserved in the fourteenth century through an unbroken oral tradition linked to Old English poetic practice, or whether fourteenth-century poets shaped the line from a continuum of alliterative writing, remains an ongoing debate" (*Gawain* xiii). As far as the meter of ME alliterative verse reveals in its line boundary, it is a complete *remodeling* of the meter in accordance with linguistic peculiarities that the language acquired between the two periods.

Notes

1 *Beowulf* lines are from Klaeber's edition while other OE lines are quoted from *A Guide to Old English* by Mitchell and Robinson.

2 English meter has been analyzed by means of the foot and its substitution, and various scansions have been proposed in order to reveal the foot and its boundary, which often results in a refusal of scansions by others. Different scansions of ME alliterative verse can be found in Chapter Two.

3 Attridge's method marks stress quality above the line and metrical features below it. Stress quality is not indicated for the present analysis.

4 The tendency to keep the time-interval between stressed syllables equal is called isochrony. The tendency toward isochrony started in the early ME period, and has been one of the peculiarities of English verse since then. See Chapter One.

5 The following lines contain seven unstressed syllables in a row between the two half lines:

```
R 114 biteres onbyrigan,    swa he ær on þam beame dyde.
                     B          o7                  B

WL 41 ne ealles þæs longaþes    þe mec on þissum life begeat.
                         B            o7                B
```

The following lines contain six unstressed syllables in a row between the two half lines:

```
M 235 wigan to wige,    þa hwile þe he wæpen mæge
                   B          o6            B

B 723 onbræd þa bealohydig,    þa he gebolgen wæs,
                     B           o6          B
```

Chapter 17

The Meter of *The Alliterative Morte Arthure* and the Special Position of King Arthur's Round Table

The excessive repetition of identical sounds makes *The Alliterative Morte Arthure* (*MA*) unique among the alliterative poems of the fourteenth century. Sound repetition, particularly the repetition of /r/ in *MA*, is illuminating because it reveals the special treatment of the phrase *the round table* within the verse line. This chapter reexamines /r/ in alliteration of *MA*, which has been discussed in Chapter Twelve, and expands the research into an analysis of the lines that contain *the round table*. The analysis will prove that the poet requires this phrase to receive full metrical significance. The fixed location of *the round table* in the second half-line of *MA* is due to the metrical constraints which impose overwhelming alliteration of the /r/ sound. Through various observations of /r/, the chapter argues that the *MA* poet exerts his talent on excessive repetition of the same sound more than required by alliterative meter, multiplying sound repetition beyond the verse line. At the same time, he is extremely inflexible regarding the alliteration of a line that contains *the round table*, even though he could have chosen a different word order or different alliteration sounds, as seen in other ME works on King Arthur.

Intricate sound repetition plays a vital role in creating unity not only within the line but also in a group of consecutive lines in *MA*. Through the examination of /r/ in alliteration and lines that contain *the round table*, it becomes clear that the poet always requires the phrase, *the round table*, to form two metrical beats. This chapter also compares *the round table* in *MA* with *the round table* in other ME alliterative works about King Arthur such as *Sir Gawain and the Green Knight* (*G*), *The Stanzaic Morte Arthur* (*SMA*), *Merlin*, and Sir Thomas Malory's *Le Morte Darthur*. While the poets of the other works allow the adjective *round* and the noun *table* to appear in the reversed order, the *MA* poet never does so. The other texts are flexible in the selection of the noun that precedes *the round table* while *MA* always chooses the noun that alliterates on /r/. After considering if this inflexibility can be interpreted as a formulaic expression, the chapter postulates the metrical framework used for the *MA* line containing *the round table*.

17.1 Excessive Alliteration and the Repetition of *r* in *The Alliterative Morte Arthure*

The base rule of alliterative meter is to alliterate a certain number of metrical beats within the verse line. In many cases, the number is three out of four per line, but the number may also be more or less, as seen on different poems in the previous chapters. The verse line may be in five-beat meter, of which three or four beats commonly alliterate. Repetition of the same sound in stressed syllables is rare in ordinary speech, and thus offers special aural effects, as discussed in Chapter Fourteen. *MA* extends this alliterative device beyond one single line, stretching the same alliteration sound over several consecutive lines. This phenomenon, analyzed in Chapters Eleven and Twelve, may be realized in various sounds and numbers of lines as seen in the following passage:

MA 362	And *r*aas it from his *r*iche men and *r*yfe it in sondyre,	/r/
MA 363	Bot he be *r*edily *r*eschowede with *r*iotous knyghtez.	/r/
MA 364	I sall en*f*orsse ȝowe in þe *f*elde with *f*resche men of armes,	/f/
MA 365	*F*yfty thosande *f*olke apon *f*aire stedys,	/f/
MA 366	On thi *f*oo men to *f*oonnde there the *f*aire thynkes,	/f/
MA 367	In *F*raunce or in *F*riselande, *f*eghte when þe lykes.'	/f/
MA 368	'By Oure *L*orde' quod sir *L*auncelott 'now *l*yghttys myn herte–	/l/
MA 369	I *l*oue Gode of þis *l*one þis *l*ordes has avowede!	/l/
MA 370	Now may *l*esse men haue *l*eue to say whatt them *l*ykes	/l/
MA 371	And hafe no *l*ettyng be *l*awe. Bot *l*ystynnys þise wordez:	/l/

The first two lines, *MA* 362 and *MA* 363, alliterate on the same /r/. Starting from *MA* 364, identical alliteration in four consecutive lines appears twice in a row. The same alliteration sound in two and four lines is frequent in *MA*, but identical alliteration over more than six lines is sometimes observed. The two passages below exemplify extreme cases of identical alliteration in six and ten consecutive lines, respectively:

MA 2790 Bot thane a *r*enke, sir *R*ichere of þe *R*ounde Table, /r/
MA 2791 One a *r*yall stede *r*ydes hym aȝaynes; /r/
MA 2792 Thorowe a *r*ownnde *r*ede schelde he *r*uschede hym sone, /r/
MA 2793 That the *r*osselde spere to his herte *r*ynnes. /r/
MA 2794 The *r*enke *r*elys abowte and *r*usches to þe erthe, /r/
MA 2795 *R*oris full *r*uydlye, bot *r*ade he no more. /r/

MA 3509 'Me awghte to *kn*owe þe *k*ynge; he es my *k*ydde lorde, /k/
MA 3510 And I, *c*alde in his *c*ourte a *kn*yghte of his chambire. /k/
MA 3511 Sir *Cr*addoke was I *c*allide in his *c*ourte riche, /k/
MA 3512 *K*epare of *K*arlyon vndir the *k*ynge selfen. /k/
MA 3513 Nowe am I *c*achede owtt of *k*yth with *k*are at my herte, /k/
MA 3514 And that *c*astell es *c*awghte with vn*c*owthe ledys!' /k/
MA 3515 Than the *c*omliche *k*ynge *k*aughte hym in armes, /k/
MA 3516 *K*este of his *k*etill-hatte and *k*yssede hym full sone, /k/
MA 3517 Saide 'Wel*c*om, sir *Cr*addoke, so *Cr*iste mott me helpe! /k/
MA 3518 Dere *c*osyn of *k*ynde, thow *c*oldis myn herte– /k/

The overwhelming repetition of the same sound in stressed syllables inevitably creates distinct unity among adjacent lines. This method of alliterating several consecutive lines on identical sounds seems a deliberate manifestation, and is called with various terms including *identical alliteration* (Oakden, *Alliterative* 233), *grouped alliteration* (Hamel 32), *running alliteration* (Schmidt, *Clerky* 55), or *consecutive alliteration* (Vaughan 2). As discussed in Chapter Eleven, about three-quarters of the *MA* lines are linked with their adjacent lines by the same alliteration sound.[1]

The intense network of identical alliteration produces certain metrical peculiarities other than excessive sound repetition. For instance, alliteration in certain lines may be weak since the surrounding lines sustain the alliteration. *MA* 2791 and *MA* 2793 quoted above contain only two alliterating metrical beats. Since alliteration often appears in the first three stressed syllables, these lines may look deviating due to their alliteration patterns of [axax] and [axxa], respectively. Yet other members of the identical group provide enough information about alliteration in order for these metrically weak lines to remain alliterative. The absence of rigid alliteration causes deliberate metrical blurring, but the excessive sound repetition in a group of lines does not allow these lines with weak alliteration to become metrically insignificant. This may be even interpreted as a device to prevent monotony if the lack of regular alliteration is considered a significant deviation from the norm (Hamel 19).

The alliteration on /r/ in *MA* illuminates certain features peculiar to this poem. As observed in Table 11.1, identical alliteration on /r/ appears in 258 lines of *MA*: seventy-five times in two lines, five times in three lines, fourteen times in four lines, once in five lines, four times in six lines, and once in eight lines. Alliteration on /r/ in a single line that does not remain in identical alliteration with adjacent lines is observed in seventy-one lines, which makes the total number of lines alliterating on /r/ 329 (7.6% of the entire lines of *MA*). The maximum number of lines for the identical alliteration on /r/ is eight, which is quoted below:

MA 1523	Thare myghte men see *R*omaynez *r*ewfully wondyde,	/r/
MA 1524	Ouer*r*edyn with *r*enkes of the *R*ound Table;	/r/
MA 1525	In þe *r*aike of þe furthe they *r*itten þeire brenys,	/r/
MA 1526	Þat *r*ane all on *r*eede blode *r*edylye all ouer.	/r/
MA 1527	They *r*aughte in þe *r*erewarde full *r*yotus knyghtez,	/r/
MA 1528	For *r*aunsone of *r*ede golde and *r*eall stedys,	/r/
MA 1529	*R*adly *r*elayes and *r*estez theire horsez;	/r/
MA 1530	In *r*owtte to þe *r*yche kynge they *r*ade al at onez.	/r/

The sound /r/ is not most frequently used in identical alliteration. The groups of the /s/ sound, the /k/ sound, and the /f/ sound are more frequent than /r/. However, /s/, /k/, and /f/ may take a form of different consonant clusters, even though the same sound initiates them. For instance, alliteration in /s/ is realized in fourteen variants: *s*, *sc*, *sch*, *schr*, *sh*, *sk*, *sl*, *sm*, *sn*, *sp*, *spr*, *st*, *str*, and *sw*. The total number of 329 lines that alliterate on the single consonant /r/, which cannot initiate any cluster, suggests how conspicuous its repetition is.

The sound /r/ cannot initiate any consonant clusters, but acts in a distinct way because it can be a second or third constituent of different consonant clusters. In other words, /r/ may appear in different consonant clusters as a final constituent. For instance, /r/ in the following lines recurs not as the word-initial sound but as a second or third constituent of a consonant cluster:

MA 786	Thane the *dr*agon on *dr*eghe *dr*essede hym aȝaynez,	/dr/
MA 1141	*Wr*othely þai *wr*ythyn and *wr*ystill togederz,	/wr/
MA 1230	One a *str*enghe by a *str*eme in þas *str*aytt landez.	/str/
MA 2844	*Pr*ike home to theire *pr*ynce and theire *pr*ay leue,	/pr/

In these lines, the recurrence of the same consonant cluster, /dr/, /wr/, /str/, and /pr/, creates a peculiar rhythm. Many consonant clusters include /r/: *br*, *cr*, *dr*, *fr*, *gr*, *kr*, *pr*, *schr*, *spr*, *str*, *thr*, *tr*, and *wr*. These consonant clusters in alliteration generate a different web of /r/ when combined with the alliteration of /r/ itself. For example, /r/ constantly appears in metrical beats of the following two passages. To highlight the repetition, /r/ in metrical beats is underlined:

MA 3212	We will by þe *Cr*osse-dayes en*cr*oche þeis londez	/k/
MA 3213	And at þe *Cr*ystynmesse daye be *cr*ownned theraftyre;	/k/
MA 3214	*R*yngne in my *r*yalltés and holde my *R*ownde Table	/r/
MA 3215	Withe the *r*entes of *R*ome, as me beste lykes.	/r/
MA 3216	Syne *gr*aythe ouer þe *Gr*ette See with *g*ud men of armes	/g/
MA 3217	To *r*euenge the *R*enke that on the *R*ode dyede.'	/r/
MA 3218	Thane this *c*omlyche *k*ynge, as *cr*onycles tellys,	/k/
MA 3219	*B*ownnys *br*athely to *b*ede with a *bl*ythe herte;	/b/

MA 3753	Thus thas *r*enkes in *r*ewthe *r*ittis theire brenyes	/r/
MA 3754	And *r*echis of þe *r*icheste vnreken dynttis,	/r/
MA 3755	Thare they *thr*onge in the *th*ikke and *th*ristis to þe erthe–	*th*
MA 3756	Of the *thr*aeste men *thr*e hundrethe at ones!	*th*
MA 3757	Bot sir *G*awayne for *gr*efe myghte noghte a*g*ayne-stande;	/g/
MA 3758	Vmbe*gr*ippys a spere and to a *g*ome rynnys	/g/
MA 3759	Þat bare of *g*owles full *g*aye with *g*owtes of syluere;	/g/
MA 3760	He *g*yrdes hym in at þe *g*orge with his *gr*ym launce,	/g/
MA 3761	Þat þe *gr*ownden *gl*ayfe *gr*aythes in sondyre;	/g/
MA 3762	With þat *b*oystous *br*ayde he *b*ownes hym to dye:	/b/

Identical alliteration unites *MA* 3212 and *MA* 3213 by the identical /kr/ sound and *MA* 3214 and *MA* 3215 by /r/. The subsequent four lines do not remain in identical alliteration, but /r/ continuously echoes in them. In the second passage starting from *MA* 3753, /r/ is heard constantly, even though these lines belong to different groups of identical alliteration. The sound /r/, thus, plays two roles in alliterative meter: to appear as an alliterating word-initial sound and be part of an alliterating sound preceded by other consonants.[2] This repetition of /r/ is reinforced if the ME /r/ is assumed to be "strongly trilled" (Vantuono, *Texts* 87). The language was still rhotic in the ME period, and /r/ was never dropped as is done in modern varieties. The *MA* poet was able to create a new sound network with /r/ by fully utilizing the multiple roles that the sound /r/ could play in different consonant clusters.

17.2 The Metrical Make-Up of "the Round Table" in *The Alliterative Morte Arthure* and Alliteration on *r*

The repetition of /r/ in the alliteration of *MA* shows a special feature. Namely, the phrase *the round table* appears only in the second half-line while the line with *the round table* always alliterates on /r/. The round table plays an important role in the Arthurian legends, and a considerable amount of research has been made on its source, meaning, and symbolic significance (Lacy and Ashe 392–93). However, the location of *the round table* in alliterative meter has not received much attention. *MA* contains forty-eight occasions of the whole phrase *the round table* and five occasions of the single word *table*. The following lines exemplify how the phrase appears:

MA 17 Off the *r*yeall *r*enkys of <u>the *R*ownnde Table</u>,
MA 726 *R*ewlys before þe *r*yche of <u>the *R*ounde Table</u>,
MA 2641 And *r*ollede the *r*icheste of all <u>þe *R*ounde Table</u>.

The round table always occupies the entire second half-line, *round* and *table* fulfilling the first and second metrical beat positions of the second half-line, respectively. This can be explained by the metrical make-up of the phrase itself. Since the adjective and the noun do not alliterate with each other, the alliteration inevitably deviates if it appears in other positions. Having the phrase in the middle means that the adjective will not alliterate if the line alliterates on /t/, or that the noun does not alliterate if the line alliterates on /r/. Neither case was favorable to the poet, though it was possible for him to place an unalliterating beat in the positions other than the line-final position as seen, for instance, in *MA* 3212 through *MA* 3215 above. He seems to have consciously avoided placing *the round table* in the line-initial or line-medial position. Indeed, there is no line in *MA* that contains *the round table* and alliterates on /t/. It seems that *the round table* is such a fixed phrase that the poet did not want the word *round*, whenever it accompanies *table*, to be unalliterating and thus to become metrically insignificant.

If *the round table* occupies the second half-line or the third and final metrical beat positions in the four-beat meter, the first and second positions must alliterate on /r/ in order for the line to achieve the common alliteration pattern, [aaax]. That is what happens, and those words that start with /r/ tend to be a certain group of /r/ words. The most frequent are *reall* (royal), *renk(e)* (man), and *ryche* (powerful). The following lines are similar in their lexical structures, as well as in their metrical structures. The initial sounds of all the metrical beats in the line are given between brackets in order to illuminate the repetition of /r/:

MA 17 Off the *r*yeall *r*enkys of the *R*ownnde Table, [r-r-r-t]
MA 719 Wyth a *r*eall *r*owte of þe *R*ounde Table [r-r-r-t]
MA 2902 And thane the *r*yalle *r*enkkes of þe *R*ownde Table [r-r-r-t]
MA 4072 Than the *r*oyall *r*oy of þe *R*ownde Table [r-r-r-t]

These lines indicate that the *MA* poet associates *the round table* with a special connotation of nobility that starts with /r/.

Lines that remain in identical alliteration and contain *the round table* also tend to form alliteration on /r/ with words signifying nobility and knighthood. The following passages that contain *the round table* are in identical alliteration of /r/ in two, three, four, five, six, and eight lines, respectively. The alliteration pattern is shown for the lines that contain *the round table*:

MA 3939 The *r*iche kynge *r*ansakes with *r*ewthe at his herte
MA 3940 And vp *r*ypes the *r*enkes of all þe *R*ownde Tabyll: [r-r-r-t]

MA 1882 Thane *r*elyez þe *r*enkez of þe *R*ounde Table [r-r-r-t]
MA 1883 For to *r*yotte þe wode þer þe duke *r*estez;
MA 1884 *R*ansakes the *r*yndez all, *r*aughte vp theire feres

MA 2918 *R*euertede it *r*edily and awaye *r*ydys
MA 2919 To þe *r*yall *r*owte of þe *R*ownde Table; [r-r-r-t]
MA 2920 And heyly his *r*etenuz *r*aykes hym aftyre,

MA 2921 For they his *r*eson had *r*ede on his schelde *r*yche.

MA 3892 When þat *r*enayede *r*enke *r*emembirde hym seluen
MA 3893 Of [þe]*r*euerence and *r*yotes of <u>þe *R*ownde Table</u>, [r-r-r-t]
MA 3894 He *r*emyd and *r*epent hym of all his *r*ewthe werkes:
MA 3895 *R*ode awaye with his *r*owte, *r*istys he no lengere,
MA 3896 For *r*ade of oure *r*iche kynge, *r*yve þat he scholde.

MA 1665 The a*r*aye and þe *r*yalltez of <u>þe *R*ounde Table</u> [r-r-r-t]
MA 1666 Es wyth *r*ankour *r*ehersede in *r*ewmes full many,
MA 1667 Of oure *r*enttez of *R*ome syche *r*euell he haldys;
MA 1668 He sall ʒife *r*esoun full *r*athe, ʒif vs *r*eghte happen,
MA 1669 That many sall *r*epente that in his *r*owtte *r*ydez,
MA 1670 For the *r*eklesse *r*oy so *r*ewlez hym selfen.'

MA 1523 Thare myghte men see *R*omaynez *r*ewfully wondyde,
MA 1524 Ouer*r*edyn with *r*enkes of <u>the *R*ound Table</u>; [r-r-r-t]
MA 1525 In þe *r*aike of þe furthe they *r*itten þeire brenys,
MA 1526 Þat *r*ane all on *r*eede blode *r*edylye all ouer.
MA 1527 They *r*aughte in þe *r*erewarde full *r*yotus knyghtez,
MA 1528 For *r*aunsone of *r*ede golde and *r*eall stedys,
MA 1529 *R*adly *r*elayes and *r*estez theire horsez;
MA 1530 In *r*owtte to þe *r*yche kynge they *r*ade al at onez.

The round table appears in the [r-r-r-t] alliteration pattern in all of the examples. In other words, the alliteration pattern of *the round table* is strictly limited; it always has to alliterate with words that start with /r/. All the forty-eight lines containing *the round table* in their second half remain in this alliteration pattern, even though slight deviations may be possible, as will be seen in the next section.

Adjacent lines that remain in identical alliteration with the line containing *the round table* tend to contain words of nobility and knighthood as seen in the following list. Spelling variations are not reflected:

araye, areste, ouerredyn, reall, rebell, reches, redily, redy, regne, rehetez, rekeneste, rekkynynge, releuis, renke, renoune, renownde, renttes, reschewe, retenuz, reuerence, rewlys, Richere, rollede, Romaynes, Rome, Roone, rowte, roy, ryche, ryde, ryghte, ryotte, rype, ryste, ryuere

The words that appear in lines that remain in identical alliteration with the line containing *the round table* include *renke* (man), *renoune* (reputation), *reuerence* (deference), *roy* (king), *riche* (powerful), and *realle* (splendid). Especially frequent are *renke* (16 times), *riche* (14 times), and *reale* (10 times). *The round table* is immediately associated in the line with words that signify nobility. Furthermore, it is surrounded in the neighboring lines by words that start with /r/ signifying knighthood again. About seventy-three percent of the lines containing *the round table* remain in consecutive alliteration with the adjacent lines. Since nobility and knighthood are the topics in the context in which *the round table* appears, the fixed phrase tends to appear more frequently when the poet describes warriors and conquests. The noun preceding *the round table* often denotes warriors; adding the phrase, *of the round table*, could be redundant.

17.3 Formulaic Patterns of "the Round Table" in *The Alliterative Morte Arthure*

Certain scholars have argued that the phrases such as *the ryealle renkys of the Rownnde Table* (*MA* 17) or *the ryche of the Rounde Table* (*MA* 726) are formulae to describe the knights around King Arthur's table.[3] Since the word order is always *round* plus *table* in the second half-line, it may be asserted that the phrase is a formula.[4] If a formula is defined as a recurring fixed phrase, *the round table* may be one of the typical formulae in *MA*. Lines containing *the round table* can be classified into the following three patterns:

Pattern 1: NOUN + *of* + *the round table*

1-a: NOUN [+man] + *of* + *the round table*

MA 147	Off þe *r*icheste *r*enkys of þe *R*ounde Table;	[r-r-r-t]
MA 719	Wyth a *r*eall *r*owte of þe *R*ounde Table	[r-r-r-t]
MA 1429	A*r*estede of the *r*icheste of þe *R*ounde Table,	[r-r-r-t]
MA 1994	With *r*enkkes *r*enownnd of þe *R*ounde Table,	[r-r-r-t]
MA 3571	With *r*enttes and *r*eches of the *R*ownde Table;	[r-r-r-t]
MA 4072	Than the *r*oyall *r*oy of þe *R*ownde Table	[r-r-r-t]

There are thirty-five occasions that fit in this pattern. In other words, the most common syntactic structure for the phrase containing *the round table* is that a noun signifying noble men precedes it. Furthermore, these nouns that precede *the round table* almost always start with /r/.

1-b: NOUN [-man] + ***of*** **+** ***the round table***

MA 1665 The a*r*aye and þe *r*yalltez of þe *R*ounde Table [r-r-r-t]

MA 3893 Of [þe] *r*euerence and *r*yotes of þe *R*ownde Table, [r-r-r-t]

This pattern is similar to the first one, but the noun preceding *the round table* does not denote human beings. Similar deviation is observed in the following example that is composed in this pattern. The collocation of an adjective and a noun is underlined:

MA 173 *R*ichely on þe *r*yghte hannde at the *R*ounde Table,

Realizing two metrical beats in the underlined phrase will result in an alliteration pattern that consists of five metrical beats, two of which do not alliterate. It is possible for an adjective phrase in alliterative meter to have only one metrical stress if the adjective is short and does not convey vital or new information. The following lines, for example, contain an adjective or a noun that may not receive full metrical stress. In other words, two readings are possible, depending upon whether full metrical stress in both the adjective and the noun is desirable:

MA 214-a Bot þe *br*ýght golde for *br*éthe sulde *br*íste al to péces, [aaax]

MA 214-b Bot þe *br*ýght góIde for *br*éthe sulde *br*íste al to péces, [axaax]

MA 185-a Grett *sw*ánnes full *sw*ýthe in *s*íIueryn chárgeours, [aaax]

MA 185-b Grétt *sw*ánnes full *sw*ýthe in *s*íIueryn chárgeours, [xaaax]

Both readings are possible, but reading *a* may be preferred for both of the lines for the sake of regular alliteration. In short, the alliterating constituent of a noun phrase is more likely to be realized as a metrical beat than the unalliterating constituent.[5] As for *MA* 173, the following reading that results in the rigid [r-r-r-t] pattern may be preferred since it is the most common metrical pattern for the line with *the round table*:

MA 173 *R*íchely on þe *r*yghte hannde at the *R*óunde Táble,

Pattern 2: VERB + ***the round table***

MA 53	Then *r*ystede that *r*yall and helde þe *R*ounde Tabyll,
MA 74	Thus on *r*yall a*r*aye he helde his *R*ounde Table
MA 424	Be þe *r*yuere of *R*oone halde my *R*ounde Table,
MA 3214	*R*yngne in my *r*yalltés and holde my *R*ownde Table
MA 4005	Ne *r*engne in my *r*oyaltez ne halde my *R*ownde Table

It is notable that all the lines in which a verb precedes *the round table* contain the same verb *hold*, yet alliterate on /r/.

Pattern 3: PREP + ***the round table***

MA 93	Þat thow bee *r*edy at *R*ome with all thi *R*ounde Table,
MA 2402	The *r*enke *r*ebell has bene vnto my *R*ownde Table,

There are a few occasions in which no other noun precedes *the round table.*

Scholars such as Finlayson, Johnson, Krishna, and Waldron assert that the stock of formulae supports the idea of oral composition in alliterative verse (Finlayson, "Formulaic"; Johnson; Krishna, "Parataxis"; Waldron, "Technique"). Johnson considers the structure of "FUNCTION-WORD ADJECTIVE knight" (uppercase original) as a formula in which the adjective varies according to the alliteration requirement. He even suggests that the structure of FUNCTION-WORD ADJECTIVE NOUN in general can be a syntactic formula in *MA*.

Applying the idea of formulaic composition to *MA* must be done with caution[6] because the formula has been discussed as a complicated convention. As claimed by Krishna, "repetition alone does not make a phrase a formula" (Krishna, "Parataxis"). Ritzke-Rutherford ("Macrostructure," "Microstructure") uses the term *cluster* instead of *formula* in a strict sense in order to denote a group of words that are regularly employed to express a given essential idea. Whatever term is used, the extensive and frequent repetition of certain set phrases often marks the central motifs of *MA* in a special poetic sense. Investigating the metrical positions of set phrases to describe warfare, fate, and knighthood may suggest a new interpretation of formulae in alliterative verse. At least, *the round table* remains in a unique metrical constraint, namely the strict [r-r-r-t] pattern.

Ritzke-Rutherford's examples of formula reveal a distinctive feature of set phrases in *MA*. She uses the following lines to explain that the word order may vary within a formula:

MA 1399 Bot thare *ch*asez on oure men *ch*euallrous knyghtez,
MA 1551 And for þe *ch*eefe *ch*auncelere, þe *ch*eualere noble,
MA 2990 *Ch*ases and *ch*oppes down *ch*eftaynes noble,

An alliterating word, whether it is an adjective or a noun, always occupies the first stressed position of the second half-line in these lines. The position of the adjective that is subordinate to a noun is flexible here; an adjective may precede the noun or follow it. The poet could have switched the word order and written *knyghtez chevallrous* in *MA* 1399, *the noble chevalere* in *MA* 1551, and *noble cheftaynes* in *MA* 2990. The reason for not using these orders is metrical. The so-called *Stanzaic Morte Arthure* (*Le Morte Arthur: A Romance in Stanzas of Eight Lines*) contains a line with *the round table*:[7]

SMA 9 The knightis of the table Round,

The *SMA* is not an alliterative poem, but is composed in the eight-syllable line with end rhyme in the eight-line stanza. The word *round* in *SMA* 9 above rhymes with *found* in *SMA* 11, *bound* in *SMA* 13, and *sound* in *SMA* 15.[8] In such a metrical context, the *SMA* poet did not want to write in the adjective + noun order for the sake of end rhyme. The same poet uses the order of *Round* + *table* in *SMA* 1049 because in this case the line needs to rhyme with *stable* in *SMA* 1051, *profitable* in *SMA* 1053, and *fable* in *SMA* 1055.

The *MA* poet knew that he could choose either an adjective or noun form of chivalry so that the alliterating syllable always occupied the first stressed position of the second half-line. He did not want to reverse the order of the two words in case of *the round table* to *the table round* as his contemporaries like the *SMA* poet and others, whom will be examined in the next section, did. He did so, however, in case of *cheualere noble* or *cheftaynes noble*.

If words other than *round* accompanied *table*, alliteration could occur in words that start with /t/ instead of /r/. This is not observed in *MA*, however. There are five occasions in *MA* in which the word *table* is not accompanied by the adjective *round*:

MA 1301 Reght as þey hade *w*eschen and *w*ent to þe table. [r-w-w-t]
MA 1330 Ne ware it for *r*euerence of my *r*yche table,[9] [r-r-r-t]
MA 3192 They *t*ryne vnto a *t*ente whare *t*ables whare raysede. [t-t-t-r]

MA 3198 *R*ehetez the *R*omaynes at his *r*iche table, [r-r-r-t]
MA 3201 *R*euerence[s] the *R*omayns in his *r*iche table. [r-r-r-t]

Three out of the five lines have *riche* in front of *table*. Again the alliteration occurs on /r/, forming the same alliteration pattern, [r-r-r-t], as those of lines that contain *the round table*. In other words, King Arthur's table in *MA* is almost always accompanied by an adjective that starts with /r/. *The round table* must occupy the entire second half-line, and the line must alliterate on /r/.

17.4 "The Round Table" in Other ME Works and the Metrical Template of *The Alliterative Morte Arthure*

The occurrences of *the round table* in *G*, another major poem about King Arthur, are far fewer. Though *G* consists of 2530 lines, only six lines contain *the round table* and another six contain *table* without *round*. The following lines are the ones that contain *the round table*:

G 39 *R*ekenly of þe *R*ounde Table alle þo *r*ich breþer– /r/
G 313 Now is þe *r*euel and þe *r*enoun of þe *R*ounde Table /r/
G 538 With much *r*euel and *r*yche of þe *R*ounde Table. /r/
G 905 Þat is þe *r*yche *r*yal kyng of þe *R*ounde Table, /r/
G 2458 Þat *r*ennes of þe grete *r*enoun of þe *R*ounde Table; /r/
G 2519 For þat watz acorded þe *r*enoun of þe *R*ounde Table /r/

The *G* poet uses *the round table* in a similar way to the *MA* poet, placing it in the second half-line and associating it with words of nobility. *G* 39 is an exception because it contains *the round table* in its middle. Three ways of reading in different alliteration patterns are possible, as shown in the following scansion:

G 39-a *R*ékenly of þe *R*óunde Table alle þo *r*ích bréþer– [aaax]
G 39-b *R*ékenly of þe *R*ounde Táble alle þo *r*ích bréþer– [axax]
G 39-c *R*ékenly of þe *R*óunde Táble alle þo *r*ích bréþer– [aaxax]

The first reading is the one that conforms to consistent alliteration, not realizing metrical stress in the word *table*. The second reading treats *round* as being metrically subordinated to the noun it modifies, but the resulting alliteration is deviated. Reading *c* realizes metrical beats in all the syllables that can receive stress, thus producing a line that has five metrical beats.[10] In the first two readings, *round table* does not receive full metrical stress in both of its constituents, which is not favorable to the *MA* poet.

One common phenomenon found in both *MA* and *G* is that both of the poets never fail to alliterate the line with *the round table* on /r/. This restriction is solely due to the alliteration purpose since the most common noun that denotes the noble men of the round table in the Arthurian legends is *knyghtes*. The phrase, *knyghtes of the round table*, is significantly common in a prose romance, *Merlin*, and in Malory's *Le Morte Darthur*. The following are a few examples from *Merlin* in which the word *knyghtes* precedes *the round table*:[11]

This is the trouthe, that the knyghtes of *the rounde table*, that was stablisshed and founded in the tyme of Vterpendragon, youre fader, on whos soule god haue mercy, . . . (Chapter 7)

. . . that thei were not assailled of somme maner peple, and the kynge Ban and the kynge Bohors ledde the kynge Arthur and sir Gawein and the knyghtes of *the rounde table*, and the xl knyghtes that ye haue herde named, and the newe knyghtes in to the castell of Trebes . . . (Chapter 23)

. . . and the fray of the people of kynge Rion, and of the peple of kynge Arthur; and ther dide Gawein, and Ewein, and Segramor, and Gaheries, and the knyghtes of *the rounde table* merveiles with theire handes; (Chapter 31)

Other collocations observed in prose are *felawes of the round table*, *companye of the round table*, *banerer of the round table*, *lordes of the round table*, *lordinges of the round table*, *meyne of the round table*, *barons of the round table*, *felauship of the round table*, and *party of the round table*. Especially evident is the use of pronoun in the phrase, as seen in *thei of the round table* and *hem of the round table*. If these phrases were employed, it would be possible to use other alliteration sounds for the lines that contain *the round table*. This idea, however, is never favored by alliterative poets. They, unlike the prose writers, deliberately avoid using words such as *knyghtes*, *felawes*, and *companye* because that will not allow the line to alliterate on /r/.[12]

Malory's *Le Morte Darthur* provides another point of interest. There are approximately 150 occasions in which the round table is mentioned in his prose romance. The reversed order is acceptable to Malory; many of such lines have the order of the noun followed by the adjective. Again *knyght* commonly precedes *the round table*:

. . . as moche as ye haue my cosyn at your desyre of your quest? Syr, I shalle telle yow, my name is Kyng Pellenore of the Ilys, and knyghte of *the Table Round.*
(Book Three, Capitulum 13)[13]

Thenne he said to hymself. I am a knyght of *the Table Round* and rather than I shold shame myn othe and my blood I wille hold my way, whatsooeuer falle therof. (Book Ten, Capitulum 53)

. . . and al was for to shewe outward that she had as grete ioye in al other knyghtes of *the Table Round* as she had in Sir Launcelot.
(Book Eighteen, Capitulum 3)

These examples imply that the *MA* poet could have reversed the word order of *the round table*, as Malory did. He did so for *þe renkes renownde* but not for *þe Rownd Table*, as seen in the following line.

MA 2912 Than þe *r*enkes *r*enownde of þe *R*ownd Table

If *the round table* appears in the middle or if words other than those starting with /r/ precede *the round table*, one of the constituents of *the round table* may not fully receive metrical stress. This can be described by the following schemes. Dots signify any unstressed syllables whereas the alliterating consonant is followed by a stress mark. The underline represents a separate word:

Verse → . . t ´ . . . . round táble . . t ´ . . . . x ´ . . [a(x)aax]
Verse → . . táble round . . t ´ . . . . t ´ . . . . x ´ . . [a(x)aax]

These two verse structures are possible variants of the meter if the line alliterates on /t/. It is inevitable, however, that the adjective *round* becomes metrically weak in these constructions. That is why the first *x* in the brackets showing the alliteration is placed between parentheses, which indicates that this syllable may not be realized as a metrical beat. If these patterns are not plausible, the only pattern that is used for the line that contains *the round table* is as follows:

Verse → . . r ´. . . . r ´. . . . róund táble [aaax]

The *MA* poet was ambitious in using excessive repetition of the same sound more than required by alliterative meter, generating internal unity made by alliteration within the line and external unity made by identical alliteration and secondary alliteration over a group of lines. The result is an amazing and amusing form of verbal play in layers of sound repetition. Adherence to the excessive sound repetition makes the poem unique among alliterative verse written in the same period. The poet could have shown this innovative talent throughout his work, but did not do so for *the round table*, even though his potential for word play and great abundance of vocabulary are fully proven in other parts of the poem. The metrical location of *the round table* reveals that the alliterative poets could be inflexible regarding certain phrases and their metrical structures.

Notes

1 Some examples in this section have been quoted in Chapters Eleven and Twelve, but are provided once again in order to reconfirm the excessive repetition of /r/ in *MA*.

2 The terms *primary alliteration* and *secondary alliteration* have been introduced in Chapter Twelve in order to distinguish two different roles that /r/ may play in alliteration. In primary alliteration /r/ initiates the alliterating syllable while it appears as a second or third constituent of the alliterating syllable in secondary alliteration. See Chapter Twelve.

3 Realizing the frequent association of *riding* and *round table* in *MA*, Finlayson comments, "(such an association) frequently generates an extended sequence of *r* alliterations, and the alliterative elements are so stereotypes as to suggest that they are formulas." See Finlayson, "Formulaic" 386–93.

4 Ritzke-Rutherford defines a formula as a group of words that are restricted to a half-line, hardly variable in wording, extremely structured by sound, and often connected with a motif. See Ritzke-Rutherford, "Microstructure" 70–82.

5 There are many instances of such a syntactic unit in *MA*. These instances reveal a striking similarity as to their metrical make-up; namely, it is usually the adjective, but not the noun, that alliterates. Yet the noun may carry alliteration in certain cases. For a discussion on metrical subordination in *MA*, see T. Turville-Petre, *Revival* 89.

6 T. Turville-Petre, for example, warns about the idea of ME alliterative verse as formulaic composition. See *Revival* 92.

7 Citations are from the edition by Bruce.

8 The whole stanza is as follows:

SMA 9 The knightis of the table Round,
SMA 10 The sangrayle whan they had sought,
SMA 11 Aunturs that they by-fore them found
SMA 12 Fynisshid and to end[e] brought;
SMA 13 Their enemyes they bette & bound,
SMA 14 For gold on lyff they lefte them noght.
SMA 15 Foure yere they lyved sound,
SMA 16 When they had these werkis wroght,

9 In this metrical context, the word *reuerence* seems to receive metrical stress in two places, achieving the common alliteration. The same word in *MA* 3201, however, will receive metrical stress on its first syllable only.

10 These metrically flexible lines often allow more than two different readings, depending upon the metrical context and the readers' preference.

11 By Wheatley's edition.

12 The only exception is the word *men*. The following examples show that this word can accompany *the round table*. The alliteration pattern appears after each line:

MA 1676 The *r*yotous men and þe *r*yche of þe *R*ounde Table, [r-m-r-r-t]
MA 2243 To *r*eschewe þe *r*yche men of þe *R*ounde Table, [r-r-m-r-t]
MA 2878 As was when þe *r*yche men of the *R*ownde Table [r-m-r-t]
MA 3173 This *r*oy with his *r*yall men of þe *R*ownde Table, [r-r-m-r-t]
MA 4081 The *r*ekeneste *r*edy men of þe *R*ownde Table, [r-r-m-r-t]
MA 4117 *R*edily thas *r*ydde men of the *R*ownde Table [r-r-m-r-t]

The only variation of this pattern is the use of *blude*:

MA 4282 Here *r*ystys the *r*iche blude of the *R*ownde Table. [r-r-b-r-t]

If stronger metrical stress is assumed in the adjective, these lines will remain in the common alliteration pattern, [aaax]. The poet frequently places an adjective that starts with /r/ in front of *men*.

13 By Spisak's edition.

References

Primary Sources:

The Wars of Alexander (A)
The Wars of Alexander: *An Alliterative Romance*. Ed. Walter W. Skeat. Millwood, NY: Kraus Reprint, 1990.

The Parlement of the Thre Ages (AG)
The Parlement of the Thre Ages. Ed. M. Y. Offord. EETS. London: Oxford University Press, 1967.

Cleanness (C)
The Poems of the Pearl Manuscript. Eds. Malcolm Andrew and Ronald Waldron. Exeter: University of Exeter, 1987.

Dispute Between Mary and the Cross (CR)
Legends of the Holy Rood: Symbols of the Passion and Cross-Poems. Ed. Richard Morris. Millwood, NY: Kraus Reprint, 1990.

St. Erkenwald (E)
Alliterative Poetry of the Later Middle Ages: An Anthology. Ed. Thorlac Turville-Petre. London: Routledge, 1989.

Sir Gawain and the Green Knight (G)
The Poems of the Pearl Manuscript. Eds. Malcolm Andrew and Ronald Waldron. Exeter: University of Exeter, 1987.

The Siege of Jerusalem (J)
The Siege of Jerusalem *Edited from MS. Laud. Misc. 656 with Variants from All Other Extant MSS*. Eds. E. Kölbing and Mabel Day. Millwood, NY: Kraus Reprint, 1988.

The Three Dead Kings (K)
Alliterative Poetry of the Later Middle Ages: An Anthology. Ed. Thorlac Turville-Petre. London: Routledge, 1989.

The Quatrefoil of Love (L)
The Quatrefoil of Love *Edited from Brit. Mus. MS. Add. 31042 with Collations from Bodl. MS. ADD. A 106*. Eds. Israel Gollancz and Magdalene Weale. Millwood, NY: Kraus Reprint, 1987.

The Alliterative Morte Arthure (*MA*)
Morte Arthure: *A Critical Edition*. Ed. Mary Hamel. New York: Garland, 1984.

Pearl (*PE*)
The Poems of the Pearl Manuscript. Eds. Malcolm Andrew and Ronald Waldron. Exeter: University of Exeter, 1987.

Piers Plowman (*PPA, PPB, PPC*)
Piers Plowman: *A Parallel-Text Edition of the A, B, C and Z Versions*. Ed. A. V. C. Schmidt. London: Longman, 1995.

A Pistel of Susan (*PS*)
Alliterative Poetry of the Later Middle Ages: An Anthology. Ed. Thorlac Turville-Petre. London: Routledge, 1989.

Patience (*PT*)
The Poems of the Pearl Manuscript. Eds. Malcolm Andrew and Ronald Waldron. Exeter: University of Exeter, 1987.

Somer Soneday (*SS*)
Alliterative Poetry of the Later Middle Ages: An Anthology. Ed. Thorlac Turville-Petre. London: Routledge, 1989.

The Destruction of Troy (*T*)
The 'Gest Hystoriale' of the Destruction of Troy: *An Alliterative Romance Translated from Guido de Colonna's* Hystoria Troiana. Eds. G. A. Panton and D. Donaldson. EETS. London: Oxford University Press, 1968.

Wynnere and Wastoure (*W*)
Wynnere and Wastoure *and* The Parlement of the Thre Ages. Ed. Warren Ginsberg. Kalamazoo: Medieval Institute, 1992.

Secondary Sources:

Abercrombie, David. "Syllable Quantity and Enclitics in English." *In Honour of Daniel Jones*. Eds. David Abercrombie et al. London: Longman, 1964. 216–22.

Abercrombie, David. "A Phonetician's View of Verse Structure." *Studies in Phonetics and Linguistics*. Ed. David Abercrombie. London: Oxford University Press, 1965. 16–25.

Abercrombie, David. "Some Functions of Silent Stress." *Edinburgh Studies in English and Scots*. Eds. A. J. Aitken, A. McIntosh, and H. Pálsson. London: Longman, 1971. 147–56.

Adams, Percy G. "Alliteration." *The New Princeton Encyclopedia of Poetry and Poetics*. Third edn. Eds. Alex Preminger and T. V. F. Brogan. Princeton: Princeton University Press, 1993. 36–38.

Allen, G. D. "The Location of Rhythmic Stress Beats in English Speech, Parts I and II."

Language and Speech 15 (1972): 72–100; 179–95.

Allen, G. D. "Speech Rhythm: Its Relation to Performance Universals and Articulatory Timing." *Journal of Phonetics* 3 (1975): 75–86.

Allen, Rosamund. "Performance and Structure in *The Alliterative Morte Arthure.*" *New Perspectives on Middle English Texts: A Festschrift for R. A. Waldron*. Eds. Susan Powell and Jeremy Smith. Cambridge: D. S. Brewer, 2000. 17–29.

Allen, William S. "On Quantity and Quantitative Verse." *In Honour of Daniel Jones*. Eds. David Abercrombie et al. London: Longman, 1964. 3–15.

Andrew, Malcolm, and Ronald Waldron, eds. *The Poems of the Pearl Manuscript*. Exeter: University of Exeter, 1987.

Anttila, Raimo. "Sound Preference in Alliteration." *Statistical Methods in Linguistics* 5 (1969): 44–48.

Attridge, Derek. *Well-Weighed Syllables: Elizabethan Verse in Classical Metres.* Cambridge: Cambridge University Press, 1974.

Attridge, Derek. *The Rhythms of English Poetry.* London: Longman, 1982.

Attridge, Derek. "Linguistic Theory and Literary Criticism: *The Rhythms of English Poetry* Revisited." *Phonetics and Phonology I: Rhythm and Meter.* Eds. Paul Kiparsky and Gilbert Youmans. Cambridge, MA: MIT Press, 1989. 183–99.

Attridge, Derek. "The Movement of Meaning: Phrasing and Repetition in English Poetry." *Repetition*. Ed. Andreas Fischer. Tübingen: Narr, 1994. 61–83.

Attridge, Derek. *Poetic Rhythm: An Introduction.* Cambridge: Cambridge University Press, 1995.

Bailey, James. *Towards a Statistical Analysis of English Verse: The Iambic Tetrameter of Ten Poets.* Lisse, Netherlands: Peter de Ridder, 1975.

Ballard, Kim. *The Frameworks of English: Introducing Language Structures.* Basingstoke: Palgrave, 2001.

Baltzer, Rebecca A., Thomas Cable, and James I. Wimsatt, eds. *The Union of Words and Music in Medieval Poetry*. Austin: University of Texas Press, 1991.

Barber, Charles, Joan C. Beal, and Philip A. Shaw. *The English Language: A Historical Introduction*. Cambridge: Cambridge University Press, 2009.

Barney, Stephen A. "Langland's Prosody: The State of Study." *The Endless Knot: Essays on Old and Middle English in Honor of Marie Borroff.* Eds. M. Teresa Tavormina and R. F. Yeager. Cambridge: D. S. Brewer, 1995. 65–85.

Baugh, Albert, and Thomas Cable. *A History of the English Language*. Upper Saddle River, NJ: Pearson, 2013.

Baum, Paull F. *The Principles of English Versification.* Cambridge, MA: Harvard University Press, 1922.

Beaver, Joseph C. "The Rules of Stress in English Verse." *Language* 47 (1971): 586–614.

Beaver, Joseph C. "A Stress Problem in English Prosody." *Linguistics* 95 (1973): 5–12.

Bennett, J. W. A. "Survivals and Revivals of Alliterative Modes." *Leeds Studies of English* 14 (1983): 26–43.

Benson, Larry D. *Art and Tradition in* Sir Gawain and the Green Knight. New Brunswick: Rutgers University Press, 1965.

Bernhart, A. W. "Complexity and Metricality." *Poetics* 12 (1974): 113–41.

Bjorklund, B. "Review of *The Rhythms of English Poetry* by Derek Attridge." *Journal of English and Germanic Philology* 84 (1985): 113–16.

Blake, Norman F. "Rhythmical Alliteration." *Modern Philology* 67 (1969): 118–24.

Blake, Norman F. "Middle English Prose and Its Audience." *Anglia* 90 (1972): 437–55.

Blake, Norman F. *An Introduction to the Language of Literature.* Basingstoke: Macmillan, 1990.

Blake, Norman F. *The Cambridge History of the English Language. Vol. 2: 1066–1476.* Cambridge: Cambridge University Press, 1992.

Bliss, Alan. *An Introduction to Old English Metre.* Oxford: Basil Blackwell, 1962.

Bloomfield, Morton W., and Charles W. Dunn. *The Role of the Poet in Early Societies.* Cambridge: D. S. Brewer, 1989.

Bolinger, Dwight. L. *Two Kinds of Vowels, Two Kinds of Rhythm.* Bloomington: Indiana University Linguistic Club, 1981.

Bolton, W. F. "The Conditions of Literary Composition in Medieval England." *The New History of Literature Vol. 1: The Middle Ages.* Ed. W. F. Bolton. New York: Peter Bedrick, 1986. 1–27.

Boomsliter, Paul C., Warren Creel, and George S. Hastings. "Perception and English Poetic Meter." *Publication of Modern Language Association of America* 88 (1973): 200–08.

Borroff, Marie. Sir Gawain and the Green Knight: *A Stylistic and Metrical Study.* New Haven and London: Yale University Press, 1962.

Borroff, Marie. "Reading the Poem Aloud." *Approaches to Teaching* Sir Gawain and the Green Knight. Eds. M. Y. Miller and J. Chance. New York: Modern Language Association of America, 1986. 191–98.

Borroff, Marie. "Systematic Sound Symbolism in the Long Alliterative Line in *Beowulf* and *Sir Gawain.*" *English Historical Metrics.* Eds. C. B. McCully and J. J. Anderson. Cambridge: Cambridge University Press, 1996. 120–33.

Bradbury, Nancy M. "Literacy, Orality, and the Poetics of Middle English Romance." *Oral Poetics in Middle English Poetry.* Eds. Mark C. Amodio and Sarah G. Miller. New York: Garland, 1994. 39–69.

Bradford, Richard. *A Linguistic History of English Poetry.* London and New York: Routledge, 1993.

Brinton, Laurel J., and Leslie K. Arnovick. *The English Language: A Linguistic History.* Oxford: Oxford University Press, 2006.

Brock, Edmund, ed. Morte Arthure: *or, The death of Arthur Edited From Robert Thornton's Ms. in the Library of Lincoln Cathedral by Edmund Brock.* London: Early English Text Society, 1961.

Brogan, T. V. F. "Generative Metrics." *The New Princeton Encyclopedia of Poetry and Poetics.* Third edn. Eds. Alex Preminger and T. V. F. Brogan. Princeton: Princeton University Press, 1993. 451–53.

Brogan, T. V. F. "Rhyme." *The New Princeton Encyclopedia of Poetry and Poetics.* Third edn. Eds. Alex Preminger and T. V. F. Brogan. Princeton: Princeton University Press, 1993. 1052–64.

Brown, Arthur C. L. "On the Origin of Stanza-Linking in English Alliterative Verse." *Romanic Review* 7 (1916): 271–83.

Brown, Calvin S. "Monosyllables in English Verse." *Studies in English Literature 1500–1900* 3 (1963): 473–91.

Bruce, J. Douglas, ed. Le Morte Arthur: *A Romance in Stanzas of Eight Lines*. London: Oxford University Press, 1959.

Bunt, Gerrit H. V. "Alliterative Patterning and the Editing of Middle English Poetry." *English Historical Metrics*. Eds. C. B. McCully and J. J. Anderson. Cambridge: Cambridge University Press, 1996. 175–84.

Burling, Robbins. "The Metrics of Children's Verse: A Cross Linguistic Study." *American Anthropologist* 68 (1966): 1418–41.

Burrow, John A. "Redundancy in Alliterative Verse: *St Erkenwald*." *Individuality and Achievement in Middle English Poetry*. Ed. O. S. Pickering. Cambridge: D. S. Brewer, 1997. 119–28.

Burrow, John A, and Thorlac Turville-Petre. *A Book of Middle English*. Oxford: Blackwell, 1992.

Cable, Thomas. "Timers, Stressers, and Linguists: Contention and Compromise." *Modern Language Quarterly* 33 (1972): 227–39.

Cable, Thomas. "Middle English Meter and Its Theoretical Implications." *Yearbook of Langland Studies* 2 (1988): 47–69.

Cable, Thomas. "Standards from the Past: The Conservative Syllable Structure of the Alliterative Revival." *Standardizing English: Essays in the History of Language Change in Honor of John Hurt Fisher*. Ed. Joseph Trahern, Jr. Knoxville: University of Tennessee Press, 1989. 42–56.

Cable, Thomas. *The English Alliterative Tradition*. Philadelphia: University of Pennsylvania Press, 1991.

Cable, Thomas. "The Meter and Musical Implications of Old English Poetry." *The Union of Words and Music in Medieval Poetry*. Eds. Rebecca Baltzer, Thomas Cable, and James I. Wimsatt. Austin: University of Texas Press, 1991. 49–71.

Cable, Thomas. "Grammar, Spelling, and the Rhythm of the Alliterative Long Line." *Prosody and Poetics in the Early Middle Ages: Essays in Honour of C. B. Hieatt*. Ed. M. J. Toswell. Toronto: University of Toronto Press, 1995. 13–22.

Cable, Thomas. "Clashing Stress in the Metres of Old, Middle, and Renaissance English." *English Historical Metrics*. Eds. C. B. McCully and J. J. Anderson. Cambridge: Cambridge University Press, 1996. 7–29.

Cain, Christopher M., and Geoffrey Russom, eds. *Studies in the History of the English Language III: Managing Chaos: Strategies for Identifying Change in English*. Berling and New York: Mouton de Gruyter, 2007.

Camargo, Martin. "Oral Tradition Structure in *Sir Gawain and the Green Knight*." *Comparative Research on Oral Traditions*. Ed. John M. Foley. Columbus: Slavica, 1987. 121–37.

Campbell, Alastair. "The Old English Epic Style." *English and Medieval Studies Presented to J. R. R. Tolkien on the Occasion of his Seventieth Birthday*. Eds. N. Davis and C. L. Wrenn. London: Allen and Unwin, 1962. 13–26.

Campbell, J. J. "Oral Poetry in *The Seafarer*." *Speculum* 35 (1960): 87–96.

Carroll, Benjamin H., Jr. "Metrical Resolution in Old English." *Journal of English and Germanic Philology* 92 (1993): 167–78.

Carter, Ronald, and Peter Stockwell, eds. *The Language and Literature Reader*. London and New York: Routledge, 2008.

Cassidy, Frederic G., and Richard N. Ringler, eds. *Bright's Old English Grammar and Reader*. New York: Holt, Rinehart and Winston, 1971.

Cawley, A. C., ed. Pearl, Sir Gawain and the Green Knight. London: Dent, 1970.
Chamberlin, John S. "What Makes *Piers Plowman* So Hard to Read?" *Style* 23 (1989): 32–48.
Chapman, Coolidge Otis. "The Musical Training of the Pearl Poet." *Publication of Modern Language Association of America* 46 (1931): 177–81.
Chatman, Seymour. "Comparing Metrical Styles." *Style in Language*. Ed. T. A. Sebeok. Cambridge, MA: MIT Press, 1960. 149–72.
Chatman, Seymour. *A Theory of Meter*. The Hague: Mouton, 1965.
Chatman, Seymour. *An Introduction to the Language of Poetry*. Boston: Houghton Mifflin, 1968.
Chism, Christine. *Alliterative Revivals*. Philadelphia: University of Pennsylvania Press, 2002.
Chomsky, Noam, and Morris Halle. *The Sound Pattern of English*. New York: Harper and Row, 1968.
Chomsky, Noam, Morris Halle, and F. Lukoff. "On Accent and Juncture in English." *For Roman Jakobson*. Eds. Morris Halle et al. The Hague: Mouton, 1956. 65–80.
Clark, Arthur M., and Harold Whiteall. "Rhyme." *Princeton Encyclopedia of Poetry and Poetics*. First edn. Ed. Alex Preminger. Princeton: Princeton University Press, 1974. 705–10.
Clark, John W. "On Certain 'Alliterative' and 'Poetic' Words in the Poems Attributed to 'The Gawain-Poet.'" *Modern Language Quartery* 12 (1951): 387–98.
Cochrane, Robertson. *Wordplay: Origins, Meanings, and Usage of the English Language*. Toronto: University of Toronto Press, 1996.
Coleman, Joyce. *Public Reading and the Reading Public in Late Medieval England and France*. New York: Cambridge University Press, 1996
Coleman, Joyce. "Aurality." *Middle English*. Ed. Paul Strohm. Oxford: Oxford University Press, 2007. 68–85.
Conner, Jack. *English Prosody from Chaucer to Wyatt*. The Hague: Mouton, 1974.
Cooper, G. W., and L. B. Meyer. *The Rhythmic Structure of Music*. Chicago: University of Chicago Press, 1960.
Cooper, R. A., and D. A. Pearsall. "The Gawain Poems: A Statistical Approach to the Question of Common Authorship." *Review of English Studies New Series* 39 (1988): 365–85.
Cosmos, Spencer. "Kuhn's Law and the Unstressed Verbs in *Beowulf*." *Texas Studies in Literature and Language* 18 (1976): 306–28.
Couper-Kuhlen, Elizabeth. *An Introduction to English Prosody*. London: Edward Arnold, 1986.
Couper-Kuhlen, Elizabeth. *English Speech Rhythm: Form and Function in Everyday Verbal Interaction*. Amsterdam: John Benjamins, 1993.
Creed, Robert P. *Reconstructing the Rhythm of* Beowulf. Columbia: University of Missouri Press, 1990.
Cureton, Richard D. "Review of *The Rhythms of English Poetry* by Derek Attridge." *American Speech* 60 (1985): 157–61.
Cureton, Richard D. *Rhythmic Phrasing in English Verse*. London: Longman, 1992.
Cureton, Richard D. "Rhythm and Verse Study." *Language and Literature* 3 (1994): 105–24.
Cutler, Anne. "Syllable Omission Errors and Isochrony." *Temporal Variables in Speech*. Eds. Hans W. Dechert and Manfred Raupach. The Hague: Mouton, 1980. 183–90.
Dauer, R. M. "Stress-Timing and Syllable-Timing Reanalyzed." *Journal of Phonetics* 11 (1983): 51–62.
Day, Mabel. "Strophic Division in Middle English Alliterative Verse." *Englische Studien* 66

(1931): 245–48.

Dogil, G. "On the Evaluations Measures for Prosodic Phonology." *Linguistics* 22 (1984): 281–311.

Donaldson, E. T. "Chaucer's Final *-e*." *Publication of Modern Language Association of America* 63 (1948): 1101–24.

Donaldson, E. T. "View Points." *Twentieth Century Interpretations of* Sir Gawain and the Green Knight. Ed. Denton Fox. Englewood Cliffs: Prentice-Hall, 1968. 98–100.

Donner, Morton. "A Grammatical Perspective on Word Play in *Pearl*." *Chaucer Review* 22 (1988): 322–31.

Donner, Morton. "Word Play and Word Form in *Pearl*." *Chaucer Review* 24 (1989): 166–82.

Duggan, Hoyt N. "Strophic Patterns in Middle English Alliterative Poetry." *Modern Philology* 74 (1976–77): 223–47.

Duggan, Hoyt N. "Alliterative Patterning as a Basis for Emendation in Middle English Alliterative Poetry." *Studies in the Age of Chaucer* 8 (1986): 73–105.

Duggan, Hoyt N. "The Shape of the B-Verse in Middle English Alliterative Poetry." *Speculum* 61 (1986): 564–92.

Duggan, Hoyt N. "Notes Toward a Theory of Langland's Meter." *Yearbook of Langland Studies* 1 (1987): 41–70.

Duggan, Hoyt N. "Final *-e* and the Rhythmic Structure of the B-Verse in Middle English Alliterative Poetry." *Modern Philology* 86 (1988): 119–45.

Duggan, Hoyt N. "Scribal Self-Correction and Editorial Theory." *Neuphilologische Mitteilungen* 91 (1990): 215–27.

Duggan, Hoyt N. "Stress Assignment in Middle English Alliterative Poetry." *Journal of English and Germanic Philology* 89 (1990): 309–29.

Duggan, Hoyt N. "The Role and Distribution of *–ly* Adverbs in Middle English Alliterative Verse." *Loyal Letters: Studies on Medieval Alliterative Poetry and Prose*. Eds. L. A. J. R. Houwen and A. A. MacDonald. Groningen: Egbert Forsten, 1994. 131–54.

Duggan, Hoyt., and Thorlac Turville-Petre, eds. The Wars of Alexander. London: Oxford University Press, 1989.

Duncan, Edwin. "Weak Stress and Poetic Constraints in Old English Verse." *Journal of English and Germanic Philology* 92 (1993): 495–508.

Duncan, Edwin. "Metrical and Alliterative Relationships in Old English and Old Saxon Verse." *Studies in Philology* 91 (1994): 1–12.

Dunn, Charles W., and T. V. F. Brogan. "Celtic Prosody." *The New Princeton Encyclopedia of Poetry and Poetics*. Third edn. Eds. Alex Preminger and T. V. F. Brogan. Princeton: Princeton University Press, 1993. 177–79.

Dunn, Charles W., and Edward T. Byrnes, eds. *Middle English Literature.* New York: Garland, 1990.

Eadie, J. "*The Alliterative Morte Arthure*: Structure and Meaning." *English Studies* 63 (1982): 1–12.

Easthope, Antony. "Review of *The Rhythms of English Poetry* by Derek Attridge." *Language and Style* 16 (1983): 244–46.

Ebbs, John Dale. "Stylistic Mannerisms of the Gawain-Poet." *Journal of English and Germanic Philology* 57 (1958): 522–25.

Everett, Dorothy. *Essays on Middle English Literature.* Oxford: Clarendon, 1955.

Fabb, Nigel. *Linguistics and Literature: Language in the Verbal Arts of the World.* Oxford: Blackwell, 1997.

Fabb, Nigel. *Language and Literary Structure: The Linguistic Analysis of Form in Verse and Narrative.* Cambridge: Cambridge University Press, 2002.

Facchinetti, Roberta, and Matti Rissanen, eds. *Corpus-Based Studies of Diachronic English.* Bern and Berlin: Peter Lang, 2006.

Faure, G., D. J. Hirst, and M. Chafcouloff. "Rhythm in English: Isochronism, Pitch, and Perceived Stress." *The Melody of Language.* Eds. L. R. Waugh and C. H. Van Schooneveld. Baltimore: University Park Press, 1980. 71–79.

Fennell, Barbara A. *A History of English: A Sociolinguistic Approach.* Oxford and Malden: Blackwell, 2001.

Finch, Casey, trans. *The Complete Works of the Pearl Poet.* Berkeley: University of California Press, 1993.

Finke, Laurie A., and Martin B. Shichtman. "Introduction: Critical Theory and the Study of the Middle Ages." *Medieval Texts and Contemporary Readers.* Eds. L. A. Finke and M. B. Shichtman. Ithaca and London: Cornell University Press, 1987. 1–11.

Finlayson, John. "Formulaic Technique in *Morte Arthure.*" *Anglia* 81 (1963): 372–93.

Finlayson, John, ed. Morte Arthure. London: Edward Arnold, 1967.

Fisiak, Jacek. *Studies in Middle English Linguistics.* Berlin and New York: Mouton de Gruyter, 1997.

Fisiak, Jacek. *Advances in English Historical Linguistics.* Hawthorne: Mouton de Gruyter, 1998.

Foley, John M. *Traditional Oral Epic:* The Odyssey, Beowulf, *and the Serbo Croatian Return Song.* Berkeley: University of California Press, 1990.

Foley, John M. "The Implications of Oral Tradition." *Oral Tradition in the Middle Ages.* Ed. W. F. H. Nicolaisen. Binghamton: State University of New York at Binghamton, 1995. 31–57.

Fox, Denton. "Introduction." *Twentieth Century Interpretations of* Sir Gawain and the Green Knight. Ed. Denton Fox. Englewood Cliffs: Prentice-Hall, 1968. 1–12.

Frankis, John. "Word-Formation by Blending in the Vocabulary of Middle English Alliterative Verse." *Five Hundred Years of Words and Sounds: A Festschrift for Eric Dobson.* Eds. Eric G. Stanley and Douglas Gray. Cambridge: Brewer, 1983. 29–38.

Frankis, P. J. "The Syllabic Value of Final -*e*s in English Versification about 1500." *Notes and Queries* 212 (1967): 11–12.

Fraser, G. S. *Metre, Rhyme and Free Verse.* London: Methuen, 1970.

Freeborn, Dennis. *Style: Text Analysis and Linguistic Criticism.* London: Macmillan, 1996.

Frye, Northrop, ed. *Sound and Poetry.* New York: Columbia University Press, 1957.

Fudge, Erik. *English Word-Stress.* London: George Allen and Unwin, 1984.

Fulk, Robert D. *A History of Old English Meter.* Philadelphia: University of Pennsylvania Press, 1992.

Furniss, Tom, and Michael Bath. *Reading Poetry: An Introduction.* London: Prentice Hall, 1996.

Fussell, Paul, Jr. "English I. Historical." *Versification: Major Language Types.* Ed. W. K. Wimsatt. New York: Modern Language Association of America, 1972. 191–203.

Fussell, Paul, Jr. *Poetic Meter and Poetic Form.* New York: Random House, 1979.

Gardner, John. *The Complete Works of the "Gawain"-Poet.* Chicago: University of Chicago Press,

1965.
Gasparov, M. L. "A Probability Model of Verse (English, Latin, French, Italian, Spanish, Portuguese)." *Style* 21 (1987): 322–58.
Giegerich, Heinz J. *Metrical Phonology and Phonological Structure: German and English*. Cambridge: Cambridge University Press, 1985.
Giegerich, Heinz J. *English Phonology: An Introduction*. Cambridge: Cambridge University Press, 1992.
Gilligan, Janet. "Numerical Composition in the Middle English *Patience*." *Studia Neophilologica* 61 (1989): 7–11.
Gilmour-Bryson, Anne, ed. *Computer Applications to Medieval Studies*. Kalamazoo: Western Michigan University, 1984.
Gimson, A. C. *An Introduction to the Pronunciation of English*. London: Edward and Arnold, 1970.
Glowka, Arthur Wayne. *A Guide to Chaucer's Meter*. Lantham, MD and London: University Press of America, 1991.
Gollancz, I., intro. Pearl, Cleanness, Patience *and* Sir Gawain and the Green Knight *Reproduced in Facsimile from the Unique MS. Cotton Nero A. x. in the British Museum*. London: Early English Text Society, 1923.
Göller, Karl H., ed. The Allitertive Morte Arthure: *A Reacessment of the Poem*. Cambridge: Brewer, 1981.
Görlach, Manfred. *The Linguistic History of English: An Introduction*. Basingstoke: Macmillan, 1997.
Görlach, Manfred. *Text Types and the History of English*. Berlin and New York: Mouton de Gruyter, 2004.
Graddol, David, Dick Leith, and Joan Swann. *English: History, Diversity and Change*. London: Routledge, 1996.
Gradon, Pamela. *Form and Style in Early English Literature*. London: Methuen, 1971.
Grant, Judith, C. Peterson, and A. S. C. Cross. "Notes on the Rhymes of *Pearl*." *Studia Neophilologica* 50 (1978): 175–78.
Green, Richard H. "Medieval Poetics." *Approaches to Teaching* Sir Gawain and the Green Knight. Eds. M. Y. Miller and J. Chance. New York: Modern Language Association of America, 1986. 102–08.
Guéron, Jacqueline. "The Meter of Nursery Rhymes: An Application of the Halle-Keyser Theory of Meter." *Poetics* 12 (1974): 73–111.
Guest, Edwin. *A History of English Rhythms*. London: Pickering, 1838. Ed. Walter W. Skeat. London: Bell, 1882.
Hagen, Karl. T. "Adverbial Distribution in Middle English Alliterative Verse." *Modern Philology* 90 (1992): 159–71.
Halle, Morris, and Samuel J. Keyser. "Chaucer and the Study of Prosody." *College English* 28 (1966): 187–219.
Halle, Morris, and Samuel J. Keyser. *English Stress: Its Form, Its Growth and Its Role in Verse*. New York: Harper and Row, 1971.
Halle, Morris, and Samuel J. Keyser. "English III. The Iambic Pentameter." *Versification: Major Language Types*. Ed. W. K. Wimsatt. New York: Modern Language Association of America,

1972. 217–37.

Hamel, Mary. Morte Arthure: *A Critical Edition*. New York: Garland, 1984.

Hamilton, Marie P. "The Pearl Poet." *A Manual of the Writings in Middle English 1050–1500*. Vol. 2. Hamden: Archon, 1970. 339–53.

Hanna, Ralph, III. "Defining Middle English Alliterative Poetry." *The Endless Knot: Essays on Old and Middle English in Honor of Marie Borroff*. Eds. M. Teresa Tavormina and R. F. Yeager. Cambridge: D. S. Brewer, 1995. 43–64.

Hanna, Ralph, III. "Alliterative Poetry." *The Cambridge History of Medieval English Literature*. Ed. David Wallace. Cambridge: Cambridge University Press, 1999. 488–512.

Harding, D. W. *Words into Rhythm: English Speech Rhythm in Verse and Prose*. Cambridge: Cambridge University Press, 1976.

Hartle, Paul N. *Hunting the Letter: Middle English Alliterative Verse and the Formulaic Theory*. Frankfurt am Main: Peter Lang, 1999.

Hascall, Dudley L. "Trochaic Meter." *College English* 33 (1971): 217–26.

Hascall, Dudley L. "Triple Meter in English Verse." *Poetics* 12 (1974): 49–71.

Haugen, Einar. "The Syllable in Linguistic Description." *For Roman Jakobson*. Eds. Morris Halle et al. The Hague: Mouton, 1956. 213–21.

Hayes, Bruce. *A Metrical Theory of Stress Rules*. New York: Garland, 1981.

Hayes, Bruce. "The Phonology of Rhythm in English." *Linguistic Inquiry* 15 (1984): 33–74.

Hayes, Bruce. "Review of *The Rhythms of English Poetry* by Derek Attridge." *Language* 60 (1984): 914–23.

Hayes, Bruce. "Metrics and Phonological Theory." *Linguistics: The Cambridge Survey*. Vol. 2. Ed. Frederick Newmeyer. Cambridge: Cambridge University Press, 1988. 220–49.

Hayes, Bruce. "The Prosodic Hierarchy in Meter." *Phonetics and Phonology I: Rhythm and Meter*. Eds. Paul Kiparsky and Gilbert Youmans. Cambridge, MA: MIT Press, 1989. 201–60.

Hayes, Bruce. *Metrical Stress Theory: Principles and Case Studies*. Chicago: University of Chicago Press, 1995.

Haynes, John. *Style*. London and New York: Routledge, 1995.

Hieatt, Constance B. "The Rhythm of the Alliterative Long Line." *Chaucer and Middle English Studies in Honour of Russell Hope Robbins*. Ed. Beryl Rowland. London: Allen and Unwin, 1974. 119–30.

Hobsbaum, Philip. *Metre, Rhythm and Verse Form*. London and New York: Routledge, 1996.

Hogg, Richard, and C. B. McCully. *Metrical Phonology: A Coursebook*. Cambridge: Cambridge University Press, 1987.

Holder, Alan. *Rethinking Meter: A New Approach to the Verse Line*. Cranbury: Associated University Presses, 1995.

Hoover, David L. *A New Theory of Old English Meter*. New York, Bern, and Frankfurt am Main: Peter Lang, 1985.

Horobin, Simon, and Jeremy Smith. *An Introduction to Middle English*. New York: Oxford University Press, 2002.

Hulbert, J. R. "A Hypothesis Concerning the Alliterative Revival." *Modern Philology* 28 (1931): 405–22.

Huntsman-Mc, Jeffrey F. "The Celtic Heritage of *Sir Gawain and the Green Knight*." *Approaches to Teaching* Sir Gawain and the Green Knight. Eds. M. Y. Miller and J. Chance. New York:

Modern Language Association of America, 1986. 177–81.

Hutcheson, Bellenden R. "The Scansion of Old English Weak Verbs in *-ian*." *Notes and Queries* 38 (1991): 144–46.

Hutcheson, Bellenden R. "Accidental Alliteration in Old English Poetry: A Reconsideration." *English Language Notes* 30 (1992): 1–10.

Hutcheson, Bellenden R. "The Realizations of Tertiary Stress in Old English Poetry." *Studies in Philology* 91 (1994): 13–34.

Hutcheson, Bellenden R. *Old English Poetic Metre*. Cambridge: D. S. Brewer, 1995.

Hyde, Douglas. *A Literary History of Ireland*. London: Benn, 1967.

Jakobson, Roman. "Closing Statement: Linguistics and Poetics." *Style in Language*. Ed. T. A. Sebeok. Cambridge, MA: MIT Press, 1960. 350–77.

Jakobson, Roman. *On Language*. Eds. Linda R. Wauch and Monique Monville-Burston. Cambridge, MA: Harvard University Press, 1990.

Jassem, W., D. R. Hill, and I. H. Witten. "Isochrony in English Speech: Its Statistical Validity and Linguistic Relevance." *Intonation, Accent and Rhythm*. Eds. D. Gibbon and H. Richter. Berlin and New York: Walter de Gruyter, 1984. 203–25.

Jefferson, Judith A., and Ad Putter, eds. *Approaches to the Metres of Alliterative Verse*. Leeds: University of Leeds, 2009.

Jespersen, Otto. "Notes on Meter." *The Structure of Verse: Modern Essays on Prosody*. Ed. H. Gross. Greenwich: Fawcett, 1966. 111–30.

Johnson, James D. "Formulaic Thrift in the Alliterative *Morte Arthure*." *Medium Ævum* 47 (1978): 255–61.

Jones, Charles. *An Introduction to Middle English*. New York: Holt, Rinehart and Winston, 1972.

Jones, Daniel. *An Outline of English Phonetics*. Cambridge: Heffer, 1964.

Jordan, Richard. *Handbook of Middle English Grammar: Phonology*. Trans. and rev. Eugene Crook. The Hague: Mouton, 1934/1974.

Kaluza, Max. *A Short History of English Versification from the Earliest Times to the Present Day*. Trans. A. C. Dunstan. London: George Allen, 1911.

Kane, George. "Music Neither Unpleasant Nor Monotonous." *Chaucer and Langland: Historical and Textual Approaches*. Ed. G. Kane. London: Athlone, 1988. 77–89.

Kane, George. "The Text." *A Companion to* Piers Plowman. Ed. John A. Alford. Berkeley: University of California Press, 1988. 175–200.

Kaye, Jonathan. "Do You Believe in Magic? The Story of *s* + *C* Sequences." *A Festschrift for Edmund Gussmann from his Friends and Colleagues*. Eds. Henryk Kardela and Bogdan Szymanek. Lublin: University Press of the Catholic University of Lublin, 1996. 155–77.

Kean, P. M. "Numerical Composition in *Pearl*." *Notes and Queries* 210 (1965): 49–51.

Keiser, George R. "Narrative Structure in the Alliterative *Morte Arthure*, 26–720." *Chaucer Review* 9 (1974): 130–44.

Kelly, M. H., and D. C. Rubin. "Natural Rhythmic Patterns in English Verse: Evidence from Child and Counting-Out Rhymes." *Journal of Memory and Language* 27 (1988): 718–40.

Kendall, Calvin B. *The Metrical Grammar of* Beowulf. Cambridge: Cambridge University Press, 1991.

Keyser, Samuel J. "Old English Prosody." *College English* 30 (1969): 331–65.

Kiparsky, Paul. "Stress, Syntax and Meter." *Language* 51 (1975): 576–616.

Kiparsky, Paul. "The Rhythmic Structure of English Verse." *Linguistic Inquiry* 8 (1977): 189–247.

Kiparsky, Paul, and Gilbert Youmans, eds. *Phonetics and Phonology I: Rhythm and Meter*. Cambridge, MA: MIT Press, 1989.

Klaeber, Fr., ed. Beowulf *and* The Fight at Finnsburg. Boston: Heath, 1950.

Knott, Thomas A., and David Fowler, eds. Piers Plowman: *A-Version*. Baltimore: Johns Hopkins Press, 1952.

Knowles, G. "The Rhythm of English Syllables." *Lingua* 34 (1974): 115–47.

Koff, Leonard M. *Chaucer and the Art of Storytelling*. Berkeley: University of California Press, 1988.

Krishna, Valerie S., ed. The Alliterative Morte Arthure: *A Critical Edition*. New York: Franklin, 1976.

Krishna, Valerie S. "Parataxis, Formulaic Density, and Thrift in the Alliterative *Morte Arthure*." *Speculum* 57 (1982): 63–83.

Kuryłowicz, Jerzy. "Accent and Quantity as Elements of Rhythm." *Poetics: Third International Conference of Work-in-Progress Devoted to Problems of Poetics* 2 (1966): 163–72.

Lacy, Norris J., and Geoffrey Ashe. *The Arthurian Handbook*. New York: Garland. 1988.

Lanier, Sidney. *The Science of English Verse.* New York: C. Scribner's Sons, 1907.

Lass, Roger. *Old English: A Historical Linguistic Companion*. Cambridge: Cambridge University Press, 1994.

Lass, Roger. *Historical Linguistics and Language Change*. Cambridge: Cambridge University Press, 1997.

Lawrence, R. F. "The Formulaic Theory and Its Application to English Alliterative Poetry." *Essays on Style and Language: Linguistic and Critical Approaches to Literary Style*. Ed. R. Fowler. London: Routledge and K. Paul, 1966. 166–83.

Lawrence, R. F. "Formula and Rhythm in *The Wars of Alexander*." *English Studies* 51 (1970): 97–112.

Lawton, David A. "Larger Patterns of Syntax in Middle English Unrhymed Alliterative Verse." *Neophilologus* 64 (1980): 604–18.

Lawton, David A., ed. *Middle English Alliterative Poetry and Its Literary Background: Seven Essays.* Cambridge: Brewer, 1982.

Lawton, David A. "Middle English Alliterative Poetry: An Introduction." *Middle English Alliterative Poetry and Its Literary Background: Seven Essays.* Ed. D. Lawton. Cambridge: Brewer, 1982. 1–19.

Lawton, David A. "The Unity of Middle English Alliterative Poetry." *Speculum* 58 (1983): 72–94.

Lawton, David A. "The Diversity of Middle English Alliterative Poetry." *Leeds Studies in English* 20 (1989): 143–72.

Lawton, David A. "The Idea of Alliterative Poetry: Alliterative Meter and *Piers Plowman*." *Such Werkis to Werche: Essays on* Piers Plowman *in Honor of D. C. Fowler*. Ed. M. F. Vaughan. East Lansing: Colleagues, 1993. 147–68.

Leech, Geoffrey. *A Linguistic Guide to English Poetry*. London: Longman, 1969.

Lehiste, Ilse. *Suprasegmentals*. Cambridge, MA: MIT Press, 1970.

Leonard, William. E. "The Scansion of Middle English Alliterative Verse." *University of Wisconsin Studies in Language and Literature* 11 (1920): 58–104.

Le Page, R. B. "Alliterative Patterns as a Test of Style in Old English Poetry." *Journal of English and Germanic Philology* 58 (1959): 434–41.

Lester, Godfrey A. *The Language of Old and Middle English Poetry*. Basingstoke: Macmillan, 1996.

Levy, Bernard S., and Paul E. Szarmach, eds. *The Alliterative Tradition in the Fourteenth Century*. Kent: Kent State University Press, 1981.

Lewis, C. S. "The Alliterative Metre." *Selected Literary Essays*. Ed. W. Hooper. Cambridge: Cambridge University Press, 1969. 15–26.

Liberman, Mark, and Alan Prince. "On Stress and Linguistic Rhythm." *Linguistic Inquiry* 8 (1977): 249–336.

Lloyd, D. Myrddin, and T. V. F. Brogan. "Cynghanedd." *The New Princeton Encyclopedia of Poetry and Poetics*. Third edn. Eds. Alex Preminger and T. V. F. Brogan. Princeton: Princeton University Press, 1993. 265.

Lucas, P. J. "Some Aspects of the Interaction Between Verse Grammar and Metre in Old English Poetry." *Studia Neophilologica* 59 (1987): 145–75.

Macrae-Gibson, O. D. "*Pearl*: The Link-Words and the Thematic Structure." *Neophilologus* 52 (1968): 54–64.

Macrae-Gibson, O. D., and J. R. Lishman. "Computer Assistance in the Analysis of Old English Metre: Methods and Results-A Provisional Report." *Prosody and Poetics in the Early Middle Ages: Essays in Honour of C. B. Hieatt*. Ed. M. J. Toswell. Toronto: University of Toronto Press, 1995. 102–16.

Magoun, Francis, P., Jr. "The Oral-Formulaic Character of Anglo-Saxon Narrative Poetry." *Speculum* 28 (1953): 446–67.

Malof, Joseph. "The Native Rhythm of English Meters." *Texas Studies in Literature and Language* 5 (1964): 580–94.

Markus, Manfred. "Spotting Spoken Historical English: The Role of Alliteration in Middle English Fixed Expressions." *Corpus-Based Studies of Diachronic English*. Eds. Roberta Facchinetti and Matti Rissanen. Bern and Berlin: Peter Lang, 2006. 53–78.

Matonis, Anne T. E. "Middle English Alliterative Poetry." *So Meny People, Longages and Tonges: Philological Essays in Scots and Medieval English Presented to Angus McIntosh*. Eds. M. Benskin and M. L. Samuels. Edinburgh: Authors, 1981. 341–54.

Matonis, Anne T. E. "A Reexamination of the Middle English Alliterative Long Line." *Modern Philology* 81 (1984): 339–60.

McCarthy, John J. "On Stress and Syllabification." *Linguistic Inquiry* 10 (1979): 443–66.

McColly, William. "Style and Structure in the Middle English Poem *Cleanness*." *Computers and the Humanities* 21 (1987): 169–76.

McCully, Chris B. "Domain-End Phenomena and Metrical Templates in Old English Verse." *English Historical Metrics*. Eds. C. B. McCully and J. J. Anderson. Cambridge: Cambridge University Press, 1996. 42–58.

McCully, Chris B. *The Sound Structure of English: An Introduction*. Cambridge and New York: Cambridge University Press, 2009.

McCully, Chris B., and J. J. Anderson, eds. *English Historical Metrics*. Cambridge: Cambridge

University Press, 1996.
McCully, Chris B., and R. M. Hogg. "An Account of Old English Stress." *Journal of Linguistics* 26 (1990): 315–39.
McGalliard, John C. "Links, Language and Style in the *Pearl.*" *Studies in Language, Literature and Culture of the Middle Ages and Later: Studies in Honor of Rudolph Willard.* Eds. E. B. Atwood and A. A. Hill. Austin: University of Texas Press, 1969. 279–99.
McIntosh, Angus. "Early Middle English Alliterative Verse." *Middle English Alliterative Poetry and Its Literary Background: Seven Essays.* Ed. D. Lawton. Cambridge: D. S. Brewer, 1982. 20–33.
McIntyre, Dan. *History of English.* London and New York: Routledge, 2009.
McKay, David. *Metrical Phonology and English Verse.* Cambridge, MA: MIT Press, 1997.
Medary, Margaret. "Stanza-Linking in Middle English Verse." *Romanic Review* 7 (1916): 243–70.
Meredith, Joel L. *Adventures in Alliteration.* www.Xlibris.com: Xlibris, 2000.
Miller, Miriam Y., and Jane Chance, eds. *Approaches to Teaching* Sir Gawain and the Green Knight. New York: Modern Language Association of America, 1986.
Milroy, James. "*Pearl*: The Verbal Texture and the Linguistic Theme." *Neophilologus* 55 (1971): 195–208.
Minkova, Donka. "The Prosodic Character of Early Schwa Deletion in English." *Papers from the Seventh International Conference on Historical Linguistics.* Eds. Anna Giacalone Ramat et al. Amsterdam and Philadelphia: Benjamins, 1987. 445–57.
Minkova, Donka. *The History of Final Vowels in English: The Sound of Muting.* Berlin: Mouton de Gruyter, 1991.
Minkova, Donka. "Non-Primary Stress in Early Middle English Accnetual-Syllabic Verse." *English Historical Metrics.* Eds. C. B. McCully and J. J. Anderson. Cambridge: Cambridge University Press, 1996. 95–120.
Minkova, Donka. "Constraint Ranking in Middle English Stress-Shifting." *Journal of English Language and Linguistics* 1 (1997): 135–75.
Minkova, Donka. *Alliteration and Sound Change in Early English.* Cambridge: Cambridge University Press, 2003.
Mitchell, Bruce, and Fred Robinson. *A Guide to Old English.* Chichester, West Sussex: Wiley-Blackwell, 2012.
Moore, Samuel. *Historical Outlines of English Phonology and Morphology.* Ann Arbor: G. Wahr, 1925.
Moorman, Charles. "The Origins of the Alliterative Revival." *Southern Quarterly* 7 (1969): 345–71.
Morris, Richard, ed. *Early English Alliterative Poems in the West-Midland Dialect of the Fourteenth Century.* London: Oxford University Press, 1965.
Nespor, Marina, and Irene Vogel. *Prosodic Phonology.* Dordrecht: Foris, 1986.
Noble, J. "Typological Patterns in the Middle English *Joseph of Arimathea.*" *Chaucer Review* 1 (1992): 177–88.
Northup, Clark S. "A Study of the Metrical Structure of the Middle English Poem *The Pearl.*" *Publication of Modern Language Association of America* 12 (1897): 326–40.
Oakden, James P. *Alliterative Poetry in Middle English: The Dialectal and Metrical Survey.*

Manchester: Manchester University Press, 1930, 1935.

Oakden, James P. "The Survival of a Stylistic Feature of Indo-European Poetry in Germanic, Especially in Middle English." *Review of English Studies* 9 (1933): 50–53.

O'Loughlin, J. L. N. "The Middle English Alliterative *Morte Arthure*." *Medium Ævum* 4 (1935): 153–68.

Osberg, Richard H. *Readings in Medieval Poetry*. Cambridge: Cambridge University Press, 1987.

Osberg, Richard H., ed. and trans. Sir Gawain and the Green Knight. New York: Peter Lang, 1990.

Osberg, Richard H. "The Prosody of Middle English *Pearl* and the Alliterative Lyric Tradition." *English Historical Metrics*. Eds. C. B. McCully and J. J. Anderson. Cambridge: Cambridge University Press, 1996. 150–174.

Pearsall, Derek A. *Old English and Middle English Poetry*. London: Routledge and Kegan Paul, 1977.

Pearsall, Derek A. "The Origins of the Alliterative Revival." *The Alliterative Tradition in the Fourteenth Century*. Eds. B. S. Levy and P. E. Szarmach. Kent: Kent State University Press, 1981. 1–24.

Pearsall, Derek A. "The Alliterative Revival: Origins and Social Backgrounds." *Middle English Alliterative Poetry and Its Literary Background: Seven Essays*. Ed. D. Lawton. Cambridge: Brewer, 1982. 34–54.

Peters, Timothy, and Eugene Green. "'P' Alliteration and Latin-English Contrasts in Langland's *Piers Plowman*." *Neuphilologische Mitteilungen* 93 (1992): 193–97.

Petronella, V. F. "*St Erkenwald*: Style as the Vehicle for Meaning." *Journal of English and Germanic Philology* 66 (1967): 532–40.

Pope, John C. *The Rhythm of* Beowulf*: An Interpretation of the Normal and Hypermetric Verse-Forms in Old English Poetry*. New Haven: Yale University Press, 1966.

Preminger, Alex, and T. V. F. Brogan, eds. *The New Princeton Encyclopedia of Poetry and Poetics*. Third edn. Princeton: Princeton University Press, 1993.

Prior, Sandra P. *The Pearl Poet Revisited*. New York: Macmillan, 1994.

Putter, Ad. *An Introduction to the Gawain-Poet*. New York: Longman, 1996.

Putter, Ad. Judith Jefferson, and Myra Stokes. *Studies in the Metre of Alliterative Verse*. Oxford: Society for the Study of Medieval Languages and Literature, 2007.

Putter, Ad, and Myra Stokes. "Spelling, Grammar and Metre in the Works of the Gawain-Poet." *Medieval English Measures: Studies in Metre and Versification*. Ed. Ruth Kennedy. *Parergon* 18 (2000): 77–95.

Quirk, Randolph. "Poetic Language and Old English Metre." *Early English and Norse Studies Presented to Hugh Smith in Honour of his Sixtieth Birthday*. Eds. A. Brown and P. Foote. London: Methuen, 1963. 149–71.

Renoir, Alain. "Oral-Formulaic Rhetoric: An Approach to Image and Message in Medieval Poetry." *Medieval Texts and Contemporary Readers*. Eds. L. Finke and M. Shichtman. Ithaca: Cornell University Press, 1987. 234–53.

Richards, I. A. "Rhythm and Metre." *The Structure of Verse: Modern Essays on Prosody*. Ed. H. Gross. Greenwich: Fawcett, 1966. 42–51.

Richardson, F. E. "*The Pearl*: A Poem and Its Audience." *Neophilologus* 46 (1962): 308–16.

Riddy, Felicity. "The Alliterative Revival." *The History of Scottish Literature Volume 1: Origins to 1660.* Ed. R. D. S. Jack. Aberdeen: Aberdeen University Press, 1988. 39–54.

Ritzke-Rutherford, Jean. "Formulaic Macrostructure: The Theme of Battle." The Alliterative Morte Arthure: *A Reassessment of the Poem.* Ed. Karl H. Göller. Cambridge: Brewer, 1981. 83–95.

Ritzke-Rutherford, Jean. "Formulaic Microstructure: The Cluster." The Alliterative Morte Arthure: *A Reassessment of the Poem.* Ed. Karl H. Göller. Cambridge: Brewer, 1981. 70–82.

Roach, Peter. "On the Distinction between 'Stress-Timed' and 'Syllable-Timed' Languages." *Linguistic Controversies: Essays in Linguistic Theory and Practice in Honor of F. R. Palmer.* Ed. David Crystal. London: Arnold, 1982. 73–79.

Roach, Peter. *English Phonetics and Phonology: A Practical Course.* Cambridge: Cambridge University Press, 1991.

Robertson, Michael. "Stanzaic Symmetry in *Sir Gawain and the Green Knight.*" *Speculum* 57 (1982): 779–85.

Røstvig, Maren-Sofie. "Numerical Composition in *Pearl*: A Theory." *English Studies* 48 (1967): 326–32.

Russom, Geoffrey. *Old English Meter and Linguistic Theory.* Cambridge: Cambridge University Press, 1987.

Russom, Geoffrey. Beowulf *and Old Germanic Metre.* Cambridge: Cambridge University Press, 1998.

Russom, Geoffrey. "The Evolution of Middle English Alliterative Meter." *Studies in the History of the English Language II: Unfolding Conversations.* Eds. Anne Curzan and Kimberly Emmons. Berlin and New York: Mouton de Gruyter, 2004. 281–304.

Russom, Geoffrey. "Evolution of the a-Verse in English Alliterative Meter." *Studies in the History of the English Language III: Managing Chaos: Strategies for Identifying Change in English.* Eds. Christopher M. Cain and Geoffrey Russom. Berlin and New York: Mouton de Gruyter, 2007. 63–87.

Sadowski, Piotr. "The Sound-Symbolic Quality of Word-Initial GR-Cluster in Middle English Alliterative Verse." *Neuphilologische Mitteilungen* 102 (2001): 37–47.

Saintsbury, George. *A History of English Prosody from the Twelfth Century to the Present Day.* New York: Macmillan, 1906–10.

Salmon, Paul. "Anomalous Alliteration in Germanic Verse." *Neophilologus* 42 (1958): 223–41.

Salter, Elizabeth. "The Alliterative Revival." *Modern Philology* 64 (1966): 146–50; 233–37.

Salter, Elizabeth. "Alliterative Modes and Affiliations in the Fourteenth Century." *Neuphilologische Mitteilungen* 79 (1978): 25–35.

Salter, Elizabeth. "A Complaint Against Blacksmiths." *Literature and History* 5 (1979): 195–215.

Sapora, Robert W., Jr. *A Theory of Middle English Alliterative Meter with Critical Applications.* Cambridge, MA: Mediaeval Academy of America, 1977.

Schane, Sanford A. "The Rhythmic Nature of English Word Accentuation." *Language* 55 (1979): 559–602.

Schiller, Andrew. "The Gawain Rhythm." *Language and Style* 1 (1968): 268–94.

Schipper, Jakob. *A History of English Versification.* Oxford: Clarendon, 1910.

Schmerling, Susan F. *Aspects of English Sentence Stress.* Austin: University of Texas Press, 1976.

Schmidt, A. V. C. *The Clerkly Maker: Langland's Poetic Art.* Woodbridge: D. S. Brewer, 1987.

Schmidt, A. V. C., ed. Piers Plowman: *A Parallel-Text Edition of the A, B, C and Z Versions.* London: Longman, 1995.

Schreiber, Earl G. "The Structure of *Cleanness.*" *The Alliterative Tradition in the Fourteenth Century.* Eds. B. Levy and P. Szarmach. Kent: Kent State University Press, 1981. 131–52.

Shen, Yao, and Giles Peterson. *Isochronism in English.* Studies in Linguistics Occasional Papers 9. Buffalo: University of Baffallo, Department of Anthropology and Linguistics, 1962

Shepherd, Geoffrey T. "The Nature of Alliterative Poetry in Late Medieval England." *Proceedings of the British Academy* 56 (1970): 57–76. Rpt. in *Middle English Literature: British Academy Gollancz Lectures.* Ed. J. A. Burrow. Oxford: Oxrord University Press for British Academy, 1989. 141–60.

Sievers, Eduard. "Old Germanic Metrics and Old English Metrics." *Essential Articles for the Study of Old English Poetry.* Eds. J. B. Bessinger, Jr. and S. J. Kahrl. Hamden: Archon, 1968. 1–38.

Silverstein, Theodore, ed. Sir Gawain and the Green Knight: *A New Critical Edition.* Chicago: Chicago University Press, 1984.

Sisam, Kenneth, ed. *Fourteenth Century Verse and Prose.* Oxford: Clarendon, 1955.

Smith, Jeremy. *An Historical Study of English: Function, Form and Change.* London and New York: Routledge, 1996.

Smith, Jeremy. *Essentials of Early English.* London and New York: Routledge, 1999.

Smith, Jeremy. "Semantics and Metrical Form in *Sir Gawain and the Green Knight.*" *New Perspectives on Middle English Texts: A Festschrift for R. A. Waldron.* Eds. Susan Powell and Jeremy Smith. Cambridge: D. S. Brewer, 2000. 87–103.

Snell, Ada L. F. "An Objective Study of Syllabic Quantity in English Verse." *Publication of Modern Language Association of America* 33 (1918): 396–408; 34 (1919): 416–35.

Southworth, John. *The English Medieval Minstrel.* Suffolk: Boydell, 1989.

Spearing, A. C. *The Gawain-Poet: A Critical Study.* Cambridge: Cambridge University Press, 1970.

Spearing, A. C. *Readings in Medieval Poetry.* Cambridge: Cambridge University Press, 1987.

Spisak, James W., ed. *Caxton's Malory: A New Edition of Sir Thomas Malory's* Le Morte Darthur. Berkeley: University of California Press, 1983.

Stanley, E. G. "Rhymes in English Medieval Verse: From Old English to Middle English." *Medieval English Studies Presented to George Kane.* Eds. Edward D. Kennedy, Ronald Waldron, and Joseph S. Wittig. Woodbridge: D. S. Brewer, 1988. 19–54.

Stanley, E. G. "*Pearl*, 358, *And þy lurez of lyȝtly leme*: Metanalyzed Tmesis for the Scale of Alliteration." *Notes and Queries* 37 (1990): 158–60.

Starr, David. "Metrical Changes: From Old to Middle English." *Modern Philology* 68 (1970): 1–9.

Stein, Robert M. "Multilingualism." *Middle English.* Ed. Paul Strohm. Oxford: Oxford University Press, 2007. 23–37.

Stevenson, Charles L. "The Rhythm of English Verse." *Journal of Aesthetics and Art Criticism* 28 (1970): 327–44.

Stevick, Robert D. *English and Its History: The Evolution of a Language.* Boston: Allyn and Bacon, 1968.

Stewart, George R. "The Meter of *Piers Plowman*." *Publication of Modern Language Association of America* 42 (1927): 113–28.

Stewart, George R. *The Technique of English Verse*. New York: Holt, 1930.

Stillings, Justine T. "A Generative Metrical Analysis of *Sir Gawain and the Green Knight*." *Language and Style* 9 (1976): 219–46.

Stockwell, Robert P. "On Recent Theories of Metrics and Rhythm in *Beowulf*." *English Historical Metrics*. Eds. C. B. McCully and J. J. Anderson. Cambridge: Cambridge University Press, 1996. 73–94.

Stockwell, Robert P., and Donka Minkova. "Old English Metrics and the Phonology of Resolution." *North-Western European Language Evolution* 31/32 (1997): 389–406.

Stratyner, Leslie. "The Middle English Romance and the Alliterative Tradition." *Teaching Oral Traditions*. Ed. John Miles Foley. New York: Modern Language Association, 1998. 365–72.

Strohm, Paul. ed. *Middle English*. Oxford: Oxford University Press, 2007.

Suzuki, Seiichi. "The Role of Syllable Structure in Old English Poetry." *Lingua* 67 (1985): 97–119.

Sweet, Henry. *A History of English Sounds: From the Earliest Period*. London: Trübner, 1874.

Tamplin, Ronald. *Rhythm and Rhyme*. Buckingham and Philadelphia: Open University Press, 1993.

Tarlinskaja, Marina. *English Verse: Theory and History*. The Hague: Mouton, 1976.

Tarlinskaja, Marina. "General and Particular Aspects of Meter: Literatures, Epoches, Poets." *Phonetics and Phonology I: Rhythm and Meter*. Eds. Paul Kiparsky and Gilbert Youmans. Cambridge, MA: MIT Press, 1989. 121–54.

Tavormina, M. Teresa, and R. F. Yeager, eds. *The Endless Knot: Essays on Old and Middle English in Honor of Marie Borroff*. Cambridge: D. S. Brewer, 1995.

Thun, Nils. *Reduplicative Words in English: A Study of Formations of the Types 'Tick-Tock,' 'Hurly-Burly,' and 'Shilly-Shally.'* Lund: Carl Bloms, 1963.

Tolkien, J. R. R., and E. V. Gordon, eds. Sir Gawain and the Green Knight. Rev. N. Davis. Oxford: Oxford University Press, 1967.

Toswell, M. ed. *Prosody and Poetics in the Early Middle Ages*. Toronto: University of Toronto Press, 1995.

Townsend, Peter. "Essential Groupings of Meaningful Force: Rhythm in Literary Discourse." *Language and Style* 16 (1983): 313–33.

Treiman, Rebecca, Jennifer Gross, and Annemarie Cwikiel-Glavin. "The Syllabification of /s/ Clusters in English." *Journal of Phonetics* 20 (1992): 383–402.

Turco, Lewis. *The New Book of Forms: A Handbook of Poetics*. Hanover and London: University Press of New England, 1986.

Turville-Petre, Joan. "The Metre of *Sir Gawain and the Green Knight*." *English Studies* 57 (1976): 310–28.

Turville-Peter, Thorlac. "'Summer Sunday', 'De Tribus Regibus Mortuis', and 'The Awntyrs off Arthure': Three Poems in the Thirteen-Line Stanza." *Review of English Studies, New Series* 35 (1974): 1–14.

Turville-Petre, Thorlac. *The Alliterative Revival*. Cambridge: D. S. Brewer and Totowa: Rowman Littlefield, 1977.

Turville-Petre, Thorlac. "Emendation on Grounds of Alliteration in *The Wars of Alexander*."

English Studies 61 (1980): 302–17.

Turville-Petre, Thorlac. *Alliterative Poetry of the Later Middle Ages: An Anthology*. London: Routledge, 1989.

van Gelderen, Elly. *A History of the English Language*. Amsterdam and Philadelphia: John Benjamins, 2006.

Vantuono, William, ed. and trans. Sir Gawain and the Green Knight. Notre Dame: University of Notre Dame Press, 1999.

Vantuono, William, ed. *Old and Middle English Texts with Accompanying Textual and Linguistic Apparatus*. New York: Peter Lang, 1994.

Vantuono, William, ed. and trans. Pearl: *An Edition with Verse Translation*. Notre Dame and London: University of Notre Dame Press, 1995.

Vaughan, M. F. "Consecutive Alliteration, Strophic Patterns, and the Composition of the Alliterative *Morte Arthure*." *Modern Philology* 77 (1979): 1–9.

Verdonk, Peter. *Stylistics*. Oxford and New York: Oxford University Press, 2002.

Waldron, Ronald A. "Oral-Formulaic Technique and Middle English Alliterative Poetry." *Speculum* 32 (1957): 792–804.

Waldron, Ronald A., ed. Sir Gawain and the Green Knight. London: Arnold; Evanston: North Western University Press, 1970.

Wells, J. C. *Accents of English*. Cambridge: Cambridge University Press, 1982.

Wesling, Donald. *The Scissors of Meter: Grammetrics and Reading*. Ann Arbor: University of Michigan Press, 1996.

Wheatley, Henry B. ed. Merlin *or the Early History of King Arthur: A Prose Romance*. London: Kegan Paul, Trench, Trübner, 1938.

Whitman, F. H. *A Comparative Study of Old English Metre*. Toronto: University of Toronto Press, 1993.

Williams, D. J. "Alliterative Poetry in the Fourteenth and Fifteenth Centuries." *The New History of Literature Vol. 1: The Middle Ages*. Ed. W. F. Bolton. New York: Peter Bedrick, 1986. 119–67.

Wilson, Peter. "Word Play and the Interpretation of *Pearl*." *Medium Ævum* 40 (1971): 116–34.

Wilson, Peter. "Reading a Line Metrically: The Practical Implications of Using the Halle-Keyser System." *Language and Style* 12 (1979): 146–57.

Wimsatt, William K., ed. *Versification: Major Language Types*. New York: Modern Language Association of America, 1972.

Wimsatt, William K., and Monroe C. Beardsley. "The Concept of Meter: An Exercise in Abstraction." *Publication of Modern Language Association of America* 74 (1959): 585–98.

Wrenn, Charles L. "On the Continuity of English Poetry." *Anglia* 76 (1958): 41–59.

Wu, Duncan, ed. *Old and Middle English Poetry*. Oxford and Malden: Blackwell, 2002.

Youmans, Gilbert. "Introduction: Rhythm and Meter." *Phonetics and Phonology I: Rhythm and Meter*. Eds. Paul Kiparsky and Gilbert Youmans. Cambridge, MA: MIT Press, 1989. 1–14.

Youmans, Gilbert. "Reconsidering Chaucer's Prosody." *English Historical Metrics*. Eds. C. B. McCully and J. J. Anderson. Cambridge: Cambridge University Press, 1996. 185–210.

Zesmer, David M. *Guide to English Literature from* Beowulf *through Chaucer and Medieval Drama*. New York: Barnes and Noble, 1961.

Ziolkowski, Jan. "A Narrative Structure in the Alliterative *Morte Arthure* 1–1221 and

3150–4346." *Chaucer Review* 22 (1988): 234–45.
Zumthor, Paul. *Toward a Medieval Poetics*. Minneapolis: University of Minnesota Press, 1991.

Index

【著者紹介】

守屋 靖代（もりや やすよ）

国際基督教大学教養学部卒業（学士）、同大学大学院博士前期課程修了(修士)、オハイオ州立シンシナティ大学大学院修士課程修了(MA)、同大学大学院博士課程修了(PhD)。国際基督教大学教養学部教授、同大学大学院心理・教育学専攻教授。

〈主な著書・論文〉

「中英語頭韻詩における繰り返しの技巧と連語」南雲堂出版(2010);「中英語頭韻詩にみる繰り返しとリズム」(共著)南雲堂出版(2006); "Vertical Alliteration in Middle English Alliterative Poems: Sound Repetition Beyond the Verse Line." *NOWELE* 48(2006); "Alliteration Versus Natural Speech Rhythm in Determining the Meter of Middle English Alliterative Verse." *English Studies* 85(2004); "The Line Boundary of Middle English Alliterative Meter Compared to That of Old English Alliterative Meter." *Neuphilologische Mitteilungen* 101(2000).

Hituzi Linguistics in English No. 20

Repetition, Regularity, Redundancy
Norms and Deviations of Middle English Alliterative Meter

発行　2014年2月14日　初版1刷
定価　13000円＋税

発行者　松本功
印刷所　株式会社 ディグ
製本所　株式会社 中條製本工場
発行所　株式会社 ひつじ書房
〒112-0011 東京都文京区千石2-1-2 大和ビル2F
Tel.03-5319-4916 Fax.03-5319-4917
郵便振替 00120-8-142852
toiawase@hituzi.co.jp　http://www.hituzi.co.jp/

ISBN978-4-89476-683-9　C3080

Hituzi Linguistics in English

No. 16 Derivational Linearization at the Syntax-Prosody Interface
塩原佳世乃著　定価 12000 円+税

No. 17 Polysemy and Compositionality: Deriving Variable Behaviors of Motion Verbs and Prepositions
磯野達也著　定価 12000 円+税

Hituzi Linguistics in English

No. 21 A Cognitive Pragmatic Analysis of Nominal Tautologies
山本尚子著　定価 8800 円+税

No. 22 A Contrastive Study of Responsibility for Understanding Utterances between Japanese and Korean
尹秀美著　定価 8400 円+税